SEAVIEW

D1569378

BY TOBY OLSON

Novels
The Life of Jesus
Seaview

Poetry
Maps
Worms into Nails
The Brand
Pig/s book
Vectors
Fishing
The Wrestlers & Other Poems
Changing Appearances: Poems 1965-1970
Home
Doctor Miriam
Aesthetics
The Florence Poems
Birdsongs

SEAVIEW a novel by TOBY OLSON

A NEW DIRECTIONS BOOK

Copyright © 1982 by Toby Olson

All rights reserved. Except for brief passages quoted in a newspaper, magazine, radio, or television review, no part of this book may be reproduced in any form or by any means, electronic or mechanical, including photocopying and recording, or by any information storage and retrieval system, without permission in writing from the Publisher.

The author wishes to thank Temple University, for its aid and support, and Lou Thibeault, PGA professional, for his golf tips.

Portions of this book first appeared in somewhat different form in *Sun and Moon.*

The epigraph quotation by Gabriel García Márquez, from *One Hundred Years of Solitude,* translated by Gregory Rabassa (Translation © 1970 by Harper & Row, Publishers, Inc.), is reprinted by permission of Harper & Row.

The extract quotation from *Cape Cod: Its People and Their History,* by Henry C. Kittredge, 2nd edition, Houghton Mifflin Company, 1968 (Copyright 1930 by Henry C. Kittredge; Copyright renewed, 1958), is reprinted by permission of Houghton Mifflin.

Manufactured in the United States of America
First published clothbound and as New Directions Paperbook 532 in 1982
Published simultaneously in Canada by George J. McLeod, Ltd., Toronto

Library of Congress Cataloging in Publication Data
Olson, Toby.
     Seaview.
     (A New Directions Book)
     I. Title.
PS3565.L84S4   1982   813'.54   81-22359
ISBN 0-8112-0828-1   AACR2
ISBN 0-8112-0829-x (pbk.)

New Directions Books are published for James Laughlin
by New Directions Publishing Corporation,
80 Eighth Avenue, New York, 10011

For Morris and Smitty,
Dennis and Rich,
Julian and Ollie

. . . the search for lost things is hindered by routine habits and that is why it is so difficult to find them.

—Gabriel García Márquez

I am determined not to live until I have no country!

—King Philip (Wampanoag Sachem), 1675

Part One

TEA DREAM

He no longer wondered where to lay down blame or whose was the responsibility or what the responsibility was. Her body, finished with its rage, had settled in the cancer the way one slips into a tub in a dark bathroom, into hot water, and soon the skin is no longer a barrier, an integrity and definition; one becomes part of the water, the cancer. The skin goes in the way the breath does, out like a ripple of the surface of a still pool; part of a quota, it does not return. She lay in the tub, and under the water, crossing the rise of her belly, a place that was darker than water: a dark towel, taken from the blankets and pillows and towels in the back seat of the car, because it gave her some comfort. Her head rested on a rolled towel, placed where the tile and the porcelain met; chalk of the small hollow valley of her left cheek, her lips slightly parted, her shallow and stertorous breathing. The glass doors in the wall of the room beyond her were a field of light, reflection cast from the side of the rented car, up from the white gravel outside the motel room in Arizona. Occasional figures of yucca advanced, danced, and faded in the opaque field. He sat in a chair, in the dark in the side of the room, watching the gun.

The gun lay on the bed in the middle of a white towel. She sighed in the distance. It was a small, blue-metal instrument with symmetrical indentations on its surface. He liked the romance of it, his privacy and her groggy sound. He reached out with a finger and touched the tip of the butt, better aligning the L-shape with the towel's edge.

And then he thought of the two bags of cocaine, each pressed in a Diamond Kitchen matchbox that was taped shut, in the trunk of the car, under clubs, blankets, and clothing. He thought of the way Melinda would give it up, her body slipping as her quota of breaths left her: neck, chin, and upper lip, her nose blowing feeble air against the water's surface (small indentations, minute waves), then going under. He lifted the gun up from the towel then and put the barrel between his teeth and pulled the trigger on the empty chamber.

3

"Melinda, are you okay in there?"

"Yes, I'm okay, honey, fine."

He came back from the click as he had come back from the Tea Dream that time. In the Tea Dream, he was sitting on a bench to the side of the blue markers at the back of a narrow tee. The tee was long enough to accommodate all the markers, and from where he sat he could see the white ones halfway up, and near the foot of the tee, where it dropped off into rough and the slope started up to the high par-three green about a hundred and eighty yards away, the red, women's markers, were set in. He had his cap and his glove on, and he was holding a seven-iron, the head resting in the grass to the side of his right foot. He looked from the club head, down the row of markers and up to the green. Beside the flagstick, gripping the shaft in her left hand, there was a woman standing in full view and facing down at him. She was wearing a white bathrobe, and she wore no jewelry. Her hair was dark and uncombed, and she was holding hazy implements in her free hand at her waist. There was a smoky fog, a thick cloud that began coming up behind her, rolling over the green's surface. It got to her, and her feet and legs were enveloped in the smoke, and he couldn't see them clearly anymore. But he could see their changing bulks and her right foot rise a little and paw at the low, delicate carpet of grass.

The fog rose up around her; she seemed to recede back into the cloud. It cowled her head, and then she disappeared completely. He started to get up, to go and find her, though he feared her, but as he rose the smoke-fog began to clear. It gathered up from where her feet had been, and when he followed its path, he saw the place of the cowling shrink and the smoke gather and disappear into two rings, and as the final billows were sucked in, he saw the head of the horse appear where her head had been, and he realized that the rings were the horse's nostrils, the smoke his breath blowing in the suddenly cold air. The horse was white and large, very stately and very powerful looking. There was a device attached to its side, a leather trussing, and the long stick with the small red flag with the white number 3 sewn into it was standing, straight up above the horse's broad back, the little flag waving. The horse pawed at the green, scarring the surface, kicking little divots out. It blew its heavy steam. And then it dipped its head once and started down the hill toward him. It pranced a little, slowly selecting places for its hoofs as it came down through the rough. He fell back on the bench and waited for it. It was massive and getting larger in its coming, but he did not fear it, not in the way he had feared the woman. He had tightened his grip on the seven-iron when he had seen her, but now he released it, his knees parted a little, and he relaxed.

The horse reached the far end of the tee and started down between the markers as if they were running lights. He could hear the creak of the trussing, the hoof-thuds, and the sound of the nostrils blowing. It got to him, and he could smell its sweat and see the doe-leather look of its soft muzzle, its powerful grinding jaws. It stood for a moment over him, moving its head from side to side, looking around. Then its thick neck began to arch over, and it brought its huge head down to him. He sat very still. He could feel the blow of the nostril smoke on his cheek, and he could smell it at the same time. It had the smell of jasmine, slightly sweet and musky.

And in the dream he seemed to open his eyes as if they had been closed, and he turned his head slightly toward the horse and looked up into its face. And the horse's eyes grew smaller, and through the smoke between the two of them the face of the horse began to change into the face of a woman. Melinda began to appear to him as he woke up. She was sitting on the floor beside the bed, at a level with his head, and between them, on the night table, was a steaming cup of tea. And he saw the oval of Melinda's lips as she lightly blew the rising tea smoke across his face. Her mouth changed to a smile as his eyes came into focus. He had risen gently from his dream; it was the smell of tea and its touch against his cheek, insinuating itself into the dream without breaking it, that had awakened him. And the dream and what he might have chosen to call reality had come together like a kind of smoke net to lift him up. He had moved to his elbows, turning his head toward her. He had never come to himself so gently. And Melinda had seemed to know this, and that is why she smiled and did not speak for a while but only looked at him as the tea smoke lifted.

"Melinda, are you okay?"

"Yes, I'm fine. I'm ready to come out now."

He wrapped the gun in the towel and put it in the suitcase and then he went to the bathroom. She smiled up at him from the dark water in the tub.

"Should I put the light on?"

"No. Leave it off, okay?"

He put his hands down into the warm water beside her body. "The towel," she said. He pulled back and reached to her belly and lifted the wet towel off of it, wringing it out as he took it from the water and placed it in the sink. He took a dry towel, folded it, and put it over the edge of the tub. Then he reached into the water with both hands and arms to his elbows, sliding one arm under her back and the other under her knees. He knelt down on the floor and lifted her up carefully out of the water and swung her legs over the edge of the tub until she was sitting on the towel. He took another towel and draped it over her shoulders. She began to rub herself with the towel, and he took another towel and dried her legs and feet. Then he got up and stood over her, looking down at her matted hair, her huddled body. He steadied her with one hand on her shoulder. He pressed her after a few minutes.

"Are you ready?"

"Okay," she whispered softly and with effort. She held the towel with a white hand across her breasts, and he reached under her again, making a chair for her. He lifted her and carried her into the other room and sat her down on the edge of the bed. The reflection in the glass doors had changed slightly. It was mid-day, and the light now brightened the foot of the bed. The glass doors were still opaque. He made sure she was steady; then he left her sitting and went over and pulled the drapes. He returned to her and helped her recline on the bed. He took a blanket from the shelf in the closet and offered to put it over her.

"No. No thanks," she said, raising her arm slightly. "But could you turn down the air conditioner a little? You can leave the blanket here." She motioned to the bed beside her. He did these things. He bent over and kissed her forehead.

"I'm going out for a while. Do you want anything?"

"No, just a little rest is all."

"Not long," he said.

"Oh, I don't think I'll sleep."

"I mean, I won't be gone long."

"Oh, I see. Okay." She let her head down on the pillow and looked at the ceiling. He went to the door, opened it, and left the room.

The motel was a long rectangular building, with a brief aluminum awning running over a narrow sidewalk the length of it. At the far end was a slightly larger building, a restaurant, and in front of the restaurant were two banks of gas pumps. Across the wide gravel drive in front of the motel was the old highway, now a secondary road, and across that, beyond the shoulder that was lined with a few yucca, and scrub he could not identify, the desert began. In the distance were the low mountains, very distinct in the sun. It was hot and dry. Across the road from him, about seventy yards away (a half-wedge, he thought), there were two Indians in rough clothing working at a shallow ditch with shovels. Between the ditch and the road, two women sat on blankets with a few pieces of what looked like jewelry spread out in front of them. They were very close to the road, and when an occasional car went by, their loose, faded shirts stirred on their arms and around their necks and the corners of the blankets rippled.

He stayed under the awning and walked the length of the sidewalk, past the two cars in front of other rooms, the two air conditioners fixed in the window casements, humming. He walked across the few feet of gravel and entered the restaurant. There were a dozen or so formica tables along the windows, facing the old highway, and a long counter. He sat on a swivel stool and ordered coffee. A girl of about sixteen got it for him. He heard a car on the gravel behind him, and a middle-aged man in Western clothing, who had been sitting at a table near the door, went out. Along the counter to his right sat two men; one looked to be a truck driver; the other was an Indian. The Indian looked his way and smiled. Like the men working across the road, he wore a faded chambray shirt and khaki pants. A red polka-dot handkerchief circled his head, tied in the back with two tails that touched his neck. The truck driver was bending over a plate of eggs and home fries; he gave his attention to his eating and did not look up. Pinned on the wall behind the counter, above the coffeemaker and glass shelves with pieces of pie on them, were a few post cards, a dollar bill in cellophane, and a small photograph of the restaurant taken from across the highway. He could make out two figures in the picture, a man and a woman about to enter the door. In the left corner of the photograph, standing at the end of the building, was a tall, erect man. He was facing into the camera. His figure was hazy and slightly out of focus, but he looked something like the Indian down the way.

He stirred his coffee and thought of the way the one had moved in behind him. The other was on the couch before him, sitting, hips at the edge, legs spread, and he was on one knee between them, touching her waist and breasts, biting her carefully, looking at her, putting his fingers in the sides of her mouth. Richard reclined in the orange chair watching; he was naked also, and the shadow push of the dim lights elongated his compact body, forcing the angles; he looked like a wasted El Greco, one arm on the back of the chair behind his head, his smile, the slant of cheekbone and dark hair. A small, plastic, crescent moonlight, with a face with little red eyes, sat on a shelf above Richard's head, and music was playing. He felt the tips of her fingers, her nails, on the small of his back, down over his buttocks, as she moved in behind him; she nipped his leg. The legs of the one he was in came up to gather his hips. The music was Santana, Little Feat, and the Doobie Brothers, various driving and loping popular pieces to which the three of them adjusted their movements. But really it was the two of them: he was in the middle, and though treated as he imagined a god might want or a man of wealth and power, it was the two smaller creatures who had control.

The one behind him squeezed something and ran cool fluid on him; he felt a thin line, delicate, but with a gravity like mercury, run down his inner leg, some gathering at his anklebones; the other one squealed and talked. He pulled her hair, held handfuls of her flesh; her heel bumped down his spine. For all he knew, the one behind him, in her somewhat mechanistic approach, could have brought the gun with whatever container held the cool liquid, could have placed them on the floor beside his foot. And then she could have caressed his flanks with one hand and taken the gun in the other, and what he felt of metal and thought was rings or hard nails or the edge of some instrument would be the barrel touching the delicate meat there. She could have been moving his passage toward some emblematic action as the other urged him on. And when he exploded or arrived some place they knew of, or almost arrived there, she could have pulled the trigger, and he would have seen the final eyes in the plastic moon before he saw snow.

He came back to the cup in his hands, lifted it, and finished the coffee. Then he took the yellow check to the cash register at the end of the counter. He dug in his pocket and brought his hand out; in his palm was some change and two white golf tees. He picked out the amount of the bill and handed it to the girl. Then he turned and left the restaurant.

He walked on the crunching gravel past the two cars and toward his own. It was very hot and still, the sun at its apex, and he could see that the two men across the road had quit working and were drinking liquid from a gallon jar. They were talking with the women, who had turned halfway from the road and were looking at them. One of the men saw him looking and nodded. The two women turned to look but gave no sign.

The light on the trunk lid made him squint, and when he opened it it took him a few moments to focus on its contents. There was a suitcase, a garment bag, and a couple of blankets in the bottom. On top of the blankets was a wide-brimmed plantation hat. He took it out and put it on. Shielded from the sun, he felt much cooler. He lifted the blankets and put them on the suitcase. Under them were the heads of four golf clubs sticking out of the canvas mouth of a narrow, white Sunday bag. He pulled the bag free and leaned it against the car's bumper; it had been resting on a canvas tarp that covered the odds and ends of clothing and household goods which filled the trunk's bottom. Tucked in the fender well was a gunny sack with a number of golf balls in it. He took the sack out, glimpsed the bulk of the two match-boxes in a pillowcase wedged up behind it, and put the sack on the gravel beside the clubs. He felt somebody behind him and turned around.

"Hi," said the Indian from the restaurant. "You like this place?"

He was not sure if there were any layers in the question, but the Indian had a very open face and his smile was not forced, so he answered him directly.

"Not much," he said.

"That's good, I don't like it either. You play golf?" The Indian was eyeing the clubs and the gunny sack. Close up, he looked older than he had seemed in the restaurant. His face was heavily lined from the sun, and he looked well worn. He was about mid-fifty. His teeth were uneven but very white, and his eyes were clear and sharp.

"Yeah, I play a little."

"I have a relative in golf," the Indian said, "name of Frank Bumpus, back East, but they call him Wingfoot. He owns a golf course. You headed back East? I see your plates."

"This is a rental car. Where is your relative?"

"Name of Seaview Golf Links, on what they call the Cape there, in Massachusetts. You headed back East?"

"If I get there," he said. "If I get there I'll look him up. What's your name?"

"Right, look him up. Bob White, relative from out West. What you gonna do now?"

"Well, I thought I'd go over across the highway and hit some balls out in the desert."

"I don't play golf," the Indian said.

"Right," he said. He reached down to pick up the two bags, but the Indian was not finished yet.

"Tell you what," the Indian said. "How many balls you got in that bag you gonna hit?"

"About a hundred."

"Tell you what, who's gonna get those balls after you hit 'em?"

"I am," he said.

The Indian looked off across the highway at the two men who were back at work and the two women. A car had stopped, and the women were showing the jewelry to an old couple who were standing together in front of the blankets. The working men had shed their shirts; their bodies were lean but rounded and not muscular. They were sweating heavily, the bands around their heads very dark with moisture. Their shovels shooshed in the heavy sand. Their hands spread along the shovel shafts as they cast it out. They were up to their thighs in the ditch.

"I could use just about two dollars and fifty cents," the Indian said, still looking off across the road. "Tell you what, I'll get those balls after you hit 'em."

"Fine," he said. "You want the money now?"

"Nope," the Indian said, and he moved to the trunk of the car and picked up the clubs and the gunny sack. "Where you wanna go?"

"Over there, I guess."

The Indian walked a little behind him as he crunched across the gravel toward the highway, heading for a place about a hundred yards from where the men and women were working, a place that would put the restaurant windows out of eyeshot. Though the highway was empty for miles in both directions, they stopped at the near side of it before they crossed. He had seen a place on the other side where the desert started a little below the shoulder of the road, a spot that would be protected from the vision of any cars that might pass.

"Is that you in that picture in the restaurant?" he asked.

"May be," the Indian answered. "Don't remember it though."

He had begun to remember the particular texture of the Tea Dream often recently. When she was sitting or occasionally standing beside some structure, holding it for support, he'd feel himself slide into a kind of awakening, a clarity that rendered most of the rest dreamlike. That she was dying before his eyes, and would certainly do so soon, were the words; and that he might stay alive beyond her was another consideration. But the experience, the flavor of the dream transition, had to do with immediacy, and it did something for him, though he couldn't say what that thing was. He couldn't say he liked it, but he thought that might be a good, if trivial, way to put it. He would be sitting beside her on a couch in some place or other, and he would begin to feel, in small increments, the intricate mechanisms of her body working with the cancer; he'd feel it in her skin temperature, the brush of hair tips against his arm, the tentative rhythm of her pulse, but mostly it was her breath that got to him. It had a smell, not jasmine, but sweet and close to that, like subtle exotic tea anyway. And when she dropped her head to his shoulder and he felt her breath pushing against his cheek, he'd smell and feel it at the same time. And then her smell was touch to him, and when he'd get up to get her water or something, and they were in different parts of the room or in other rooms or she was in the back seat of the car and he was driving, he felt that in smelling her he touched her, was attuned in some way to her. The alveoli in her lungs, the small wet sacs, were the place where blood, breath, and cancer systems joined. He imagined them as little sacred chambers in which, like intricate arguments, the elegant battle took place. It was a systems battle, an attempt, in those small globes, for the three energies to dovetail and link, and with each small failure a small accommodation was made. And she was running out of accommodations, so that each new one became more crucial. She knew the result would be her death, but this, in its way, freed her to live in the elegance of the struggle. At least, this was the way he saw or imagined it at times. She was very much alive now, all the time, and he was jealous of her. And yet he was grateful to her, for the inhaling of her. He wanted her often; he had great lust for her. He didn't want to cure her. She seemed the healthy one.

They crossed the road and the shoulder beyond it and moved over and down to where the desert floor began. They moved to the left a little, locating a place that was fairly flat: slabs of shale, with a thin layer of sand blown away from them in various places and some seed spill from the road's shoulder that had sprouted into feeble grass. The Indian put the gunny sack and the clubs down, leaning the clubs against a low rock so that the heads were elevated slightly off the ground. He stood back a little and looked out into the desert. The sun was still high but a little over their shoulders now; the hard lines of their shadows had begun to cast shade to their left. There were a few giant saguaros staggered out in the distance ahead of them and a few barrel cactuses in the spaces between, some clustered and some loners. This and the very spare brush and the sand was all there was from there to the distant mountains.

"I mark that one at about two hundred yards, that big one

almost three," he said, not looking back at where the Indian stood. "You know, this will take a while."

"Big one's two city blocks, about," the Indian said. "I got a while."

He glanced back sharply, and then he shrugged at the Indian's way of measurement and at his resolve. He reached into the gunny sack and took out a small grasslike mat, a piece of Astro-turf. In a corner of it, a small one-inch length of thin hose stood up. He found a flat place and spread the mat out. He reached back to the gunny sack and pulled it over to the right of the piece of turf. Then he lifted the closed corners and let the balls flow out onto the sand. The balls gleamed in the sun. A few had red stripes around them. Some were cut. Others were marked with black paint. The clubs in the Sunday bag were only of fair quality. There was a driver and a four-wood and two irons, a three and a seven. The woods had black, composition heads with red inserts and gold screws; their grips were dark red. The irons had black grips, were noticeably step-shafted, and came from another set. He took a light-blue golf glove from his back pocket and put it on, pushing between his fingers to snug it up. Then he took the four-wood by its head and pulled it free of the bag. He turned it around and used it to poke one of the balls onto the middle of the piece of turf.

He took his stance, his feet square to the ball, toes slightly out-ward for stability, knees bent. With his right hand he pushed his hat down on his head. He looked out across the desert, and then he addressed his attention to the ball. The club head rested on the turf; his hands, at crotch level, held the grip. He moved his hands slightly to the left, bringing them an inch in front of the ball. Then he began. The club head moved back from the ball as the shaft came up in the sun and lifted; the shaft paused for a mo-ment, hanging parallel to his shoulders in the air above him. Then it moved over and downward, coming through to the ball and back over his shoulder from the other side. There was a small sharp click a moment after he had hit. The ball lifted in a low trajectory from the mat. It kept rising until it peaked about forty yards above the desert, and then it gradually sank, and then it hit into the sand. It rolled about ten yards and came to rest on a straight line out from where he had hit it, about halfway between the two large saguaros. It was very easy to see against the desert floor.

"Two-fifty," he said and put the four-wood back in the bag and took the driver out.

"Long game," the Indian said from where he sat on a low rock behind and to the left of him.

He placed a ball on the rubber tee in the corner of the piece of Astroturf and addressed it. This time he started the ball out to the right, but it did not stay there. He had put a slight draw in it, and near its peak it began to bend back left. When its roll had stopped it was twenty feet to the left of the first ball. The third ball hooked even more than the second, but he had started it even further right, and it came back also. When it landed it formed a triangle with the other two, equally close to them. He hit about twenty balls with various degrees of draw in them. They gathered together in their small space in the distance. Then he began to start the balls off to the left, slicing and fading them back in so that they gathered with the others. Some of the time he would come off the ball, dropping his left foot back off his stance after he had hit it, even stumbling occasionally. The balls continued to drop in the cluster. About five times he topped his shot, squirting the balls out only thirty to forty yards; these balls formed a cluster of their own.

He liked to let it come in this way, very casually, and not to force it. He was halfway through the bag and working with the seven-iron when he knew it. He began to be able to feel the club head in the tips of his fingers through the shaft and grip and the difference in his right hand and in his gloved left. When the club face struck the ball, he could feel it in the hair on the inside of his thighs. The swing he had to take to hit the ball seemed very perfunctory, a kind of ritual movement only, and even hitting the ball seemed unnecessary. He simply put the ball where he wanted to put it, and the thing was that no matter how far away he put the ball, or how he got it there, he still felt connected to it. The balls constantly changed their tight pattern in the desert, the pattern he felt he held in him; the balls were out there as a part of the way he was. And he toyed with it. He hit the balls in slightly different places, almost imperceptibly altering their trajectory and final placement.

Behind him, the Indian sat on his rock watching. "Short game," he thought, as the head of the seven-iron put the balls to rest at the side of a barrel cactus a hundred and seventy yards out in the desert. He took a folded post card from his shirt pocket, opened and studied it, listening to the sharp clicks and the occasional sounds of birds. On one side of the post card was a photograph of a road leading up to a lighthouse. On the left of the road was a small building with two figures standing in front of it. To the right was a brief golf course fairway, with a green at the end of it; a flagstick with a red flag stood up from the center of the green. The lighthouse was prominent and white in the background. In the sky to the left of it a small, precise arrow, pointing downward, had been penned in. At the top of the arrow were the words *my place.* On the other side of the card, beside the address and stamp, was the message: *My dear Relative, this is my place. I am doing well. You can send my best regards to all. You can enjoy this view of my place on the other side of this, under my arrow. I wish you well out there. I remain yours truly Frank Bumpus.*

The Indian looked at the picture again for a while, then he folded the post card carefully and placed it back in his pocket. The man had finished hitting the golf balls, and he was now standing with the seven-iron hanging along his leg, looking out into the desert. He was tall, and his blond hair was cut short. He had a broad back, but his posture was poor. "Would not sit a horse well, I'd say, and he doesn't look like a golfer," the Indian thought. The man stood there for a while, just looking, and then he turned away and put the club back into the bag with the others. The sun was now well behind him, and the man's shadow was longer and almost in front of him. The day birds had changed places with the evening birds, who were here a little early. There were no more morning birds around. The man turned to the Indian sitting on the rock.

"Okay," he said. And the Indian got up, lifted the limp gunny sack, and walked out into the desert.

When he entered the room again he had been gone for over two hours. Melinda was covered with the blanket, huddled near the edge of the bed, and sleeping.

NIGHT

There were no lights on the side of the road, and only a few houses, set back, with lights in them. There was a bright half-moon that gave light to the shapes of the cactuses, and occasionally they would pass a lit truck stop with a few low, dark buildings to either side of it. A few trailing clouds seemed blue in the half-moon light, and the dash lights, faintly blue also, lit the knees of the Indian in the seat beside him, over close to the far door. He could see the corner of her shoulder behind him in the rearview mirror. She was not stirring and seemed asleep. Bob White's hands were at rest in his lap. His head bobbed on his chest; he was sleeping also. A marker came up in the window: *Tucson—46 miles.* He was thinking of when he had given her the Laetrile in the motel a few hours ago, before they left. And this trailed him back to Richard and the two women.

In the shadows of the vacant lot next to the house he approached were three young Chicanos smoking marijuana, leaning against the side of a gutted Ford Falcon, making inaudible sounds in the still warm air of the late June evening. One of them was a girl, and he could make out the shape of one long leg, naked below shorts, tucked against the thigh and buttocks of one of the boys. The boy was pressing her against the car. The other one leaned beside them, the glow of a joint where he must have been holding it in his mouth.

"Git off it, Manny," he could hear the girl whine as he got closer, and then, seeing him over the boy's shoulder, "Hey, meester, help me, help me, huh?"

"Yeah, yeah, meester, come help thees leetle girl, yeah, yeah," Manny crooned, "oh yeah, oh yeah." And the three laughed, and the one with the joint removed it from his mouth and spat in the dust.

The house was located in West Los Angeles, the Chicano section, on a numbered street. It was surrounded by a new cyclone fence, the gate well oiled; it had made no sound when he had opened it. Like most of the houses there, it was small and boxy, flat-roofed and stuccoed, and had a wooden porch running the width of its front. On this porch, to the left of the door, was a wicker chair with a large empty clay planter beside it, and next to the planter, its tank and seat covered with a small tarp, was a black, evil-looking, Harley 600. He could see the shine of its lacquered fender and the hard chrome emblem on its transmission cover. Its wheels were silver. Its spokes shone in the dusk like needles.

He reached the porch still feeling the intimidation of the three kids. They ignored him. He glanced over his shoulder, catching a glimpse of the car he had driven there. The screen door rattled a little when he rapped it. The inner door was open, and he could see into the dim light of a small foyer, and then Gerry entered the space and came up to the door, squinting.

"Yeah?" she said.

He had not seen Gerry in over ten years, and he had not expected to see her there. She looked like a ghost. She had always been small and thin, but now she looked totally wasted, much older than the woman in her early thirties he figured her to be. She did not recognize him.

"Richard called me," he said. "I'm Allen, remember?"

"Sure," she said, remembering nothing. "Hey, Richard, there's a dude named Allen here," she called over her shoulder, and let him in.

When he saw Richard, sitting in an easy chair in the living room of the house, he began to realize why he had come there. It was not only for the Laetrile; though that held its desperation, he could have gotten it without much trouble elsewhere. He had not seen Richard in over ten years, and yet there was a feeling of unfinished business between them. He was not sure how he knew this. The chair was orange and cheap. There were no curtains on the windows, and some of the Venetian blind slats were broken loose. There was an old threadbare, Oriental rug on the floor.

"Hey, Allen, still fucking those school kids up?" Richard said, and then "Sit down, man, we'll rap."

He took a seat on the couch across from him. Gerry left the room. Richard was dressed in much the same way he had when they had known each other in the past. He wore jeans, sandals, and an expensive print shirt. There was a thick gold chain with a heavy medallion at the end of it around his neck. His dark hair was still cut in a shag style that looked a little womanish, but his face and body had changed. Though his face was still sharklike, angular Roman nose and narrow chin, it was harder than Allen had remembered. The large change was in his body. He had remembered him as being lean but smooth, having a swimmer's body; now he was much thicker. He had obviously been lifting weights over the years. His arms strained at the sleeves of his shirt. He was smoking a cigarette, and he was looking at Allen in a way that seemed to give recognition to the sense of reunion that he was experiencing, but he seemed to want to refuse to talk about old times or the distance they had both traveled since they had last seen each other. Allen stiffened his body, fearing that he might look too much older than he was. He reached up and touched the side of his face. He had a feeling that there would come a time when he would have to fight Richard. He was big, and he felt he kept himself in pretty good shape, but he wondered if he would have any chance against him.

"So, what's the story?" he said, the words coming out tougher than he had expected, and waited for Richard to talk. Gerry came back into the room with a tray of beers and another woman. She handed them each a can. She looked at Allen's eyes as their hands touched, but he could see nothing in hers. The other woman was a little heavier than Gerry, a little less wasted, and younger, about twenty-five. Her hair was long and dark and a little ragged. She had what looked like numerous small freckles on her arms, tiny scabs. She took her beer and sat on the floor beside Richard's orange chair. Gerry sat on the couch, at the far end of it, away from Allen. The new woman picked absently at her arm, cocked her head to the side, and stared between Allen and Gerry at the wall behind the couch. Allen was tempted to turn and look at the wall, but he figured there was nothing there.

"You remember Gerry, right? She was gone a long time, but she came back. This here is Wendy." He touched the head of the woman on the floor beside him. "I call her 'hot and juicy' sometimes, but I don't do it very often, and nobody else does it."

He figured he could not ask where Gerry had been. He saw in the hardness of Richard's look that the point was that she had come back because he had wanted her there.

"I dig you need the Laetrile, man, and I got it. It was easy, but that's because I been at it a while, right? Now here is the bit . . ."

As Richard talked, Allen listened to the way he chose his words. His language was odd, theatrical, and a little old-fashioned. He figured it for a mix of Chicano inflection and, probably, words and phrases picked up from Gerry. It struck him that Gerry had been in prison while she was away. He remembered her use of heroin from the beginning. That would account for the dated quality of Richard's speech. What had not changed was the sharpness of Richard's intelligence; even through the jargon Allen could hear his wit and intensity. Though he had gotten his language from outside of himself, he was in charge of those who he had gotten it from. Still, there was this room in this house and the two women. Regardless of his power and ability, his situations always seemed seedy and smalltime. And he often got caught at what he did. Allen remembered two drug busts early on when they were still in college. He suspected it was the strangeness of some deep and hidden moral sense in Richard that caused him to put himself in situations where he would fail. He suspected also that it was this moral sense that was the link between them. Coming from similar backgrounds, connecting in the Medical Corps in the Navy, attending college together, they could have become each other easily. Even after the added covering of ten years, he could sense it—this accident of their directions—and he felt tenderly about it. It was clear from Richard's composure that he owned Gerry, probably the other woman as well.

". . . so you drop one of the boxes in Tombstone, the other off in K.C. The bread goes to my mother's house in Detroit. You can cop the Laetrile and the works now, or you can wait till later. It's an easy gig. So that's it for business. Wanna snort a line?"

The sex had more power for him when it came back in memory. The little plastic moon only became apparent when Gerry had dropped the Venetians and dimmed the lights. The one behind him was Gerry, though he had wanted her in front. It had not been appropriate to indicate this, because he had given over all control. He had at first felt the fact of Richard's watching in a tender way. He had seemed, for the first time in their long acquaintance, relaxed and centered. He had not seemed vulnerable, but he had seemed in tune. But that had changed after a while, and Allen began to be aware of something dark and a little uncomfortable in the watching. The rest of it was a kind of intense activity, practiced to some rules that he was unaware of but was guided through. He recalled he had avoided the touch of Wendy's arms, had not wanted to call her by that other name, and that Gerry had kept her face hidden along his flanks.

They came through a cut in the low hills and started their slow descent into Tucson. The moon was still to their left. Much of the city was dark, but there were flickers of light enough to define its shape in the shallow cup of its valley. Fingers of lights trailed off from it up into the foothills, and closer to them, where the valley emptied into the lower hills and the desert, the broadest finger, the rows of motels and neon shopping plazas of the city's haphazard expansion, reached toward them. "Tucson," Bob White whispered, his fingers opening and flexing in his lap, his palms running slowly back and forth over his knees. She stirred at the sound of the spoken word, shifted her position slightly in the corner of the backseat behind him; he caught an edge of her shoulder in the rearview mirror. He noticed his left hand clenched tight to the wheel, his white fingers. He relaxed it slightly and shifted his body in the seat. Bob White handed him a lit cigarette. He took it across the space between them, looked over and nodded. Bob White settled back against the door, his hands now at rest on his thighs. Allen adjusted the vent to keep the smoke from filling the car. He slowed down a little.

She sat in the chair in the motel room facing him, her head propped up on a pillow, five little drops of sweat symmetrical on her forehead, the ends of her hair still wet, but beginning to curl, where they had touched the water of her bath. Small in his terry-cloth robe, which seemed darker in shadows alongside the light, adjusted to bathe her right arm from the wrist to the biceps: the arm bent, the palm open on her knee, the crook at the front of her elbow in half-shadow, as if blood gathered there and she was in post-mortem lividity.

"Squeeze," he said, and her fingers came up and gathered around the red ball he had placed in her palm, pressing it so that her thin biceps flexed and the rubber hose around it tightened. The ball was the one he used to improve his grip strength; he could squeeze it flat in his hand. He could see she could not make a dent in it. Sweating more profusely now, drops in the outside corners of her eyes, one on the bridge of her nose, she turned her head slightly, away from the spot touched more by the light, now that he took her wrist and extended her arm a little. He slapped her with two fingers, sharply, and the vein rose and the artery that crossed it, the pattern as particular as her palm lines, shallow streams around the ball in her hand running with perspiration. He lifted the needle, the syringe attached to it; he took a cotton swab damp with alcohol and brushed it over the vein. Outside, on the eave of the breezeway, a mockingbird was singing other people's songs. He placed the needle along her forearm in line with the vein, the bevel up. With a quick jab he inserted it. Her flinch was almost imperceptible, a small intake of breath only. The bird quit singing, a car ground on the gravel in the distance, some Spanish was being spoken. The slight surge of her blood pushed back on the plunger against his thumb; he let a little of it into the syringe. She opened her hand slowly when he told her to. The red ball sat wet on her palm. He snapped the tourniquet from her biceps; the pressure against his thumb diminished. When he detached the syringe from the needle, a few drops of blood fell out on her arm. He attached the thin clear hose connected to the glass bottle hanging from the lamp and opened the clamp. Blood entered the hose, then the clear liquid from the bottle cleared it. He stood up from where he was kneeling before her. He adjusted the clamp so that a slow regular dropping of the liquid entered the hose near the neck of the bottle. He taped the needle to her arm. He wiped up the few drops of blood with a tissue, which he folded and then wiped her brow with it. She turned back and smiled at him. For a moment he had felt a release of intensity when the act was finished; he had felt suddenly very tired. When she smiled at him, he surged again.

"Okay?" he asked.
"Okay," she said.

He liked the feather touch of her fingers on his spine playing
some light music. She made little sounds when he sucked a piece
of flesh on her arm into his mouth, making a circle. He bought
her a silk scarf to keep her collars from chafing against her neck.
She bought him a snakeskin wallet. He bought her pieces of
Indian jewelry. She cooked him fancy desserts on occasion. When
he carried her from place to place he kept his hands open and flat
against her flesh. She had a way of giving herself over to his carrying. He carried her often. He stood while he made love to her,
sometimes, so as not to injure her body by pressing too hard
against it. She bought him a silk robe, Japanese style, and turned
her head away shyly. She ate everything still but favored things
that were spoonable. He spoke to her while she was sleeping. Her
skin had grown slack in its struggle, but there were no significant
lines in it. He bought her a small flashlight. He liked the way her
voice trailed off at the ends of her sentences. She bought him
Johnny Walker Scotch and took an occasional puff on his cigarette. He found that even her thin waist had grown thinner when
he placed his hands around it. She placed her lips on his neck
when he carried her. He liked to buy her pieces of fruit.
  She bought him a knit shirt with an alligator on the pocket, and
they laughed about it. He put the tips of his fingers into her
mouth when he made love to her. She pointed things in the land-
scape out to him from the corner of the backseat. He had a way
of moving to her before she called him. He liked to leave her
alone and then return to her. He gave her money. She gave him
room on her pillow. He bought her pieces of hard candy to suck
on. She bought him small tools. She leaned against him when she
walked. He gave her towels to press on her stomach. She made
little sounds when he lifted her: air forced out of her lungs when
his hand took her weight through her back. He liked to prop her
up with pillows in chairs. She sang very quietly in the dark in the
tub. He thought of her, walking to his ball after he had driven.
He bought her a curved shell from Africa to file her nails with.
He liked the way she had given over control to him. She seemed

very strong in the stolid way she accepted the places of her help-lessness. He liked it that she was a real burden. She gave him a small hemostat. He bought her thin yogurt in small containers. He liked the feel of her arm across his back when he carried her, her hand like a soft hook on his shoulder. He bought her loose under-wear. He liked to watch her in her glasses, reading, framed in the rearview mirror. She seemed to like to catch his eye in the mirror and smile. She bought him a small notebook in which to keep their accounts. He liked the strange smell of her breath. Some-times her fingers would caress the arm of the chair in which she sat. They drank tea in the evenings. He made a picnic of fruits and vegetables at a rest stop. They did not talk about things in detail. She made liver pâté when there was a kitchen. They wrote no letters and received no mail. They had no friends.

He bought her a pair of warm socks. She read many books. She seemed to be waiting for something other than her death. He took her to a baseball game in a small town in southern Arizona. They did not travel much on the super highways, and he drove slowly. He liked the way she dressed herself with such care. He bought a gun. He liked the smell of the medicine bag. She bought herself a thimble after she had pierced her finger with a needle and it would not heal. He bought himself bright-yellow cheap headcovers for show. She had some trouble when she swallowed. He liked the way she was lighter each time he lifted her up. He bought her a stuffed stocking with the smile of a fat snake sewn into it for the small of her back. He told her stories of adventure and other details about golf. He told her stories about his child-hood. She told him about the way sand drifted along the Cape. He bought her a music box the size of a matchbook. She liked the seriousness in his eyes when he was studying. He read very little, but he went over books in his mind. She bought him range balls at a market. She was pleased that he liked it that she was finally reading *Moby-Dick*. He liked the way she understood the be-havior of other people. She liked the way he sweated when he made love to her. She was no longer curious about his secrets. He felt she had no secrets.

She thought of his psychological insides as a series of mystery boxes, some transparent, others only half opened, the rest opaque and totally closed, shut off from his entrance completely. He was strong on the complexity of details. He rolled his eyes and laughed with her when she told him about his boxes. She liked the ways in which she had become physical with the cancer. He bought her books about the Indians of the Southwest. They both stopped taking each other so much for granted. She bought him a Coltrane tape, *Meditations*. He took her to see a pottery exhibition and found he was moved by it. He liked the way she liked to bathe in the dark. She thought seldom about the other possible men, lost days, and her lovers (so many years ago) back East; it's all right, good-bye and no regrets. They walked short distances some evenings, but like young lovers or old people. She appreciated his sadness when he was sad; she left him alone with it, realizing it was proper and necessary. He was taken by the hardness of copper jewelry against her vulnerable skin. She liked the way, in her memory, he put a small red boat out from a dock. They talked about the congruence of their traveling dreams.

TUCSON

In the twenty years of increased expansion into the foothills, the javelinas had for the most part kept out of sight. Still working the Sangre de Cristos, those distant mountains that turned red in the sunset to the pleasure of the rich who had built on the other slope of the wide low valley in which the city sat, they had grown thin and increasingly vicious in that spare, high country. When they did come down, visibly, into the foothills, their packs were smaller, usually no more than thirty in number, and they usually came in quick raids, hitting the cultivated cactus and the feeble gardens of those who lived highest up in the hills. They weren't a problem if they weren't stirred up. On a few occasions they had killed dogs who had tried to attack them. They could run quickly for short distances. There was a time when people ate them; they had been thought a delicacy when they were healthy and fat. It is doubtful if the rich who now lived there would ever have eaten these small wild boars. They were not numerous enough to be an embarrassment to the developers; they had become an instance of local color. Bob White thought he'd like to see some of them. He also wanted to see about getting a few rattlers.

Melinda had slept well and was feeling stronger. The cancer was taking a break, was the way she thought of it. Neither she nor Allen thought that the Laetrile had anything to do with it. They had stopped at a motel at the mouth of the valley before entering the city itself. The only available room had twin beds in it, and Allen thought that this had in part accounted for Melinda's good sleep. Bob White had demurred at the offer of sharing the room with them. He had slept in the car, said he would like being able to see the road and the lights. The three of them had coffee in the room, and Bob White had told them a couple of stories, one about his childhood, the other about hunting rattlers. Melinda had found pleasure in the stories. She liked the childhood one most. Its message was conventional, and she felt she had heard the story, or some version of the story, before. But he had a way of telling it that was both ritualized and personal, and added to that was the humor he brought to it, a humor that joked both on the form of the telling and, in a very sweet and wise way she thought, on the trials of growing up. She thought this humor could have some application to what she was doing as well. And Allen had liked the story also.

Bob White said he would like to be let off near the foothills; he would like to use the gunny sack the golf balls were in. They had laughed some at trying to figure what to do with the balls. Finally, they had decided to put them in the bottom of the shower stall. Allen had taken his shower among them. Melinda said she would stay and read, would order some lunch at the pool, would spend the day relaxing. He said he would call her around noon. He and Bob White drove off at nine.

When he dropped him off at the crossroad at the bottom of the foothills, Bob White immediately began walking. As he turned the car around, he saw him turn and stick his thumb out to the first two cars that passed him. He drove to the parking lot of a supermarket a few blocks away. The lot was already half full, and he parked between two cars. He got out, opened the trunk, and transferred the four clubs he had used the day before into his own brown-and-white vinyl golf bag. He folded the limp Sunday bag and stuck it in the left wheel well. He checked the larger golf bag, the small zipper compartment, to see that he had enough balls and tees. Satisfied, he got back into the car and drove out of the parking lot.

He thought three of the six courses in the Tucson area were possible. One was a public course, and he only toyed with trying that one for a moment. One of the others seemed good, but when he checked its location on the map he saw it was close to a retirement section of the city, and he decided against it. The third was called Tucson Hills. It was a par-seventy, sixty-three-hundred-yard course, and it was rated as having average difficulty in *Golf Digest*. It was located fairly close to the residential areas that were in turn close to the professional and business complexes of the city.

At the entrance, a few yards in from the blacktop road, was a crushed-stone drive with a wooden archway at the foot of it. Hanging from the crosstie was a piece of wood that swung free on screw eyes and woodburned into it were the words: *Tucson Hills Country Club (Private)*. He passed under the sign and along the drive, which was lined with a hedge high enough that from his car he could not see beyond it. The drive went on for a quarter-mile, and when the hedge ended, it opened up onto a crushed-stone parking lot to the left. At the end of the parking lot was a low rectangular building, adobe, in the Spanish style, with a red tile roof. There were three archways, equally spaced, in the side of the building, and above each was a sign: *Restaurant, Patio, Pro Shop*. He parked and walked across the gravel through the archway marked *Patio* and into a space open to the sky in which there were a few metal picnic tables with umbrellas in the middle of them. At the left end was a bar that lead both into the patio and the restaurant on the other side of it. Three men sat on stools on the patio side of the bar with their backs to him, and facing him was a man in a white jacket behind the counter. The man looked at him curiously as he entered. He paused for a moment, then walked to the right through the open courtyard to a screen door with a small sign above it: *Pro Shop & Office*. He opened the screen door and entered. The pro shop was large and carpeted in green. It contained the usual gear. There were two metal tables to the left of the door, a couple of easy chairs, and a TV set on a platform attached to the wall. A man in his early thirties, muscular and blond, wearing an expensive tan knit shirt, stood behind the glass case of the counter, a hand resting on the case, a low modern cash register to his right.

"Hello," he said, not smiling. "Can I help you?"

"Thought I might play a little golf," Allen said, reaching into his back pocket as he crossed to the counter. He took a card out of his wallet and handed it to the man.

"Redwood?" the man said. "Never heard of it." He reached under the counter to his left and took out a small printed pamphlet. "These are the course rules; we keep them here. Green fees are eighteen dollars for guests. You've got to take a power cart; that's twelve bucks for eighteen. It'll cost you thirty to play. You still want to do it?"

He reached into his wallet and took out a twenty and a ten and handed them to the man.

28

"Okay," the man said, his spirits rising a little. "Carts are to the left as you go out; they don't need keys. First tee around the back."

"Might have a cup of coffee first?"

"Sure. The way you came in. Juan'll take care of you."

He took a score card and wooden pencil from a container on the counter. The card had a small, rough map of the course on the back of it. He folded the card and put it and the pencil in his shirt pocket and went out into the patio to the end of the bar. He ordered a cup of coffee when the Mexican waiter walked over to him. He took the score card out of his pocket and opened it on the counter with the map facing up. Then he checked the three men. Two of them looked to be in their early fifties; their golf clothes were conservative, and they were very well groomed. One had a thin mustache and graying hair. He was the larger of the two, and his hands suggested that he had once done physical labor. The other was short and stocky, thick through the chest and arms. He had a small paunch pushing out over his belt against the edge of the bar. The third man was younger, maybe thirty. His clothes were a little flashy. He had a golf cap tilted back a little on his head and a mod haircut. He was more animated than the other two, a little ingratiating and brash at the same time. He would laugh at a statement made by one of the others, then he would get quickly serious. Both of these behaviors were slightly exaggerated. On occasion he glanced down the counter in an automatic way, looking for approval, simply because there was someone there. He also seemed a little curious.

"Hey," he said after a few minutes. "I see you're checking the card. You from around here? You'll like the course, if you're lucky that is—it's a tough one. Ever play it?"

The other men looked over at him also. The shorter one nodded and smiled slightly. The other just looked.

"I'm just traveling through," Allen said. "Thought I'd get some golf in."

"Good luck," the younger one said, and laughed. "You'll need it." He glanced at the other two to catch their reactions. Then he returned to his conversation with them, but in lower tones.

After a few more minutes, Allen could see that the three were getting ready to leave. He got up, put a dollar bill on the counter,

and walked through the archway and out to his car. He opened
the trunk and sat on the edge of it and put on his golf shoes. He
toyed with the shoes until he saw the three men come out through
the archway. The younger one was moving his arms and leaning
toward the other two as they walked to the side of the building.
The carts were carefully lined up there, and two of them had
golf bags in them. The larger man and the younger man got into
one of the carts, and the stocky man got in the other.

He pulled his bag out of the trunk, shut it, walked over to the
carts, and adjusted his clubs in a carrier. Then he drove around
the building to the first tee. It was a large tee with a cart path
beside it, and by the time he had pulled up to the path the three
men were standing behind their carts, readying their clubs. The
young man glanced over at him. Then he spoke to the others,
softly, his head close to theirs. The large man nodded, and the
stocky one shrugged.

"If you want you can play along with us," the young man
called over to Allen. "This is Steve," he said, opening his hand in
the direction of the larger man. "Frankie," indicating the other.
"I'm Lou."

The young man had made the introductions before Allen had
any chance to respond to his offer. He let it go. He said his name
and shook hands with the three of them. The larger one remained
a little reserved. The stocky one was looking him over.

"Throw your sticks on," he said, indicating his cart. "Tim'll
take yours back."

It was clearly the prerogative of the larger man, Steve, to hit
first, and he did not rush it. He took his time washing his ball in
the red container that stood on a post to the side of the cart path,
and he wiped it carefully. Then he walked to the back of the
tee, to the blue markers, and took some time looking for a spot.
Finally, he teed the ball up.

"We play the blues," Lou said.

Steve looked over to where they were standing, and Lou shut
up. Then he lifted his driver and took a look at the club face,
flicking at it with his thumbnail. Then he addressed the ball,
looked up a few times to check his line, and with a short back
swing and a fluid motion struck it. The hit was straight and low.
The ball carried about two hundred yards out in the middle of

the fairway, and it came to rest a good thirty yards beyond that.

"That's a good hit, Steve," Lou said seriously. "Do it good, Frankie."

Frankie scowled a little, as if the young man had been a little too familiar with him. He went to the back of the tee, teed up, and took a practice swing. He had a full if slightly inside-out back swing, and when he hit the ball it hooked a little, coming to rest short of the first shot, near the rough to the left of the fairway.

"Good place to come in from, Frankie," Lou said.

"Yeah?" Frankie said, and then as if to cover the sharpness of his response, "Could be worse, I guess."

Allen figured the younger man for a hot dog, a fair to good college player who had lost some of the sharpness of the practice which went with that. When he saw Lou hit, he thought he was probably right. He outdrove the other two by a good thirty yards. He was straight but a little high, and he did not get as much roll as Steve had. He had gotten his shoulders through the shot a little too quickly. His swing was economical, but he had muscled it a little, trying for too much power.

Then it was his turn. The first hole was a par four. For all practical purposes it was straight; there was a slight dog leg to the left, but it would not come into play unless his shot was short and to the extreme left. The green, visible from the tee, was slightly elevated, with a trap to the right front. Along the left of the fairway was a stand of trees about two hundred yards out. He figured to come through nicely on the first shot but to get it high and short and play a bit of a slice. He started the ball off to the left in the direction of the trees; when it got near the top of its arc, it curled in a little. He had put a little less than he had wanted to into it, and it got closer to the trees than he had figured, but it took a good bounce, and when it came to rest, it looked to be sitting where he would have a possible shot, along the trees, around the slight bend, and into the right of the green. It was a bit shorter than the other three balls. Nobody said anything after he had hit.

When he got to his ball, he saw that if he brought it in slightly he could come around the edge of the line of trees and make the green; he would be right of the flag, but there was a down slope, and he figured it would, with a little bite in it, wind up close enough to the cup. The three waited for him to hit, Frankie sitting in the cart behind and to the side of him with his arms crossed over his chest; the other two were to the right and back in the middle of the fairway, in line with their balls. The proper club would be a five-iron, but he went back to the cart, took a four out of the bag, paused for a moment, looked toward the green, and then put the club back and took out a three.

"I think a three, can't quite tell how far I am," he said.

"Can't help; don't know how ya hit," Frankie said. "There's the one-fifty marker over there." He lifted his chin in the direction of the other side of the fairway ahead of them, indicating a red stick at the edge of the rough.

Allen approached his ball and stood behind it, sighting down the row of trees, then he stepped up to it. When he hit it, he caught a little grass behind it, meeting it fat. It was low, along the line of trees, and straight.

"Trap," Frankie said matter-of-factly behind him before the ball landed. It hit in the middle of the sand trap to the right of the green.

"Right," he said, and he got back into the cart with Frankie.

Frankie was next. He hit a shot, again with a slight hook in it, that was high and stopped where it landed, on the green to the left of the flagstick, pin high, about twenty-five feet from the cup. Steve hit a seven-iron; the shot was as straight as his drive had been. It hit about ten yards short of the green and ran up to within six feet of the hole. The hot dog used a wedge, less club than he needed. He came through it smoothly and with considerable snap; it clicked off the club face, and a good-sized divot rose up a few feet in the air ahead of where it had rested. It was high and true. It landed to the back of the green, bit, and shot back about three feet, coming to rest on the high side of the hole, about twelve feet away, leaving him with a tricky downhill putt.

When they got to the green, all of them got out of the carts, and the three others waited for Allen to hit from the trap before they walked up onto the putting surface. The trap was wide and flat; good sand, he thought, and his ball sat up cleanly, a thin furrow in the sand running from the back of the trap, where the ball had hit, to where it now rested. He was about ten feet from the lip, which was low and would not come into play. There was about fifteen feet of green between him and the cup. The first five feet or so were level, and then the green sloped down a little. On the other side of the cup there was another thirty yards of level green and another ten feet of good apron before the slope down into the thicker rough. He hit the ball thin, lifting only a little sand, and the ball flew most of the green, hitting near the far edge, and trickled to the back of the apron and just over into the beginning of the rough. He looked up to the others and shrugged in an embarrassed way, then raked the trap and walked around their lines on the green to the far side. He had forgotten to get a club, had his sand wedge in his hand, and he trotted back to the cart to get one.

"Take your time," Steve said, smiling for the first time.

He got three clubs out of his bag, a wedge, a seven-iron, and his putter, and crossed the green again. He looked the shot over, took a practice chip with his seven-iron, then dropped it beside the putter in the grass and selected the wedge. He did not want to mess with roll on this shot. He could see enough level green near the pin where he could lay it down. He had a good lie, and he decided not to bring the ball back at all. He lifted it carefully, quite high; it landed and rolled a few feet and came to rest five feet from the hole. Lou missed his putt and took a tap-in for a four. Frankie missed his also, had a tricky three-footer coming back, but knocked it in with some authority. Allen took a bogey five. Steve ran his into the heart of the cup for a birdie three. It was not until they got to the back nine that they began to gamble in earnest.

It was hot in the foothills, but the air was dry. When he got to where the road ended abruptly beside a staked-out lot, he sat on a rock and took a sip of water from the small cough-syrup bottle he carried in his shirt pocket. From his back pocket he took out a piece of cloth and tied it around his forehead as a sweatband. While he was resting he checked the gunny sack for holes, and in the bottom of it he found an old golf cap with the words *Redwood Links* stenciled on a patch above the brim. He put it on, and his face felt cooler.

He had gotten a ride from two Indians in a pick-up truck who were headed over the foothills to their reservation. They had passed a few words, and they had let him out where the last of a series of dirt roads spurred off from the blacktop, heading deeper into the hills. When he got to the end of the road, where he rested, he was above all the development, though the two men had told him that that would not last and that the white men were planning more roads further up. After he'd rested he walked off into the wilds of the foothills, snaking back and forth though moving significant distance away from the developed land. He stopped occasionally to listen and watch birds and to sip some drops from his bottle. Much of what he was walking through was sand, red clay, and shale, with low cactuses and occasional desert flowers growing here and there. He found four small arroyos where there was a little shade and greener growth, and he came upon two caves where he found what he took to be javelina spore, but it was not fresh and he did not see any javelinas.

He gave up his search for the javelinas after a while and sat down to think about the rattlers before hunting them. It was well into July, so it would be a little tricky, though not as bad as August. In August, the snake shed his skin; he was blind then, and he would strike out at anything that moved, without any kind of warning. He was a little skittery in July, so you would need a good stick. He found one about four feet long, broke the twigs off it, and waved it a little for feel. Then he began looking for the snakes.

He poked the stick around the bases of cactuses. When he came to places where the shale was a little elevated, he circled them, checking for sunny resting places. After about a half-hour, he found his first one. It was good size, about five feet long he guessed, and good and fat. It lay flat, strung out from tail rattles to a point about eight inches from its broad head, where there was a bend in it, a little slack it used when it raised up some to check things. Its head was flat on the rock, its eyes half open and a little glazed. The piece of red shale it was on was about two feet off the ground; it protruded in a shelf out from a configuration of shale that was about ten feet in diameter. He was standing off to the side of it. "Good afternoon," he said to himself and moved slowly away and to the left to get a look at what was behind it.

Though the rock to the rear of the snake's tail was in shade, it seemed darker than it should be there, and he suspected that there was an opening between rocks where the snake, if he startled it, could go. He would not want to mess with it if it got in there. He moved slowly, a little more to his left, aiming to come close to getting between the sun and the snake. When he had moved far enough back and to the side, he was about thirty feet from the snake, a little to the left of its head. He raised both of his hands, linking his fingers together, and moved them slowly into the path of the sun. He was humming softly, a kind of cricket whistle, disjointed and without any clear rhythm. When his hands got in the sun's way, they threw a shadow on the ground about six feet from the overhang on which the snake rested. He altered his fingers slightly, forming the shape of a small rodent on the ground. He tested it by rippling his fingers slightly; the shadow undulated like some injured thing. He bent quickly to the left, his hands still in the air, and then moved back again. For a moment he had thrown a shadow across the snake's head. The snake's head lifted in a quick fluid gesture, its eyes snapping open. For a full two minutes, it looked slowly around, shifting its body slightly. Then it lowered its head to the same place on the rock, but its eyes remained open.

Bob White began to move the shadow slowly back and forth on the ground. It was not in clear sight of the snake, but it must have done something to the temperature of the air or to the small insects it passed over or to the attitude of the few places where there was grass, because the snake began to inch its way slowly forward toward the edge of the shale ledge. In ten minutes it got there, and when Bob White saw that it was getting close, he stopped the movement of the shadow and began to twitch it slightly at intervals of about five seconds. The snake looked at the shadow intently. After twitching the shadow for a while, he began it edge it away from the snake slowly, with little flutters and jerks. The snake stayed where it was, but when the shadow was about eight feet away from it, it dropped its head over the end of the ledge and began to slide off the shale, curling to other pieces of shale below it, until all of its body was on the sandy ground. It had added twists to itself, and it began to glide slowly over the sand, head slightly erect now, the small trough where its body had been leaving a shallow trail behind it.

When Bob White had the shadow about ten feet from where he stood, he stopped it, making it quiver in place. About six feet from the shadow the snake stopped moving, then began to edge forward again to reach striking distance. When he thought he had the snake close enough to him, out in the open enough, he pulled his hands out of the sun's path. The snake stopped moving immediately and was poised, as still as a piece of twisted pipe. He left it there, and walked quickly back and got the gunny sack and the stick. When he moved, the snake jerked its head in his direction and began to rattle. He returned to where he had been, held the gunny sack in his left hand, and began to rap with the stick on the ground in front of him.

"I've got you now, old salt," he said aloud, and then he yelled out, "Hoo!" and rapped the stick sharply against a piece of shale. The snake jerked his head up higher and began to rattle more furiously, and Bob White moved in. He tapped the tip of the stick between the snake and the opening of the gunny sack in his hand. When he saw the snake tighten its body, shortening it like a compressed spring, he stopped moving the stick toward the sack and just tapped it in place on the ground. The snake was now about three feet from the stick, and he moved the gunny sack in closer. When the snake struck, he jerked the stick away, and at the same time he thrust the gunny sack toward it. The snake landed in the sack up to the midpoint of its body. Bob White lifted the sack, and the snake fell into the bottom of it, twisted and turned for a moment, and then was still.

By the time he had gotten two more snakes into the sack, the sun was high above him and it was very hot. He found a shaded place and drank what water remained in his small bottle. Then he untied the piece of twine from the mouth of the sack and let it rest on the ground. He found a few good-sized stones and took his stick and prodded the snakes until they began to emerge from the sack. He killed each one by dropping a stone on its head. Then he cut off the heads and the rattles, throwing the heads into the desert and putting the rattles in his pocket. When he had done that, he took out his knife again and skinned the snakes on a rock. He put the skins, rolled into loose coils, into small plastic sandwich bags that he took from his back pocket. From the fold of bags, he extracted three larger ones and put the snake meat into them. Then he packed the bags into a corner of the gunny sack and folded it into a square. He put the sack in the shade and sat on a rock, smoking and looking at the few flowers around him and listening to the birds. The smoke curled up from his lobster-claw pipe, gathering in a thin cloud in the still air above his head. After a while he got up, knocked his pipe empty against a rock, fetched the bag from the shade, and set off in the same zigzag manner he had used to get where he was, back by a different route toward the dirt-road spur and the lower foothills.

There was a hint that something might materialize when they reached the ninth hole, a short par three with a tee that was elevated so that one hit considerably downhill to the green. Because of the shortness of the hole (about a hundred and sixty yards) the green had been made small, and there were traps guarding it on all sides.

"Farthest from the pin buys lunch?" Steve said, as they were climbing out of their carts. Frankie had loosened up some as they played the front nine. He was not as good as the other two, but he was close enough in skill to keep himself in things, and he seemed pleased there was someone playing with them whom he was better than. Steve and Lou were playing about even, near par. Frankie was four over, but he had missed three short putts, rimming the cup. Allen was five over and had dropped three long putts to save pars.

Steve had the honors, and he dropped his shot in close, about eight feet from the hole. Lou was next; he pushed his shot slightly. It hit and trickled to the rough on the other side of the green, far to the right. Allen was pleased to see that Frankie had a good chance. His shot was short, hitting in front of the green, but it had been rather low, and it rolled up, finishing about four feet from the cup.

"All right!" Frankie said.

Allen dropped his shot to the right of the two close balls, between them and Lou's. Lou had lost, and he joked about it a little. When they had finished the hole, they parked their carts to the rear of the Clubhouse and entered the back arch that led into the patio.

Lunch had been no small wager. He could see from what they ordered that the tab would come, with drinks and tip, to more than fifty dollars. They asked him a few questions about where he was from and what he did. His answers were direct but sufficiently comprehensive so that they did not feel they were pushing for information. He asked Frankie what he did, figuring that would be the easiest way to get to the associations. Frankie owned a small, executive flying service. Steve was in real estate and "speculation," and whatever he did it was big. He kept a plane of his own at Frankie's place, an eight-seater. Lou was the youngest vice-president that one of the local banks had ever had; he found a way of making this known to Allen. He, and Frankie to a lesser extent, seemed clearly dependent on Steve in ways that were not spoken of but apparent in their behavior. Frankie just held to a lower station. Lou remained obsequious.

Before they were finished, Allen let it drop that he did not think the course was very tough. (He had checked the map of the back nine, noting that the fairways were quite a bit narrower than on the front.) Now that he had gotten used to the way it played, he said, he thought he could beat it without too much trouble. He had worked the front nine by spraying a lot. He had seldom been off the fairways, but he had seldom been down the middle. Steve looked up sharply at him when he spoke.

"Steve's on the board here," Lou chuckled. "Them's fighten' words!"

It was better and easier than he had thought it would be.

"Still," he said, "not much water, the greens aren't too tricky, the holes are a little short, no problems with sight lines." That seemed to do it.

"Well, what would you say to some friendly wagering on the back nine," Steve said, bending slightly forward, looking at Allen across the table. "Say twenty a hole for outright winners and a hundred for the match; unless that's a little too steep for you?" Allen demurred slightly, backing up at the force of Steve's intensity.

"That *is* a little steep," he said.

"Thought it might be," Steve said dryly.

"But okay, sure, why not," Allen said.

"Good," Steve said, "very good." He smiled benignly, sipped at his whiskey and water, wiped his mouth delicately with his napkin. It was getting close to noon. Allen excused himself and went to call Melinda.

She hung up and went back to her poolside chair at the table under the beach umbrella. There were two children at the shallow end playing in the water, a boy and a girl about seven and ten. Their mother lounged in the water up to her chest, leaning her back against the pool's side, her arms resting on the edge. The children played well together, and the mother seemed relaxed; she watched, but she did not interfere or direct. Occasionally a high giggle would come from the girl when her brother splashed water at her, but their play never got too frantic. They had a float in the shape of a dolphin with an inflated ring that could be gotten inside of and a beach ball. At times the dolphin was used in their play, but at other times it bobbed off by itself, oddly commanding a space in the pool; moved by their wake, it often seemed ready to dive under the water. It stayed close to them, though the beach ball floated away at times.

There was a middle-aged man with a paunch, his wife next to him, sitting in a deck chair beside a poolside table. He was very white, and both he and his wife were sipping at tall drinks and watching the children play. One thin young girl lay in the sun on one of the beach lounges, getting her tan.

When she came back from the phone, the sun had shifted a little; but the walk back and forth had tired her, and in addition she was not worried about the longevity of her skin anymore, so she did not move the chair but let the sun hit her face and arms and her chest above her one-piece suit. "Wither away," she said to herself. She was very thin, and she knew she looked good this way; she had always tried to keep her weight down, but in recent years she had been unsuccessful. When she fell ill, the weight had begun to drop off. After a while it had leveled off, and now she was the way she had always wanted to be. She thought of this as a fringe benefit. The major benefits included this trip, the fact that they had no money to speak of, and the fact that he could earn some through his skill: a skill connected to his body.

This made him very desirable. Over the years she had not really known how little he thought of himself, though he spoke of what he felt as inadequacy in his work. He was a physical person who had denied that part of himself too much, and what he had been always desperate about, as she saw it, was the futile search for a body component in the mind work that he had to do for his teaching. The heart of the benefit was a time thing, very ironic of course. He had found his body when her need arose. She had found hers beneath the added weight she had carried. Her new body was the evidence of her need for him to connect to himself in the way he had. His body had gained some weight, all muscle, from his practice. She felt she had given him some flesh. They had a beginning, though it was near the end.

She did not think of the cancer as a foreign element in her anymore. What it had done was to make real the delicacy she had always asked him for in their sex. Sex with him before had always been a little desperate, as if he were reaching for something beyond and not in her; he always passed over what was there. Now that had changed, and she still had some hope that more inclusive change, the kind that would extend beyond the sex, was possible because of it. Her mind's delicacy had become a delicacy of body; her weakness was physical. When they made love he was attentive to this. He lifted her and placed her carefully in different ways. She directed him and moved him by talking. He did not talk much while they were making love or otherwise, but she could see often, afterward, how overcome he was. They made love often, usually once a day, when she was up to it. She had not felt so alive in a long time. What is this thing called love, she thought. Making it, mostly. Much of the rest is dross. How good to feel so self-involved.

And she was reading a lot of books now, books she had always wanted to read. She read them with care and fine attention, and she learned a lot from them. But what she learned was not material to be used anywhere. She read them for what they contained because they had been written by people who knew how to write. She felt the purity of doing this, the sense of authentic leisure. She loved the books, and she loved him. She loved herself in her test of power, a test that she was passing. She almost thought she loved her foe, the cancer, too: it provided the good test. She had put her water colors and her oils away for good; she had no more interest in representation. She was having the best time of her life.

When the play of the children in the water became very quiet because their game now was about making small ripples with their hands, she heard the crunch in the gravel over her shoulder to her left. She turned her head and saw Bob White coming, wearing a golf cap and carrying a gunny sack. She smiled, and he entered the gate of the fence surrounding the pool, walked over, put the sack on the pool deck, and sat in the chair beside her. He smiled and pointed to his cap as he looked at her. She laughed lightly.

"Nice," she said. He nodded, very seriously.

"Good for the sun," he said, and she laughed again.

"Very hot day," he said. "I got some snakes here." He tilted his head in a secret, conspiratorial manner in the direction of the bag. "Quite good to eat," he said. "You ever fix snake?"

"No," she said. "You?"

"No," he said, "woman's work." But he smiled and added, "A very skillful and artful thing to do, I think. You wanna try it?"

"Absolutely," she said.

He gathered her hat and purse for her and helped her up and into her robe. Then he gave her back her purse and picked up the gunny sack in his other hand. Then they went back to the room.

He had been there before he had gone to the pool. He had cleaned out their hibachi and put fresh charcoal under the grate, and he had placed the grill in the corner of the small patio outside the sliding glass doors in the rear of the room. Tucked under the edge of it, held so that breeze would not scatter them, were a few pieces of torn newspaper. Inside, over the formica counter to the right of the sink in the small mirrored alcove between the room and the bath, he had spread some newspaper with waxed paper over it. In the sink was a square plastic container with the name of the motel on its side, the ice bucket full of chipped ice. On the counter to the other side of the sink was more waxed paper, and on top of it, beside small restaurant packets of salt and pepper, was a small pile of odd-looking plant clippings. Among them was a tiny, delicate blue flower at the end of its own cut stem. His knife rested beside the clippings. It had a bone handle and looked like some kind of fish knife. Both the clippings and the knife blade were touched with drops of water from the washing he had obviously given them.

"What a beautiful little flower," she said.

"Very beautiful," he said. "Very good with snake."

She was a very good cook, and he was very good with his knife. After he had put the snake meat in its bags on top of the ice and had hung the skins to dry over the latticework that separated the patios in back of the rooms, he began to work at the pile of clippings. He cut the small flower off first and put it to the side. Then he stripped some of the greener stalks of their side growths, putting them between his thumb and the blade at their bases, then squeezing and turning his wrists slightly. When he had finished this, he slit each stalk down the middle, revealing its greener inside; the stalks looked a little like leeks. Then he cut them in two-inch sections.

"Don't know about this salt and pepper," he said.

"I can take care of that," she said. "Is snake dry or oily? It *looks* dry."

"Snake is very dry," he said.

"We'll need some oil," she said. She got oil from the styrofoam picnic basket they carried with them.

"Is it open or closed when they cook it?"

"I remember they do it open, I believe," he said.

"I thought it might be," she said. "We can do it on foil with holes in it, to let the smoke through and keep the juices in."

The story Bob White had told about hunting rattlers had to do with using hand shadows to get them away from holes. In the story he had told of the one time he had felt very close to a snake. This had happened as the snake watched the shadow, becoming in its fury and intensity sort of hypnotized. What had happened was that he had gotten himself kind of lost in watching the snake's eyes watch the shadow of his hands. It was almost as if the eyes drew him closer, the sheer will of the unblinking force causing the shadow and his hands with it to move too close to the snake. He had awakened in time, and the snake just missed his hands when it struck. He had felt very close to the snake that time.

While they were working, he with the clippings, she with the foil with the holes in it for cooking the snake and with the oil and the salt and pepper, she thought about the other story, the one she had enjoyed most, the familiar one about his childhood that had reminded her, in its way, of her own.

It is said that I was born Robert Whitelaw in nineteen and twenty-three. They say this was before much development out this way, and things were pretty good for Indians, almost as good as they are now, but in the middle there things went downhill. My grandmother, who was a Pamet Wampanoag, had come from the East with her father after her mother had died. She married my grandfather, a Pima, and my father was born to them. When my father got ready to begin to think about getting married, my grandmother fixed him up with a Pamet woman who had come out West for other reasons. This woman became my mother. I begin to remember very well about the times when I was seven years old and up. Maybe I remember the tail end of those good times they say were going on in 'twenty-three. But this story is about a time when I was ten years old, so you can forget about what I have just said and listen to what I am going to tell you. My family was not too poor; my father had a few horses, and he worked some on the railroad there. On this day we went in to that place where you picked me up. It was different then, that road was the highway then, and that place was a store with a lot of supplies in it and a place where people who drove along stopped to buy souvenirs of the Southwest. Behind that place they had rattlesnakes and armadillos and some prairie dogs in cages. I think they had a coyote there, but he was very scrawny if they did. People I knew sold them snakes sometimes.

Well, on this day my father took me and we went there, to that place. My father wanted to get some rope there or something. When we rode up, there were a few cars there, maybe five of them, old cars like they used to drive then, but then the cars were new. I wanted to stay outside and watch the people stretch and go out back to see the snakes and things, so I did that while my father went inside to shop around. It was a hot day, and I had an old derby hat on my head. I believe I found that hat along the highway one day. There were two families there who had stopped there in a fairly big car. There were two men and two women and four or five kids. The kids were older than I was.

The grownups were younger than my father. One of the men had a camera and a stand for it, and he was taking pictures. He would tell the people to move around so he could take their pictures in front of things. They kept moving around, and once he even had them stand in front of the big car so he could take their picture there. Hell, I thought, that man is nuts with that camera. I used to talk to myself in that way. It was the way my father talked sometimes about white men, and I loved my father and the way he talked. I was leaning against the side of the building there, and I had a weed in my mouth to keep it wet, and I had my derby hat tilted down on my forehead against the sun, but because I thought it looked good that way too. I think I must have looked very funny there, the way kids can do when they stand around like that.

Anyway, those people were looking over at me sometimes, whispering to one another, laughing sometimes, looking the other way. The man with the camera wasn't seeing me though, though he might have when he pulled up, because he was busy moving the people around for picture taking. Finally, he did see me though, and when he did he just stopped everything, left his camera sit on his stand, put his hands on his hips, and just stared at me. I looked away from where I was looking at them, but I couldn't keep my head away, and when I turned it back, the man spoke to me. He said something like, Hey, kid, come here a minute. I thought I had nothing to do so I went over there. He said he would give me a quarter if I would take some pictures with them. I said okay. The first one was for me to push the button while he lined up with the others in front of the car. I did that one. Then he said I should get in line and he'd take my picture with the others. After that he wanted to take a picture of me in my derby. Then one of the kids talked to one of the women, who told the man I should put on one of those headbands they sold in the store with a feather in it. I took that picture with the kids. They too put headbands on.

Now this is where it starts to get good, if you want to say that about it. The man running the camera said that the other man should lift me up on his shoulders for a picture. I got up there, and the man with the camera got ready, but then he stopped and ran over to the car and got one of those small toy tomahawks out of it. He gave it to me, reaching it up above the other man to where I sat. He said I should hold the tomahawk up in the air and look mean. Well, I did that one, and then pretty soon they were telling me to do all sorts of things for pictures. In one time, they told me to pretend to scalp one of the women. I didn't know where to put the tomahawk, but they showed me. In another one they had me point a little bow and arrow at the kids, who they had hold up their hands and lean back as if they feared me. It was when they were having me do the one with the rubber knife, in which I held it across the throat of one of the girls—I had to stand on my toes to reach her, because she was very tall— that my father came out of the store and saw what was going on with me and the people there.

He had some rope and some few bundles, and I don't think he would have broken his stride coming out of the place when he saw me, but he did drop one of the bundles and had to pick it up. When he did that he didn't look my way, but he went right over to the horses. He tied his bundles onto the saddle straps and put the rope over the horn. The man took the picture then, and I dropped the rubber knife and walked away. My father was on his horse, and he walked it to the edge of the highway, where he stopped it. Then both my father and the horse, it seems to me, looked both ways down the highway as he had taught me to do. Then my father crossed the road on the horse. When he got to the other side, he pulled up. He kept his horse facing away from me and the people and the cars. He just sat there on the horse, aiming in the direction of the desert there and over in it to where we lived at that time. I know for sure that there was no talking right then or calling out.

I climbed onto my horse, and when I threw my leg over it, I could tell by the way the sun hit my face that I had forgotten my derby. I walked my horse over to the edge of the highway. After I stopped and looked both ways and when my horse's hoofs started to click on the highway, my father started his horse up, and when we were both over there in the desert, I was about thirty feet behind him. I knew I had to stay there and go the whole way like that on the ride home. We didn't pass too many people, but we did pass some, people we knew and ones we didn't.

All these people looked at us riding this way. I was always thinking that they all knew I had done wrong. By the time we got home I was very tired and hot and sad. My father never said a word about all this when it was over. Maybe that evening he patted my back or smiled at me or some such thing. When the times of a thing were over with my father they were over. Even now and at this somewhat significant distance from the events told in what I have just spoken about, I cannot append some powerful moral to this tale beyond the obvious. I would say, though, however vaguely I might put it, that there was something about disentanglement and walking away that has stayed with me from it. Sometimes, I guess, in some circumstances, there is no other hope for it, no help on the inside. I remember that trip home behind my father as a kind of purgatory passage. I bore it with some lessening of pain, I guess, because there was a kind of light at the end of it.

She was shaping the foil, each piece with the edges slightly turned up to catch the oil. He was cutting beside her. She was getting a little tired from standing. She reached a little too quickly for one of the bags on the ice; she wanted to measure the snake against the foil containers. She felt a little dizzy from the motion. There was some oil on her hands, and the bag slipped out of them and fell to the floor. He put his knife on the counter and reached down at her feet to pick it up. Her hand touched his shoulder lightly for balance.

"Hell, that snake is nuts with that slipping," she said.

He came up with the bag, put it back on the ice, then turned and smiled at her. They both laughed lightly, and she put her hand up on his shoulder and leaned a little against him. He reached down and picked her up and carried her to the bed. He placed her gently on it and put a pillow against the headboard. Then he took her under her arms and lifted her to a half-sitting position.

"Just have to rest a little," she said.

"You rest a little, while I finish up with the cutting," he said. "Then we can get to work with the good stuff." She nodded weakly as he looked down at her. Then he turned and walked back to the counter.

Even before they got to the tenth he was beginning to feel a little down about the situation. Earlier he might have considered the hot dog as someone to deal with, but Lou's desperateness, exacerbated now by the difficulty he would have to face in betting with Steve at a game of skill, made him feel something for the younger man. As for Frankie, he had come to like him. Whatever the density of his tie to Steve, he seemed to be his own man. He might be a little freed by the fact that he was simply not as good at golf as Steve was and could, therefore, go all out without worrying about winning big. But more important than that, while he was respectful he was not a panderer, and Allen liked him for his apparent clarity in the relationship. Among other things, Steve was a prick, he thought. The meanest thing about him was that he showed his power but acted as if he were above using it on someone as inconsequential as Lou. He let him, the outsider, know that he could step on either of these two others anytime he wanted to do it. He could step on Allen too, but he liked better to show him what his power was all about.

The tenth was a long par four with a dog-leg right; a stand of thick, beautiful oaks at the knee obscured sight to the green. A man-made stream ran along the right rough, starting at the tee and opening and cutting into the fairway about two hundred yards out, short of the bend. The stream formed a small pond there, complete with lilies. There was some fairway remaining to the left of the pond, about fifty feet of it, guarded by a long, lateral trap at the edge of the left rough. It was the number-one hole on the course. Its difficulties were these. If you played up short of the pond too far to the right, you would have a blind shot over the oaks to the green. That shot was sufficiently long from there that it would be hard to clear the trees and have enough left to get to the pin. On the other hand, if you played to the left, between the pond and the trap, you would have to hit a very controlled shot that was quite long; from the tee, that fifty-foot space was very narrow looking. If you got it close to the trap and a little short, you could see the green; close to the pond and short, you might still be blinded. Halfway between the two would be good, if the shot were long enough.

The hole was a four-hundred-and-seventy-five-yard par four; the fairway to the dog leg beyond the pond was slightly uphill;

the green was small and elevated, and the rough started thick, very close in behind it. Regardless of pin placement, it was one hell of a golf hole. He almost laughed at the absurdity of finding it on this course. He wondered who in the hell had designed and built it, who kept its foreign growths in such good shape here in the desert. He did not figure to par it. He felt very ready to play it.

The entrance of a new element, one that did a lot for Allen's spirits, occurred with the first two hits. Steve automatically took the honors, and Lou followed him. Steve was smiling faintly as he teed up at the blues. He took a practice swing and then looked back at the three of them, still smiling, before he hit.

His drive was the longest he had hit that day. He had a deeper backswing, and he clicked through the ball with force. The drive must have been at least two hundred yards on the fly. It dropped on the far side of the pond, coming to rest about twenty yards beyond it. Lou was next. His ball was a little higher than Steve's, but it was longer. It had a very slight tail on it, and it carried a good two hundred and fifty yards, stopping a couple of feet from where it hit. It finished well beyond Steve's ball, in the middle of the fairway, in clear and unobscured sight of the green. Frankie seemed a little nervous, and he took his time getting set. He lined up a little to the left, and he hit his ball where he aimed it, playing for the far left of the fairway. The ball wound up short of the trap, with a very long but fairly open shot to the green. Then it was Allen's turn.

He knew now that they were hustling him. This did a lot for him. It cut him free of his concern for Lou; it allowed him to begin to dislike Steve in a very comfortable and unambivalent way. The fact that they were as good as they were helped also. It would be difficult to beat them, and that warmed him. He felt that he had two very distinct advantages over them now. The first was that it had been they who had abandoned golf as a sport of individual skill. They were going to try to play him as a team. That would hurt them in two ways. It would hurt them, simply, because golf is not a team sport, and he knew that the diffusion of attention that came from such thinking would take an edge off. It would also hurt them because it would introduce more material from their relationship into the game. A lot would be dragged in, and some of it would have to get in their way.

The second advantage he had, had to do with money. For them, for Steve at least, the money was no more than a kind of whip or a term of humiliation. He was sure Steve did not care about the money, but he was also sure that what the money represented was a very serious thing having to do with self-esteem, which was much harder to lose and much harder to win also. For him, on the other hand, the money was very important. If he won it, he would be pleased to have it. He needed it; it would buy things that he needed. But if he lost it, and he certainly did not want to lose it, it would be no more than the money he was losing. He could imagine himself going back without it; he would be sad about it, but that was all.

"That was a wonderful shot," he spoke softly to Lou, who stood a few feet from him. Steve was sitting in the cart, ready to go, while Frankie was getting ready to hit.

"You think so?" Lou said, a new coldness in his voice. Allen ignored the tone and pressed it a little, as a start.

"A really wonderful shot!" He kept his tone warm and open, his eyes clear.

"Right. Thanks," Lou said. He was uncertain about how to take the statement. He would think about that a little. Allen was not sure yet how he might work on Steve, if it became necessary. He thought he would give it some time.

When he got up to hit, he was feeling very loose and good. He knew that after a while he would lock into the game in the way he liked, and the anticipation was very nice. He also liked very much to play a golf course for the first time. Whenever he played a new course, he was careful not to study the upcoming holes too carefully, check the map out too much. There were things he might have articulated to himself about this, but they were so close to the bone that there were no good words for them. Very practically, in this case especially, ignoring the map and the distances spelled out would help him to concentrate not on pictures and symbols but on the tangibles.

When he drove, he pushed his follow-through a little, enough to make it look as if he had tried to power the ball, and he stepped back a little with his left foot as he finished, a little off balance. He sliced the ball slightly, but he had started it off to the left, and it came back and hit close to Frankie's ball, rolling about twenty feet to the right of it, but too far in that direction to have any clear shot to the green.

"I guess that's a little right," he said, looking up the fairway.

"I guess it is," Steve said as he started the cart up. Allen got in the cart with Frankie, and when they reached their balls, Steve and Lou were sitting behind them, waiting. They had parked well back of his ball, a little to the right, but just close enough so that he might see them out of the corner of his eye as he hit.

Frankie hit a really quite beautiful second shot. He used a four-wood, but he hooded it, took a three-quarter backswing, and punched the ball just enough as he came through it. It was low and straight and long. It pulled up about forty yards from the green, right in front of it. He could see from where he had parked the cart that the pin was cut in toward the back of the green, behind the trap on the right. Frankie would have to fly the edge of the trap, and he thought he would have to stop the ball pretty quickly, but he was not sure about that. He could not read the slope of the green from where he was.

He decided not to go for the green. To do that, to be sure to hit it, he would have to play for the left of it, and since he could not tell what kind of putt that would give him—it might be a very difficult one, and he might not hold the green anyway on that side—he chose to play for the trap. He figured if there was enough space between the trees and the trap, he might come up short of it, in good position for a chip. If he hit the trap, that was okay; he had been in traps three times on the front nine. They had been well raked, the lips had been reasonable, and he had liked the texture of the sand. He used a four-iron, a little more than he needed, but they were close and would see his club selection. He decided not to toy with the fact that they were closer to him than was appropriate. That kind of thing could wait until he might need it. He caught the ball slightly fat, carried the trees, and though he couldn't see it hit, he suspected he had reached the trap.

Steve hit his shot stiff at the pin, but he had a slightly fluffy lie, the ball flew on him, and he did not get enough bite into it. The ball stopped about ten feet above the flagstick, and from where Allen was he thought he would have a very tricky downhill putt. Lou made it known, by considering his shot and then switching clubs, that he was close enough for an eight-iron. He hit the ball crisply, straight and very high; it sat down about twenty feet away to the left and a little above the pin.

Frankie pitched up with a wedge. He bladed it slightly, and it hit the lip of the trap and stopped there, in the bit of fringe between the trap and the green. He was the closest to the hole, only seven feet away, but the fringe he was in was thick, and the shot he would have was downhill and would run away quickly to the right.

When Allen got to the trap, he saw that he was well back in it, with a good lie, and that from his angle it would be possible to get the ball to sit down on the green. He checked the other three, figuring what they might do. Frankie's shot was close to impossible, he was lying three and would take, at best, a five. Both Lou and Steve had chances for birds, but he doubted that either of them could make their putts. He figured them for pars. He knew that they would not play it that way though. If they tied, nobody would win money on the hole. If he hit up and was away, he would have to putt first, and that would help them make an easier decision. If he got too close the decision would also be too easy for them. He decided to try to play the shot fat, catch the down slope to the left of where Frankie's ball was, hoping to stop it before he got outside of Lou. He dug his feet into the sand and played the shot. He lifted a thick fan of sand onto the green, and the ball hit close to the lip in the fringe and rolled down and to the left, stopping about fifteen feet out. Lou was away.

Lou took some time in lining up the putt. Once he glanced over at Steve. About four feet beyond the cup there was a low down slope. He stroked his ball a little too firmly; it rolled wide, above the cup, reached the down slope, and did not come to rest before it was a good six feet away.

"Shit," he said, and let his putter slip from his hand to the green. He picked it up with resignation and walked around the others' lines to where his ball had come to rest.

"Who's away?" Allen asked, looking in Frankie's direction.

"Steve is," Lou answered, a little too quickly.

Steve touched his putt with a delicate stroke, but firm enough to negate some of the undulations that faced him. It was a sound putt, and it pulled up about fifteen inches beyond the hole, about the best he could have done with his line without sinking it.

"That's a gimmie," Allen said, smiling at Steve. "Nice putt." Steve ignored him and stroked the ball firmly into the hole.

They all looked at him. He thought he knew what they were thinking. He would miss his putt. Lou would miss his intentionally. The hole would not be halved. They would take him for the first twenty bucks. He very much wanted to stick it to them with this putt.

When he got set to hit, he saw that being a little below where Lou had been made the putt easier. It was more uphill than Lou's, and this would take a lot off the break. He could see Frankie's ball in the fringe when he addressed his ball, and he did not like seeing it. He stepped away from his putt.

"Mind hitting first, Frankie?" he said.

"Fine with me," Frankie said, and Allen reached for the flagstick and put it back in the hole. He stepped back off the green, glancing at Steve and Lou, seeing that they had no objections.

Frankie took a square stance on the fringe, his weight well back on his right foot, the leg stiff. He addressed the ball with a seven-iron. When he hit it, it jumped up and landed about eight inches out on the green. It rolled straight at the heart of the hole, struck against the flagstick, and dropped in.

"Well, I'll be damned!" Frankie said, shaking his head.

"That's a hell of a par, Frankie," Allen said, and grinned at the other two. They both smiled tightly. Frankie and Steve had halved the hole, and nobody could win any money on this one. Frankie had no part in the conspiracy. Allen got up to his ball, lined it briefly, stroked it, and missed the putt by a good four inches on the high side. He grinned at the two again, but they did not smile back. He tapped in for his five. Lou studied his six-footer briefly. He stroked it in for a par.

Allen birdied the next three holes, a par three, a four, and a five. The three he managed with a long straight putt, the other two by hitting his approach shots very close to the pin. He used a little play on the five, duffing his second shot, then coming in stiff with a five-wood. He was a hundred and eighty dollars up at the end of four. Lou was coming apart, struggling to save pars.

Steve seemed as brittle as a piece of ice. He was not talking to Lou, and he was not nodding when Lou made a particularly nice recovery, chipping close in from the trap with a six-iron on the par five. Steve had rimmed two particularly difficult putts, and his rage and the need to keep it in check, to remain dignified and powerful, were doing just enough against him. Frankie was playing his own game. He, like the other two, was even at the end of four.

Allen had to be careful about not getting carried away. He had stuck it to them good with the three birdies, but then he backed off some, realizing that if he wanted to get any mileage out of this place, he had to be a little cozy about what he was doing. If he won too big, Steve would get the drift of it, and it was clear that he had sufficient power around the place that he could close him off from further play here. He got a little too cozy, found trouble on the next few holes, and Steve stiffened some, pulling up on him. He got a hole up on the sixteenth, but dropped it on the seventeenth. Coming into the eighteenth, a long par five, he and Steve were even.

While they were driving their carts to the tee, he figured the possibilities in order to clear that business away. He knew it would be him or Steve or even. Lou would be pressured out of it, and Frankie didn't have the ball to play a hole of this distance well. If they halved the hole, he would be up three from Frankie and two from Lou. He'd take a hundred dollars, and that minus the thirty it had cost him for cart and green fees would put his winnings at seventy; not too good, but something. If Steve won, he'd owe him twenty for the hole and a hundred for winners. The hundred from the other two would cover most of it, but he'd be fifty dollars down. If he won, he'd be in much better shape. He'd get a hundred from each for winners, and a hundred and twenty for the holes. That would give him three hundred and ninety net. That would make this a very good day.

He got a little surprise when the four of them gathered on the tee. Steve had teed up but had gone back to the cart to dig in his bag. When his head was turned, Lou spoke, though a little reluctantly.

"How about a little pepper to finish up, say an extra half hundred for best ball?" It was obvious that Steve had put him up to this on the way from the seventeenth.

"Why not," Frankie said. "I could get a little back." Allen agreed, and so did Steve.

The hole was a sharp dog-leg right, longer but not as difficult as the par-four tenth. It was not possible to reach the turn in the dog leg in one. The green was out of sight from the tee. From the card it was hard to tell what the hole was really like beyond the bend.

"Anything one should know about this one?" he said. Frankie seemed about to speak, but Steve cut him off.

"Just play it," he said. It was the first really direct and sharp words Steve had spoken to him. There was a moment of embarrassment for the other two, but he covered it by saying, "Right, I guess that's golf, isn't it." And then he smiled at Steve. Steve did not acknowledge his smile, but turned to address his ball. The other two stepped back and were still.

Steve's drive was a good one. He played it to the right of the fairway. There were trees on that side, running around the dog leg. He found it hard to figure just why Steve had kept it up that side, and he watched to see how the other two played it. Lou skyed it slightly, but his power was enough so that he got out almost as far as Steve, a little to the left of him but still to the right of the middle of the fairway. Frankie hit a good drive, right down the middle, coming up about thirty yards short of the other two.

Before he hit, he took the card out and looked the hole over again. On the map there was an odd circle of quotation marks past the dog leg in the middle of the fairway, about halfway between the green and the knee, if anything a little closer to the green. It could be a tree, he thought, and he looked along the right of the fairway and over the tops of the trees beyond the curve. If it was a tree, it was not a big one, he thought; he could not see any distant branches. He wondered if it was water. If it was, it did not look too significant. Still curious about Steve's drive, he stepped up and addressed his ball. For a moment he thought about going up the right side with Steve and the other two. It would seem reasonable to follow the lead. But he liked the terms that came with playing the course blind, and he did not much like following Steve in anything. It just did not seem proper, from what he saw, to play the hole down the right. Whatever that thing was around the bend, if the card was in any way accurate, it could not be too important as a hazard. So far the card had been fair, as had the course, with the possible exception of the difficulty of the tenth hole. He decided to play his drive to the left of the middle of the fairway and to really get into it. He took a full back swing, his left arm stiff, and when he came down through the ball, the hard muscle in his forearm snapped his wrist through it. The ball clicked off the screws, the tee jumping up behind it. It rose gradually, and when it looked to be at the top of its arc it kept rising. Then it peaked and began to drop. When it landed and finished its long roll, it was a good two hundred and seventy yards out, between the center and the left rough, no more than thirty yards from the bend, with a possible sight line down the turn toward the green.

He stopped short of his ball and got out of the cart. Frankie had taken a few clubs and climbed on the back with Steve and Lou. There was a large distance between their three balls and his. He had hit far enough to the left that he knew that though his ball was the longest, he would be away. He walked over behind his ball, checking his lie. When he looked up and sighted around the bend, some things became clear.

He knew he should have seen it when he started the round. The eighteenth green finished near the first tee, at right angles to it, and beyond the green, which he could now see, was the clubhouse. When he began, he had been too intent on getting involved with the three, and he had not looked around much. In the middle of the fairway, about two hundred and fifty yards from where he was and another hundred or so from the green, was a massive, domed mound of earth. It spanned the entire fairway, was pretty close to being circular, and there must have been a distance of at least a hundred feet from the flat of the fairway to its highest point. If it was the same on its far side as it was on this one, its diameter would be a good seventy-five yards. There was rough growing on it that looked from this distance something like Eastern hog cranberry. The rough looked thick, but it was very even, probably kept that way by a grounds-keeper, and the evenness accentuated the symmetry of the mound. It did not look like any natural upheaval of land; it looked distinctly man-made.

On top of the mound, bright in its colors and at the dead center, was the largest totem pole Allen had ever seen. The pole rose a good thirty feet up in the air. Its painted shaft was three times the size of a telephone pole, and it had six brightly painted faces, with hawknoses, scowls, smiles, and appendages to their sides (ears or wings) that stood out yards away from it. On the very top, and not like any totem pole he had ever seen, was a larger than life-size figure of an Indian, dressed rather simply in a fringed outfit, a band with one feather in it around his head. He was standing very straight and still, arms at his sides, in his left hand what looked from this distance like a small tomahawk. In the other was a quiver of arrows, and there was a bow hanging from the shoulder.

Allen shifted his eyes to the side of the mound and over it to where he could see part of the green with the clubhouse beyond it. Then he looked back at the stolid figure. Though the mound protected the green, the figure did not seem to be standing there for that purpose. It was as if he were apart from any concern. If he had some interest in events having to do with playing the hole, that interest was directed back to the potential of tee shots reaching the bend. He was high up and as such seemed apart from developing clusters of relationship that might occur below him. In this sense, the figure had a strange and distant austerity about him. He looked, also, extremely funny, like something from a miniature golf course designed for giants. On impulse, Allen yelled across to the others and pointed.

"Look at that!" he said. He saw Frankie nod. Steve just looked over at him. Lou was busy in his bag, and he acted as if he did not hear.

He felt he wanted to just stand there for a while, to just take the thing in, to fit it into the day, but he knew he did not have time for this. He looked over to check the rationale behind Steve's shot. The three of them had trees to go over, but the trees were lower near the bend than the ones that had obscured them from the tee. There was, in fact, a kind of passage of low trees that one could get a three- or a four-iron over from where they were. A fairly good shot over the trees would fly the right side of the mound, and he judged that such a shot would bring the player to within seventy-five yards of the green, out in the open, with an easy wedge into it. If—and this was about the worst that could happen—the shot came up short, there was sufficient room between the edge of the mound and the right rough that the player could come down there and be left with no more than a hundred or a hundred and twenty yards in, again with an open shot. He, on the other hand, had trouble.

By playing to the left, for what he thought was the clear line in, he had made the hole play very long. He was almost three hundred yards out from the tee, but he had over three hundred left to the green—well over it, he guessed. From his angle, he did not have the play the others had to the right of the mound. He thought he could reach the side, but if he did, the ball could well jump down or roll into the trees. They were thick there, and he could get hung up badly. If he played to the left of the mound, a longer shot, he would surely wind up in the trees on that side of the fairway. He could see the white out-of-bounds stakes, pretty close in on that side, and he could not think to risk that shot either.

He looked over and saw that Steve was getting impatient. He was taking abbreviated practice swings with a three-iron, stopping that every few swings, putting his hands on his hips. Allen decided to prolong it a bit. He took a three-wood out of his bag, took a couple of practice swings, then walked back and sighted his line. Then he shook his head and started to walk over to where the other three were standing. It was a long walk, and he took his time. Steve took a short and vicious little swing with his club as Allen walked up to them.

"About this obstruction out there, what are the rulings?" he asked, looking from Lou to Steve.

"What do you mean?" Steve said, looking down at his club head, chipping at the top of the grass.

"I could mean, what's gonna happen if I hit it."

"You'll probably loose," Steve said, still chipping away.

"But what I mean is, is it in bounds, and what's the ruling if I hit that cute pole?" Steve looked up sharply, obviously angered at his use of words.

"Up to the redskin on the top—that's King Philip; that's an authentic copy of a Pima pole; that's a *real* Indian burial sight under there— If you hit the pole, you play it where it drops, as long as it falls in bounds. The mound is a natural obstruction; it's played as rough. You play the ball where it lands. Rub of the green. You got that?"

"Got it," Allen said, smiling into Steve's anger, and walked back across the fairway to his ball. He had made his decision before coming over to them, but he wanted to get everything articulated before he hit. He did not much like hearing that it was a burial sight. He did not think the Pimas had been Mound Builders, nor did he think they had used poles. He was not sure though. He did think he remembered that King Philip had something to do with events not out here but back East.

He had taken the three-wood out so that Steve would see it and anticipate his shot. When he got back to the cart, he replaced the wood and took out a three-iron. He stepped up and addressed the ball, and he felt the rush coming as he locked in. The ball was a Golden Ram, the highly compressed one. He liked to play it because it felt like a stone when he hit it. It was especially good for chipping. He saw that the ball had come to rest in the grass so that only the *Go* of the letters on it were showing. He felt his chest begin to hum as he saw the crisp gold lettering on the dimpled white surface of the sphere that sat like a found egg in its grassy nest of green at his feet. He lay the silver of the club head down carefully to the right of the ball, the face with its straight horizontal etched lines and its slight pitch.

As he shifted his feet and got set, he looked into the geometry of the grass, a few blades touching the ball, the rest growing in the direction he would hit. He would caress a little of the grass on his way to the ball, but he would not bruise it, and it would affect nothing. In front of the ball, about two inches from it, was where his small carpet of divot would be cut cleanly and lifted. He would see sky as the ball left him, then he would see the fine carpet rise up, then he would see the ball again about fifty yards from him, flying, then the carpet would re-enter his vision as it reached its peak of flight, then it would drop out of his field as it fell to the ground.

He addressed the ball with the club shaft held by its grip at a level with his crotch. He held it as firmly and safely as he would have held himself there in other circumstances. Then he moved his hands slightly to the left, bringing them over the ball, angling the club shaft slightly so that the head was behind the ball, his hands over it, and when he came through it and hit it the whip at impact would give it backspin, the letters of its name spinning toward him as it left the club face, and it would stop close to where it landed.

Then he was ready, relaxed, still, and set. He made of his head the fixed center of his body, picturing a plumb line hung from a point below the fossa containing his pituitary gland in the center of his skull, standing in space and ending at his crotch, with the line held still by the weight of his scrotum. The club head and the glint of the shaft left his field of vision; his left hip turned inward slightly, his right back, but his head remained still in the pivot. He reached the top of his backswing, and the shaft paused for a fraction in time before starting down. As it moved into its arc, he could feel in discrete increments the growing weight of the club head as the centrifugal force increased. His body compensated, the plumb line swinging fractions to the left as his hip moved toward the potential line of flight. Then the shaft and the club head entered his vision again, moving toward the waiting ball. The ball swelled out and hardened as the head approached it. Then there was the click and the bite of the blade cutting the back of the divot. The ball lifted, the divot rose, his head began to turn on its axis; he saw the ball and the totem pole, large and imposing and silly in the sun, then the divot came up, showing its green side, then it floated away. When it was gone, the ball was at the top of its arc. It stopped there, and then it started its gradual decline. When it hit, it stirred nothing, it simply disappeared into the top of the mound, six feet to the right of the pole.

He sighed. Then he inhaled. Then he lowered his club from where he had brought it to rest on his left shoulder after finishing his swing. He walked up a few feet and picked up the pelt of divot. He came back and fitted it into the space from which he had cut it. He stepped on it and tapped its edges down with the head of his club, folding the edges of grass together. Then he walked back to the cart and replaced his club in the bag. He stood beside the cart and looked over at the others.

"Are you all right?" Frankie called over to him. All three were looking at him. From where they were they could not see where his shot had landed; they had no vision of the mound top and the pole.

Frankie addressed his shot then and hit it. From where Allen was he could see it come down. As he expected, it came to rest to the right of the mound, between its base and the rough, an open shot to the green. Frankie looked over at him. He made a circle with his thumb and index finger, raised and shook it in the air.

Lou's ball came to rest somewhere in front of the mound; it was obvious from the trajectory and force of his hit that it was well out and safe. Lou looked over at Allen quickly, but before he could give any sign, he looked as quickly away. Steve hit the best shot of the three. He was to the right of Lou, well out in the fairway beyond the mound and visible from where Allen stood. Steve gave him no glance at all, letting him know that he knew where his shot had gone and did not need any confirmation.

When they came around the turn in their carts, the mound loomed even larger than it had appeared from the openness of the fairway before the turn. It was monstrous, and the totem pole, he thought, must have been a good six feet in circumference. Looking up at it from the base of the mound, it stood against the clouds in the sky. They stopped their carts short of Frankie's ball.

"Am I away?" Frankie asked Allen.

"Depends upon height," he laughed, "but maybe so." The other two refused any hint of curiosity, and when Frankie looked over at them, they did not look back.

"I'll hit then," he said. He used a seven-iron, hit his usually low, short iron shot, but he hit it too firmly. It landed on his side of the flagstick over the small trap, but it had a lot of roll in it, and it crossed the green and moved well into the rough on the other side.

"Shit," he said, and rammed his club back into his bag.

Allen reached to his bag and selected a nine-iron; then he put it back and took out an eight. He put that club back and unbelted his entire bag from the cart. He slung it over his shoulder and started up the slope of the mound. When he got to the top, he slung his bag from his shoulder and rested it in the grass. At its crest, the mound was still curving, and he could see that the massive totem pole had been set directly in its navel. He glanced down to where the others were waiting. He was about twenty yards to the right of the pole, and the three below him could see most of him. At the same time that he was about to suggest that one or more of them come up, he saw Steve bend over and talk sharply and briefly to Lou. He guessed the reason. Steve thought he might be partly out of sight when he found his ball, and he did not want him improving his lie. Lou jumped from the cart and trotted up the mound, slowing to a walk when he was about halfway up. This was the first time he and Lou had been alone, and he decided to use that. He knew that any prolonged talk between them up there would get to Steve.

"Hey, Lou," he said, "good view from up here, huh?"

"Right," Lou said, then quickly, "where's your ball?"

"Somewhere over there," he said, waving vaguely with his arm but keeping his eyes on Lou, and then looking past him to where Steve was sitting in the cart watching. He reached down and got a club out of his bag, a five-iron, and toyed with the grass at his feet while he talked. He figured Steve might think his ball was where they stood. He would surely wonder what he was doing with the club. He took a practice swing, not touching the ground.

"You like coming up here on an errand?" he said. He was surprised at Lou's directness.

"Fuck no, I don't like it! Come on, let's find your ball."

"We'll find it. Let's talk a little."

"Look man, this is my livelihood we're dealing with. You wanna talk, we'll talk later, okay?" He had started his statement strongly, but there was a slight tone of pleading as he ended it. Allen could see that he had underestimated Steve's pressure. He also knew that Lou's opening up in this way, though he may not have intended to, was a measure of disaffection. He felt himself wanting Lou out of this hole; he hoped that Lou's putt was of sufficient difficulty when it came to remove decision from him. For a moment, he felt helpless in having no control over that aspect of what would follow.

"Okay," Allen said, "I get it." He turned away, his five-iron still in his hand, and walked up toward the base of the pole. About ten yards from it, to its right as he approached the crown of the mound, he saw his ball, a part of it visible through the low growth it sat firmly in. He moved on up to it to check his lie, but before he got to it something else caught his attention. He laughed to himself, visibly shaking his head as he came to the mound's crest. Down on the other side, at the foot and running out a good thirty yards toward the green, was a sand trap. The trap must have been at least fifty yards wide; it covered a good portion of the green side of the mound, stopping on either side only a short distance in from the rough. Its size was remarkable, though it was on scale with the size of the mound and pole. More remarkable was its depth; its front lip must have been a good five feet high. He realized that had he played his shot a little longer or tried to clear the mound, he would have wound up in the trap, either by roll or on the fly, and he would have had one hell of a difficult shot to the green from there.

"The forces of evil will stop at nothing," he said under his breath as Lou came up to him.

"What did you say?" he said.

"Not much to say about that," he said. "That speaks for itself." He looked up from the trap to the green. He was about a hundred yards away from it, but it would play quite a bit shorter than that because he was well above it. From where he was he had an open shot to the pin, which was cut in close to the middle of the green, with an uphill slope between him and it. He walked back to his bag and got out his wedge. When he came back, he stepped up and addressed the ball, moving his feet and tamping them down, working to get a good stance. Before he got set to hit, he looked over at where Lou was standing and past him down to where Steve still sat, looking up. He motioned with his head a little, and Lou stepped back some and to the right, getting out of his field of vision.

He had to think of this shot as a touch shot; a full wedge would be too much. At the same time, his lie was airy, the ball would jump out a little ahead of the club, and he could not get any backspin on it. Also, he would have to hit a bit of the weed before he got to the ball. He figured that the slope of the green between him and the cup would slow the ball down some, but not enough; he would need more than that to get it to stop on the down side. The clipped fringe in front of the green was about four feet wide and looked well cared for and true. He figured he would need a little roll in that to slow the ball down. At the edge of the fringe, the longer grass of the fairway tucked in nicely. If he landed in the fairway, about three feet from the fringe, he ought to get a bounce into the fringe, a little slowing roll onto the green, and then the quicker roll up to the cup.

He picked a spot. He placed the club head, slightly elevated in the air, behind the ball. He elected a short backswing and a punch shot with very little wrist in it. The club came up smoothly, pausing a moment when its head was at a line near the top of his own, and then the head came down sharply and jammed the ball up out of the rough. His follow-through was abbreviated also, the club head finishing and stopping at the height of his left shoulder. He held that position as he watched the ball fly. He could see a wing on the side of the totem pole out of the corner of his eye. The ball hit close to where he had played it. It hit fairway and bounced once in the near edge of fringe, finishing the fringe on the roll. It had roll in it when it reached the shorter carpet of the green. It began to slow down halfway between the cup and the fringe. It quit no more than eight feet below the hole, a little to the left of it.

"Good out," Lou said behind him when the ball stopped. He watched the ball sit there a moment, then he quit his position and looked at Lou. Lou was smiling at his own quiet understatement, and he smiled at Lou.

They walked back down the slope of the mound to the carts. Frankie was standing with his hands on his hips, shaking his head and smiling.

"That was really something," he said.

"Thanks," he said. He expected nothing from Steve, but Steve nodded slightly as Frankie spoke. He got out of the cart and went to his bag for a club. He found what he wanted and stood away as Lou got ready to hit.

Lou's shot was firm, but it drifted a little to the left, stopping about twenty-five to thirty feet from the hole, on the left, pin high, on the side hill. Steve went directly at the pin, but he was a little long and wound up fifteen feet above it.

When they got to the green, Frankie took the cart and went around behind it. He made a good shot from the rough. He was below and out of sight of the green from where he had landed, but he got the ball up to the fringe on a good line. The ball took an odd bounce—he had shanked it a bit—and it quit to the right of him, outside of Lou's ball. He putted very close and tapped in for a bogey six. Lou lagged up to within a foot, and Steve told him to take it away for par.

Steve took a lot of time in studying his position. It was clear that he was trying to lock into the putt, but he could not keep himself from looking up, briefly checking the other ball and the man who had hit it. When he came around to the front of the green to check his line from that side, he said, "Mark yours," and there was no request in his voice.

He's locking in incorrectly, Allen thought. He's used to giving orders; he didn't mean to offend this time. He went over and marked his ball with a copper Danish krone he carried with him. The small, etched mermaid of the harbor nestled down in the close-clipped grass. He liked the sense of respect for occasion the coin gave to his game, respect for the green, its difficulties, and its social forms. The game could be compartmentalized that way into various forms. There were tee forms and fairway forms for iron shots and longer woods. The tee and green forms were the most social, and the codes of behavior for the green play were the most distinct and separate. Coming to the green was like a group of people arriving at a cocktail party or, depending on the kinds of events that got them there, like souls arriving at shelter in a storm. Once over the apron and onto the putting surface, there was room for some talk about modes of arrival, breakdowns, and sights seen on the way. But there was a time, very soon after the gathering in that circumscribed space, when that talk had an appropriate ending and the brief and intense party began.

There were responsibilities on the green, and there were space limitations and injunctions, and though these things could be seen from a distance only in physical movements and tasks, they were all social, matters of good taste, posture, and manners. Steve glanced up at him as Allen marked his ball and lifted it, then he went around to the other side of the green again, looking the putt over, plumbing it, checking to see in what direction the grass grew. Lou was standing on the back apron, his hand on his hip, one foot planted casually in front of the other. Frankie anticipated the task of replacing the flagstick in the hole when they were finished. He stood well away from Steve's lines of study, but he would be quick to reach for the pin when the putting was over. These two had putted out, and having done that they thickened the social atmosphere.

Before anyone putted, the imaginary lines running from where the balls rested on the green to the cup were multiple and complex; they dictated where one might walk, and this in turn dictated who might stand by whom. There was little if any talk from one side of these lines to the other. Each player was intent on his own line and the study of the possibilities of break and pacing. As each putted and got down, he was free to give full attention to the putts of those who followed him. The limitations on movement in the physical area diminished as the amount of attention given to each putt increased. There were exceptions to this rule, but most often the last to putt was he who was in the position of winning the hole if his putt fell in, and it was he whom the others, freed from any concern with putts of their own, were watching with various unspoken desires and wishes. The way such self-interest was handled and denied was through silence, demure standing back, in physical stillness, in postures of unconcern.

Allen felt that right now he could win it without putting. The fact that Steve was ready and aware of the psychological game possibilities was enough to make it likely. All he needed to do was speak. He was thinking, this is a speed putt, there's too much break and trickiness in his line for him to risk trying to leak it in. If he had spoken this thought, he would have thickened the social matrix by interrupting Steve's attention to the putt. The break in the attention would have been insignificant. Steve was good enough at golf for that not to bother him. It would have been Steve's sense of the motive behind the talking that would have thickened things. He could have stood in crucial places, could have altered his expression in various ways, could have coughed or cleared his throat. But he did nothing, and it is possible that that in itself took its toll, because it was contrary to Steve's expectations.

And he began to think, while Steve was working at getting ready, that this may well be the sense in which this game today was at bottom characterological. It was just that Steve could not possibly imagine that the man he was playing against now had certain standards that would not allow him to reduce the grandeur of the game they were playing to something that had to do with relationships between people. The stakes, the money, was something he accepted as the catalyst to what they were doing. For him, at one end of the hierarchical scale on which the money stood was the game played for pleasure, for practice and enjoyment. On the other end was the game played for life and death. With the stakes as given, the morals of the game entered. These had to do with the other man and the ball and the ground to be covered. And that complex of tensions and chemistry was sacrosanct to him. At least he thought it was. It was not to be messed with, and he would not violate it. Steve's limitations were moral; but at bottom his morals, those of business and power, were contradictory to those of golf. At least, this was the way Allen romanced it; this was why he knew Steve would lose, why he had already lost.

Steve stepped up to his ball finally, took a few smooth practice swings, and addressed it. He moved his head slowly from the head of his putter to the ball and down the imaginary line where he intended to send it. Out of the corner of his eye as he sighted he saw nothing. There was no opponent there, nothing for him to deal with, no one for him to exert power over. Even before he took his putter back for the stroke, his concentration was without attentive focus. When he struck the putt, he pushed it slightly, sending it out too far to the left. It caught the middle and not the down side of the slope that he wanted it to hit; it bent in toward the cup as it turned, but it did not bend enough. He missed the cup by a good two inches on the high side, his ball coming to rest only a foot beyond it. When the ball stopped he tried to shrug, but he could not manage it. The shrug was like a tick in him. He stepped up and punched the ball home for his par.

Then it was Allen's turn. Always his turn came. He never minded slowness of play, because his turn would always come up, and when that happened he would be alone again. It would be something else altogether. He never minded waiting for it, because of what it was. This one was for all of it, this one putt.

Nobody else was involved in it. The mower had cut the green; he could hear it cutting another one in the distance. He could feel the slight wind. The birds were singing, and he picked out red-winged blackbird, brown thrasher, and catbird, isolating the differences in voice between the last two, then he released them. He looked back up the fairway to the top of the mound. The faces in the pole looked away from him, the Indian at the top was turned away, high up, distant, and uninterested. He glanced at the other three. They were very still, very unimportant. He smiled. He walked up to the putt, saw that it was straight with a slight curl to the left, just at the hole. He was close enough that he could just drive it home, with speed, taking the curl out of the putt. He decided instead to play the curl. All he had to do was hit the ball so that it would stop about a foot on the other side of the hole, play it into the right side. He stepped up to it. He sighted it, and then he stroked it. It came off the putter with some speed. About a foot from the hole it began to die. Six inches out on the right it slowed enough so that it could catch the break. It entered the middle of the cup, and fell in with that nice hollow sound. It never touched the back of the hole.

It was only after he was halfway to the motel that he began to come back to himself, to the matrix of real life and the structures he was involved in. First the gas gauge took his notice; it was below half full, and he pulled into a self-service station and filled up. He had worked in gas stations when he was a boy, and he liked to fill his own tank, to catch the smell of the gas fumes as he pumped. The station was at the side of a small shopping mall. He saw a liquor store with its light on, even though it was only six-thirty and still light, between two other stores in the mall's crescent, and when he had finished with the gas and paid the attendant, a young woman in white overalls, he drove over to the liquor store, where he bought two bottles of good chilled champagne. Melinda liked champagne, and he liked to surprise her with it. When he left the liquor store, he saw that there was a flower shop near the far edge of the crescent, and leaving the car with the champagne on the front seat he walked over and bought some roses. Then he left the mall and got back on the road that ran in front of it.

When he drove onto the gravel drive of the motel, dusk was beginning to come on. There was a nice reddening sky near the horizon above the Sangre de Cristos; the mountains were beginning to become shadows that would get back light when the sun lowered behind them. He heard the sound of voices as he approached the door.

"Here I am," he said, knocking and speaking at the same time, the paper bag with the champagne in it in his hand and the bouquet of roses held in the crook of his arm. Bob White opened the door, smiled, and bowed slightly from the waist, extending his left arm, his palm open, directing him into the room.

The voices had been the two of them talking. Melinda was sitting in her robe in the roughly upholstered chair; a straight-back chair had been pulled up in front of her. She had her back to them. She turned in her seat as he entered, smiling.

"Hi," he said. "Look what I got here." He handed her the flowers, and put the bag with the bottles of champagne in it in her lap.

"Terrific! You did it good, huh?"

"I did it very good," he said, and he sat on the chair in front of her and reached his head over to her and kissed her, a rose brushing the tip of his chin.

"What have you two been up to today?"

She smiled in the direction of Bob White, who stood somewhat behind him, and nodded. Bob White came into the side of his vision when he went over to the drapes that covered the large sliding doors in the back of the room. He looked over at Melinda when he had located the lines tucked behind the fabric. She nodded again, laughing softly, and Bob White slowly pulled on the lines, opening the drapes, revealing the small lit patio on the other side of them. He had turned in the chair, and he laughed when he saw what the patio contained.

They had put the low, dark, imitation-wood formica table from the motel room out in the center on the bricks. On it, on top of a white towel and to its right, were the ice bucket and three of the plastic glasses from the room. In the center of the table was the rectangular motel room tray. Melinda had covered it with aluminum wrap, pinching bits of the foil along the edges to create a scalloped pattern. From the ends of the tray inward were rows of small cherry tomatoes, olives, slices of cucumber, and radishes. There was a large rectangular pocket left in the center of the tray, and this was lined with crisp lettuce leaves. On the far right of the table was a tall, fat candle covered in foil, with a foil lip about the wick as a wind guard. The candle was lit. To the right of the table, in the corner of the patio, was the hibachi, the coals ashen but with a glow of light emanating from their center. On top of the hibachi, in the boat of aluminum foil, in the bed of odd and colorful clippings, the strips of snake meat were cooking. Above and away from the hibachi, to its right, the carefully hung snakeskins shone in a row over the latticework at the end of the patio.

"Snake," Bob White said softly, looking down into the carefully formed boat of foil.

"Allen, it's rattlesnake!" she said, touching him lightly on the shoulder.

"Fantastic!" he said.

While he was showering, standing among the golf balls, Bob White and Melinda tended to the preparations. They put paper plates and plastic knives and forks on the counter outside the bathroom door. They put a bottle of the good champagne down among the cubes in the ice bucket. They waited for him, watching the snake cook and smelling it.

When he was finished drying himself, he put on a pair of shorts and a blue terry shirt, brushed his teeth and brushed at his hair. When he came out he went to the champagne and opened it. Beside it on the now crowded table were the roses, standing in a plastic pitcher. He popped the cork and filled the three glasses with the wine. He handed one of them to Melinda and one to Bob White, who was over close to the hibachi, keeping an eye on the cooking.

"To the snake," he said, lifting his glass.

"To the snake," the other two said in reply, and then they drank.

"Snake's ready," Bob White said, and he and Melinda, using white washcloths from the bathroom, lifted the boat of foil to the table. When they got it there, Melinda put her end down in the corner of the waiting space, and Bob White, using his knife, held the snake and the cuttings back while he pulled out the foil, letting the snake come to rest in the place they had prepared for it. Then the three of them just stood and looked at the rare and delicate strips of snake meat and the cuttings.

"Let's eat 'em," Bob White said, and he stepped up with a slight flourish and took the small blue flower he held in his hand and dropped it among the strips of meat. It was a soft blue in color, but it was the only blue thing on the arrangement, and it seemed to command its small portion of space, distinct in its petals and stamen. Melinda got the paper plates and the plastic knives and forks. He got the upholstered chair from the room. When Melinda returned, he helped her to sit in the chair, and Bob White served her snake and brought her a fresh glass of champagne. He and Bob White remained standing, holding their plates in their hands. They ate, making sounds of pleasure and smiling at each other between bites.

When they were finished and the coals from the hibachi glowed brighter as night came on, he sat on the arm of the chair with his hand on Melinda's shoulder, holding his glass, full of champagne from the second bottle. Bob White squatted on his haunches on the patio bricks, taking occasional sips from his glass, which he replaced at the side of his right foot without looking at it. They talked a little, quietly, about the snake, the pool, the golf course, and the weather, the look of the Sangre de Cristos that day. After a while, Bob White told a kind of story that had to do with what Allen had told them about the play. When he was finished, Melinda raised her glass to him, and she and Allen toasted him and his grandmother. Then Bob White raised his glass, and he and Melinda toasted Allen on his win. After that, chatting and laughing softly, they cleared things to the sides of the patio, making a place for Bob White to bed down. Soon after that, Bob White said he thought he might retire, and bidding them good night, he went outside, pulling the glass doors shut behind him. He did it in such a comfortable manner that neither Allen nor Melinda were concerned that he not be sleeping in the room with them. When Bob White had left, Allen and Melinda caught each other yawning, laughed a bit about it, and decided that it was time to go to bed. They decided to leave the end of the cleaning up until the morning. Allen waited until Melinda was in bed and set, and then he turned the light off and got into bed himself.

Hunting snakes can be difficult, but doing it is understandable. Playing golf may be understandable too, but you understand I don't play golf. I wouldn't know anything about that then. I don't really hunt snake either, you understand, but I did it a lot when I was a boy, and a little after that, and I think I can understand it pretty well. Now Indians always talk a lot, it is said, about how the white man sometimes doesn't understand things too well, and it is true that Indians do talk like that. I know that for a fact, because I have heard them do it, and I apologize to say that I have done it too sometimes. Indians don't understand things too some-times, so you see we don't get very far with this. That is okay, however, because this is not what I am going to talk about here. A couple of years ago I made a trip to Lake Havasu City to see that London Bridge they have over there. Lake Havasu City was not a city or a lake when they started in there. First they made the lake, then they made the city. Then they put that London Bridge there so they could get across the lake to the other side. They put part of the city on the other side of the lake so they could use the bridge to get to it. When I went there, I didn't understand what was going on there. I went there because people I knew who had been there told me I wouldn't understand it when I saw it. They were right. But it was not a waste of time going over there to it.

This is about the time I was hearing about the mound you talked about over here at the golf course. It was a while ago, and I knew somebody who worked up around here, and when he came back he told me about it. There was that Mount Rushmore and that place where that man is building that mountain into a statue of Crazy Horse. I hear he is not finished doing that yet. Anyway, he said that they made the mound bigger, big enough to put the whole Pima nation in it if they wanted to. That would be pretty big, of course, and I knew that that man that I knew made things bigger than they were when he talked. Still, I knew that it had to be pretty big for him to get it that big in his talk.

That's why we talked about Mount Rushmore and that Crazy Horse statue at the same time. One thing we understood when we talked about the mound was that we both thought that the way they had made it part of their game was a pretty fucking shitty thing to do, excuse me, but that's exactly what we said and how we felt about it.

One day my grandmother came up while we were talking. Now this man I'm talking about was a little bit of a dummy; that is to say, he didn't have good sense. My grandmother asked us what we were talking about, and this man piped right up. The big mound over at Tucson, he said. You mean Lake Havasu City? she asked. I poked at him, but he didn't get it. No, no, the big burial place at the golf course over there, he said. What are you talking about? she said. What place is that? This one, he said, and he took a post card of the mound, a colored one with that big prick of a phony pole stuck in it, out of his breast pocket and showed it to her. She didn't understand it I don't think for a little while, but she pulled the post card away from me when I tried to get it. What *is* this? she said. It's nothing, Grandma, I said, and tried to get the card away from her again, but she pulled it away again. They say that's one of our people's burial places over there by Tucson, that dummy said. They say that's King Philip, some Eastern Injun, on the top there, he said. Then my grandmother got it. King Philip? she said, the Sachem? They stuck him in there? They stuck a pole in there! a pole! Then she dropped the card down on the ground, and she sat right down alongside of it. She sat there a long time, but she didn't look at the card any more.

That night my grandmother died. It was the pole in the mound with her own King Philip from the East that got to her, I think. She was old, and she was going to die pretty soon after that time anyway. In the evening before she died we had a long talk. I mean all of my family that was still alive then sat around the place, and we talked to my grandmother. She was very old, and I understand that before she died she had forgotten about the mound and the pole altogether. I believe that she was very happy when she died. She had a good life as those things go. This is not really a sad story that I have finished telling you. I thought of it because you mentioned that mound.

RAIN

The adjoining room became vacant, and he insisted that Bob White take it. The Indian had slept on the patio, using Melinda's egg-carton mattress, the night of the snake dinner. At midnight it had started to rain, and he had come in, to a corner of the room by the door, and finished the night there. In the morning it was still raining, and they had run back and forth from the car to Bob White's new room, carrying his few belongings into it. When he was set up, he went with Allen and got cartons of coffee and fresh donuts from the restaurant and brought them back to the room, walking close to the building, under the narrow canopy, in the rain.

It was still raining up in the Sangre de Cristos where it had started. The clouds had come in black and low, and it rained as though when the clouds hit the mountain tops they had been ripped open. In the first three hours, the sand had held the water, but then it became saturated, and the remnants of old stream beds started to flow again. Before too long, before morning, the water coming off the mountains had entered the washes and streams below at the foot of the mountains, swelling them. After they had finished their coffee, by ten o'clock, some of the streets of the city were flooding. The road Bob White had taken into the hills to find javelinas was a shallow river, and the rich in the houses in the foothills were marooned. At noon, the rain slowed and settled from a flood to a steady downpour. The radio talked about isolation, closed businesses, accidents; it said it was going to rain for a while.

"I have heard it can rain here for quite a while," Bob White said as they stood at the front glass doors, watching the sheets of rain. By one o'clock they had ordered the room. Allen had wiped each of the golf balls in the bottom of the shower stall and put them back in the gunny sack. Melinda had straightened up, discarding the remnants of the snake dinner, had made up one of the twin beds, had rested between jobs for a few minutes. Bob White had gone to his room to organize his belongings.

Allen backed the car in under the canopy, close to the door, and organized the trunk. He checked to see that it was dry, no water leaking between the seams, and he took the Tombstone Diamond matchbox and put it in a place in the wheel well where it would be easy to get at. Then he moved the car back off the sidewalk, getting soaked when he hopped out from under the canopy to move it. At one-thirty Bob White came back, and they had a smoke together, and then Bob White excused himself and went back to his room. It was still raining. It was getting damp in the room, and the clothes he had taken off and hung on the shower rod to dry were not drying. He wore a robe, and he put the small space-heater on in the bathroom to get some humidity out of the air. Melinda rested in her unmade bed, her head turned to the side, watching the rain come at a slant, keeping the glass doors opaque. By two-fifteen the only job left was the Laetrile. Allen got the works out, moved the table to the side of the bed, and tried to hang the bottle, the tubing dangling down, from the lamp fixture on the wall at the bed's head. It would not hook up, and he finally put the bottle down between Melinda's knees.

The insertion of the needle was quick and easy. Melinda's small intake of breath as the needle entered was lost in the sound of the rain. He put the strips of adhesive, crisscrossed, holding the needle to her skin with one hand, and in the other he held the bottle above her. When the strips were secure, he reached up to the bottle and adjusted the drip, his two hands, with the bottle in them, elevated. He was sitting on the bed at her hips, and before he could lower the hand he had raised to the bottle, she lifted her left arm and put her hand under the fold of his bathrobe at his chest and put the tip of her index finger into his hair and moved it until she touched his nipple. She then rotated her finger in small circles, outling the hardening flesh. He looked down at her face; she was smiling. Lying on her back like this, gravity pulled at the skin on her cheeks, deepening the hollows in which the shadows in her pale skin rested. Her fingers moved in a twisted line through the hair on his chest, heading for the other nipple. He anticipated, and the hairs on the back of his neck stood up.

"Snake trail," she murmured, an edge of her smile twisting.

She reached the other nipple and circled it, then brought her thumb up and squeezed it. Her right hand moved to the bathrobe, along his leg. The needle was in at the front of her elbow, and she had little play, had to keep the arm from bending, but her hand could move from the wrist. She got it under the robe, flipping the fold off his leg, and ran her fingers inside his knee and just above it. He lowered his right arm slowly, leaving the bottle in the air, elevated, held in his left hand and dripping, and put his hand on the knot of her robe and disengaged it. His hand went under her robe; he lay it flat, his fingers spread on her lower belly in the deep hollow, the heel just touching the hair at the rise of her pubis. He gathered his fingers a little, holding and squeezing a span of her loose flesh. She shuddered fully, but with a shallowness that was indicative of her profound weakness, and he was at the dull edge of despair for a moment, but as she shuddered her fingers hit spasmodically at the tip of his nipple, and he was aroused away from it.

"Snake bite," she whispered, and pushed her hips up into the heel of his hand. He moved the whole hand down, and she parted her legs a little, and he pushed up into the hair. She took the flesh on the inside of his thigh for support, keeping herself where she was. Her left hand slid from his chest to his crotch; she traced another snake line in the soft flesh above his penis. She brought her hand out from under his robe, crossing her own body, allowing her left shoulder to settle into the bed, and arranged her arm in an L, her hand open and palm up on the pillow beside her head.

"Do it," she said, and he looked up at his left hand in the air, holding the bottle, and checked the drip; it was regular and steady. And the rain outside was regular and steady, and the steady drops hit against the glass doors. He had not pulled the heavy curtains across them, and some of the drops sat there, and others made abbreviated snake trails in the glass. The sky was dark and cloud covered, and he could see the suggested outline of the car beyond the glass doors, but he could see nothing else.

He put two of his fingers into her and moved them from side to side; she was wet and healthy there, and he pushed deeply into her, and she opened her legs wider and tucked her chin down to see his hand on and in her, but the effort was too much for her, and she let her head fall back on the pillow and pushed into his hand, her eyes closing, then opening, and looking into his eyes.

He smiled and took a third finger and touched her clitoris and brought his thumb to it and squeezed and rolled it. "Snake bite," he said, and she growled, and ground a little against him.

And then she was rising. She squeezed harder into his right thigh, keeping her arm with the needle in it as straight as she could. She moved in a small space, did not flail or kick out; she shuddered and rose and shuddered. The back of her left hand moved back and forth beside her head on the pillow. Once she moved the hand to her mouth and sucked at her fingers and bit them. When she came, she came long and delicately, and before she could reach the peak of it, she was tired from it, but she was able to begin to relax near it, and her sighs were strange and ethereal. They were a mixture of passion and giving in to the failed effort of passion at the same time. They hurt her, and they hurt him. His hurt was the hurt of loss impending made into an emblem from the future as he felt and heard her coming. Hers was the hurt of fulfillment coming from the diminished quota of fulfillments. She felt another one going as it went. She wanted to rise up to it completely, to say good-by to it, but she could not make it. It went above and beyond her, and when it was almost gone she slipped back from it into the tiredness that had, almost insidiously, its own reward. For a while she would not have to struggle against the cancer, to win the small holding-action battles that gave her the little moments that were left to her, if she wanted to fight for them. And she did fight for them, always; they were living, and she felt very alive. But they were hard won, and she was tired, and the guilt-free and long resting after such times with him had their own value; they renewed her a little.

He checked the bottle. It was half empty, his arm was tired, but he could hold it there. She was relaxing now; her breath was returning. The last thing she released was the flesh inside his thigh. When her hand went loose the drip quickened a little, the pressure she had given her veins, their blood pushing against the Laetrile, diminished, allowing the fluid in. He was still hard above her hand, but he began to fall, and when the head of his penis hit the tips of her fingers, he lurched up and became hard again. She looked up at him out of her half-closed eyes. They both knew that there was not much left that she could manage, maybe nothing. He needed more, but he knew the trip and the time at the pool, the snake dinner, and now the rain had taken a lot out of her. She looked wasted and on the edge of a kind of sleep.

"It's okay," he said. "You go to sleep; I'll unhook you when the bottle's empty."

She sighed and settled deeper. Her left arm moved from the L down to her body, her hand coming slowly to rest on her stomach. Her legs came together, and he reached to her and adjusted her robe, covering her breasts and legs. When he tucked the collar of her robe at her throat, she said "No," and she reached her hand up and pulled her robe back from her breasts, tucking it around them, so that they stood free and accentuated, very white and brown tipped against the green of the robe's fabric. She reached up a little and took him in her right hand and ran her fingers over his penis; she shifted slowly, and her breasts moved a little, swaying. She smiled faintly below her lids, looking at his face he thought, but he could not see her eyes. "Let me see it," she said, and that aroused him further, and he moved closer to her and half stood, one knee on the bed. As he moved, the clamp on the tubing hit with a light click against the bottle as he lowered it to get to her, and he glanced up and elevated it again.

When he looked back he found he cast a shadow cutting into the light and that her right breast was now darkened, the left the more prominent in contrast. He caught his breath to hide his response from her, though she was occupied and would not have noticed. The fear of mastectomy, and the odd wish for it, hit into his stomach briefly. There had been a biopsy and some time of dazed fear in waiting before the call came. And he remembered it and how they had looked not quite at each other, neither able to incorporate the idea of it. And now he saw that negative image on the right. It was like a boy's chest. There was a place below her breast, just under it, where he liked to put his hand flat against her ribs while she was on her back, with arms on the pillow above her head, her breasts pulled up. To move his hand down the ribs to her waist and back up again, to the edge of her breast on that side. And in this light, he could imagine the breast gone, could almost see it that way, but without the scar tissue, and could think of the way her boy's chest would feel on that side, his hand moving to touch ribs all the way up, stopping and changing the fingering of bone only when it reached her clavicle and the cup's indentation above it before it reached her chin and cheek. He would take her head then, his palm holding her lower mandible, and would be rising up himself, beginning to lift and turn her face toward him. He would want her eyes in his eyes before he kissed her, and he would be looking at her face up until the final moment before his lips touched her lips. Their flat, bare chests would touch against each other as they embraced; there would be no protuberance to keep them apart.

Then his hand moved, in the imagining, up cheek to ear, and the hard, gold bullet in the post driven through her lobe scraped against the pad at his hand's edge, and she came back to him as who she was. He backed up slightly, lifting his eyes up from her shadowed chest. She shifted as he moved, and their linked actions brought her right breast into the light. And she was symmetrical and ordered again and conventionally lovely.

She tossed a fold of his robe to the side, exposing him; she put the tips of her fingers under his scrotum and ran them out to his tip. She shook her breasts a little, and he reached down and took the whole of her right breast in his hand. He was hunched over, his left hand in the air above them holding the bottle, his right arm fully extended as he held her breast. Her head shifted a little, her lids still half closed over her eyes; her breath was very shallow. She brought her hand to her mouth and stuck out her tongue a little and wet her palm and her fingers. He watched her mouth, straining in himself in his position. She was weak and fading; she was half conscious, but the corner of her mouth was up, half twisted, leering, beautiful, and spacy. Were it not sickness it would be drug-lust, he thought. Or lust from desire he imagined; lust after desire fulfilled, lust from thankfulness, from the purest kind of relaxation. He squeezed her breast harder, ran his index finger over her nipple. She moved her wet hand and took his penis, her fingers cool and slippery. She pulled gently, watching herself do it. He watched her breast in his hand, her face, her hand moving. He looked to the glass doors and saw the rain and the shadow of the car and a new shadow the size of a man standing. The hair on the inside of his thighs raised up, though he was not sure of the shadow at all. He looked back at her breasts, her face, and her hand. His semen began to flow out, the first drops falling to her wrist, the rest running down her hand to reach them. As he came, the bottle high in his left hand was quaking; it was lighter, almost empty.

"Almost empty," he grunted softly, and when she looked from her hand to his face, he nodded up to the bottle, directing her eyes there. She followed his look, and when she saw the bottle she got the point and shook a little in weak laughter. He laughed softly with her; he was still shaking and quivering, still coming, his penis lurching. And then the lurches had more space between them. He glanced at the glass doors. The figure was gone. They stayed as they were for what seemed to both of them a long time, his body bent over, her hand holding him, the semen slowly drying, the bottle in the air.

After a while he said, "Let me get a Kleenex, before it dries." She had drifted off to sleep, but just to the edge of it, and she woke up without much transition. She let her hand fall from him.

"Let it stay there," she said weakly. "I want it there."

He got up carefully. He had some muscle pains. His left arm was stiff, and it hurt at the elbow as he lowered the bottle. He clamped the tubing off and placed the bottle on the bed beside her. Her sweat had loosened the adhesive, and the tape came off easily. He took a piece of cotton from the alcohol container on the floor at his foot. When he withdrew the needle he pressed it against the point of exit to keep the blood in, the hematoma from forming. After he had pressed it there for a while, he used a piece of the adhesive to secure it. She was sleeping, her breath regular and shallow again. The semen had begun to dry into crystals on her hand and wrist. He closed his robe and tied it. He adjusted her pillows and her robe, put her right hand over her left on her stomach. He stood back from the bed, the bottle and the tubing with the needle in the end of it in his left hand, the metal alcohol-sponge container in his right. For no good reason he could have articulated, he smiled, and then he bowed to her, deeply and from the waist. As if she knew somewhere in her early sleep that he was doing something odd and possibly extraordinary, she shifted a little and she smiled too. He walked to the glass doors, the materials still in his hands. It was still raining, a little harder than before; the glass doors were sheeted and running with it. He could not see the car beyond them. He put his face close to the glass, trying to see out. He could see nothing. He put his forehead against the glass. The glass was cool, and it felt good.

After he had put the Laetrile materials away, he took a shower, missing the feel of the golf balls around his feet, and dried and dressed himself. Then he got paper and pencil and wrote a note to her:

Melinda: had to go out. you know. be back by seven.
Call Bob White if you need anything. I'll get dinner.
I love you of course. Allen.

He put the note on the pillow beside her head, then changed his mind and propped it up with a glass on the motel room table. He got the gun from between the folds of white towel in his suitcase. He loaded a clip into it carefully. He looked at it, then took the clip out and checked the chamber; it was empty, and he pulled the trigger. It did not click. The safety was on, and he made a note of its position and snapped the clip in again. He put the gun into the pocket of his raincoat and put his arms into the sleeves and settled the coat on his shoulders and buttoned it. It hung heavily to one side, pulling the collar against his neck. He looked around the room, checking, a thing he always did before leaving a place. He looked down at peaceful Melinda sleeping. Then he turned away, opened the door, and stepped out into the rain.

By the time he had left the stones and turned onto the blacktop, the rain had diminished, and after he had driven for a few minutes it had stopped. The radio told him there were some flooded cars, a few had slid into the washes, a bus with children coming home from a summer trip had skidded and fallen over, but no one had been injured. His wipers were off, and he passed people with hoods up and rags in their hands, working to dry plugs and points. The road leading out of the city to Route 80 was still fairly empty. At one point he had to slow and wait while the cars in front of him crept, wheel deep, under a viaduct. There were some people in yellow slickers walking along the roads. When he hit the highway and started the slight rise out of the city, all evidence of the rain fell away. He could see the edge of the cloud cover ahead of him; he pushed the car up to seventy, and before long he drove from under the clouds, entering the sunlight, the shafts of which made the highway in front of him sparkle. The sky was clear, but there were no heat waves shimmering on the road in front of him. He opened the vent and felt the warm, dry desert air come in.

In twenty minutes he slowed to enter Vail, and after he'd passed through it and come to a place where the shoulder widened, he pulled off the road and got the Tombstone matchbox out of the wheel well in the trunk and put it under the front seat. While the trunk was open, he decided to put the gun in it, and he took it out of his raincoat pocket and slid it between two of the towels on the trunk floor. He had bought the gun in Los Angeles, on impulse, and he had later thought that the reason he'd bought it had to do with a slight sense of romance in the delivering of the cocaine, a kind of vague old-movie, underworld feel. He knew better than that, but once he had gotten the gun, he had kept it; he hadn't wanted to let it go. And he hadn't wanted to let Richard go either, once he had gotten back in touch with him. He knew he could have gotten the Laetrile elsewhere; he need not have agreed to the bargain that had him here on his way to deliver the Tombstone matchbox of cocaine. Something about Melinda's wish to go East, to head back into something, urged a need in him that had to do with Richard and his own past. This need, like his need to keep the gun, was at this point only pictorial for him, vaguely emblematic, not at all clear.

It took him a little over an hour to get the seventy miles to Tombstone. As he got closer to it, things along the road became increasingly familiar. The first thing he noticed were the small white crosses at the roadside, markers for the places where accidents had occurred in which people had been killed. When he saw them he remembered how he had seen them when he was in high school, living in Bisbee, twenty-five miles the other side of Tombstone. He knew the road between Bisbee and Tombstone better than this stretch, but he had traveled here some too. He remembered a place, a looping turn from a long downhill slope, where there were more than twenty crosses clustered like a small graveyard at the roadside. Driving into Tombstone with friends, they had dared that turn in the road often, laughing and joking but not untouched by the danger and its evidence in the crosses. Mostly, he had driven to Tombstone with his father for his quack arthritis treatments, baths and massages, that were supposed to produce wonders. They had moved from Chicago to Bisbee for his father's health. When he was in his second year of high school, his father had died there.

He remembered the last turn into Tombstone, and he slowed down as he entered it. There had been considerable building on the edge of town since he had last been there close to twenty years ago, but after the turn, Boot Hill still sloped up to the left, a low-brush rise with its wooden and stone markers, now with an out-of-place cyclone fence surrounding it. A little farther down on the right was the O.K. Corral, and by the time he reached it he had slowed to a crawl. The O.K. had changed also; it had been "restored" with new paint and a new sign, and some boards had been replaced, and the grounds had been worked on. Down the streets beyond the O.K., little signs had been hung out in front of the various stores, markers with historic names woodburned into them. He turned at the corner of the Crystal Palace Bar, drove down a half block, and parked. There were tourists walking the streets, cars with various out-of-state plates, but there were not a lot of tourists, and the town did not look to be thriving. Across the street from the Crystal Palace, he saw the vaguely remembered Bird Cage Theater and the *Tombstone Epitaph*, the old newspaper, beside it. He turned into the Crystal Palace, pushing one of the swinging half-doors and slipping through it like a hesitant cowboy.

There were six men sitting at the bar, five facing the long glass mirror behind it, the other at a place where the bar turned in an L to the wall, a position where he could see the door. In front of the mirror, obscuring its lower part, were hundreds of bottles of liquor, about half of which were phonies, empty bottles with Old West labels on them. The mirror was high, long, and beautiful, its edge framed in gilded wood or plaster. The bartender had a striped shirt and a handlebar mustache. He nodded to him as he entered. Two of the men at the bar were cowboys, real ones, in boots, Levis, pearl-button shirts and Stetsons. The three men beside them were tourists, all of them heavy and dressed in various combinations of searsucker and brushed cotton. The man at the turn of the L—he thought this was his man the moment he entered—was young, about thirty; he wore a tailored cowboy shirt, dark blue, but he was hatless. A beer bottle stood on the bar in front of him. He smiled as the stranger approached. Allen got there, sat down, and ordered a Lone Star.

There was the sound of gunfire outside, and the two cowboys sitting beside him laughed when it came, shaking their heads.

"The bloody Chisholm battle is on again," one of them said.

"No, that's Gunfight at the O.K. Corral, I think," the other said.

"Maybe so."

"Think it is," the bartender said.

He remembered the Frontier Days weekend that occurred each summer in Tombstone, in August he thought. There were re-enactments of all the famous Old West battles that the town in its heyday had witnessed, at least twenty of them. All of the historic businesses would be enlivened by people in traditional Western costumes. The Bird Cage Theater would be open, presenting the shows that had been popular in the middle of the last century. And there would be a lot of beer drinking, some real fights, and a lot of barbecues. He remembered that one of the traditions was to try to get enough beer drunk on that weekend so that by the end of it the block at the center of main street would be covered, from curb to curb, with empty cans and bottles. This end was usually accomplished.

"Frontier Days?" he asked.

"Naw, that's not till August, the twelfth this year, isn't it Ray?"

"That's right, I think," one of the cowboys answered the bartender and looked over at the stranger. The cowboy was about forty-five years old; he looked very strong and hard. His face was sun-leathered, his eyes a little milky. The man in the L of the bar tipped up his beer, paid for it, and left. The tourists finished up and left too. The bartender went to the end of the bar and gathered their glasses and started to dunk them into a vat of water behind the bar. The cowboy was still looking at him.

"Leak," he said, and he got up and headed for the door under the sign that said *Hombres* in the far corner of the large room. When the cowboy got off his stool, Allen saw that the other one was hunched down over his beer, sipping at it by lifting it only a couple of inches off the bar. His hat was cocked back on his head, and he was looking straight ahead into the mirror.

When he saw that the cowboy had reached the door in the corner, he slipped off his stool and followed him. When he entered the wood, tile, and porcelain room, he saw the cowboy standing at a urinal, and he stepped up to one, two urinals away from him. The cowboy looked over sharply at him.

"You know Richard?"

"I know him," he answered.

"We'll do it in fifteen minutes. It's three-thirty now. There's a place up the street, a sign says *Rose Tree*. You turn left. The other side of the rose tree is a house with a lot of bottles on the roof, I mean *hundreds* of them. Behind that house. You can't miss it. You better walk over."

"I know the place," he said.

"Do you," the cowboy said, raising his eyebrows a little. "Fifteen minutes." He zipped up his fly and left.

Allen waited a moment and then left too. He went out the swinging doors of the Crystal Palace, turned left, and headed for the car. He got into the driver's seat, reached under it, and got the matchbox. Then he got a small, plastic shopping bag, with hand holes cut into it, out of the glove compartment and put the Diamond matchbox into it. The bag was black and had the name of a store printed on it. He began to get out of the car but changed his mind. He started the car and drove it around the block, parking it parallel to the road in a space with a driveway in front of it. It was pointed with the traffic, on the street that led out of the town to the highway, back in the direction of Tucson. He got out of the car, the plastic bag in his hand, and walked to the corner, turned left, and headed for the street on which the Crystal Palace was located. He was a block away from the Palace, at the corner where the rose tree sign was, when he got there. He checked his watch. It was three-thirty-seven.

He remembered the rose tree and the house with the bottles because it was near them that his father had come for his treatments. The rose tree had been called "The Largest Rose Tree in the World"; it had cost a quarter to see it, and it had been surrounded by a high fence. The bottle house had belonged to a woman who had for years put bottles on her roof to let the sun stain them. It took close to twenty years to get a good bottle that way, but he remembered them as being very beautiful, and she had sold them for what was then good money, about ten dollars apiece, more for the special ones.

When he had crossed the street and passed the rose tree sign, he saw what he thought was the rose tree fence enclosure on his side about halfway down the block. Above the fence, and further down at the corner, he could see the tops of some bottles sticking up. There was a parked car on the other side of the street, about where the fence was. He saw a man in a cowboy hat sitting in the driver's seat. The car was in front of a white frame house, and there was another man standing in front of the door. He wore a summer suit. He was pretty sure that the house was the one in which his father had gotten his treatments, but he remembered a sign on the side of the house, something about the kinds of treatments given, and there was no sign as far as he could see where the man now stood. The walkway to the house looked like the one he had carried his father up, but he was not sure of it.

When he got to the fence surrounding the rose tree, he was almost across from the car. A bench had been added to the enclosure, bolted to the fence itself, and above the bench was a sign, the words burned into a piece of heavily lacquered wood; it read: *howdy, pardner. rest a spell*. He moved to the bench and sat down on it under the sign. He checked his watch; it was two-forty. He looked across the street at the car. The man at the door looked over his shoulder at the man sitting in the driver's seat. The man in the seat lifted a hand. The other man turned and walked back to the car and got in. The man in the cowboy hat started the engine, and the car drove to the corner, stopped there, and then turned right.

He put his hand on the shopping bag on the seat beside him and got up. He walked along the rose tree fence, passed a house, and then came to the one with the bottles on its roof. There were not as many bottles as he had remembered, but there were still plenty of them; they covered the entire roof, but now there was more space between them. The sun hit against the bottles; there were some flashes where the few newest bottles stood, but most of the light was absorbed; the older bottles had a way of doing that. He suspected that the market for the fine things that the bottles were had slipped some over the years. The colors in and on the bottles were amazing in their gradations and shades, and the reflective and absorptive qualities of the bottles lit the roof up with similar variety. The sun gave a solid and sharp light to the day, but the roof was a complex of shadows, twinkles, and colors.

He moved to the back of the house. There was a dirt road running behind it, and beyond the road, though he could see a few scattered houses in the distance, there was mostly open desert, and he was on the literal edge of the town. He stood there for a minute, then he saw a pickup truck turn into the dirt road, about a block away from him from the direction of the town. The truck came slowly up the road. When it got about twenty feet from him, it stopped. He could see the cowboy through the dirty windshield, his Stetson square on his head. The truck stopped short of the edge of the property of the house with the roof of bottles. There was a low picket fence and a small yard with a meager cactus garden behind the house. A sand path ran between the cactus to the stoop; the door was a screen door. The cowboy had his arm out the window of the pickup cab resting on the doorframe; he lifted his hand from where it gripped the frame and motioned. Allen walked over to the window of the pickup. On the seat of the cab beside the cowboy, he could see a re-volver, what he thought was a six-shooter.

"Never mind that," the cowboy said. "Give me the shit."

He lifted the bag up. As he extended his hand to the cab of the truck, he noticed that the cowboy was not looking at him, but past and behind him. Then the truck lurched forward, the rear frame of the door hitting his hand, spinning him around and send-ing the bag flying off beyond the dirt road and into the edge of the desert. The truck was already well underway when it got to the corner of the house, and its tires squealed some when it bent to the right and shot down the blacktop in the direction of the rose tree.

He saw the car slide to a stop about forty yards from him, the man in the summer suit jump out, and the car, with the door still open and flapping, accelerate after the truck. The man, in jump-ing from the car, had tripped; he fell, went with his roll, and came to his feet. A sleeve of his jacket was ripped, and he jerked at it with his other hand as he ran, breaking his stride. There was a gun in the hand of the arm with the ripped sleeve, and as Allen turned toward the house he saw the gun disappear as the man pulled at the sleeve to rip it away and free himself.

In two strides Allen was over the low picket fence and in the sand. When he got to the screen door, he ripped it off its hinges as the hook lock pulled loose, and it flew back behind him. The force of the wrenching set the house into slight motion.

"Shit!" he heard, and then a crashing, as the man with the torn sleeve and the gun got tangled in the flying door.

He could see the light at the end of the house, and he headed for it. He could hear the bottles fall and roll and break above him. He passed an old woman who was half risen from her crocheting of a tablecloth at a large oak dining-room table. He hit the screen door at the front of the house with both of his hands out; his right hand ripped through the screening, and the other hit against the left frame, sending the door free of the latch and open. It slapped like a rifle shot against the side of the house. He cleared the front stoop in the air, heard the tinkle and crash of bottles above and behind him, ran down the front walk, crossed the street, hit along the side of the house across from the bottle house, and then came to the rose tree fence. He vaulted over it, using the *howdy pardner* seat bench, landing on both feet in the dirt near the rose tree itself, its huge trunk in front of him. There were no visitors, and he grabbed onto a low limb and climbed up into the rose tree, scrambling into the higher branches, where he saw that he could reach the roof of the house against which the enclosure was built. He reached for the eave, the hot shingles burning his fingers, and hoisted himself up and over. There was a large, uncapped chimney rising a good six feet up from the middle of the peaked roof, and he headed for it. He moved around the chimney; it was a good three-and-a-half-feet square, but he felt exposed on all sides, and he grabbed at the edge of the chimney above him and pulled himself up to the top of it. It had one flue; it was open, and he saw light below. He climbed down into the chimney, searching for a purchase on the edges of the brick interior. He found small narrow ledges for his feet, and then he crouched down.

He was breathing heavily, but he could hear the bottles. They were still falling over, some breaking, some rolling around on the flat roof; some hit against each other, tinkling. They sounded like a massive and airy wind chime at times, at others like a piece of odd contemporary music. His breathing was the base line, the rhythm. A line of bottles would fall like dominoes, some ringing others—the darker ones, he thought, having a hollow sound, the newer ones like crystal. They fell, rolled, crashed against each other, dropped from the roof with dull thuds. And then he held his breath.

He heard the man coming, could hear him opening the door in the rose tree fence, could even hear his breathing. The breathing settled quickly as the man moved around the tree. He heard the final ripping away of the sleeve and a small click. The safety or the hammer, he thought. He heard the man scuffling as he climbed the tree. Then he felt a small quiver in the chimney as the man came up over the edge of the roof and onto it. He heard his feet sliding and scraping on the shingles as he moved to the peak of the roof, then a firmer thudding as he walked along the caps to the chimney. Then the man stopped, and all he could hear was his deep, regular breathing.

He stood very still where he was, looking up. Above him he could see the open sky, and as he watched it, a dark element of clouds began to drift across it into the framed field of his vision. The clouds were very dark, almost pure black and as thick as oil smoke. He heard the man shift around a little as he looked, felt him circle the chimney still looking. Then he stopped. He imagined him looking up at the clouds as he was, their attention focused on the same issue. They were very close together, and he felt embarrassed in his secrecy, wrong and shy. The clouds had moved in, and the patch of sun that had entered the chimney, oddly exposing him, was gone. He felt his hair lifted slightly, his scalp touched by a cool breeze. Then he heard the sound of gunfire. He thought at first that it was thunder or more mock Old West battling, but he heard the man suck in his breath and shift quickly and pause; he could feel his attention.

"Christ!" he heard the man say sharply, and then heard him scrambling down from the peak. He felt the roof return to its architecture as the man left it. He heard the tree groan and the dull thud as the man's feet hit the ground. The door to the rose tree fence ground on its hinges a little as the man opened it, and then he could not hear anything at all.

He waited. He remembered living in Bisbee, twenty-five miles from here, when he was in high school. Bisbee was at the top of the low mountains, the southern end of the Continental Divide before it dipped into Mexico. In the winter, it got cold and snowed in Bisbee. But he did not think that it got so cold in Tombstone, at least not cold enough to warrant a chimney of this size. He was not sure about that, though. Another odd thing was the locked screen doors. It was the middle of the day, and he could not figure why she had them locked. He shook himself back, realizing he was beginning to daydream. The first question was, had they got any significant look at him. Second, did they have any line on his car. He did not take time to figure the chances. The car would tell the story; if they got that he was sunk. There was enough in the trunk and the glove compartment to nail him. Hysteria began to creep up in him as he thought of Melinda, the possibility of not making it East with her, but he pushed it back down.

He rose from his crouch, put his elbows on the brick outside of the flue, and hoisted himself up until he was sitting on the bricks with his legs dangling into the hole. He could see the top of the rose tree and the street a few houses away. He knew if he looked around he would be able to see back to the place where the truck had stopped. He was too exposed, and he got his legs out of the hole, turned, and lowered himself down the side of the chimney to the peak of the roof. He saw there was still nobody visiting the rose tree, and though the enclosure made him uneasy, he climbed from the roof to the tree's limbs, working his way down, and dropped to the ground. It was much darker than it had been before in the rose tree enclosure; the dark clouds hung high and heavy up through the branches. They had moved in over the town and stopped.

He went to the fence in the wall and opened the gate, stepped out and moved to the sidewalk, starting back in the way he had initially come. There were a few tourists walking the street on which the Crystal Palace was located a block away to his right. He crossed the street and continued on toward where his car was parked. There were a couple of people walking the other side of the street, but they took no notice of him. When he got to the corner, he did not turn toward the car but waited while the traffic passed. Coming into the town and leaving it to get to Route 80, the traffic was heavier on this street, and he had to wait for some time for the light to change. He saw that no one was around the car. Another car had parked behind, but it was empty. It was not the car that belonged to the two men, he thought, but he wasn't sure. He crossed the street when the light changed, went another block, and turned to his right, walking until he came to the corner of the street that would lead him back to the Crystal Palace. He realized he was holding back from approaching the car and that he had no good reason for doing so. They either had a line on him or they didn't, whoever they were, and he had better just go to the car and see what happened. He turned toward the Crystal Palace, walked the block to the street on which he was parked, and turned right again, getting the keys out of his pocket as he moved. When he reached the car, he unlocked the door, got in, started it up, and when there was a break in the traffic, pulled out into the street and drove away.

When he hit Route 80, he brought the car up to sixty miles an hour, lit a cigarette with the dashboard lighter, and settled himself into the seat. Then he began to relax a little and to think things over. He felt a quick chill as the realization hit him that he could have left the car where it was and hitched back to Tucson. If they had a line on the car, leaving it there would have given him some time, maybe even enough to get away East. This was not his line of work, that was sure; he had been lucky. There was one thing he knew then. There would be no drop off of cocaine in Kansas City. He would put more miles between them, then he would get in touch with Richard. A few minutes after the rain had begun hitting the windshield, pelting the town behind him in a heavy wash, he drove the car out from under it, into the light of a clear sky and the edge of the beginning of twilight.

RICHARD

What trees there were outside could bend their boughs, their twigs reaching, in that green aching intensity they wear, out to touch each other in the night, and he wouldn't care. There were, in fact, two walnut trees, because in the late eighteen-eighties this had been a walnut grove: black walnuts, their small protected satellites, in green jackets, scattered under the boughs. The flesh within those meaty jackets, under those hard, brainlike shells, he could have eaten, sat beside a fire, in a soft chair, with a cat and a bottle of good wine, some cheese. Even a small spaceheater, because this was California, little change, and in the winter just small bites at times; he could have faced it in against his legs, the way his father had put feet up on ottoman, before the fender, felt toasty warm, hearing the little crackles. The trees had made their peace so many years ago, much like the large rock in Idaho into which pioneers had carved their names, those of their wives and children, and their dates of passage. In the failed and now intractable bark: hearts, initials, and gang names, some spray paint on the trunks and lower limbs. He could have trimmed the bark and sprayed the holes with sealer, done some small amount of pruning, gathered up the fallen nuts before the birds got to them, but the fact was he had never set foot beside the entrance path, running from the cyclone gate up to the porch, had only seen the backyard while shaving, and not because he had in any way intended to look there. He had lived in the house for one year. The man there before him had put up the cyclone fence to keep his dogs in, two Dobermans who roamed the yard at night, dark, aware, and silent, keeping the place safe. He didn't need the fence, he had certain powers, and the kids stayed away.

There were raspberries along the back fence and a small lemon tree, four feet tall, in the corner, feeble but surprising in its fruit. There were flowers, mostly hidden, but not choked off, by the variety of weeds around them. And the weeds themselves were beautiful. He could have brought some in and dried them, put them in a container on a window sill, noticed the way they looked in sun and shade. The flowers were poinsettias, (oddly) a few columbines, and morning-glories. Once, a century plant had come to bloom for a few days, but he had not seen it. Along the fence running the sides of the house, through windows by which he only passed, could have been seen remnants of rhubarb and the orange vines that are often found in the company of poison oak, and poison oak as well. To both sides of the front gate were shrubs, and in among them the new shoots of an avocado tree were coming on strongly, and maybe in a few years a large tree, with its green and bulbous fruit, would be growing there. Even had he known of all these things, he would not have thought of the grounds around the house as all potential and realization; he would not have thought of the place as a yard at all. It was another world; he had no knowledge of, nor care for, its seedy warmth and complexity.

He did not even go about that daily business any more of small pleasures: food, the way of his bowels, and specifically for him, the sound of good jazz. Though he still played it, he didn't tap his foot or hum tunes. He didn't buy clothes, nor did he look at the bodies of women in them; they held no surprises that he was capable of. He knew there was another kind of world of feeling that he was outside of, but he could not quite believe that it was any more than sham, and he was beyond the possibility of touching it. It was like the quiet cooking of the yard around the house. He would have accepted its occurrences as knowledge, but he could in no other way have awareness of them. A week ago some kid had thrown a stone that thumped into the side of the house wall of the living room. He had been rolling joints at the card table when it happened. The sharp report had startled him, and a place in his mind began to uncoil like a snake finding a new pathway through fixed stones; the sound, the cause of the sound, the possible human hand in it, the vision of the kid running away: the unencumbered freshness of the stately thought-trail. He had felt a welling-up from somewhere, but his mind had quickly closed it down, and he backed up to think if he would have to get onto the kid, and he was grooved again.

He stood in the middle of the shower now. His arms hung at his sides. He accepted the thick jets of water pounding heavily into his chest. Above the open stall of the shower was a mirror, a small tilted oval he had rigged there in which he could see himself, the dents in his water-pounded chest, the hanging arms, the sodden, half-erection. He had begun lifting weights because it was something to do; he had felt that there was little left to do, and there had been some new pain in it. But the pain had gone, and he continued with the weights because of the definition and not the strength. As the muscles pushed out of his body, he could both see and feel them individually, and pain could be isolated; he could be struck, and he could strike the specific bulks of his body against things. He had started with the weights four years ago, at the time she had returned from prison and had begun to whip him. She had learned whipping in prison, and she had liked it, and she taught it to him. He whipped her also, but she did not understand why she liked it. When he had met her, twelve years ago, she had been searching for a definition of herself, and he knew immediately that she was so damaged (there was so little of her there) that she would take anything that would give her any sort of integrity in the eyes of anyone.

He had hooked into that; she was holding to voracious sex at the time, out of some recent desperateness, but the conventional devouring was soon exhausted, and as the pathetic integrating had become concretized she had begun to think of herself as "kinky"; anything in any way different in sex defined her. Finally she had come to think of herself as what she called a "kink," and whenever he battered her, she thought she became who she was. She thought she liked the whipping because it was odd and different; he knew better. But though, as he thought, he insulted her about it often, above her intelligence, playing with irony, it was a weak game, and he did not care to try to deal with her mistaken sense of herself. He liked her the way she was. She had whipped him, and he had cried out "Mother, Mother," and then he had often beaten her, heavily, pounding her with the sand sock and wet towel. And it was true that there were other ways of living going on around them the interstices of which they came into, but not often. And when they did find themselves in situations, he smirked inwardly to himself about them and pointed out their phoniness to her; that way, though at different levels of consciousness he thought, they both shut them out. And perhaps the largest irony was that, for both of them, it was within the parameters of what might be called the conventional, where the deep and real unknown abided, that the thing feared at its very roots was incomprehensible to them because it was not grooved for them and was beyond their context. But such quality of fear was beyond their articulation also; so, they did not know of it.

At certain angles the water beat into his chest as if he were a hollow gourd, the tight skin over his muscles a drumhead. He turned to feel an individual jet bite into his nipple, scalding him though the water was cool. He thought of the image of the slab of stone on his chest, his stepfather standing over him with the sledge, the heavy, concussive thud as the sledge dropped, the veins in the muscles bursting, the way a rib broke from his sternum and dove into his heart, the deeper and more satisfying pain as he was cracked and split open. He smiled under the spray. He knew all about it: the systems of psychology, the old marquis, the sickness in the smiles at pain. Her whipping him had been really the last thing that had lifted him up, and that had not been successful for him for a number of years. The image of his stepfather with the sledge coming down on the stone was a toying, a distance in history. It did not move him. Nor did the sex, the risk of selling drugs, the chances taken on the Harley, the occasional busts, the intimidation of the narcs.

She was lying in the other room on the bed, waiting for him. Soon he would go in there and fuck her; that was the only way he could now think of it, and there would be nothing new or imaginative to it. She had little imagination, of this he was sure, and if he just wore something, a piece of her underwear, some lipstick or eye-liner, it would lift her. She would say when she saw him coming, "That's kinky," and she would be moved some when he entered her. But he had gone the limits of his imagination with her, and many times what he had proposed and accomplished was well beyond her. She would just stare at him then, not understanding, and so he would whip her again, and she would like that and call it kinky. For him she was now like a strip of rag, some half-rotten piece of fruit, and he would gain little pleasure as he ripped into her, pounded her, and the only thing that would keep him in any way erect would be the very slight pain of the loss of desire in giving and taking pain, and even that would be fading.

He had thought recently of killing her. He had never killed anyone, and she was still close to him and was appropriate. The killing would have to be right, because it would be near the end, and he would have to plan how he would get himself killed afterward. He had begun, casually, to think of a possible plan for it. They had seen some snuff movies, and she had been dimly interested in them. They were kinky she thought, but she had been heavily zonked on scag at the time, and she could not really see through to the fact that that would be the final kinky act. Whatever else she was, she was a survivor in her passivity. This he saw clearly, and had he ability to do so, he would have admired her for it as he might have admired her for other things beyond his image of her. With him it was more ironic; he survived in spite of himself. He was too smart to get caught seriously in the web of pain that he found ways of arranging. The drug deals with the vicious, desperate Mexicans in Ensenada, his cheating them on their own turf, his touches with the more dangerous big buyers in West L.A.—whatever net he got himself into his intelligence forced him to solve and get out of. He had the pleasant bruises and the rushes of danger to remember, but he had stayed alive.

He stepped back in the stall a little, letting the water strike down against his penis, hit into his testicles, and hurt them; it made him a little harder. He would go into her soon and do the thing, be done and finished with her for now, in that way at least. In the morning the two of them would get up early and get ready to leave. He felt good thinking of the new start. He would go East, beyond even Detroit where he had come from. Maybe it would take some time. But he would find and then he would kill his old friend Allen, who had cheated him. He knew that Allen's wife was from that Cape out there, and he would take his time and would probably find them there. He would kill him not so much for the cheating but for the surge of it and the pain that would follow, possibly a new kind of pain, a mix of what they would do to him when they caught him and the hurt that might

come a little from the loss of Allen. He had not ␣
desperate or unhappy; he had been numb and bored. He kn␣
was close to burned out at thirty-three, but now he would ␣
alive again for a while. Maybe this fresh feeling would get him
up enough so that he could visit his mother in Detroit on his way
East. The fact that he had arranged the drop at her place, and
the pain in having involved her in his life again, gave him some
little hope that it might be so. The way she would look at him
and the way he would behave with her stirred in him a bit.

He turned the shower off and let the water run from his body,
down through his creases. He waited while he drained, and then
he stepped out of the stall, took a towel from the rack, and began
to dry himself. He rubbed each muscle that he could identify
individually, dabbing at his chest and his angular face. When he
was finished and while he was splashing cologne on his inner
thighs, he heard her voice, whining he would have called it, from
the other room.

"Come on, Daddy, come on." She sounded bored and a little
flat. It was as if her voice and its performance could make the
desire real, the request urgent and sincere, though it was incapable of that.

He reached up and took the watch cap from its place and put
it on. Then he hung his thick chain and medallion around his
neck. Then he soaked his towel in the sink and rang it out into a
wet, thick rope; he tested it by slapping it into his leg. Then he
checked to see how he looked in the mirror. He was fine, he
thought, if a little uninteresting. He was getting older, he thought,
but most of him was hard and firm.

"Time enough," he said softly, "time enough." And then he
turned from the mirror and went in to her. It was dark in the
room, and he could not see her very well. But he knew she was
ready and waiting. Outside, the sad and injured walnut trees, as
if from a kind of instinct, reached out and fought against their
peace.

MELINDA

Born Melinda Prada in the warm August, she grew up on a young sandspit of land that pushed into the Atlantic like the fragile arm of a young boy. The arm might have been diseased, at least a mutation or birth defect; it lacked fingers, a positive hinged and mobile elbow; it seemed eaten away in some places, one of them an inlet where Melinda lived. The name was pronounced pray-da, the slight pathetic anglicizing of the Portuguese that the women had accepted and the men had forced, historically. For the women had changed their names anyway, but the men had work to do among Yankee fishermen and thought to become Americans, against their skin color and language. It could not have been a young girl's arm, with its welcoming or slight defiance, because it was a public gesture in the sea, and there was no public act for women to perform. And yet the calm and yielding, but resilient nature of the spit was surely feminine and not to be controlled, and this was the geological irony, confronted and not solved: there was no manipulation of the spit possible to good ends. There was, as with the women, a fragile working relationship.

She was an only child, to her father's chagrin (her mother's pleasure), and she came to his dragger and to the sea when she was twelve years old, at the same time as boys came to her. Her father knew his sources were circuitous. They shamed him, and he made no mention of the following passage when he found it, even put the book away out of eyeshot.

Every returning New Bedford whaler brought home a few bravas, or black Portuguese, among its crew. These Cape Verde savages—a cross between exiled Portuguese criminals and the aborigines of the Islands—began to drift into Mashpee and marry into the hybrid of Indian and African Negro that they found there. This vicious mixture caused what Mr. Pocknet called 'a drift of disgust against Mashpee' . . .

When the other boats came zigzag in to see, at first her father hid her (as he had hid the book) below decks, but this was futile, since news traveled among the fishermen, who were like old folks with nothing to do when it came to rumor. She was revealed, and she was good enough at the nets to become quickly integrated. And, though not approved of, she was his daughter and was accepted as an oddity.

On the way in from the Georges Bank she used water colors sometimes, oils occasionally, and pastels, and she wrote stories. The boys saw she could do all this well and the dragging too, and they could see their own dim, secret wishes for the joining of tenderness, sensitivity and strength in it, and they feared and shunned her. Her stories were sea stories and like her painting, very clear and comprehensive and tough. She saw the way the water came in against the boat, the way it looked at a distance, the colors in the various cloud covers and the light in them. She had insight into the lives around her, and what she wrote affected those who read it. She took up with girls then, who knew their places and were full grown and integrated. And when she was sixteen and her parents drowned, ironically, on a pleasure cruise to Boston, she took up with an older woman, an artist in the town at the Cape's end, who taught her things about technique and taught her to mourn her parents properly, and loved her and let her go with grace when she was eighteen, and she went to art school in Boston.

There had been some women there, but the times were not right for it, and she was thwarted, and when this happened she turned more intensely to her studies and her art. She wrote stories and sold them to magazines, and her water colors were a success in small galleries, and she knew she was on to things important. She quit the writing after a while, making a choice for the visual. There had been men there too, usually older ones whom she had come out to a bit, but they had learned to fear her intelligence and skill, though more slowly than the younger ones, and things hadn't worked out. She finished school and went to work, teaching young children art. She kept the circle around her own art very tight, knowing what she was doing, and then she found that she was twenty-three years old.

That year she met Allen and went out with him. She slept with him, cooked for him on occasion; they had long talks, and she discovered no shocks to her expectations. She was smarter than he was, and he balked at this like the rest, conventionally, but she was older now, and he was younger than he was, and before too long, in a way that she did not understand (and she liked that she did not understand it), she found out a familiar quality in him. Her way of loving him became unintimidating to him when she found it out, and they had married and lived good and reasonable years together. Then she had been introduced to the cancer.

This was the past Allen had put together from what she had told him and from his own romance of it. He felt she had no secrets in the way he did, but she did have a few. There was the closed circle in which her art stood; he was shown the product openly, and he thought he understood intention and process through it, but he had no sense of her strength manifest there. He took the clarity he saw as a kind of openness and transparency, but that was not it. And when the cancer started, and he saw some depths in her revealed, he saw them as feminine depths, that is, to him, depths of gentle sensitivity and attunement. He did not see that what they were were instances of clarity, certainty, and a steel-hardness of character. They joined anew in the occasion of the cancer. She found his weakness and childishness, and it endeared him to her. He saw what he thought was the bud in her unfold into certain womanhood, not realizing that it was a purer power, and neuter.

"It's like a web," she said, "or a net. But it's a circle. There is no up and down to it; it's in and out. Think of all of those sticks making it up as being people. If you were a disconnected stick lying on the table beside it, you'd feel, possibly, lonely. No. There'd be no *place* for loneliness then; you'd just be disconnected. You'd be very still. If you push one of those sticks, one on the other side will move. They'll *all* move a little, like people, each in its own way, but because you pushed one of them. The one on the other side could be a person out of your past, or somebody that you don't know very well, or somebody you do know well, but he's far away right now. I don't mean mind control or telepathy. When you push that stick the other one doesn't move the moment you push it; it takes a while. I mean that things you do always change the fabric or net or web you are in. It comes around to affect the other sticks in time. The small wires between the sticks are the processes that cause behavior. One end is head process, the other end is, well, you know, the other end, another kind of consciousness—D. H. Lawrence, et cetera. And it could be something as small as a symbol or a photograph you look at, after many years, that starts the chain, the net, reaction. The focus of the thing, its integrity, is the matrix; this is what we call 'meaning.' Out here we analyze it. But in there, when we are one of the sticks, we can't do that. A breeze pushes against one stick or wire, and we, on the other side, or in the middle, or very close to the one that the breeze pushed, are moved a little. There is no help for it, and we're moved before we know it. So that knowing is always after the fact of definition. But look how the sticks seem to ache when they are still. They want moving; that's about all they really have. That is the story I wanted to tell you," she said, glancing up at Bob White. "I call this story The Integrity Sphere."

She was out of breath from talking, so she stood quietly beside them, looking into the window. They both seemed able to see the sphere as she saw it; at least, they attended to it. They were in front of an architect's window in Aspen, Colorado. It was after he had gone to the river where he had let out the cocaine from the plastic bag that had been in the Kansas City Diamond matchbox, let it mix its rush with that of the swift stream. It was after noon. The Buckminster Fuller Tensegrity Sphere was on a piece of dark felt covering a table. It stood there, airy and both powerful and fragile. It was made of quarter-inch pieces of pine doweling five inches long, screw eyes, and thin wire. None of the sticks touched each other, and the wires in the screw eyes did not touch the sticks. Gravity seemed to play no part in its structure. It was the structure that was powerful, the materials that were weak. He held her shoulder. Bob White stood on the other side of her. There seemed no room in the sphere for free movement. Open as it was, an open matrix, it seemed claustrophobic to him. He wondered if he could push on it hard enough to break it. He thought he probably could, quite easily. But what would be left then? She leaned against him. He pressed her shoulder when she finished talking.

"That was a pretty good story," Bob White said, and then he moved his hands from where they hung at his sides and began a soft clapping in front of his waist. She turned to him, away from the window, and when she did that Allen took his hand from her shoulder and began his own soft clapping also. People passed by them, but the clapping was so soft that they did not notice it. They both bobbed a little as, from either side, they turned in to face her, clapping lightly. They were smiling, breaking into light laughter, and she stepped back from the window a little and bowed a little to each of them as they clapped. As they began to finish they moved closer, in to one another, making a kind of circle. When they were done, they were touching against each other in various ways.

THE GAME

They drove out the end of the town at five-thirty in the morning, before it was completely light, and headed up Independence Pass. At the top they would come to the ridge of the Continental Divide, the watershed; they would be leaving the West then as they descended, and after they had passed through Denver they would enter the plateau entrance into the Great Plains. They rose up from the town, but before they were high enough to see back to it in its wholeness, they were closed off from it by the mountains.

"It's gone," Melinda said as she turned her head back from the rear window.

The pine stands were thick and grew close to the road. There were small meadows of aspen, their leaves shimmering silver as the sun came up. At one point, well back in a meadow behind other trees, they had a glimpse of a ripe cottonwood, like a huge dandelion gone to seed, dropping its puffs in drifts on the light morning wind. The forks of small rivers ran down to turn along the road or go under it, falling away on the other side. After a while, at about eleven thousand feet, they came to timber line; the large trees were gone, and the high meadows of wild flowers and moss and low scrub began. Near the top they passed a ghost town, a long-abandoned mining village: dozens of log buildings returning to the meadow they were in, reclaimed very slowly, a peaceful and nonviolent death, though perhaps of a passionate history. Then they came to the top of the mountains.

There was a sign and a marker and a place to park. Off to the left, up a gradual slope, there was a pile of boulders on a hill, a place that seemed to be the ultimate top of things. With the exception of the hill, at the parking place everything seemed to slope away from them, gradually. The sign said: *Independence Pass, elevation 12,095 feet*. They got out of the car and sat at a redwood picnic table near the parking area. They drank hot coffee from the thermos they had brought with them. The air was very crisp and thin, and Melinda was very pale in the sun.

"This is very high up," she said.

"It is, indeed, very high up," he said to her.

"Could be higher," Bob White said, and he took his coffee cup with him and started to stroll up the slope to the pile of boulders.

When he was gone, Melinda put her cup down and began to talk. For the first time in a month, she talked extensively about her dying. She said she thought it was time to take stock some: a lot had happened, and a lot was going to happen. She mentioned the Tensegrity Sphere with a wan smile. She talked about his getting rid of the cocaine, the close call in Tombstone, the sense she had from what he had told her about Richard. Nobody would let this slip, she thought, least of all him. She said she knew there was more to come. She turned toward Allen on the bench, under the few high clouds and the sun. He sat hunched over, elbows on the table, hands cupping his coffee. She said she wanted to get back to the Cape. He said he knew that.

But she said she had to go beyond her concern for him. She had that, but she had really only herself at the bottom. He was a concerned party, but the party he was concerned with would not be there long, and he would have to make his decision, finally, without regard for her. She said all this sounds very romantic, but it is not romantic; it is the way things can be when you are going to die and you know it. Whatever else, she would not use the gun, and she did not want him to use it on her, even if things got really bad. And if somehow he had to leave her, that was okay too. She said she did not mean to sound callous about it; it was simply the way things were.

While he listened to her, looking over at her at times, he thought in part of the impossibility of reading another's feelings and thoughts in their behavior, in their face and posture and the movements of their body. At least for him it was a difficult thing, difficult to be sure of. Only when he played golf was it all clear and sure. Elsewhere he avoided it, because when he tried to do it he found he was most often wrong. It was especially hard, he thought, with people one had some closeness with. He had had a friend once who had asked it of him, and his inability to see is what had choked off the friendship. If his friend were troubled, he would not speak of it and confide until he was asked about it, and the way you were supposed to know that he was troubled, to unlock him, was to read it in his expression, the way he carried himself, the subtle tones in his voice. If you did not read him, it was because you were insensitive to his feelings. But he had never been able to read people in this way, except on the golf course, where somehow there was a kind of objectivity, a set of brackets, in which he could see behavior clearly and understand it. Too often when his friend sent out his cues, he saw them as a desire for privacy, and he did not engage him.

But Melinda talked to him, had always done so, and he did not have the burden of being judged for missing the nature of her feelings in her behavior. He felt himself as an isolate person all the time, but Melinda broke into that with her talking; she knew how to talk, and she had learned not to ask him to reciprocate in the talking, knowing how hard a thing it was for him, and she knew that when he did speak, he meant what he said. He thought, were he to put all this into words between them, they could both say that this understanding kept them together.

"If we get to the Cape in a while, I'll die there, and then you'll have to figure the rest for yourself. If somehow we don't get there, we'll have to play it by ear. What I want to say is that I think it's a good idea to lay it out here and now, because we could get separated, and we might not have talked. It's not that I really have much to say to you that I haven't said. God knows, we've said it enough recently. It's just, now we've talked and we don't need to feel that there were things we should have said and didn't get to. You know what I mean?"

"I know what you mean," he said.

"Well, is there anything you want to say? You really don't need to. But I thought, maybe, well, this might be your chance if there were anything."

"I can't think of anything right now," he said, "but it would be good for me if I held you."

"Come on," she said.

As he slid awkwardly along the bench to her, he felt selfish. He *did* have things to say to her, but he despaired of the possibility because he could not articulate them, and if he did say anything it would not be the thing he wanted to say. He knew that all talk was of this kind, but at his very core he could not participate in it, could not begin to speak his feelings. It was as if he *were* his feelings and utterance would be to lose that part which was uttered: small bits of his being jettisoned, dissolving in the air, like pieces of flesh cut from his arms with a paring knife, peels cast into a fire. She saw much of this as he came over to her.

"It's all right," she said, "it's all right." And like the child he was, who at bottom was dumbfounded and bewildered at the talk and behavior of adults, he came and put his head down under her arm, his ear against her warm breast above her shallow breathing, and he did a thing that was like weeping somewhere inside himself; he could not wear it on the outside. It was too much like talking, the possibility of the dumb and stupid image made real: his literal heart torn from his chest, to lie still and gushing and bloody on his shirt sleeve. But he felt very close to her, and she felt very close to him. They felt somewhat in common, because what they had removed from between them was forms. They both knew that this was what the talking and the inability to talk were designed to do; they were nothing but catalyst for this touching. He had thought to hold her, still thought he was doing so, but it was she who was holding him. She put her palm against his cheek, pressed him into her breast. He put his left hand on her knee. They sat in the open place on the top of the mountain at Independence Pass, and after a while they heard the scuffing of Bob White as he kicked a few pebbles loose on his way down from the boulders, and they released each other.

"What did you see up there?" Melinda asked him when he reached the table, and he smiled at them before he gave what he knew to be both the real and the cliché answer.

"More mountains," he said, "higher ones."

They dropped down in the east of the watershed into the steep cuts and the broader valleys below and headed by way of Boulder into the outskirts of Denver. They drove through the heart of the city and out the other side, down into the foothills, and made the decision to head north into Wyoming, up to Cheyenne. They got to Cheyenne at midday, saw some posters announcing a rodeo, found a motel in which they unloaded and changed, and were at the rodeo by one-thirty. They spent the afternoon watching the cowboys ride broncos and Brahma bulls and rope calves. Bob White spoke about rodeos in his neck of the woods.

At one point, between events, Allen took Melinda back to where they stabled the animals in split-rail pens, so that she could see them up close. There was a place where the pens were set in a U-shape, and by walking into the U they were almost surrounded by them. The animals' smell was strong, but they were not at all skittery; they seemed very placid and very wise, in a way very professional. One horse came over to the fence and put his nose on the top rail. He and Melinda felt the horse's muzzle. It felt like kid glove, but the best part was the feel of the soft hot breath touching their palms and tickling between their fingers.

They spent the night in Cheyenne and were up and back on the road early in the morning, heading out into the flat lands of the Great Plains. They were not in a hurry, and they drove the old highways and secondary roads, passing close to farms and through small towns. In one town in Nebraska, just the other side of the Mountain-Central time-zone line, they saw a marker announcing that the local agricultural college had restored a piece of prairie as a project. An arrow on the sign pointed the direction, off the main drag, into the few blocks of residential area. The street was on the far side of the town, and they turned into it. At first it was lined with two- and three-story brick houses from the 'twenties and 'thirties. There were large, old trees in the yards. Two blocks in, the newer, frame ranch houses started. The prairie was between two of the ranch houses, on the other side of the street. They parked across from it, got out, and went over to it.

It was less than a half-acre in size, and it too would have been a ranch house, so the plaque in front of it said, had it not been for a young professor and his class at the college. They had discovered that it was land that had, somehow, never been cultivated or farmed. They had acquired it and let it return to its natural state. It was what the Great Plains had been like at the time of the dominance of the Comanches and the coming, or attempted coming, of the Spanish. The weeds, grasses, and flowers growing in it were well over their heads when they entered it.

There were paths cut through it, and they walked these, separating. Though the paths cut back across themselves, they could not see each other, even though they were often no more than a few feet apart. They sounded to each other like small animals or birds in brush, out of sight, as they came close to each other. They talked into the air to each other, over the high growth. Melinda found dew glistening on a spider web across a path and announced this, ducking carefully under it. Allen came upon very strange flowers, small and blue, on thin stalks.

"On a horse, I could see over this," Bob White said at one point. "That's why the Comanche succeeded. Until he didn't," he said.

They spent close to an hour in the prairie, humming and studying whatever they came upon. They spoke less and less as time went by. Each felt enclosed and attentive. There were telephone wires visible from the paths, up in the sky, and they used these to keep their bearing, realizing that were the wires not there, they could well get lost and turned around and confused. Melinda finished her travels first and found her way back to the mouth of the prairie. A few minutes later Bob White joined her there. After another few minutes, Melinda called out. Allen answered her, and soon they heard him coming through the paths toward them. Soon they were together again.

They passed through two more small towns and then jogged back to an old highway and traveled it for three and a half hours. Melinda slept in the corner of the back seat behind him, and Bob White read sections from *Moby-Dick* and studied the road atlas, giving close attention to the Eastern seaboard. Then they headed north again on two-lane country roads. At a gas stop, Allen called Richard from a phone booth to the side of the old building. The conversation was short, and Richard's voice was strangely flat.

"We're talking about twenty-thousand dollars so far, man. When you hit K.C. do it right. We'll see about the other. Call me when it's done."

Allen didn't tell him what he had done with the Kansas City package, but he did say he didn't plan to risk going to K.C. He started to mention Melinda, but he changed his mind and didn't do it. Richard would have none of the K.C. risk talk. He spoke as if he hadn't heard it, and when he was finished he hung up.

In another half-hour they were as far north as Sioux City, Iowa, about seventy-five miles west of it, and they came to a town where they agreed to stop. Even as they approached the far reaches of the town they could tell that it was one of those places whose economy had depended in large part on the road passing through it being well traveled. The coming of the big highway, a good four miles from it, with no exit roads or signs, had taken the traffic away, and now the town lay waste. It had to get what it could from truck traffic and occasional sightseers. Weeds grew in the small town square; many of the buildings in the short central block of Main Street were boarded up. Few people were on the sidewalks. They went through the town, and about a block after the stores quit and the seedy motels began, across the street from a small, closed Dairy Queen, they found a place that seemed adequate. There was an office in front, a small unconnected building with a driveway on either side. The drives lead between the sides of the office and the two low, severe, rectangular blocks of rooms extending back from the road. Between the rectangles, the rooms facing into it, was an empty swimming pool with grass growing between the slate of its decking. He parked and went into the office to check them in. When he came out he had a slight smile on his face.

"What's up?" Bob White said when he got back into the car.

"A little surprise," he said, and he drove the car across the cracked blacktop to their adjoining rooms. He and Bob White unloaded their gear. Melinda checked the bathrooms, finding them clean enough, and tested the springs on the bed on their side. It was four-thirty by the time they were finished getting settled. They were sitting in the chairs in Bob White's room. They had eaten a late lunch, and they had decided that a drink and snack would be enough. They drank watery Scotch and ate cheese and crackers. All the time they had been unloading, Melinda and Bob White had been watching Allen, wondering about the surprise and playing the game of not asking about it.

"Are you two ready for a little action?" he asked them finally. They both nodded, enjoying his withholding.

"Okay, wait here, I'll be right back," he said, and he left the room and headed over to the office. Bob White got up and opened the drapes that covered the window, and they watched him enter the office. He came out a few moments later, carrying something.

"What's he got there?" Melinda asked.

"Looks like golf clubs," Bob White said, "looks like putters."

When he entered the room again, he was grinning broadly; he had the three putters in his left hand, and he raised a finger on his right, indicating that there should be no questions yet. He went to the gunny sack in the corner of the room, flipped its neck over, and pushed on the bag to get a few balls out of it; about ten rolled out into the room. He ran his hands over them, turning them, and selected three: a nearly new Golden Ram and two range balls, one with a red stripe around it, the other with a large black circle on its side. He put the three balls on the bed and turned to Melinda, holding the three putter heads in his hands, fanning the shafts out and presenting them to her for selection. By this time she was grinning too, and she chose one of the putters. Then he turned to Bob White and did the same thing with the remaining two clubs.

"Now we had better practice some before we go out to the links," he said, and he pushed a good number of balls out of the gunny sack onto the carpet and began to show them how to hold their putters and how to stroke. Melinda already knew how to hold a putter, and Bob White had seen enough golf in his time so that he too had no trouble with this. The three of them began to putt balls around the room, aiming for the legs of furniture, thudding balls against the wall and the door. Allen gave them various clipped phrases of instruction: head down, feet well planted, accelerate through the ball, hit on the sweet spot, don't push. The room was a small space for such activity; they had a lot of balls on the floor, and they hit balls into each other and bounced them off each other's feet at times.

"This is a crowded green," Bob White said, and the other two agreed, laughing, and they all said excuse me when they got in each other's way. After a while, he suggested that they quit, that they were ready now, and he pointed to the bed, suggesting that Melinda take her pick of balls. She selected the Ram, and Bob White took the ball with the red stripe around it.

After he had rounded up the golf balls on the rug and put them back in the gunny sack, he led them out the door and down to the end of the rectangle in which their rooms were located. At the end, where the cracked sidewalk ended, there was a dirt path leading around the back of the building, and he motioned for them to follow him down it. When they got to the back of the building, he stopped. Melinda and Bob White came up beside him, and they looked at what was before them.

The upper mandible of the whale stood as an archway of entrance into the grounds of the miniature golf course. At either side of the jaw's hinges, where they pressed into the ground, a low white picket fence went out and around the ragged oval of the course. The fence dipped half into ruin in various places where the course descended into the bottom of its cavity behind the whale's jaw, and weeds curled into the fence, making it an awkward crown of thorns. The jaw of the whale had the shape of a massive wishbone; it was at least eight feet high at its apex, and he wished the feel of the place did not remind him so much of Tombstone, the bag lying at the edge of the desert, the man coming up off the ground like a crab toward him, the gun in the torn sleeve. This place too was at the edge of things, the course a kind of exaggerated instance of the slow ruin of the town that had been passed by. Beyond the course were the wasted grainfields moving in from the hum of the highway, a good three miles away, and the fields seemed to be reclaiming the ground the course stood on. The weeds and obscure offshoots of the dead stalks of old corn had crept back into and over the course, and they were touching up against the back of the cinder blocks of the motel itself.

The jaw of the whale was pinioned with a large bolt where the wishbone joined at its top; the head of the galvanized bolt protruded on one side, the nut on the other. The entire surface of the jaw was marked with initials carved into its bone and the peeling remnants of fingernail polish and other paints that had been used by those who had no knives or chisels. Weathering had turned the carvings into signs and emblems, and away from words, and when they stepped into the tortured archway, Melinda thought of the mutilation of goosefish on the bay beaches of the Cape. When she was a child, she had seen other children stab and hack at the horny skin of the beached monsters in outrage at their ugliness, leaving them with pointed sticks standing like quills in their hides. The difference was in the bone quietness of the whale's jaw and the fact that it was in Kansas. It seemed ancient here and beyond any quality of pain. Its shape stood out of the carvings and the paint, its power within its stillness hardly diminished, and the three of them were a little nervous standing within it.

They stood for a long time, under the jaw, somehow in the whale's presence, not as a live whale but one so single-minded in its power that the marrow in the bone retained a force beyond its long-ago death, as if it had pushed up out of the earth of Kansas, its mysterious place of burial.

They moved out from under the jaw in time and approached the slab of rubber, scuffed and worn, that was the first tee, about eight feet the other side of the archway. As they looked up to study the hole, a straight par two in a keyhole shape, they could see the remnants of the sea theme of the course beyond it. Slightly to the left and down near the bottom of the cavity, about ten holes away, was the figure of a small dolphin, its body bent in an arch, under which they thought they would have to hit when they got there. Three pelicans, one with its head missing, stood on the green of another hole. There was a shark, a small sperm whale, a barracuda, and configurations they would not be able to make out until they got nearer to them. They flipped a coin, and Melinda won the honors. The keyhole was outlined with one-by-three pine, and there were no hazards to negotiate. The only hint of a sea theme were the few shells left glued to the boards surrounding the square green: quahog shells, some mussels, and a few oysters. Melinda putted on the warped surface. Her shot went past the cup, thudded against the board beyond it, and rolled back two feet, stopping only a foot from the hole. Allen and Bob White both missed their putts also, and the three of them managed to get down in two, even at the end of one.

As they moved from hole to hole, considering each putt carefully, they began to feel themselves descending. They had made a rule that each ball would be putted out, were engaged in a kind of medal play, and such was the decayed condition of the course that they would often find themselves flying off the green or the fairway of the hole they were playing, having to come in from the scarred ground of other fairways, chipping into their proper pathway from stones and sand. It was not unusual for holes to be won with sevens and eights, and as they descended and the competition moved them, they began to become exhausted. Behind them, up the narrow and winding crushed-stone path that ran through the course from hole to hole, they could see the cracked and mutilated figures of sea life: a giant lobster with a broken claw, a seahorse with a crushed muzzle, fish painfully twisted. Allen was just a little ahead. Melinda was on his tail, and Bob White was still within striking distance. They had finished the ninth hole, and they felt half submerged.

At the tenth, the dolphin hole, the course seemed to level off and bottom out. They were under the sea, various levels of sea life around and above them, behind and ahead. Their alliances fell apart and came together as their scores altered. At times Allen was engaged in a struggle with Melinda and she with him. At times Bob White surged, and one or the other of them felt threatened. The oval of the picket fence seemed to lean inward. Standing on the tenth tee, they felt pressed down in the middle of the purgatory of a sea garden, one that was the mirrored reversal of the health of the real sea, that romance of paradise. Even their putters felt like burdens, tools they had to carry as a kind of penance. They felt too comfortable now with their grips, and this was an embarrassment, as if a hint of some indulgence in sin, so that they often hid the putters along their legs or hung them down from clasped hands, like European walkers, behind their backs.

They were catalyzed, and they rose a little when they saw the situation of the tenth hole. The tenth, the dolphin hole, was a par four, with a right-angle dog leg near its end. The dolphin, about four feet long and bent into a graceful arc, crossed over the narrow two-foot fairway of worn green carpeting. Where from a distance they had thought they could go under the body of the dolphin, there was no opening at all but a sculptured and chipped blue wave on which the dolphin was riding, having leapt up on it, its head slightly on the decline, as if it would soon plunge, come up, and catch another. The end of its nose was

gone, and the paint that might have marked its pupil had worn
away. Its mouth had a smile in it, but it could see nothing, and
this turned it away from any hint of motivation or pleasure, and
its dive seemed totally insouciant. It would go down into the
wave, and the structure and attitude of its body would cause it to
curl and come up again. Then it would enter another wave, and
another. It was locked in its motion and could not turn out of
the waves. Cute as it might have once been, it was no dolphin
from an aquarium show. The human and weather damage done
to it, and the neglect had given it a history of seriousness they
each felt as being not much different from their own.

The dolphin guarded the way to the getting down, the finality
and the repose of the satisfied click of the ball as it fell into the
cup and settled. It seemed impossible that the concentration of the
dolphin could be passed. Beyond the dolphin was the square of
green on the upper level with two holes in it, and these were the
entrances to tunnels that ran under the upper green and would
drop balls that rolled through them onto the lower, final green
surface to the left. One tunnel exit was at the side of the lower
green, about five feet from the cup and around a corner. From
that point a bank shot off the rotted boards might well be re-
quired. The other tunnel came out directly in front of the cup,
about two feet away from it, and the best shot coming out of
that tunnel might fall in. But the greens were in the future, the
cup at the very bottom of the groin of the sea, and first they
must negotiate the upper waves and the dolphin riding on them.

At the end of the narrow incline of the fairway, at the base of
the ascending curl of wave, there had once been a slide, a half-
tube of corrugated metal pipe that had arched up through the
wave and into a groove fashioned gently in the dolphin's side.
The lower bit of pipe was still there, but a good eight inches
were missing between that bit and the groove, and time and the
set of the wave had shifted the dolphin's body some, and it bent
inward slightly toward the rubber of the tee. Bob White thought
he would try that path. He had the honors because he had won
the ninth, and he placed the ball with the red ring around it on a
flat place on the rubber of the tee. He addressed a place slightly
behind the ball, took a practice swing, then set his feet again,

addressed and stroked firmly through the ball, keeping his head down, accelerating through the putt. The ball clicked sharply off the blade of the putter, rolled true to the broken tube, and was kicked into the groove in the dolphin's side. But the dolphin had bent over enough so that the ball, instead of sliding over the dolphin's body and dropping onto the upper green, spun up into the air, arched back a bit and fell and clattered into the crushed stone to the side of the fairway. Bob White's putter was still elevated, pointing toward the dolphin, the shaft following the putt, but when the ball spun off and landed, he lowered the club and shook his head.

"Difficult to negotiate," he said, and he stepped back to let Melinda have her shot at it. She had been standing back and watching the dolphin intently, and when it was her turn, instead of settling in and putting, she walked around behind the upper green, bent over slightly, and squinted at the body of the dolphin from the other side.

"There's something here," she said, and she beckoned to the two of them to join her to see what it was. They walked around and came up beside her.

"There," she said, and they both looked where she pointed and saw that there was a small hole in the left of the snout of the dolphin, about two inches below its vacant eye.

"We'd better check the other side," Allen said, and they went around to the fairway, moved up close to the foot of the wave, and studied the dolphin's body. He ran his hand from the curve of the tail up the dolphin's side, and about halfway up he discovered there was indeed a hole there too, and that it had been stuffed with a bit of cloth which had been packed carefully into it, so that it was not apparent from a distance. He pulled the cloth out, revealing the hole, and he pointed to a place below it where there was a remnant of a second piece of corrugated piping. The hole was a good eight inches up from the top of the wave, and that put it about two feet from the surface of the fairway. They could now see that this had once been the desired way of playing the hole, that the proper shot had gone through the dolphin and not around or over it.

Melinda touched her face and thought for a few moments.

Then she decided on a way to play her shot. She lined up behind the rubber tee, but she aimed to send her ball through a break in the rotted boards at the side of the fairway. This would take it, if she hit it well, out and alongside the upper green a little past the dolphin. There were broken boards around the upper green also, and a steep incline to the little hill the upper green was on. She figured that she might be able to roll her second shot up the embankment and onto the flat surface. Her first shot was a good one; the ball went between the broken boards, clicked among the gravel, and quit beside the embankment, a good approach-shot placement.

Now it was Allen's turn. He took a handful of gravel from the path beside the fairway and ran a finger through it in his open palm until he found a proper piece. He put this piece on the rubber of the tee and placed his ball on it, so that the ball was a little elevated off the rubber. It would be an extremely difficult shot, and he would have to hit it hard enough to take most of gravity's pull out of it. He figured he'd miss the hole at least once before getting the range. He stepped up over the ball, adjusted his line, glanced up at the body of the dolphin over and over again as he shifted his feet. When he thought he had the line just right, he settled in and placed the head of his putter on the rubber. He glanced up a few more times, and then he held his head steady, looking down over the ball. His hands shifted slightly, moving a couple of inches in front of the ball on the stone. Then the club head moved back to the top of his quarter swing, and then it accelerated down, and the ball shot off the stone and struck against the dolphin's body a few inches to the side and below the hole. His second shot failed also, but it was closer, and when he sent his third, the ball hit the hole, clattered and vibrated in its entrance and fell in out of sight. He walked quickly to the other side of the dolphin to see where the ball would come out and how it would fall, but nothing happened. He waited a moment. Still nothing. The other two came around beside him and waited also.

Because of the intensity of their study of the dolphin and the attendant difficulties of the hole, they had lost track of time, and only when the three of them stood together waiting did they discover that dusk was advancing and the course beginning to darken. The far side of the dolphin's body now had shadows within it; its skin was darker, and it seemed more seaworthy. The shadows masked the peel of paint, and the eye above the hole no longer seemed vacant to them. Over the body of the dolphin they could see the rise of the figures they had worked their way through as they had played the first half of the course. The failure of the sun and the coming of shadow enlivened them also; the shark seemed fresh from the sea, and the penguins looked like a trio of small children in formal wear watching them at play. At the very top of the expanse behind them stood the whale's jawbone. It looked immaculate and unsullied, very skeletal and bone hard and very white. They could see the sky around it and through it. It stood like a firm, stylized rendering in the air, but it seemed to have incredible weight at the same time, to be permanent in its place, as if it had never had another. Clouds moved and shadows shifted around it; the first coming of points of stars were in its arc, the moon's sliver was above it and to its left. But its outline and its surface were untouched by any movement or magnitude. Though it was entrance to this place, it seemed pivotal, the still center of something, and they found they could not and did not want to pull their eyes away from it. They stopped for a long time, looking up at the jaw, and then Melinda touched him lightly on the bone of his elbow and whispered below and behind him into his shoulder.

" 'But miles to go before I sleep,' " she said. And Bob White grunted, and Allen moved his elbow from her touch, and the three disengaged themselves from the matrix of their placement, though very slowly, each stretching almost imperceptibly, waking themselves.

"The ball," Allen said. And he walked slowly around to the front of the dolphin and knelt down on the fairway, getting his head at a level with the hole and peering into it. It was darker now, and it was hard to see, but he thought the hole went straight into and through the dolphin's body. Still on his knees, he turned his head and reached back and motioned for Melinda's putter. He had left his leaning against the embankment on the other side, and he took hers; holding the club head in his hand, he slowly insinuated the shaft into the hole in the dophin's side. It's like a strange injection, he thought, and he took his time, and he was careful not to hit the shaft against the sides of the hole as he entered the dolphin's body, and his left hand felt a brief need to elevate above the dolphin, to hold the bottle up. When the shaft was almost a foot in, he struck something. It was hard; it was surely the ball, but it gave way a little when he hit it and then pushed back a little and caused the head of the putter to shake a little in his hand. He pushed again, a little harder this time, and he heard a slight whisper of sound, a kind of scraping, from deep in the hole; there was a strong spasm along the putter shaft, and the head pressed back into his palm. Bob White was still on the other side of the dolphin, and he spoke softly.

"Come here," he said. And Melinda put her hand on Allen's shoulder and squeezed, and he got up from his knees, leaving the putter imbedded in the wound, and they both walked slowly around the dolphin to the back of the upper green. As they got close to where Bob White was standing, he raised his arm, indicating that they should move even slower, and they did that, watching Bob White and not the dolphin. When they got beside him, they turned and looked to where he was looking.

Below the place containing the recessed ring of the dolphin's eye, in shadow and behind its fixed smile, the snake's head and its encumbrance had unfurled and stood transfixed in the air a good three inches from the surface of the dolphin's body. The encumbrance was a small bird. A nestling, it was too young for coloring and its fear petrified it. The snake's black head was very large, and with its mouth open and the bird locked in its jaw, it was hard to see how it had managed to come from the hole, but it had done so, possibly releasing its grip a little on the bird's body after exit. The snake's head was very black, its wide-open eyes were very small and bright red. The body of the bird was sideways in the snake's mouth; its outer wing was open and hanging down and over the snake's lip. The wing opened and closed slowly and repetitively, like a feathered fan or a sail touched in the rhythm of a wave-action breeze. The bird was like a carried banner, or a war bundle, or a burden of shame. The head of the snake moved slowly from side to side, scanning, and the three watchers felt guilt and immediate failed responsibility, and they surged forward imperceptibly and recoiled from the vision at the same time.

He thought about the ball in the hole behind the body of the snake. He wondered if it would have enough roll left in it if the snake left the hole. Would it be able to bounce out and possibly reach the first tunnel opening in the upper green? He already lay three, having missed two attempts to get his ball into the dolphin's body. With the right bounce and a good roll he could reach the passage to the lower green and have a putt for par. Was the snake a movable obstruction? Was it a natural hazard? What could the P.G.A. rules be in a case like this? He focused on the delicate body of the bird and came back and away from his quick retreat. The automatic crazy movement of his thought-train startled him and quickly made him sad. He saw the wing and the closed eyes and the bird's head in repose, and over the bird's back, the top of the snake's snout and its small red-blazing eyes. He reached beside him and took Melinda's hand; it was cool and dry, and it did not respond. He looked at her face and saw that her head was fixed, her mouth slightly open. As he watched her, he saw her head turning very slowly from side to side, in mimic of the snake's own movement.

Inside her head there was really very little control going on. There was a foregrounding of brief visions and flickers: snatches from dreams and potentially harmful past realities. What was locked in to its own control was her chemistry, her methodically dying body. Her breath exchange was shallow, expelled and sucked in through her open mouth, through parted lips, held by her fixed jaw. She felt her nostrils closed and a little parched. She held the life of the bird in her own mouth. If she opened her mouth and released it, they could step forward and kill the snake. The life they valued would have escaped from harm, and the other they would find dispensable. But if she pressed down too hard, she would crush the life from the bird, and then they would kill her in rage, though she would be already dead, because surely it was the life of the bird that was her own. She thought of the way she took his penis into her mouth to give him and herself pleasure. The same structure of vulnerability was involved here. She felt she was looking into the face of death, and though it was a composite face—the snake's head and the bird's body forming, in the increasing darkness, a silhouette emblem—it was not a face at all, but a structure, a fitted machine, mechanized by two past lives conjoined. And so it was a face, like her cells in their matrix were: the face of death then, a place, simply, of meeting.

They stood like the three penguins on the slope behind their play. She was like the decapitated one, her head, like that of the snake still mostly in the hole, separated in its intensity from her body. Bob White was the one standing a little to the side of the other two, looking slightly away, part of the group in his shape and black-and-white outfit but separated in name and ability. He saw the snake's head and the bird, saw it could be a totemic emblem, but he had seen such things before; and though the vision had power to stiffen him, he could work within its familiarity, and he was calculating. The way the bird was turned it would be difficult for the snake to get it back in the hole if he chose to do so. Snakes ate young birds in a way that was a kind of birth reversal. In birth, the child's head emerged then turned to allow the shoulders' exit vertically through the stretched opening. When a snake took a young bird from the nest, he grasped him in a way that allowed a good purchase, gripping the bird sideways at right angles to the jaw. This was a king snake, a constrictor, and he could not chew the bird but would have to swallow and digest it alive. To swallow it, the snake would have to turn it, getting it parallel to his mouth, take it in headfirst, the reverse of birth.

Bob White could see some matting of feathers on the top of the bird's head. He knew that this must be the snake's secretions. The snake had begun to swallow the bird when they had disturbed him with the ball. Surely he had stopped swallowing when the ball hit. He had waited, and when the shaft of the putter had pushed the ball, he had come out of the hole with the bird so that he could get the bird out of his throat and turn it. If the snake were caught with the bird in his throat, he would be defenseless. With the bird out and crossways again, he could drop it if he had to. He could use his mouth and the power of his body then; he would stand some chance. Bob White knew the snake did not really feel like dropping the bird. Probably he did not really feel at all in the way that we think of such things, but he could taste the bird and did not feel like losing that taste and the beginnings of fullness he had experienced when he had the bird's head in his throat. His head stood now out of the hole to the side of the face of the dolphin. He held the bird very gently but firmly in his mouth, and he moved his head slowly from side to side, scanning. Bob White thought he understood him.

He motioned to them with an open hand that they should stay where they were, and because he knew the snake could not pull his head back and withdraw into the dark safety of the hole as long as he held the bird in his mouth this way, he did not hesitate or try to dissemble or trick the snake. He walked slowly around the embankment of the upper green, withdrawing his knife from the sheath inside his shirt as he moved. When he got to the fairway and the other side of the dolphin, he crouched slightly and crept to the face of the wave. The dolphin was hip-high, and he could see the head of the snake over the dolphin's head. The head of the snake had followed his movement until he was out of its peripheral vision. Then it had returned to the other two, stopping its scanning. Bob White took the blade of his knife and rested it behind the head of the dolphin. Then he slid it over the dolphin's head and moved it swiftly under the neck of the snake, just back of its jaw. When the snake felt the steel, it tried to withdraw, but Bob White lifted the knife blade, pinning the head of the snake to the top of the hole.

They could see the glint of the knife blade below the body of the bird, parallel with it. It seemed that the snake's red eyes blazed out as they contracted. Bob White's head was above the head of the snake and the head of the dolphin. It was too dark for them to see his eyes, but they thought that he was looking at them. The knife blade seemed to stay where it was for a long time; then, suddenly, it was above the head of the snake. Then the snake's head with the bird in it fell from the hole, skimming down the dolphin's body, and tumbled onto the green, to the left and away from the wave. There was a furious shaking inside the body of the dolphin, and when they looked up from the vision of the severed head with the bird still in its mouth, they saw the body of the snake coming out of the wound. It was very long, and it spilled over the side of the dolphin, staining it, and fell like a coiled placenta, and came to rest in an almost perfect ring, still vibrating, on the surface of the upper green.

There was a moment in which they could see the placenta and the tableau of the head with the bird in it, and all was very fixed in place and silent. Then the ball came. It appeared, white and swollen, in the mouth of the hole. It seemed to linger there enough to turn, so that its black spot appeared, an intense large pupil that changed the mouth into an eye in the dolphin's side. And then it fell out, bouncing once on the dolphin's body and once on the green. When it quit bouncing it rolled four inches, and then it disappeared again, this time into the tunnel. They heard it rattle in the tube as it descended. Allen moved to the lower green to watch it come out. When it came it had good speed, and it skipped past the final hole and rolled to the board lining the green. It hit the board and started back, crossing the warped green surface. As it was losing its energy it reached the hole, rimmed it, hesitated on the back of the hole's edge, and then it fell in. From where Bob White stood on the other side of the dolphin, he could not see the ball enter the cup. But he could hear the click.

"Birdie," he said, very dryly and very softly. The two looked up and over at him. He had not smiled when he spoke. Then Melinda started to laugh a little. Then all three of them were laughing softly and tentatively in the increasing darkness.

Bob White came around from the body of the dolphin and climbed the embankment to the upper green. The coil of placenta was now still, and the black-leather sheen on the scales shone in the little moonlight and the dim artificial light that came from the backs of the rooms over and across the sea course. The strange cross formed by the head of the snake and the bird was also still, the snake's eyes still open, but glazing and without any intensity of rage left. The shocked bird seemed dead. It was very quiet, its outer wing gathered back to its body. It was unmarked, but it was still held fast. Bob White knelt down beside the strange small figure. It looked like a lost charm from a crazy bracelet. He put his thumb and index finger over the eyes in the snake's head, holding it fast to the green. Then he insinuated the tip of his knife blade under the body of the bird, between its small downy belly and the snake's lower jaw. When he felt the hardness of the lower jawbone and the leathery bottom of the mouth, he pressed the blade into the leather and through the scales until he had pierced the jaw, pinning it to the green.

Holding it there, he moved his thumb and finger to the front of the head's snout and slowly opened the mouth. With his ring finger, he gently urged the bird's body out, till it lay in front of the head. Then he released the open jaw, letting it shut. He picked up the bird then and cradled it in his palm and got up from his knees and slowly turned, looking for a place to put it. He knew there would be no snakes coming now for a while, and he wanted a place where, in the morning, sun would shine on the bird when it came up, a place where the bird would be touched or surrounded on all sides, but a place that from the top would be open to the sky. He stopped turning when he faced the dolphin, and then he climbed down the embankment, holding the bird in his hand. When he got down, he reached and tore a handful of weed from where it grew in the gravel of the sea-course path, and he took the weed and the bird around to the fairway side of the dolphin. When he reached the dolphin's side, he took a bit of the weed and scrubbed at the stains on the far side of the dolphin's body with it, mixing grass stains with the snake's fluids, changing the smell. Then he threw the bit of weed down on the coiled placenta. He took what remained of the weed and gathered it in the clean, faded blue-check handkerchief he took from his back pocket. Then he rubbed the handkerchief and the weed slowly along the ball groove that ran in the side of the dolphin, pressing hard, staining the handkerchief and the groove.

When he was finished, he gathered the weed and the handkerchief into a crinkled low pocket, fitting it near the top of the dolphin's side where the groove was almost horizontal to the ground. Then he placed the small body of the bird into the pocket, tucking it in and spreading the sides of the pocket slightly away from the feathers and head. When he was satisfied, he stood up from his crouch and looked down at the bird. Then he reached down and made a final adjustment, putting the pocket a little bit farther away from the bird's tail.

They had been watching him intently from where they were.

Melinda was still behind the embankment of the upper green. Allen was standing where his ball had fallen in. And now they watched him coming away from the fairway and the dolphin's body and climbing back up the embankment. He could have stepped easily over the dolphin to get to where he was, but it was clear that that would have somehow been inappropriate, and they stood where they were and waited for him. When he got to the upper green and the placenta and the severed head, he reached down and picked the head up and took it with him down the embankment again to where his ball and Melinda's lay among the gravel of the walk, both distinct in the limited light. He took the head of the snake and wedged it down among the stones, so that it stood up with its closed jaws pointing toward the sky, a gesture not unlike that of the whale's jaw, and though diminutive, its recent history might have held a similar complexity. Then he took his knife and opened the mouth of the snake, and holding it with the blade twisted, he picked up a good-size piece of gravel and used it to wedge the jaw so that the snake's mouth stood up wide open when he removed the knife.

"Wait," Melinda said softly from the other side of the embankment. "Let me." And she came around to where he was and reached down beside him and picked her ball from among the stones. When she came up with it in her fingers, her hand held up a little in front of her so that the ball shone in the half darkness, she could see Allen, the upper half of his body only, mouth open and looking at them across the embankment and the upper green. She moved over and down to the snake's head and placed her ball where the bird had been. Bob White stood back and to the side.

She was at the side of the snake's head and the ball now, intent on the coming break of the perceptible structure that had grown up around them. She wanted to finish it. It was not real life. She felt she was now a living monitor of such things. As she addressed the snake's head with the blade of the putter, she stopped breathing, holding a brief modicum of air in the fragile domes of her alveoli. The blade was square to the head of the snake. The ball stood in the open jaws. The configuration was now like the handle of a garish cane. She brought the shaft of the club back, keeping her left arm and wrist stiff, and with no other move in her body, she stroked down and into the side of the snake's jaw, below where the ball was. There was a dull thud, followed by a slight click as the blade struck the jaw and the ball afterward. Both the ball and the head lifted up from the stones, the head spinning and falling and the ball continuing. The head landed and bounced on the embankment, and the ball bounced on the upper green, and then it bounced again, clearing the rotten board lining the far side and falling and landing on the lower green, coming to rest four feet from the cup.

"That's a good shot," Allen said, finishing the game of the structure and beginning to end it at the same time.

"I'll pick up," Bob White said, and he reached down and lifted his ball out of the stones. She made her putt. Bob White took an X on the hole. It had gotten too dark for them to continue further, and with no real discussion they agreed to quit. Bob White checked the bird a last time, adjusting the handkerchief pocket where it rested. Then he took the body of the snake, like a coiled hose, in one hand and its head in the other and walked across the sea course to where the weeds and the corn pressed in as the desiccated fields began. When he got there, he stopped. He set his feet. Then, turning like a discus thrower, he spun and released the coiled snake's body into the air. It unwound as it lifted, straightening for a moment like a spear. Then, as it descended, it telescoped in on itself, becoming increasingly smaller and inconsequential as it disappeared. He threw the head out in the same direction he had thrown the body.

When he finished, he came back to them, and they started together back up and out of the dark, broken sea, past the pelicans and the shark and the other fish figures, until they passed under the whale's jaw. They stopped there, turned, and looked back under the massive archway. It was quite dark now, and though they could see the form of the dolphin behind them, they could not see the place where the bird rested upon it at all.

When they got back to their rooms, Melinda said she was very tired and thought it would be a good thing if she slept alone that night. Allen said he thought they could arrange that, and maybe she should take Bob White's room and bed, and he and Bob

White could sleep together in their room. They did that, and though the walls were thin, Melinda wept very quietly in Bob White's bed, and Allen did not hear her. And though Allen was very tired, Bob White lay so still beside him that he kept feeling and listening for movement and breath, so it was a long time before he was able to fall asleep.

Early in the morning, at the beginning of first light and while they were still sleeping, Melinda got up and went back out to the whale's jaw and the sea course. She was in her bathrobe and slippers, she was too intent to notice the way the day changed the look of things, and she stepped carefully down between the sea figures, retracing the way to the dolphin. When she got to the dolphin's side, she saw that the small pocket was empty, the bird was gone. She went back to the room, and when the three were sitting together having coffee in Bob White's room later, she mentioned to them that she had gone out and that the bird was no longer there.

"What do you think?" she asked Bob White.

He looked at her, hesitating a moment before answering, thinking that he could lie to her. But then he thought that the lie would be feeble, and also that to lie to her would be the wrong thing to do. And he said:

"I do not think that bird has come to a good end."

Part Two

DAY

There were two pictures hanging in the clubhouse, side by side, on the wall behind the glass case. The one on the left, put up with tape and brown and peeling at the edges, was a mock blueprint rendering of an eighteen-hole course, and scribed in between the lines denoting the location and shape of the new clubhouse were the words *Seaview Links Proposal* and below that *Baron Associates/1955*. The other was an old and faded photograph, about a foot square, in a glass frame. It was a picture of the seventh green, taken from the fairway close in front of it, with the lighthouse in full view in the background. Four men, all of them in baggy knickers and jaunty tams, stood on the green. One was tending the flagstick, while a second addressed a putt of about fifteen feet. The other two stood to the side, both with hands on hips, each with one foot planted a little ahead of the other. Off the green to the right stood a fifth figure, more faded than the others. It was hard to tell what he was wearing, not golf togs surely, but his posture was very erect and formal, and he seemed not to be in any way involved in the proceedings. He was looking away from the green in the direction of the camera. On the surface of the glass, in felt-tip marker, various hands had drawn little arrows pointing to the figures, and there were names and statements beside the arrows: *Fred Borker considers a putt, The Chair watches critically, John Hope holds stick.* Around the head of the figure standing off the green, a small feathered headdress had been carefully inked in, and beside the arrow pointing to the figure were the words, *Chief Wingfoot's Revenge!* and then, in very small parentheses, *Chip.* A white card had been tacked below the photograph, and typed on it were the words *Seaview Links, One of the oldest courses in America. Continuous play since 1892. Above photograph, 1920.*

Sammy winked at the photograph and the blueprint, as he did most mornings when he came in to open up. Barefoot, in old jeans and a worn madras shirt, he moved behind the glass counter to the old cash register, pushed the "No Sale" button, and gave

127

the handle a crank. The bell rang and the door slid open. He saw that there was plenty of change, enough for the traffic of the first major tournament of the summer. He closed the door and went around the counter to the stove in the kitchen area. The clubhouse was small and L-shaped. Where the two rectangles joined, and across from the door, was the glass case, about four feet long, containing balls, tees, and gloves. To the left of the case, at the end of the building, was the kitchen: a large refrigerator, formica counter and stove, a sink, and a card table. Behind the glass counter, filling the shorter rectangle, was Sammy's golf gear concession: a few windbreakers, a couple of sets of clubs, various hats and other golf equipment. Windows in the back wall of the concession overlooked the short ninth fairway and beyond that the longer, par-four eighth. Sammy fiddled with the percolator, got it loaded and on the fire, and then went to the concession room to get his hat, a large crumpled fedora he liked to wear because it kept his long hair from getting in his eyes and because it kept the sun out, but most of all because he liked the way he looked in it. He put it on and scratched the wispy hairs of his untrimmed beard.

"Right on time," he said aloud. He could see across the eighth fairway, about a hundred yards from the clubhouse, big Chief Wingfoot walking stiffly toward him. The Chief moved very methodically, and such was the monotony of his gait that he was almost upon the terns pecking in the fairway before they were aware of him and rose up in little flashes of white (it seemed from this distance), right in the Chief's face. Sammy saw the Chief stop, pick something up and study it for a moment, and then get back into his gait. He was walking the trail of the underground river, Tashmuit, that cut across and under the fairway, turning near the clubhouse and heading for the sea. The grass was greener where the river ran, and when it swelled up in winter, it was visible as a slight ridge. Even in summer, its strength was notable. The ground was softer above it, and the attentive could feel it pulsing under foot. He called it People's River when he had occasion to speak of it, keeping its ancestral name to himself. It was where the people had come for their water. They could walk to it when they had need. It was out of the way for him, but he used its path when he entered the golf course at most times. It gave him strength in its place as evidence and a time for thought to renew his purpose. When it turned seaward he quit its path and headed toward the clubhouse.

Though it was early July, the morning air was crisp and cool; there was plenty of dew on the spare grass of the eighth and ninth, and the white brick of the lighthouse shone like a new dime in the morning sun. Sammy poured the hot coffee into two stoneware mugs marked *Seaview Air Force Station*, with a little emblem on each, and went out to where the Chief was sitting on the transplanted park bench overlooking the ninth green.

"Good morning, Chief. Coffee," Sammy said, and handed him one of the mugs.

"Hey," the Chief grunted. "Feather," and he handed Sammy the clean white tern feather he had picked up.

"That's a fine feather," Sammy said, holding it up in the sun. He took his fedora off and plugged the root of the feather into the band so that it stood up straight along the crown.

"What a fine day!" Sammy said. And he and the Chief sat on the bench together, sipping at their coffee and looking out across the fairways and into the rough grass beyond.

The road that ran in front of the clubhouse separated the seventh fairway and the rest of the course behind it from the eighth and ninth. It ended in a cul-de-sac parking lot right in front of the lighthouse. The lighthouse perched on the edge of the high dunes, a hundred feet or so above the narrow beach, with the Atlantic Ocean beyond it. Earl Sawgus chugged his pickup truck along the road, saw as he usually did the backs of Sammy and the Chief on the park bench, went the hundred yards to the parking lot, turned in a slow circle, enjoying the condition of the seventh green and the eighth tee, came around and back down the road, and parked along the side of the clubhouse.

"Now where the hell is that Chip?" he said to himself as he got out of the truck.

"Yo, Sam. Yo, Chief. Morning," he called as he walked toward them. "Now where the hell is that Chip, you think?"

"Chip here," the Chief said.

"Oh yeah? Where?" said Earl.

"I'm here, ma man, I'm here!" came a voice from over by Earl's truck. "Here I come." And a young man of about eighteen, very scrawny and tan with close-cropped dark hair, started a slow and crooked walk toward the threesome at the park bench.

"That was somethin', I mean, that was *some* action Earl! I mean, that was definitely *not* on my agenda. I wonder can you dig it? Came right up to my leg then; stopped *on* a dime. Too *much!* 'Student crushed by pickup at Seaview Links.' What a routine *that* was . . ."

"Fucked up," Sammy murmured.

"Made the turn—the avenging angel—spacy day—whose thoughts were elsewhere—young boy asnooze watching the eye-lid light show—mysterious tires crunching in gravel—stopped *on* a dime. What a scenario! —Hey, Chiefie! what's happening? Hey Sam! What's up for today, Earl? Do we plant trees? Do a little, you know, green care?" He danced a little jig. "I can *dig* it!— reprieve from death!"

"Most definitely fucked up again," Sammy said. And Earl, with Chip loping behind him, walked toward the parked machines on the far side of the clubhouse. Earl was the greens keeper at Sea-view. Chip, a horticulture student at Cape Tech, was his helper. Sammy was the club manager and pro. Chief Wingfoot believed he owned the golf course.

By the time it was seven o'clock, Chair Fredricks had showered and shaved, carefully cleaned, cut, and filed his fingernails, shined his golf shoes, laid his golf clothes across his bed, broken open a three-pack of Top Flights and put them in the zipper compart-ment of his plaid bag, put up the coffee to perk on the Sears workbench in the basement, and was now standing in front of a hot cup of it, looking out at the wheel cover of his new Oldsmo-bile, framed in the basement window. The cup and saucer were bone china, with blue flowers on them; the coffee was black and hot; the wheel cover was clean and shining, because he kept it that way. It was a beautiful morning in town, and in the yard of his accounting office in the front of the house, a couple of mock-ingbirds were showing off. The Chair was dressed in a short blue robe. His woods rested beside the coffee cup on the workbench, and as he lifted the driver up and began to clean the head's grooves with a small silver pick, he was thinking about the difficulties with the Quahog People and what he hoped the day would bring to him. When he finished picking the flecks of dirt out of the grooves, he put the shaft of the driver in the small vise attached to the bench, sprayed a little polish on the head, and began buffing it with a clean white rag.

As chairman of the golf commission at Seaview, all communication with the Quahog People fell to him. It was not the kind of thing he had bargained for when he had politicked for the position five years ago. What he had wanted was to keep the operations of the course professional, and he had thought of his only major adversary there as Sammy. Now these Indians were writing him letters and calling him up. They usually called him when he was at work on somebody's books or with a client. He kept telling them that he, as chairman, had nothing to do with their claim of ownership; the course was run by the National Seashore, only leased to the town, and they would have to deal with the Seashore Commission. But every time one of them called or wrote, it was a different one. They seemed to have no leader, and he kept having to repeat himself. And then there was this Frank Bumpus person; for two years now he had hung around the course. He was not good for the professionalism of the place, and being an Indian, though he never mentioned or did a thing about it, he must have been connected with the Quahog People. The rest of the golf commission members were all too happy to let this business fall to the Chair, and since the Chair would not have trusted anyone else with it anyway, the hassle was all his.

He finished buffing his driver and reached for another club. He could hear his wife stirring upstairs. He put the club shaft in the vise, took another sip of coffee, and began to pick. Well, to hell with the Quahog People, the Chair thought. This is a more important day. It was the day of the first major Saturday tournament of the season. All the others had been tune-ups and haphazardly run by Sammy. The Chair favored these early, official tournaments, the ones that were for members only. The members rule kept most of the tourists out, and most of the players were locals. The Chair knew their ways and could keep things in line.

More important, he was set this year to get Sammy, and he was going to start things off right this season by beating him. He kept buffing at the club heads until the luster came up the way he liked it.

By ten o'clock in the morning, Chip was well into the swing of things. At nine, in the bathroom in the clubhouse, he had snorted a line of coke, using a clear plastic ball-point pen with the ink-holder removed. That, on top of the joint he had smoked around seven-thirty, had done the job. Now he was rambling down the second fairway on the mower, aiming for the second green in the far corner of the golf course.

"Out of sight of them all, ha ha!" he said to himself in the mower's hum. He stopped short of the green and turned the mower off. He could hear the dull grind of Earl on the fairway mower on the other side of the course. He got off his machine, took a look up the fairway behind him, then turned his attention to the task at hand.

The second hole at Seaview was a par-five, five-hundred-and-ten-yard hole, with a dog leg to the left. The tee was cut at the top of a hill, with a heavy rough in front of it running down about seventy-five yards to the beginning of the fairway. The fairway before the dog leg was wide open. There was a large trap to the left, on a knoll from which the ground ran down to an open area just at the dog-leg knee. The open space was where the average hitter aimed to drop his drive. From that point, the fairway turned and narrowed a little, with heavy rough running up a hill to the left and pine trees running up a steeper hill on the right. At the end was the untrapped green, of average size, closely guarded in the back by low pine and scrub running up yet another, gradual hill and toward the cliff, high at the sea's edge, about a hundred yards away.

From the tee one could see the edge of the green in the distance. A strong shot could leave the hitter under a hundred and eighty yards to the green. It was possible to get home in two. From the tee, looking up to the top of the hill that bordered the narrower part of the fairway to the right, were three massive radar domes. They looked very much like golf balls and were the property of the Seaview Air Force Station, a lookout command on the edge of the Atlantic down the coast from the lighthouse. Below the radar domes, about halfway up the hill, was a small, medieval-looking stone tower. It was called the Jenny Lind tower and had been given the name by the man who bought it when the old Fitchburg Depot in Boston had been demolished around the turn of the century. The story was that he had heard Jenny Lind sing from the tower, had fallen in love with her, and had put the tower up on land he owned at the time as a tribute to his impossible dream.

The second was Chip's favorite hole, and when he had made his "Special Seaview Map" it had gotten the most detail and attention. He liked riding the narrow fairway on his mower, the way the slopes on either side guarded it. In late July, he liked to climb up the hill and sit close to the tower, eating blueberries he had picked on the slope out of his hat, watching the golfers try for the green. The fairways at Seaview, all but the eighth, were hardpan and sand, with little grass, and he liked to watch the golfers duff their shots, yell down the cavern of the fairway, throw their clubs, and stomp their feet. They never knew he was there watching them. More than any of this, he liked the apron, the collar, and the green. He had worked hard, removing small stones and large ones, filling and leveling with fresh soil, planting what he could get to grow, cutting things to just the right length.

Though he was buzzing a little from the drugs he had taken, he was in no way distracted, and seeing his work and its results brought things into an even clearer focus. He got down on his belly and sighted across to where the apron met the green, a blade of grass tickling his nose. "One little place," he said aloud as he studied the slopes and contours leading into the manicured surface of shorter grass that was the collar and then onto the green itself. He reached into his pocket and took out a new golf ball, a Club Special, and placed it just in front of his nose, sighting along it to a small pine in the rough beyond the green. The spot in question lay on that line, and he marked it before he rose. He went to the mower and took a small trowel out of a canvas bag that hung from the seat. He returned to the golf ball, where it stood up, white and shining, and sighted down the line again. Then he crawled on his stomach along the line and to the questionable spot. When he got there he saw that some miscreant weeds had stuck their arrogant spiked heads up through the body of his work, and he shook a finger at them as he rose up to his knees. "This is it for you, little nasty fuckers," he said, and began scratching and digging, moving bits of grass, weed, and dirt with his special little trowel.

Frank Bumpus knew the tournament would begin at twelve-thirty, and he wanted to be back at the clubhouse for it. That is, he wanted to be sure to be there when the men began to gather, wanted Chair Fredricks, especially, to see him. He had worked hard to appear as an annoyance that was both harmless and very visible, and he knew that today would be a good one in which to push the plan. When the time came, such P.R. considerations would be important. Public opinion and visibility, the way the press would pick him up as a somewhat colorful fellow, would give a kind of power of its own. He figured he could get some work done before the tournament, so when he finished his coffee he left his mug on the edge of the park bench next to Sammy, said good day, and set out across the eighth fairway toward his home.

He lived in a beach shack tucked in the dunes near the cliff above the ocean. The shack had no water or electricity, and often the sand would drift against it as high as its windows and cover its porch, and he would have to shovel it out. Still, he had plenty of wood and a good stove, his people would carry water in for him from a jeep they parked on the beach, and though he was in his mid-seventies, he was very tough and in good health. He had lived in the shack for twelve years, ever since he had come back to the Cape (where he had been raised to manhood) as an organizer for his brother Pamets, and he attributed his good health in part to the Spartan existence he felt the shack afforded him. And there were other things he liked about the spot as well. The outer beach that he could see from his small porch was the one that Henry David Thoreau had walked and written about. He had read the book, and he thought that Henry David Thoreau had a good, if tight, sensibility and a way of seeing which was valuable. A mile or so out to sea was the place of numerous shipwrecks over the centuries. He had read about them, and he had a map on his wall showing the shapes of the ships, their place of sinking, and their names, countries, and dates. It warmed him to know that his ancestors had found good use for materials washed up from these shipwrecks.

It was hard to find a book that had much to do with his people out here. Massasoit's Profile Rock was little more than a tourist attraction, and when the great King Philip appeared in a text, he was only presented in the extremity of his heroic final acts. But Bumpus felt the presence of the ancestors in the white man's history books. He was only a mile or so from Corn Hill and equal distance from the waters by which the white man had first camped when he came here. He felt his people's bones under the ground. His favorite thing to read was the beginning chapters of *History of Plimouth Plantation*. This place was mentioned in the first few pages of that text. He liked the clarity of William Bradford's prose, though he had been a limited and too earnest man. In his own slow and quiet battle, Bumpus liked to think that his rather awkward adversaries could at least be traced back to William Bradford as their ancestor and that the terms of the struggle had been defined in Bradford's terms, by worthy men. He felt this gave some dignity to what he was involved in beyond the justice of the claim.

And there were men at the golf course, though not the ones he had engaged with, who gave him heart and respect for his foe. These were the Portuguese and Yankee fishermen, many of whom were now retired from the sea to golf. They were men of substance, and he liked to imagine them and himself as young men, as children, as embryos, and finally as ancestors. Back there they could have fought well against each other, killing each other as they might. Often he thought he could see these kinds of shards of racial identity in their eyes as he spoke to them on the links.

He entered his home and walked past his desk to a corner of the room where sat a table, a stoneware pitcher, and a bowl. He poured some water into the bowl, took up a sliver of soap, and washed his hands and dried them on a towel that hung on a nail driven into the wall. Then he went to his desk, sat down, and took a folder from the top of a large pile that rested there. On the tab of the folder, typed in, were the words: *Franklin M. Fredricks, CPA, Log/Correspondence.* Inside the folder, stapled to the inside cover, was a piece of lined yellow legal paper containing a calendar of phone calls and correspondence dates. Most of the papers in the folder were carbons of letters and transcriptions of phone calls. He ran a thin finger down the calendar. "Letter today, Saturday; phone call Monday," he thought. He put the folder aside and turned in his swivel chair to the typewriter that sat on the short part of the L of his desk. In this position he could see out the front window of the shack. A pair of male goldfinches were pecking at the tube of the thistle-feeder that hung from a two-by-four rig stuck in the sand.

"Hi, boys," Frank Bumpus said. "There's a bobwhite coming soon," and then he began to type.

The Chair had picked out a pair of white cotton pants with little boats on them. The boats were set a good three inches apart, so there was no mistaking that the pants were white. They had no cuffs and were double-stitched with kelly-green thread down the outer seams. On the wide belt loops, fragments of the little boats could be made out. The boats were toylike, and each of them floated on a curl of wave that was equal to their length and about a quarter-inch deep. The waves were a few thin lines of green and blue, with the white of the background showing through. The boats seemed not to be located in any clear pattern; some were at right angles with the leg, but some were set askew, and a couple were almost upside down. Their hulls were dark green, and they had bright red masts that were topped with orange sails. They did not seem seaworthy. Each one had a small porthole with crosshatched lines in its side, and each had a little pink rudder, and a pink point at its prow.

At five places on the legs there were five little whales. They were the same size as the boats, and they too floated on little waves. They were pink in color, with curvy tales, and they each spouted a curl of water from their blowholes. They each had a little eye and little green lines for smiles. Near the slit of both front pockets, but not printed in a symmetrical way, there were two dolphins. These were the same size and general shape as the whales, and only their color (they were blue) seemed to distinguish them. But at a closer look, which the Chair had taken before buying the pants, one could see that the dolphins, though they sat on similar waves, had no blowholes or curls of spout, and they were not, like the whales, riding the waves but were arched in mid-dive, halfway between the exit from one wave and the entrance into another. They didn't seem to have any pupils in their happy eyes.

Alongside the pants on the bed was the Chair's shirt, a knit pullover, kelly-green in color, with white stitching around the edge of the collar and pocket. A canvas cap and a belt were beside it. The cap was red and had a white-and-green emblem, a golf tee with a ball beside it, and the words *Seaview Links* stitched in the front of its crown. The belt was white and made of plastic, its edges stitched with black thread. It had a black, plastic-covered buckle. On the floor, below the garments, were the Chair's socks and shoes, the socks lying neatly over the shoes, not touching the floor. The shoes were two-toned, green-and-white Foot-Joys, with scalloped dust tongues (devices the manufacturer called "shawls") covering the laces. They had been brightly shined. The socks were new, green-and-black Argyles.

The Chair stood in his boxer shorts and undershirt in front of the full-length mirror on the closet door to the side of the bed. He turned in a slow circle, keeping his eyes on the mirror, checking himself out. He reached up into the legs of the boxer shorts to the tails of his undershirt, pulling it down until there were no wrinkles where the elastic waistband met the shirt. He sucked in his stomach and adjusted the straps at his shoulders. Then he sat down on the bed beside his clothing. He ran a hand along the leg of his pants, and then he reached down and lifted the socks from the shoes, rolled each one down to the toe and adjusted them on his feet, unrolling the tops until they were straight and tight to his lower calves. He twisted the left one to get the ribs and the diamonds in line.

When his socks were in order, he got up and lifted his pants, shook them slightly, lowered them, and stepped in. Pulling them up, he danced a little to get them to fall properly in the leg. He noted the way the little boats fell. He turned and took his putting stance in full view in the mirror. With his left leg extended, the right back and firm, the little whale on the inside of his thigh could be seen. He smiled at himself. Then he picked up the belt and slipped it carefully through the loops. He left it unbuckled and lifted the shirt up and shook it out. He slipped it on, and rather than pull at the fabric, he did another little jig so that it fell down around his body until he could see himself in the mirror again. He adjusted the collar, unzipped the pants, and squatted with legs apart to hold them up while he tucked his shirt over his boxer shorts, smoothing out wrinkles around his body. When the shirt was secure, he gripped the pants, stood up, and pulled them over the shirt. He zipped them and fastened his belt, adjusting the buckle over his fly. He checked the pants fold to make sure the zipper was covered.

He went to the closet and opened the mirrored door and took out a piece of rug, which he brought back to the side of the bed, and placed his shoes on, taking the spikes off the floor. Then he sat down and put the shoes on it, lifted the scalloped shawls and laced them. When this was done, he picked up the cap, smoothed back his hair, and put it on, pulling the peak down firmly. Then he stood up on the piece of carpet and looked at himself in the mirror.

At first he stood straight, then he slouched a little, casually, putting his weight on one leg, the way he would stand while one of his partners was putting or teeing off. Then he took his putting stance again, checking the inseam of his trousers and the placement of the whales, the place where his pants met his socks, the protrusion of his anklebone with a diamond directly over it, and the arc of the side of his shoes and the way the first two scallops of the shawls angled along them. One of the tips of the laces was protruding from under the shawl, and he reached down, lifted the shawl, and opened the bow a bit, and then took his stance again and nodded. He checked his right leg to see that the pants came to the tops of his shoes. Then he took another casual stance, the one with his left hand on his hip, his right arm hanging loosely, bent at the elbow, his hand in his pocket with his thumb protruding along the fabric. This is the way he would stand in the clubhouse before they went out, talking jovially and authoritatively with the men.

Then he took various stances and went through various motions. There was the motion of pulling the peak of his cap down with conviction, snugging it as he prepared to address his ball for a long iron shot only after he had studied the distance and other issues perceptively. There was the motion of picking and throwing bits of grass in the air, watching their speed and direction as they fell, checking the variations in wind conditions before he teed off. There was the stance of disapproval when someone moved while another was putting. There was the stance and look of condescending approval at a shot well made. Once he let his left arm rise up and fall in mild philosophical despair at the behavior of Sammy. Another time there was the look reserved for Frank Bumpus, a look of restrained intensity. Once he put his hand on his head, looking to the heavens in disbelief. Once he smiled warmly, very loose in his body, his clothing showing brilliantly, suggesting obviously desired friendship.

Near the end, he went to a drawer in the dresser at the foot of the bed and from among carefully stacked packages of golf balls, tees, markers, and hats—his winnings over the years in the tournaments—got out a new glove from a pile of them. The glove was dark green with a white flap of Velcro on its underside to secure it, and in the middle of the flap was an emblem, a spherical figure, a transparent matrix of parts, in the middle of which was a small green club head. At the tip of the flap was a pearl button that could be removed and used as a ball marker. He slipped the tight glove over his hand, securing the Velcro. He went back to the mirror and stood before it. He lifted the gloved hand in front of his body at a level with his chest, the back of the glove facing away from him, the sphere and the pearl button clearly visible in the mirror, in a position where all would be able to see it. He formed a loose fist with the hand, his index finger extended and pointing. He was about to speak, and they all were listening attentively and with much anticipation for what he was about to say.

CHIP'S SPECIAL SEAVIEW MAP

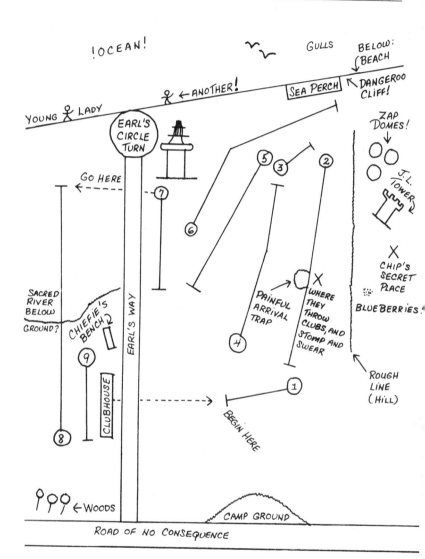

!OCEAN!

GULLS

BELOW: ↓BEACH

←ANOTHER!

SEA PERCH ↖DANGEROO CLIFF!

YOUNG ♀ LADY

EARL'S CIRCLE TURN

ZAP DOMES!

GO HERE

⑦

⑤ ③ ②

J.L. TOWER

⑥

✕ CHIP'S SECRET PLACE

BLUEBERRIES

SACRED RIVER BELOW

GROUND?

CHIEFIE'S BENCH

EARL'S WAY

PAINFUL ARRIVAL TRAP

✕ WHERE THEY THROW CLUBS, AND STOMP AND SWEAR

ROUGH LINE (HILL)

⑨

④

⑧ CLUBHOUSE

① BEGIN HERE

♀♀♀ ←WOODS

CAMP GROUND

ROAD OF NO CONSEQUENCE

FIRST TOURNAMENT

The Chief stood beside the screen door of the clubhouse, almost as still as a cigar-store Indian or like an official greeter, and nodded to the men he knew by sight and the ones he did not know, as if it were his place to welcome them to the tournament. They had a greeter in the town at the end of the Cape, that historic seaport. He was an old man and once selected he had the job for life. He wore clothes that imitated what the Pilgrims had worn, though his were acetates and vinyls, and he carried a bell that he rang as he walked the streets crowded with tourists, greeting them and crying the news of the town, *his* town, if he struck one as more than a transformed emblem of the real past. The Chief had this greeter in mind, but since he knew he wore the history of his people in his features and demeanor, he had opted for a more insidious twist, and his costume consisted of no more than a Seaview Links golf cap and an old wooden-shafted niblick that he usually held by its head and used in his brief and economical gestures as a pointer and a kind of walking stick. Otherwise, he was dressed in a pair of khakis and worn tennis shoes and a blue chambray shirt buttoned at the collar of his thin neck. His hair was black and straight, and it hung below the back of his cap, short but touching his lined neck, cut straight across. Though seventy-four-years old, tall and thin, he stood with the grace of one who was no more than fifty.

The Chair was one of the first to arrive. He parked beyond the clubhouse, a little up and across the road from it. He did not miss the Chief standing there as he passed, and he was already slightly pissed as he sat on the seat of his car, his legs out the open door, and put his golf shoes on. He got his clubs out of the trunk, left them leaning against the split-rail fence that led up to the first tee, crossed the road, stared in the eye of the Chief as he passed him, and entered the clubhouse. John Hope had arrived before him, and the Chair nodded to John and rolled his eyes a little, giving one of his head gestures toward the door behind him. John nodded in understanding and smiled.

Across the road from the clubhouse, to the right of the path leading to the first tee, Chip was putting the finishing touches on the putting green. He wanted to make sure that the apron was in good shape; a lot of men used it, standing a few yards behind it, practicing their chips on tournament days. While he was digging in his bag for his implements—his small clippers, wide-toothed comb, his bug spray—he glanced up and saw the Chief standing by the door. The Chief was looking his way, and Chip looked at him and smiled and mouthed the words "Hi, Chiefie!" in an exaggerated manner, and the Chief read them and smiled back. Chip started on the high side of the green, the place where there was the most room for the men to chip from, and began to work one side to the other, kneeling and combing the grass upward and clipping the uneven ends off. When he found ladybugs he put them on his shoulder, singing "Ladybug, Ladybug," but most of the other bugs he found got a brief shot of the spray. When he had finished with a section of fringe, combing and clipping it, he would watch as it slowly lowered itself, and when it did not lower fast enough for him, he would stand up and make his shadow fall over it. This took away the light energy of the sun and would cause it to bend over quicker. He worked carefully and methodically and with considerable skill. He was just high enough so that his attention was clear and focused; the overly intense perception time was gone, and he liked best to be this way. The Chief liked to watch the way he worked.

Back in the clubhouse, Sammy was finishing up with ordering the gear in his small pro shop. He straightened the stacks of shirts, and he pointed the brims of the hats forward in their nestled piles. The Chair was out in the small attached garage talking animatedly with John Hope. He's bugged by the Chief again, Sammy thought, and he laughed to himself as he looked down at his shoes. He had picked new ones out for the Chair's benefit. They were garish, two-toned orange-and-brown, and he had worn peds instead of socks so that it looked like he was barefoot in the golf shoes. He had ragged the ends of his cutoffs a little, and a couple of strings of white fabric hung from them. He had put his gold chain with his *save the whales emblem* on it around his neck. His *save the whales* bumper-stickers on the glass counter was another thing that bugged the Chair. His fedora, with the new white feather in its band, was ready under the counter. He thought he would save that, a final touch, just before the tournament began.

By eleven-forty-five a good number of men had rolled in. There were at least twenty of them, some standing in the clubhouse talking, others out front messing with their bags and clubs, a few across the road chipping and putting. Some laughter came from the putting green. Chip's high-pitched giggle could be heard. He hadn't quite finished in time, and the balls were bouncing around him, some hitting his legs, him grabbing some of them in flight or on a first bounce as he worked on the last patch of fringe. At twelve o'clock the Chair stuck his head out the door and yelled with a kind of impatient urgency.

"Sign up time, sign up time!"

A couple of men walked into the clubhouse. Most of the others stopped what they were doing and looked at him. A few laughed and poked each other. The Chair let the screen door slam and went to the table where John Hope was already sitting. John had the sign-up sheet ready with a few dollar bills for change beside it. The Chair took the three-by-five handicap cards out of the green-metal file box and put them on the table. He sat down beside John and began shuffling through the cards. The Chair had selected this part of the sign-up job for himself because it afforded him banter with the men. The cards listed their names and their handicaps. Every week, once the tournaments got going, Chair would spend an evening in the clubhouse going through the cards, adjusting the handicaps up or down as they were influenced by the scores the men had posted during the week. Since this was the first official tournament, the handicaps on the cards reflected the skill of the men at the end of the previous season. As they came into the clubhouse and signed up, paying their four dollars for the pot, many of them looked down at their cards when the Chair extracted them from the pile, checking to see how many strokes they had. This pausing and checking made the sign-up take a little longer, but the Chair didn't mind that. He spoke to most of the men, joking and complimenting.

"Cooky, you sandbagger, a seventeen! Tom, a twelve, good

play last year; hope you stayed sharp over the winter. Crow, you devil, a twenty-four?! You *still* hit 'em good for a fat man! A.J., *good God*, eleven!; you tough old cocker!"

As the Chair was carrying on, some of the men looked at each other and rolled their eyes. Sammy grinned behind his glass counter, selling balls, gloves, and tees. Then the door opened, and Commander George Wall entered the clubhouse.

As commanding officer of the Seaview Air Force Station, Wall was part of the matrix of troubling circumstances that touched on play at Seaview. In the first place, and probably most important to Chair, Sammy, and the other local members, Wall was a real sand-bagger. A year ago, Wall knew that this was to be his last year as commander of the Air Force Station. He was going to be transferred, a promotion, to a post in San Diego, and he had vowed that before he left he would get the trophy that went to the winner of the First Flight at the end of the summer.

From the beginning, Wall's experience in the club championship had pissed him off. He could not win it. Each year he would spend most of the winter sharpening his game, getting it honed to what he thought was its finest edge, and then one of these damn fishermen, or storeowners, or country schoolteachers would come up with some crazy, incredible round. They didn't even know how to hit a ball properly. They would hold their clubs like baseball bats. They would putt like women. They would pitch and run where they should use a wedge. They would blast out of sand traps like they were digging graves. But they would score, and they would beat him soundly. He had been assigned to Seaview as a trouble-shooter, and he had shot down the trouble. When he had arrived as commanding officer, the men had been fraternizing with the townspeople to an inordinate extent. They had used the N.C.O. club and the P.X. buying beer and cigarettes at military prices. He had even found that some of the local women were living with Air Force men, in common-law arrangements, on the base. Extra duty, frequent inspection, two field days a week, and curtailment of passes and liberty had put a stop to all this. Now the men were sharp, they respected him, the place was in order. He was forty-three years old, he had pulled an entire (if small) command into shape, he was being promoted because of the excellence of his work, but he could not beat a bunch of hick civilians in a local golf tournament.

It enraged him, and when he got wind of his transfer, he vowed that he would not leave Seaview without a trophy. He had spent the previous year of weekly tournaments padding his handicap. He had done it slowly, shaking his head each tournament day, talking about how hard he was working and how his golf game was going to hell. He had brought his handicap up to a fourteen. Sometimes in the evenings, in winter, he would come out and practice drives. He practiced his short game behind the B.O.Q. at the base. He figured his true handicap at Seaview was about a five or a six. He had set things up with care. He would come back a little this summer, getting himself down to a twelve or so. He would win the First Flight trophy at the end of the summer. He was very sure of the skill with which he had handled his strategy. What he didn't know was that the enlisted men and most of the officers at the base had no respect for him at all. In the beginning they had simply disliked him, but after the word got around that he was most probably padding his handicap, they began to think of him as a real asshole.

"Well, Frank, a fourteen; hope there's a better year for you this time around," Chair said, using his eyebrow-raising expression as he located Wall's card.

"I hope so," Wall said, and after he'd paid and nodded to the five or so men around the table who looked his way, and nodded particularly sharply to the two enlisted men from his command who were exercising their privileges at Seaview, he walked back out the door and over to the putting green to hit some.

From almost anywhere on the course the radar domes, like huge golf balls and in strange juxtapostion to the Jenny Lind tower below them, could be seen, and as Wall crossed the road and two teenagers in bathing suits and sandals passed in front of him on their way to the lighthouse and the beach below it, he thought of the difficulties that remained for him before he was free of this place and took up his new command out West.

The environment creeps had been after him for over a year about the supposed dangerous microwave emanations from the domes. In the middle of the previous summer, one of the hang-glider enthusiasts who liked to cruise out over the cliff along the sixth fairway had caught a good enough updraft to carry him inland a little. He had circled one of the domes, close into it at about a level with its top, and a couple of days later he had checked into a hospital in Boston, feeling ill. When the doctors had examined him, done a semen test, and found him sterile, the reporters got a hold of it, and in a very short time the environment creeps had started to call and write letters and show up. In the beginning he had stonewalled, but this had only caused them to switch their fire to Washington, and Washington, needing time, had dumped it back in the lap of the Air Force, into his lap. He was to do a friendly public-relations routine until Washington figured the facts and a solid position on the issue.

About the same time as the hang-glider incident, the Free the Skin Beach Coalition had pushed their own form of madness into visibility. For as long as anyone could remember, people had been swimming nude, in large groups and small, at selected, secluded spots well down the beaches from the access roads. Two years ago, some national underground magazine had gotten a hold of the fact and had given the name Skin Beach to the stretches along the Cape from the lighthouse down past the golf course and Air Force Station. The summer the article appeared, people started to come out to the beaches by the hundreds, flaunting nakedness whenever they felt like it. Things came to a head on a particularly hot August weekend when a motorcycle gang from Boston, the Devil's Advocates, had raised hell and havoc crossing people's property to get to the beaches. The towns along the beach and the National Seashore people had come down as hard as they could with local government ordinances, harassing and arresting nude bathers. In reaction, at the end of the previous summer, the Free the Skin Beach Coalition had been formed. While they and their lawyers were hassling with the towns and the Seashore, somebody got the bright idea to "liberate" the beach below the Air Force Station. This beach, one posted and used by the men at the station and their families, was neither part of the towns that flanked it nor part of the National Seashore. It was under the governance of the Air Force, and as such it fell to Wall to administer its use.

In the beginning, he tried to use sentry watches, having his men simply run the nudies off. But his men liked better to perch on the dunes with binoculars and watch the bathers, laughing and poking each other. Once he was so pissed that he went down and ran them off himself.

One day near the middle of August, a strange group had gathered on the beach early, before dawn, and when the morning watch was set, his men reported that it looked like a major confrontation was possible. In addition to Skin Beach people, a good number of Devil's Advocates were there. And these two groups were joined by hang-glider enthusiasts. Already the gliders were drifting along the cliff. The men reported that it looked like the Advocates had at some previous time made a connection with the hang-glider group. Their relations seemed friendly, and some of the Advocates were gliding in their leathers along the cliff and out over the mild breakers. The nudies sat a little apart from the two other groups, and the situation looked volatile.

Wall had acted quickly, sending his men down with unloaded but very threatening weapons. There had been a confrontation with the Advocates. His men had been rushed, and only after they had gotten their hands on the Advocate's leader, arrested him and, in their enthusiasm, beaten him soundly in front of his gang, had things come under control. They had dispersed the trespassers and then had brought the leader up the cliff to Wall's office at the station. To avoid the kind of incident the beating might have precipitated, Wall had released him. That had been the end of it, though Wall had received some very threatening, anonymous mail that he figured came from the outraged Advocates. The threats were grandiose: promises of future war with the Air Force Station. The letters were short and curt; there had been four of them, and then they had stopped, and the difficulties had seemed to cool down over the winter. But he had heard through the grapevine that things were being planned for this summer. There was the possibility of demonstrations of some kind by both the environment creeps and the Free the Skin Beach Coalition.

Wall sighed, then stiffened up when he got to the putting green. He proceeded to practice, finding a spot among the others who were putting there. Chip had finished and gone back to the clubhouse to eat his lunch. Wall made a few putts, missed some, and missed a few on purpose.

The phone kept ringing in the clubhouse, as those who were

quitting work at noon called to say they would be there for the tournament so that the Chair would hold the draw. Sammy answered the phone, speaking briefly, and before it was back in the cradle would call out the names: Ed Souza, Gordon Tarvers, Sparkie Hurd. . . . From outside the screen door, names would be called out also as those who were late pulled up. At twelve-twenty-five, the Chair had a stack of thirty-six cards in his hand, and he was tapping the corner of the stack on the table, watching the clock. At twelve-thirty he glanced over at Sammy.

"That looks to be it," Sammy said, and the Chair rapped the cards one last time and called out a little too loudly into the room.

"Draw! Draw!"

The words got to the door and out it, and as the Chair shuffled the cards and began laying them out in rows on the table, "Draw! Draw!" could be heard as far as the putting green. Those already in the room pressed in around the table, watching the cards come up, checking to see who they were teamed up with. When they saw their cards, they turned and began to look for their partners. The tournament was handled in shotgun fashion, teams starting at one, five, and seven at the same time, and by twelve-thirty-five all the golfers were headed for their assigned tees.

As the clubhouse emptied and Earl came in to take over for Sammy while he played, Sammy reached under the glass counter and got out his fedora with the feather in it. He put the hat on, pulled the brim down to tuck it tight, broke open a cellophane bag of long "Florida" tees from his special stock, and turned and smiled at Earl.

"Look all right, do I?" he asked. "I better, I drew the Chair."

"Who-ha," Earl said flatly. "Just the right start to the season."

"Better believe it," Sammy said. "See ya," and he left the clubhouse and headed for the first tee, where the other three members of his foursome—the Chair, Commander Wall, and Eddie Costa, the fisherman—would be waiting. They were going to be third in line to hit off, but the Chair would, for sure, have them up there and ready.

When all the golfers had left, Chief Wingfoot quit his place at the side of the door and walked down the road toward the lighthouse. He would turn to the right when he got there, head along the rough of the sixth fairway that ran along the ocean's cliff edge, and when he got down to the sixth tee, he would cut through the rough to the sea perch. He would sit there and watch the ocean a while, his people's golf course behind him. When the foursome that Chair and Sammy were in reached that hole—and that would be a while from now—he'd have a few things to do. When he got to the tee, he cut through the long weed to the dune's edge. He was high above the sea, the weeds tall behind him, and he sat on a ledge of shale, his feet hanging over the cliff. The tide was low: a few long clean bars, with still pools between them and the beach, were visible above the water, and a few herring gulls drifted out and along the cliff at about the Chief's level. He took a piece of weed and put it in his mouth for the moisture. Below him, a few children, small at this distance, dug in the sand, their mother watching them from under a bright beach umbrella. He began to think of the shellfish on the Cape and the Quahog People.

There was little of the conventional in the way most of the men at Seaview played golf. There had never been a real pro at the course, and Sammy had the job because he was a native, played a respectable game, and was willing to work long hours for little pay. The Golf Commission had renewed his contract each year for the past five. His father, a retired fisherman now doing a little charter-boat sport work in Florida, had been a respected member of the Cape's fishing community, and the Chair's objections each time the contract came up for review were disregarded by the other members of the Commission. They were loyal to the father, and they had a liking for the easy-going nature of the son.

In the old days, before the tourist boom, golf was one of the only recreations available down on the Cape. The shape of the course was such that most of the tourists disdained to play it when they did start coming. Though Earl and Chip had done a lot for the tees and greens, the fairways looked like somebody's backyard that had never been seeded. Earl kept the weeds low as best he could, but the fairways were mostly tufts of weed, occasional small carpets of wild rye, patches of grass, dandelions, and sand, with bits of stone here and there and shards of broken clamshells up from the beach. The shells were there because when it rained, the gulls, who dropped clams from great heights in order to break them for food, drifted in over the course with their catches and let them fall along the fairways.

When Sammy reached the first tee, the Chair was looking the other way, busily commenting on the hits of the foursome in front of them. When they had all hit, he turned and saw Sammy's hat and new feather. Fred Wall was looking too, but his mouth didn't drop open the way the Chair's did. He was able to keep his commanding officer's demeanor in the face of such things. The Chair snapped his mouth shut and kept his peace; he would not give Sammy the satisfaction of comment.

When the foursome ahead of them had reached the green, Sammy went to the tee to get ready. Sammy was a two-handicapper, the Chair had six strokes, Wall had his fourteen, and Eddie Costa had nine. Sammy had the honors, and he stuck one of his special long tees in the ground and put a new ball on it, the ball standing a good two inches above the grass. He had a wide stance and a very fluid if abbreviated swing. He cracked the ball off its high perch and curled it a good way out to the right of the fairway, where it rolled up the last rise and quit about fifty yards from the green. The Chair, though his hit was long and straight, caught a tuft of grass, bounced high in the air, and came up about seventy yards short, on a line between the two small traps on the left and right front. The Chair got a lot of hip into his swing, and just before he hit the ball he had the habit of lurching slightly in a little jump in the direction of flight.

Eddie Costa was the loosest hitter of the four. He teed up and took a stance that was very open, his left foot pointing directly down the fairway. He gripped the club like a fishing pole held for a side-style surf cast, and he got ready by turning the head in small circles halfway up into his backswing. Just before he hit, he banged the club head hard on the ground behind the ball. When he clouted it, the force of his swing caused him to come off both feet, and he would wind up in a slight crouch, his feet wide apart, his toes pointing down the fairway, his eyes intent on watching the ball. His hit, as usual, was low and straight: it kicked up a puff of sand about a hundred and fifty yards out at the top of a low hill in the fairway and shot in the air for another thirty yards. It got a good bounce and came to rest on the down side of the hill to the right, about eighty-five yards away from the green. Fred Wall had the only conventional shot in the group. His swing was very careful, practiced, and mechanical. He was a little to the left, but he was straight. He finished in a good spot, on the hill to the left of the green, about fifty yards out, with no traps between him and the flagstick.

Eddie Costa played his second shot in a style that was distinctly different from his first. Eighty-five-yards away, and with the edge of the trap between him and the pin, he elected to play a pitch-and-run shot. He had nothing above a six-iron in his bag. He never needed the loftier clubs, and for his shot he selected a four-iron. Still using his fishing-pole grip, this time he choked up significantly on the club shaft; his left hand was well down on the grip, and there was a good four inches between it and his right. He planted his feet beside each other, digging in by kicking at the sand and grass tufts. This time he did not bang the club head on the ground but instead took a series of short half-swings, moving the club back and forth from his shoulder to the ground behind the ball. The half-swings got stronger and quicker, and at the end of them he hit. The ball shot off the club face, again very low and straight. It hit about fifteen yards short of the trap, approached it, entered it, and rolled through it, jumping a little when it hit the front lip. It came to rest in the middle of the green, about twenty-five feet from the cup.

"Good shot, Eddie, good *shot!*" the Chair yelled over from where he stood behind his ball. Sammy took his hat off and waved it. Wall lifted the club in his hand slightly off the ground.

After the Chair and Wall had hit safely to the green, both finishing about the same distance away as Eddie, Sammy kicked his ball around in search of a good lie. Chair was walking up to the green, but he watched Sammy, making sure that he did not move his ball closer than it was. Sammy glanced up and saw Chair watching. He grinned, and the Chair turned away. Then Sammy found a place, a good tuft of grass, and he hit up. His wedge was high and true, and he finished inside of the other three.

"All right, all right!" Eddie Costa said when they all had

reached the green. "Off to a *good* start. Eight points at least." The Chair scowled at him. He did not like mentioning points until the putts were down; it was inappropriate, and it was bad luck.

"Come on boys, hang tough," he said. Three of them two putted for pars. Sammy stuck his in for a birdie. The Chair wanted the team points, but he also wanted to beat Sammy. He was both pissed and pleased when they walked over to the second tee. They had tallied nine on the hole. He was one down to Sammy. It was a good and bad start.

After they had hit their drives on the second, the long par-five dog leg, with the elevated tee from which could be seen the Jenny Lind tower with the radar domes very large at the top of the hill above it, they started down the path to the fairway and saw Chip up on the hill in the right rough, picking the few early blueberries he could find and popping them in his mouth. He had parked his cutter at the foot of the rough and hopped up there, giving the foursome quiet so they could concentrate on their second shots. The Chair was walking with Wall, and when he saw Chip he said, "That's a hell of a job Chip is doing on the aprons," and then he yelled out, "That's a hell of a job you're doing on the aprons, Chip!" Wall jumped away a little as the yell rang in too close to his ear, but the Chair didn't notice. Chip acknowledged the Chair's yell with a bow and a wave. Two men in the foursome ahead of them, over two hundred yards away on the green, looked up and glanced back down the fairway.

It didn't take the Chair long to get even; he birdied the second hole while Sammy parred it. The other two took bogies. By the time they reached the fifth green, Sammy had pulled ahead again, by three. Chair had a long putt for a par on the fifth, and he made it. Sammy was on the green in regulation, but he misjudged his first putt, went well past the hole, and missed it coming back. At the end of five, Sammy was two up and the team was about even for the round.

High up and out over the sea, a few cloud puffs with plenty of blue between them hung over the distant markers of lobster pots in their ragged lines in the barely swelling and receding water beyond the shore's activity. The few hunting gulls had curled out from the shore and were cruising over the deep water, occasionally folding their wings and falling into the sea for shallow bait fish. There had been a factory boat far out, close to the end of sight, but a fog bank had rolled in, creating a false horizon beyond which the boat was probably still working, though totally obscured. It was still bright and sunny over the sand and surf, and the children were still playing. The Chief had taken his tennis shoes off, and his hanging feet were touched by a light breeze. He had laid his niblick on the cliff's edge to his side, and his golf cap was cocked back on his head. He had heard the talk of three foursomes as they came up to the sixth tee to hit. He was only about fifteen feet from the tee, but the grass and brush were high and dense, and even when one of the men had lumbered into the bushes to take a leak, he had been unaware of the Chief's presence. There were no golfers on the tee now, and the Chief could hear the fluted songs of some purple finches in the thick growth behind him.

When they had discussed the relatively small issue of choosing a name for their organization, there had been a variety of views on the subject. The boys from around Niagara, the Iroquois advisers, had thought they needed something very direct and understandable, something the white man would remember because it was in his lingo and not too enigmatic. Frightening names had a strong lobby, mostly among the young fellows. They were very militant, and they wanted this to be apparent "out front," as they said. His group was not a political group as such but had considerable sway in the matter, because they were the ones whose specific ancestors had lived here (it was their own names that appeared on the land claims). They had from the beginning an agreement of intention. They wanted a name that had specific historical import and at the same time was symbolic. Once he had been elected as chairman of the steering committee, a position which for all practical purposes meant that he was the man in charge, he had suggested the name Quahog People, and he had argued for its selection with good reasons.

Part of the strength of the white man's tradition lay in the early economy of the Cape. Fishing was its backbone, and no small part of the industry was shellfishing. The oysters and clams of the Cape were famous in the Eastern United States, and whenever the locals evoked the power of their past, they would talk of the gone high quality of shellfish, saying it was even better in their grandfathers' time. That would usually get them to speak of the hard life their ancestors had led, suggesting that their own backbones had been formed by these hardy fishermen. Now it was true that the fishermen who still worked the waters off the Cape worked very hard, and it was also true that those who had moved from a fishing tradition into other endeavors were hard workers also. But many of those in power had gotten their money and influence not from a tradition that had to do with hard sea work but from the tourist trade and the sale of land. When they did work, it was during the summertime, when the tourists came, and what work they did then wasn't very hard work, though they often complained about it. In the winter the work consisted, for many of them, of a little light half-day labor and the counting of the money they had made during the summer.

That their ancestors' toil gave them right of ownership of the land was also questionable, because though shellfishing was never associated with the Indians, it had been the Pamets who had lived on the Cape before the white man took over, who had started the shellfishing industry. Talk was always that the Pamets had lived in a kind of paradise here, had simply picked up the clams and oysters and eaten them. The truth was that they had harvested and cared for the shore waters in a very diligent manner. They had farmed the sea as they had farmed the land. They had used sea clams, spading the shells in with herring to fertilize their beanfields. Many of their implements were made from quahog shells: needles, hoes, pendants, even arrowheads. Shell heaps had been in evidence from the tip of the Cape to its foot. In this the historical light, if anyone could lay claim to the name Quahog People it was Frank Bumpus, a Pamet himself, and his organization. Quahog People was a good choice because it took a noun that the white man thought was part of his tradition and returned it to its proper place—and that was just what the Quahog People planned to do with the land upon which the golf course sat.

The symbolic implications of the name had been arrived at by

Frank Bumpus himself, and when he spoke to his people about them, he spoke eloquently. He told them that, like the Indian, the quahog was always there. Each year the crop was ravaged, but each year it returned. The clams moved along the coast slightly, but they never moved too far from the integrity of their home ground. At times the red tide got to them, but enough of the seedlings always lived through so that a new crop was insured. The white man harvested and ate them, they were passive in their acceptance of this, but their numbers were large and self-renewing. They were silent and enigmatic in their thoughts, but their power to survive was beyond question. He knew, when he told them these things, that he was stretching the truth beyond the symbolic implications a bit, and they knew it too. He would have liked their name to have the consistency of the allegories in the medieval illuminations he had studied, would have liked them to have the force and complexity he had marveled at in Shiva iconography. At the same time, he had argued that the name had a trickster quality to it. It was worthy of Hare and the African Anansi. Furthermore, its meaning would remain veiled to the white man: in this sense it would be a secret name, and that was important because it would symbolize their unity and closure, and thus their strength.

Frank Bumpus knew how much of this was politics, how much rabblerousing and magic, and how much pure bunk. Still, there were a lot of small chunks and pieces that came from the core philosophy, and these kept the rest of it in proper perspective. His enigmatic buffoon role on the links at Seaview was politics and a preparing of the false adversary as communications buffer once the occupation began. The Free the Skin Beach Coalition was bunk but of a fortuitous nature, in that it would serve well as a diversionary force. The kind of victory he hoped for was territorially minimal, and they would only need to hold the land for a short time for the tactical end to be accomplished. Visibility would grease the wheels; their lawyers would begin to handle it from there. The code post card had gone off, and he trusted that his relative, the tactician, was on his way, slowly and in an underground fashion. The government's people had been watching them all for close to a year now, but Frank Bumpus was sure they had them properly confused. Soon enough Bob White would be here, and then they could begin the specifics in earnest.

The Chief was lifted from his reverie by the sound of voices. He could hear the Chair yelling out as the foursome he was in reached the top of the hill that fronted the fifth green, and he pulled his feet back from the cliff's edge, putting on and lacing up his left tennis shoe. He then took a large blue-and-white handkerchief from his pocket, tied it around his right ankle, and put his right shoe on as well. While they were over on the fifth green putting, he adjusted his cap, cleaned up his niblick by rubbing it against his leg, and stood up and dusted his clothing.

When Sammy, Chair, Eddie, and Wall were on their way over to the sixth tee, Chief Wingfoot stepped out of the bushes that bordered it. He was leaning heavily on the shaft of his niblick and limping. The handkerchief around his ankle flopped against his tennis shoe as he moved out to greet them.

"Now *what* in the hell is this?" the Chief could hear the Chair say, a little too loudly, to Wall and the others. Sammy and Eddie nodded to the Chief, and when the four got close to the tee, the Chief addressed them.

"Good afternoon, gentlemen, I wonder if you could give me some aid; I seem to have pulled up lame."

"Lame, my ass," the Chair said under his breath, and then more audibly, "Why don't you sit here and wait a little? Some of the guys with power carts will be along, and they can give you a lift in. We've gotta move on."

"That would be fine," the Chief said, "but I have business to transact, and I must get back soon. Could you not afford me some assistance?"

"Why the hell are you out here, anyway?" the Chair said sharply. "This is no place for the lame!"

"True, true," Chief Wingfoot sighed, "but I am here, and I *am* in need."

"Well, for Christ's sake!" the Chair said and rapped his thigh with his gloved hand.

Sammy had a wide grin on his face. Wall was standing off to the side, not wanting to get involved in the thing. Eddie was the only one who was busy. He was digging around in the large side pocket of his golf bag, pulling things out of it and tossing them on the grass of the tee. So far he had withdrawn a pint of Wild Turkey and a worn three-wood head cover he kept it in, a good-sized piece of fishing net, two lures with corks stuck on their hooks that he used when he plugged for bass, a paper bag full of sinkers, an obscure piece of scrimshaw, a fillet knife in a tooled leather sheath, a pair of torn undershorts, a pocket calculator, a rigid three-inch oyster measure, an ivory cue ball, and a pair of dice.

"Mother of *God!*" the Chair yelled when he saw what Eddie was up to. Sammy's grin was widening, and even Wall could not hold back. He had his hand over his mouth, his head shaking, his laughter muted.

"Got it," Eddie said, and he pulled a good length of thin nylon rope out of the deep recesses of the pouch. "We can truss up the carts together, hang the net between 'em; we'll get you in okay, Chief."

"Now wait *just* a minute," the Chair said, but Sammy and Eddie were already at work. Before the Chair could get himself organized and formalize his complaint, they had hooked their two handcarts together with rope, Eddie tying complex nautical knots quickly and automatically, had hung the piece of netting, double-folded, between the two carts, and had helped the limping Chief over to the contraption, each taking him by an arm, and had lowered him into the sling. The Chief reclined there, his niblick in one hand across his chest and his other gripping the mouth of Sammy's bag, his legs spread apart, and his feet firm on the axles of the inner wheels. He was smiling graciously.

"This is just fine," he said.

The Chair was steaming, and when he hit his drive, he shanked it badly. It sailed off into the rough on the right, between the fairway and the cliff that ran along the ocean's edge.

"Shit!" he screamed, and he jumped up into the air once. When he landed he spun around, something like a discus thrower, and flung his driver down the fairway a good forty yards; it turned end over end, and when it hit it rapped the ground loudly. He was instantly embarrassed at his loss of control, and he tried to be demure as he stepped back and waited for the others to hit.

Each of the others had hit shots like the one the Chair had

just managed. And each of them had, at one time or another, lost control in a similar way. This, and a sense of fundamental comradeship that went with golf at Seaview, prevented them from responding to the Chair's behavior in any uncharitable way.

"Tough luck, Chair; you can still get there in three, still get a par," Sammy said before he drove his ball, and the others nodded and grunted in agreement. The Chief did not say anything. He just sat in his sling.

Sammy and the two others had good drives, and the Chair found his ball easily, hit a fair shot out of the rough, and was beyond the others in three. He tried to keep away from them, to disassociate himself in some way from the mad contraption with the Indian in it that Sammy and Eddie pulled down the fairway, but this was impossible; they were clearly a foursome. The bathers who walked along the path cut in the right rough, heading for the narrow dune passage that lead down the cliff to the beach, stopped to stare and point. Somebody who was flying a kite at the edge of the cliff gawked at them, forgetting his kite for a moment, and it drifted in circles and fell in the middle of the fairway. It was a plastic skyhawk, and when the flyer tried to jerk it up again, it danced like an injured bird as the trussed-up carts passed over its line, caught a slight breeze, and rose up a few feet above the carts, flapping insanely, its line caught and twisted in the carts' wheels. The procession paused to disentangle the kite line; the bearded man who was flying it came out in the fairway to help with the mess, and the Chief reached down from where he was slung to give aid. Sammy's feathered fedora bobbed as he and Eddie worked with the knots and twists.

The foursome playing the fifth and parallel fairway came over the hill in their power carts, stopped at the top, turned to the right, and came down to see what was happening. Just then the specter of a hang-glider, huge and casting a broad shadow into the rough, lifted from below the cliff's edge near the lighthouse and began to drift along. The rider must have seen the goings on on the fairway, because he drifted a little too far inland, lost his updraft, and began to sink in wide circles, finally coming to rest about fifty yards from the cluster of power carts, kite, men, and contraption. Wall rushed over to the glider, helped its occupant to his feet, and began to talk seriously to him. A tourist bus had stopped in the parking lot of the lighthouse, and a line of senior citizens—women in flowered dresses and gray hair, with a few old men in baggy suits behind them—had made their way down the path between cliff and fairway and had stopped to watch the spectacle. A few gulls drifted in with shells in their beaks and began dropping them on the fairway's hardpan. Then the fog came.

It had been coming in slowly and for a while. It was thick, damp, and heavy. As it moved, it pushed against a clear line of sunlight. There were no clouds in the sky in front of it. When it had reached close to the beach below the cliff, the woman and her two children had packed up and left. They were tourists. It was their first time on the Cape, and the organic-looking density of the approaching fog had frightened them. The jagged lines of lobster-pot markers looked like fairy lights for a moment as the fog passed over them, the sun shining in the space between the wake and the fog bottom, and then they blinked out like small, serial firecrackers. From the cliff the fog could be seen as a distinct mass between the sea and the wispy layer of mist above it, and above the mist the air was clear and the sun still bright. When the fog got fifty yards from the shore, a young man on the path in the rough noticed it, and with his head turned back over his shoulder, he reached out and touched the young woman with him, causing her to turn and see it also. They looked at it for a moment, and then the young man struck a kind of sunworshiper pose, his arms wide apart and his head elevated in a kind of joke. They were on their way to the beach when they had stopped to watch the hang-glider float inland and fall to the fairway. Then they had, with the others, watched the goings on with the golfers, the contraption, and the kite. But now they wanted the sun to take the fog away. It would spoil their beach day, and he lifted his arms to pray to it. His young woman friend could not contain herself, and she yelled out.

"Look at the fog! Look at the fog!"

Many in the group of senior citizens heard her, and most of them turned from the sights on the fairway to look. By this time the fog had reached the sand, and after it crossed the beach and hit against the base of the cliff, having nowhere else to go, it started to fold in on itself, to thicken, and to climb. Many of the elderly people got nervous, the flowers on the dresses shifted; their line on the path broke as they looked, piecemeal, out at the cliff, over at the fairway, and back at the bus near the lighthouse in the parking lot. The fog came over the crest first where the lighthouse was, covered the bottom half of it, and then it sucked up the bus. Some of the people had started back that way, but when the bus disappeared they stopped; and others of them turned, only to find that the fog was coming over the whole length of the cliff edge, folding and moving toward them.

Out in the fairway, the golfers had disentangled the line of the kite. The Chief rested in his sling. Sammy and Eddie got up, and the kite flyer, when the line was loose, trotted back toward the rough, pulling his string, watching the kite rise quickly. The golfers watched him get up and go, and then they saw the flowered dresses and the bathers and the fog behind them. The flyer stopped when he reached the edge of the rough, but his kite kept rising, and as he watched it go it disappeared, and he was left holding a rigid string that stood up straight in the air. Most of the old women and a few of the baggy-suited men started to come together in a kind of common purpose. Their line was disheveled in the rough, but when their feet hit the fairway it firmed up again. They came to the hardpan running and hopping, occasional clamshells thumping into the ground among them.

The golfers recognized their force immediately, and they headed for the power carts, hoping to get the carts between themselves and the oncoming flowers that were now losing their colors as the fog touched them. The Chief in the contraption was out front and vulnerable. He wound his fingers in the netting of the sling and braced his feet. Sammy and Eddie held tight to the pull-cart handles, and Sammy used his other hand to hold the crown of his hat. Wall and the hang-glider pilot, though they were to one side at a place where only a few bathers would pass them, struggled to move the grounded glider out of harm's way. A little breeze had come up, and the glider was fighting them; their arms extended above it, they tried hard to hold it down. It lifted one or the other of them occasionally above tiptoe.

When the oncoming tide of flowered dresses and baggy suits

tucked in the front of the fog gained the middle of the fairway, the Chair was the first to fall. He had been caught in a moment of indecision between the possible safety behind the power carts and that at the edge of the line beyond the hang-glider. He had started for the glider, but when it began to lift, he had pulled up and watched it. Then he had turned back toward the carts, but saw that he could not make it in time, and stopped and put his hands up.

"It's okay, don't panic! Don't panic!" he yelled. But the Chair had a panicked kind of yell, and when they heard it they only came on quicker. The first to get to him were two very heavy women. One was ahead of the other. They were probably neighbors, and the one had reached back to get the other's hand so they would not get separated. Just as their hands linked, they came upon the Chair, and though their hands broke apart when they hit his chest, there was enough force in their weight and movement to lift him off the ground and throw him back. As he stumbled, trying to keep his footing, he reached out for support. What he seized was a flowered sleeve. It ripped, and the whole front of the dress came away with it. At the sound of the rip, the woman clouted him with a small pearled bag, knocking his golf cap off, quaking his skull. As he fell backward, grabbing at the bag in defense of himself, he brought the three of them down in a heap, the one with the ripped dress fighting to get her hand and the bag free of the sleeve.

Now they were all in the fog. It was like the inside of a cloud. Most of the phalanx passed and entered the next fairway and disappeared. Wall and the hang-glider were out of sight to the right. Three women had run into the cluster of power carts and stuck there, holding tight and shaking. One thin old man had run up against the Chief's contraption, shuddering the netting and ropes, swaying the Chief a little in his sling. The old man had grabbed Eddie's cart handle and held fast to it. He looked down at the Chief in embarrassment. He was the same size and build as the Chief, but he was a good fifteen years older, about ninety. The Chief could see that the elder thought it had been unseemly for him to run from fog while this younger man, the Chief himself, watched him do it. The Chief smiled reassuringly up at him, and the man relaxed some, smiling back. He had a bushy gray mustache and equally bushy gray hair.

"This is a pip; this is a hell of a note, boy!" he said to the Chief, his eyes sparkling.

"That is correct, Father," the Chief answered. "Pretty good fun too!" And they both laughed, like a flute and a piccolo, in the fog.

When the Chair had disengaged himself from the two women and had helped them get loose from each other, he got his rain slicker out of the pouch in his golf bag and tried to help the woman with the front of her dress ripped away put it on. She saw him with it, and she lifted her hands and pushed at the air in the fog before her.

"Don't look! Don't look!" she hissed at him, and he gave the slicker to the other woman, who helped the embarrassed one on with it. Then he took their arms and led them over to the power carts. When he got them there, one of the men spoke up.

"What'll we do now, Chair?" Before the Chair could answer, Sammy spoke from near the contraption that was parked in front of them.

"We'll call the tournament for a while, scores stand, we'll play the holes we're on over again. This stuff'll pass shortly. Dick, you take two of the ladies in in the cart. Crow, you take a couple, then come back and get some others. Eddie and I'll take the Chief in. The rest of us'll walk."

"I'll walk!" said the old man standing beside the Chief's contraption. Wall came up to the Chair's elbow out of the fog.

"What's going on?"

"We're going in for a while," the Chair said.

When they got to the clubhouse, the men were straggling in from various directions. The touring bus, with most of the senior citizens in it, was parked across the road, and the driver, in his slightly wilted gray uniform, was moving around, reasurring and taking count. Chip stepped off the bus, where he had been distributing styrofoam cups of coffee.

"Hey, hey; hey, *hey*," he said to no one in particular. "The Chipper becomes a help to the aged, Captain of Relief, Fog Savior. Wow! look at that lighthouse in the mist! Seaview happenings."

A couple of the women were in the clubhouse drinking coffee, talking with the golfers coquettishly. The driver came in and caught them at it, and he hustled them out and into the bus. The woman with Chair's slicker got on still wearing it. In a few minutes, the bus was fully loaded. The last one to board was the old man. He patted Chief Wingfoot on his golf cap before he left him.

"Take good care of that leg, Son," he said as he turned to go.

"Thank you, Father, I will," the Chief said, and in a few minutes the bus pulled out.

By the time all of the men had gathered in the clubhouse, were sitting and standing around, drinking coffee and soda, the fog had already begun to thin out. The Chair had taken charge again, and he was walking among the men, talking about the fog but trying to avoid saying too much about what had happened on the sixth fairway. This got plenty of play from the others though, and it took all that the Chair had to laugh heartily with the rest when the story of him and the two women came up. The minute the bus pulled out, he knew that his slicker had gone away with the woman, and for a moment he had a strong urge to chase after the bus in his car. This would have added fuel to the joke, and though he really hated to lose his slicker—a new one, with the same emblem he wore on his glove, that airy sphere carefully sewn into it above the pocket—he could not face extending the joke, and he let it go.

In twenty minutes it was totally clear again, the fog had crossed the narrow Cape and sat down on the beach on the bay side. Already there were bathers walking along the road and driving up toward the lighthouse. Some had left the bay when the fog came and would now use the beach on the sunny ocean side. The Chair called for attention and told the men the same things Sammy had told them out on the sixth. When he was finished, they all shuffled out of the clubhouse and went off in their clusters to resume play. When everyone had left, the Chair walked out. Chief Wingfoot was sitting on the park bench with the grip of his niblick on the ground, his hand resting on the club head. Sammy and Eddie were finishing the last stages of disconnecting the pull-carts.

"Okay, let's go," the Chair said, and he jerked at the handle of his cart and started across the road. In a couple of minutes, Sammy and Eddie caught up with him.

"Where the hell is Wall?" the Chair said. "Do you *know* where he is?"

"He set out ahead of us; he'll be over there," Eddie answered.

When they got to the sixth tee again, Wall was indeed there, waiting. He had come out early to look for the hang-glider and its flyer. He wondered what had happened when the man had drifted away from him, trying to pull the glider down in the fog. There was no evidence of the glider when Wall got back. The flyer had been a little scruffy and mean looking, and Wall had suspected some motive other than pleasure in his cruising along the cliff side.

Without any talk, the foursome hit off, resuming their play. The rest of the day went smoothly, but things were subdued. The Chair had little to say, and none of them played particularly well. They finished the eighteen holes at five-fifteen, a little later than usual. Two teams were in the clubhouse ahead of them, and one of these had ended with a plus five; they were the leaders, and when all the teams were in, at six o'clock, the plus five held for first place. Sammy and the Chair's team came in with a minus four, out of the money. Sammy had played poorly, shooting an eighty. Chair finished with an eighty-two, losing his private contest with Sammy. Wall and Eddie Costa had pretty much played to their handicaps. It was their play that had kept the team close to even.

When the tournament was over, most of the men left quickly. It was later than usual, and they wanted to get home and ready for dinner. Sammy had some clean-up work to do, and before the last man was out, he began to get to it. The Chair didn't linger. What little talk there was as the teams came in had more to do with the fog and the events prior to the break in play than with the golfing, and he didn't care to listen to this or participate in it; so before the last team was in, when he saw that already his foursome was out of the money, he made it known to anyone who was within earshot that he was leaving, and he left.

That evening, after he had finished dinner and it was getting dark, the Chair got his clubs out of the trunk of his car and took them down in the basement to clean them up. Fog had come in again. It had begun to rain, and the rain hit against the hubcap of his car into the small rectangle of the window high in the basement wall to the left of the workbench. He could hardly see out at all, and the light over the workbench seemed a little dimmer than usual. He was cleaning the grooves in the head of his five-wood with a small penknife, being careful not to cut into the wood itself, when it began to flood in on him. He had flashes of himself throwing his driver down the fairway, of his embarrassment and the silence of the others. He saw the huge white corset covering the breast of the woman whose dress he had ripped half off. He saw the Chief in the sling, his benign stare, and he shook his head, his rage rising. He saw the woman going away in the bus wearing his slicker. He heard the men laughing in the clubhouse, and he slumped. He heard Sammy giving instructions while he, the Chairman of the Golf Commission, stood by in ineffectual silence. He gripped the vise, his fingers hitting against the head of his five-wood, and he squeezed the unyielding steel. He looked down through the foggy haze in the darkening room and saw the drops of moisture on the waxed head of the club floating on the three white letters stamped above the face. *V I P* the club said. He began to shake and to weep in a high choking voice. The drops on the club head were joined by others in a small flood. He was addressing his ball on a fairway in a sudden rain. He was a boy, and they were laughing at him, and he had lost his jacket.

MOOD MUSIC

Sometimes in the early evenings, on days when it was slow, Sammy and Chip liked to get out and play a little Hit and Throw Ball, one of the games they had invented, Chip giving the names. On this particular day, one following four days of heavy rain and a week after what Chip had named Fog Day, the sky was bell-clear, the temperature warm and dry, and most everyone on the Cape had headed for the beaches, staying there for hours, a little glassy-eyed in wonder at the weather. In the later afternoon, as if by some plan, a lightly cool breeze had come up, very soft and just a little bracing, and most of the beachgoers, in sweet wonder exhaustion, had headed home for drinks, and evening cook-outs. A couple of foursomes, husbands and wives, had started out around four o'clock, but when they got to the sixth tee and saw the ocean from the high dune cliff, they could not help themselves. The second foursome joined the first one when they got there. They left their clubs standing like a strange committee in their hand carts around the tee and went through the brush to the sea perch and sat down, talking in low tones about the weather and the sea, counting the buoys on the lobster pots, making friends with each other.

For close to a month now, ever since the French Canadian campers, the weekenders, and the other summer tourists had been coming to Seaview Links in some numbers, Sammy had *The List* out and ready behind the counter. Sammy and Chip had started keeping it two summers before this one, writing down the most interesting questions the tourist-players asked, once they were out of sight. *The List* got longer, and only a few of the questions were the fake ones that Chip added, appending his name after them in parenthesis in his small clear hand.

THE LIST

1. Is this the golf course?
2. Are you open?

3. Where did you buy the rest room signs?
4. How do I stand?
5. Are you cutting the grass?
6. Do you sell charcoals here?
7. Do you sell fishhooks?
8. Do you believe me when I speak? (Chip)
9. Is the Coke good?
10. Is this the old building?
11. Is this the clubhouse?
12. Is this the right place?
13. If it rains, will I get wet? (Chip)
14. Do you rent balls?
15. Is that the ocean?
16. Can my friend walk with me? Can she hit my balls?
17. Are you a French Canadian too? *Sacrebleu!* (Chip)
18. Are you a native?
19. Are these the score cards?
20. Is that the foghorn?
21. Are there any places to eat?
22. How deep is the ocean? (Chip)
23. Is it going to rain?
24. How high is the sky? (Chip)
25. Can I wear golf shoes?
26. Does it get cold when it snows?
27. I'm from an elite club in Philadelphia. Can I play here?
28. Did anybody turn in a ball?
29. Are those wooden clubs old?
30. Do you remember anybody? (Chip)
31. Is this the bus stop?
32. What do you do when you play nine holes?
33. What are winter gloves?
34. Is this where you play golf?
35. Will you read this lighthouse? [The Chipper hands over a copy of JW tract to listener] (Chip)
36. Is the wind blowing?
37. Is it raining up here?
38. Do you have buffets?
39. Where is the ocean beach?

40. Who did that wonderful job on the aprons? (Chip)
41. Can we play in one bag?
42. Do you have little sticks to hit the ball off?
43. What do you do in the winter?
44. What kind of white bread is in the sandwiches?
45. Who is the best chipper on the course? (Chip)
46. Can I get married on the cliff?
47. Who makes the grass grow? (Chip)
48. Do you have to take a test to play?
49. What happens when it rains?
50. What happens when the fog comes in? (Chip)
51. Is that the lighthouse?
52. Am I right- or left-handed?

In Hit and Throw Ball, one made every other shot by chucking
the ball in the general direction of the green. If one was on the
green when a throw shot came up, one simply bowled the ball
at the cup. Sammy and Chip also played Cross Golf, Over and
Under, Change, Back Ball, and other invented variations. Chip
was waiting on the second tee, practicing his windup, when
Sammy drove up in a power cart. Ordinarily, on a day as slow
as this, Sammy would put his sign out on the door, but on this
day the Chair had come in to work at the handicap cards and
said he would watch things while Sammy went out to play. He
was very nice about offering to do it; it was that kind of day,
and ever since the Chair's encounters in the fog he had seemed a
little more relaxed, a little easier about himslf. Bob Days, an
electrician at the Air Force Station, was doing a little volunteer
wiring at the clubhouse and said he would watch out for things
too.

Sammy and Chip teed off, both electing to hit their first shots,
and when it came to the second, Chip winged his off into the
rough to the right of the fairway so that he could get to where
the blueberries were. After Sammy had thrown his and they had
had a friendly, joshing argument about whether Chip had thrown
his ball out of bounds, they both got their balls to the green. Chip
was one shot behind Sammy when they got there, so while Sammy
had a bowl, Chip had a putt. Sammy missed his bowl, complain-
ing that the green had not been well cut and that that had thrown

his ball off. Then they argued about the quality of Chip's work on and around the green, joking and trading insults. Chip said that nobody who dressed as bad as Sammy did had any right to complain about anything that had to do with quality or taste. Sammy retorted as how Chip might do a better job once he got out of Cape Tech and became an adult. Things went on this way until they, like the others before them, reached the sixth tee and saw the ocean. They could not help themselves either, and they went to the edge of the cliff, said hello to the husbands and wives, and sat and looked.

The beach was crowded, but those on it were as still and awe-struck as the ones sitting on the cliff above them. The only movement came from the curling of the edges of beach umbrellas in the breeze and the few children who played in quiet ways in the edge of surf. People sat in beach chairs looking out. Some stood, together or alone, facing the sea. It was so clear, the horizon at such a distance and yet a sharp clear line, that the sea seemed a contained massiveness, and as such dwarfed even the crowded beach, making it seem half empty. In the places between the colorful spread-out blankets and towels with the brown-and-white bodies lying on them, the sand was a clean tan, and where it joined the surf, it darkened and opened, untouched and running as far as they could see to the left, until it hit against the escarp-ment that moved up to the promontory where the hard white lighthouse stood. Gentle and foamy whitecaps kept the children back, and beyond them the water turned blue, and as it went out and deepened it became emerald green. About two hundred yards out there was a finger of seaweed rising and shifting and lowering in the swell, and beyond the weed, where the water was blue again, long lines of variously colored lobster-pot buoys were bobbing.

The whales' river appeared so gradually that the watchers on the beach took no notice of it. Those on the cliff saw it coming, a broad white line of gentle turbulence snaking from beyond the promontory on which the lighthouse stood and stretching a good two miles before them, well to the other side of the pots. Then they saw the backs, the dark islands rising, lingering in slow movement along the coast, and sinking again. There was a glitter-

the air above the whales' river: gulls and terns riding
s, diving occasionally in the whales' wake, lifting the
bait fish that were stirred to the surface. The two lines, of whales
and birds, continued far out, moving parallel to shore, and after
they had passed a mile off to the right, they turned and headed
seaward in the direction of Europe. When the drama was over,
the watchers leaned back on the cliff's edge, realizing they had
been tensed by the sight. The sea continued as if nothing at all
had happened. Below where the whales had been were the ship-
wrecked hulls the comers to the New World had left. On a day
like this, they might have risen to the surface and moved leisurely
in to the shore. Today, there was a Japanese factory boat in the
far distance, it was working the water with its indiscriminate
nets. Two boats steamed around the lighthouse point and began
pulling the lobster pots. There were no pleasure crafts on the sea,
and this seemed right. Everything was serious, unconcerned, and
real.

Back at the clubhouse, the Chair finished up with the handicap
cards, got a cup of coffee, and went into the pro shop to see if
there was anything he could use his holdover winnings from last
season to buy. Bob Days was there, working on a bad connection,
and while the Chair checked out the shirts with the alligators on
them and the various versions of the golf cap, they chatted about
nothing in particular, and both of them greeted Barney Packett,
another enlisted man, when he came in with four cases of beer
he had gotten at the P.X. and fed the refrigerator in the small
snack-bar area.

In the middle of the eighth fairway, across from the short
ninth and the clubhouse, seven Canadian geese were moving
around and pecking in the grass. They had drifted in at three in
the afternoon. The adults were fat and sleek, and the young kept
close to them. A few terns and a crane in from the edge of the
sea moved inland lightly at times, the crane dropping down for
a few moments to find food, then lifting away and sailing. From
where the Chair stood at the window, he could see the whole of
the short ninth fairway, from the tee to the two-tiered green
only a few yards from the clubhouse to his right. The fairway
was shaded a little by the building and the three pines standing
back near Chief Wingfoot's park bench. John Reuss and Tony

Worthington were lazily practicing on the ninth in the crisp air, and the Chair watched them. They would each hit a few balls from the tee, then stroll up and chip the ones that had landed around the green. When all the balls were on the green, they would putt the longest ones, joking and laughing lightly when a difficult one fell in the hole or came close. The two were in their early eighties. They had fine, casual, almost second-nature chip shots. Their game was very relaxed and very sure. They drove the short green not with conventional wedges but with low straight pitch-and-run shots, trickling their balls up through the fringe, rolling them into good positions on the green. Their clubs were old and well used. They fit their hands like good and familiar tools.

While the Chair was watching, Eddie Costa came into vision from the parking area and greeted the two players and joined them. Eddie was wearing baggy work pants and a bright red shirt. John and Tony joked about his shirt, smiling and nodding to one another. The three laughed, and Eddie dropped a couple of balls on the green and putted them.

By the time Chip and Sammy were back to the path across the road from the clubhouse, five others had joined the three in their practice on the ninth hole, and the Chair was getting ready to go out there himself. The sun was moving away, but it was still very pleasant and dry, and the light breeze had shifted to the bay side, toned down a bit, and became warmer. Bob Days had finished his electrical work and had gone out to sit on the park bench and watch the casual players. Some of them were not playing at all but were standing around, joshing the others occasionally and talking, their putters and irons hanging along their sides, an occasional can of beer in hand.

As Sammy and Chip got to the road, a large silver Cadillac with Texas plates drove slowly in front of them, heading up to the parking area at the lighthouse. A man and a woman were in the front seat, both wearing cowboy hats.

"Hey! That was Roy Rogers in that car!" Chip sang out, grabbing Sammy by the arm and pointing after it.

"Texas plates, a Cadillac, and those hats," Sammy said, "but that was *not* Roy Rogers."

"Yes it was!" Chip said, "Yes it was! Old Roy and Dale on the move! Rhythm away from the range! Good old Roy and Dale for sure!" And he dropped Sammy's arm and trotted off up the road after the car.

"Roy Rogers, my ass," Sammy said to himself, shaking his head and smiling, watching Chip trot up the road, slapping his thighs in little-boy horse-riding-play fashion. Then he crossed the road and went into the clubhouse, where he saw the Chair taking a seven-iron and a putter out of the club rack in the pro shop.

"What's up, Chair?" he said, still smiling.

"Going out back to hit a few," the Chair answered, "no business while you were gone. Have a good round?"

"Okay, Chair. Hey, see you out there in a minute."

Sammy went into the pro shop as the Chair left it, and by the time he got to the window and saw the crew gathered out on the ninth, the Chair had come around the side of the building and was already greeting this one and that one, asking about wives, children, putts and iron shots, complimenting and judging. Sammy went back to the cash register, checked the day's receipts, and locked it. Then he got a beer from the refrigerator and headed out the door himself. Before he could go around the building, the Texas Cadillac pulled up in one of the parking places next to the clubhouse and Chip hopped out of the back door. He was grinning and winking; he opened the door on the driver's side, and a rather short and broad Texan got out.

"Sammy, this here is Bobby Lee Bando," Chip said, "and this here is Melda Bando." He indicated the rather squat woman in the squaw dress who got out of the other door. Sammy noticed the woman did look a little like Dale Evans, but he could see nothing of Roy Rogers in the man.

"Hi," he said, and the man extended his hand.

"How you be?" the man said. "Nice spread you got here. Course looks good. Is it on the pro tour?" His wife smiled and looked around, nodding in agreement with her husband's comment. Sammy glanced at Chip. They both figured they would have to get that pro tour question on *The List*. Chip was a little off to the side and behind the Texans. Sammy could see him bobbing and winking, making furtive gestures.

"No, not on the tour yet," Sammy said. "Come a long way?"

"All the way from Texas," Bobby Lee Bando answered. "All right to look around a spell? Maybe hit a few?"

"Just closing," Sammy said, "but you're welcome to come out back and chip a bit."

Chip jumped a little when he heard Sammy's offer, and he stepped up and took the man and the woman by the arm, putting himself between them, and led them behind the clubhouse to where the others were gathered. Sammy was watching Chip introduce the two around when he heard a loud sputtering motor. He turned to the road and saw Manny Corea pull his old pickup into a parking place beside the Caddy.

"Hey, Manny!" he said as he went to the truck. Manny indicated the truck bed with his head, and when Sammy looked he saw four good-sized buckets, two of mussels and two of quahogs, in the back.

"Can you use these?" Manny asked him.

"Hell yes!" Sammy said, "let's take 'em around back," and the two lifted the cans out of the truck bed and carried them over to the park bench where Bob Days was sitting.

The day was beginning to fade away, and the shadows of the three pines were extending over the fairway and touching the edges of the green. The Canadian geese were still pecking over on the eighth, but they were hard put to find patches of sunlight in which to shine. Though some of the men still pitched and putted, most were by this time standing in small groups and talking. A few came over to see what was in the buckets. Chip was herding the two Texans from group to group, and when the shellfish appeared, he brought them over to the park bench. They had not seen quahogs before, and Melda Bando wondered if they were good to eat. The men standing around the buckets assured her that they were better than that even, and Manny Corea suggested that they steam them up in the clubhouse.

"Anybody for mussels and chokers?" Sammy yelled out to the crew on the fairway and green, and he was answered with assenting calls. Bob Days said he would fix some lights, and he went to his truck. Bobby Lee Bando said he had some music, one hell of a stereo tapedeck in his Caddy, and while Bob Days hooked up some spots and floods and fixed them to the trees,

Bobby Lee went to his car to select tapes. Chip and Sammy went in and put two of the buckets up to steam on the small stove in the snack-bar area. When they got inside and were alone, Chip let his agitation go.

"That's him! Old Roy!" he said, "That's him! That's him!"

"Hell, look at how short and fat he is," Sammy said, "that's not him."

"He's in *disguise!*" Chip said. "Traveling *in*cognito! But pretty old Dale can't hide her cowgirl charms and beauty! That's *her*, did'ya see her?!"

"Looks like her," Sammy said, "but, hell, that's not her."

"Old Roy and Dale. Who-ha!" said Chip.

"You're nuts," Sammy said, getting the buckets of shellfish going over the flame.

"Come here!" said Chip. "Watch this!" and he pulled the mildly protesting Sammy over to the door of the clubhouse, stuck his head out, and yelled.

"Trigger!"

Bobby Lee Bando was on the front seat of the Caddy with the door standing open, going through the tapes. When he heard the sharp yell, his head jerked up. Chip ducked back into the clubhouse, dancing around.

"See that! See that! Sound of the old hoss name! *Dear* old Trigger! Those little pistolas along his snout, stuffed and waiting for *re*-incarnation! My, oh my! Old Roy and Dale at Seaview!"

"Okay," Sammy said, "I give up."

They fixed the mussels and quahogs, adding some white wine to the broth and a few herbs that somebody managed to come up with. Bob Days got the lights up and on and carefully adjusted so that they lit the bench, the green, and a part of the fairway. Earl came in from his mowing, got his gallon jug of iced tea out, and joined the group. Bobby Lee Bando put a quiet Neil Hefti tape in the deck, with a Frank Sinatra backup. Chip was surprised at Roy's choice of music, but figured him for a low profile. The cases of beer were brought out to the park bench. A few of the men's wives, wondering why they had not come home, showed up and joined in. Chip and Melda Bando were the first to dance. They did a slow foxtrot, very gracefully and with considerable skill, around the flagstick on the lighted green. Eddie Costa grabbed his wife and joined the couple, but he kept just below the apron on the fringe, not wanting to spoil the green's integrity. They ate the shellfish and drank the beer. A small cluster of men, with the Chair at their center, practiced and talked about various short-chip techniques in the middle of the fairway, at the edge of the lighted place. Bobby Lee Bando showed them a Texas grip he knew.

It got darker, and the lights created a kind of lawn party atmosphere, a lighted space with the slight mystery of the encroaching darkness held back. The tapedeck floated Frank Sinatra's "Nancy" over the various grasses and the trees. The geese, what few were left, quietly honked in response to Frank's singing. The owner of the nearby Exxon station and his wife, who took a lighthouse drive each evening, saw the activity and stopped and joined in. They were excellent dancers, and their turns on the green were admired by all.

There was a chipping contest. Sammy talked about the whales and saving them and handed out a few bumper-stickers. Chip talked to a few men about various green-maintenance techniques that he had learned in school. Melda Bando talked to the women about Texas chili. Manny Corea told the story of the mussel find. The Chair's poses and gestures were subtle and abbreviated and unobtrusive. He felt calm and peaceful. His wife came, and he danced with her. They did a simple two-step. Chief Wingfoot came over and sat in the shadows above the green, beyond the play, and watched. Sammy brought him a bowl of quahogs. Eddie Costa sang an old Portuguese fishing song. They all loved hearing it, but he refused to translate it, saying that that would not do at all. The women gave Melda Bando recipes for kale soup.

It was a clear night, and the lighthouse was dark and silent; no warnings were necessary. Out beyond its softened whiteness, the lights of a few boats glimmered on the sea, a mile away. The surf washed almost inaudibly on the sand, sparks of phosphorous in its gentle wake. The last of the day retired, and the stars came out. Frank Sinatra sang his songs again into the night. The people moved in loose and changing clusters, talking, laughing softly, and listening. The party continued, sweetly, until after twelve.

Sammy took the last dance with Melda Bando. The two drifted formally across the green. Everyone became silent and watched them. When the song ended, a light applause rose up. The dancers bowed and smiled. When the party ended, they all went home knowing they would sleep peacefully when they got there. Once they were gone, Chief Wingfoot rose from the grass and stretched. Then he followed the throb of the underground river, Tashmuit, heading home in the dark. A light mist developed out over the sea, and the lighthouse began its sweep, its beam touching the tops of the trees and the roof caps of the clubhouse. The air was perfectly still. The course, under the warning beam, was safe in darkness. And it was quiet at Seaview, there on the edge of America.

Part Three

THE HIVE

He woke to discover he was standing at the edge of a cliff, looking at something. In the lingering tail-end rush of the cocaine,
there had been two women in his head, one silver and one gold,
and both severely battered. They were tall and pubescent and
very thin, and he had shaved the head of the silver one and driven
a slightly domed thumbtack through the flesh in the side of her
nose. The head of the tack was black lacquer, and where she reclined, naked like the other, she had been placed with cheek on
biceps, her arm extended with palm open, face tilted to keep the
tack's placement, lest it should fall away. He had left the hair on
the gold one. In places it was matted and twisted from perspiration; where it was dry it was strawlike, black at its roots and
heavily peroxided. He had placed a ring of barbed wire in an
anklet above her foot. This he saw as a kind of taming that had
something to do with animals and America. It had been the first
time for both of them, but he had known that they had the experience in their monads, and he had cracked them like geodes,
with his instruments opening the hollow crystal cores to the dark.
A bicycle chain, a small surgical bone saw, a diamond-head
needleholder, a blunt sand wedge, four atraumatic needles, a
shackle, a pair of pliers, his wet towel, four dilators, blunt and
sharp curettes.

Except for the velvet-covered platform on which they lay, the
room itself was not dark. It was the center of a glowing hive with
a chamber at the core. The chamber was like the inside of a
geodesic dome or a massive, hollow golf ball. Extending up from
the platform on the circular floor, the walls to the apex were a
grid of small, square openings, the mouths of narrow ducts
through which women were trying to enter. He stood next to
the dark platform, watching them. In various places, and in a
kind of swelling and receding rhythmic pattern, their heads darted
into the chamber or came in slowly through the squares, thrust-
ing for entrance. But the squares were too small to allow their
shoulders to pass, and they thudded and bounced back, then

darted and moved in, trying again and again. In one place a woman had managed to thrust her arm through an opening; her shoulder pressed against her agonized head at the ear, her sharp earring slicing her flesh; her arm was extended like a battering ram, in the position of a body surfer on the crest of a wave, her fingers snapping and waving and beckoning to him, her red mouth contorted, black eyes blazing. In other places the women had given up and took their lust and ambition in looking. Their heads pushed in as far as they could get them, they craned their necks and strained hard to see him and the two on the dark platform. They avoided the eyes in the heads of those in the other openings across the chamber.

He had a device with buttons in his hand, and the buttons controlled the sliding doors that could close off the glowing hive openings individually. He had ways of making his selection, and he would push buttons to activate the slow sliding, and the heads would reluctantly recede from the openings as the doors came down from above. At times the adamant would not give it up easily. The doors would press their necks like soft, slow guillotines, and only when the pressure was convincing enough would they wiggle their heads free and recede as the doors closed down. With these adamant ones he would only open the doors again when he judged that the pounding of the heads against them had caused sufficient pain and frustration. At the heart of his pleasure was the knowing that what the women desired was less the activity on the dark platform than the culmination and stasis of what he had done there. The gold one was patterned with silver cuts that were pink lipped, and with hot silver stripes. The silver one had the shapes of small copper cymbals ringing on her shoulders, her back, and her thighs. The two were unconscious and slightly entwined on the purple surface. He felt peace in their posture. If one lifted any part of her body, he would put her to rest again.

She was in the car in the parking lot at the foot of the thick shaft of the lighthouse, where he had told her to wait for him. She was neither silver nor gold, and there were no spaces on her body that he could think of as virginal, nothing for him to touch into that way; it was scars over scar tissue, a surfeit of a kind of knowledge. He did not bring her with him, and when he reached near the cliff edge, he turned away from it and watched the shadows darken and cut cavities into the fairways and the slopes of rough as the sun left them. Clear across the course, before the sun finished, he saw a hard glinting off large white objects, three of them in a cluster on the far side. Turning back, it was the feminine moon he woke to, half axed away and the color of tarnished brass, to see it moving into a black cloud, and the stars that looked to him like pulsing tattoo needles, puncturing through the skin of the dark sky. He stood erect and singular, totally unaware of the limiting romance of his perceptions and the melodrama of his visions. If there were things going on at the lighthouse or down the beach below him where a small fire flickered, he was apart from it. If the action of the moon had been a slow camera shutter, closing, he was not the one involved in the activity photographed but was standing to the side, looking into the lens. He wore a Western leather vest, tight Levis, and black leather tennis shoes. His pendant was a thick gold chain with a large coinlike object at the end of it. On the face of the object was an etched figure of small wires and rods that formed a rough circle, a complex matrix. His shoulder brushed the wood of the barricade that kept him back from the cliff's lip, an erosion-control device. He kicked the wood firmly, and bits of sand fell away at the edge.

In the morning after the miniature golf game, they had packed up and headed north. Melinda had thought of the small bird freed from the snake's jaws and its possible whereabouts and fortunes for over a hundred miles of travel, but in the end she came to suspect that Bob White was correct. Regardless of what final mystery might remain, it had most probably come to its end, and that was now over, and the way was no longer important. Wherever it was it was at peace now. And so she turned her thoughts to the traveling, and in turning from the bird, she turned from the way of her own ending. She knew the place of it, was fairly certain about the timing. The passage of the car now stirred up grasses symmetrically along the roadside, and she watched these waves for a while, dozing at times and awakening in a kind of sureness of comfort to find them continuing and unchanged. They put on considerable mileage that day, steadily working their way north, and they were up early the next morning and on the road again. In the late afternoon, after passing Niagara Falls, they moved through the outskirts of Lockport and pulled into a motel near Albion. After loading their gear into the adjoining rooms, Bob White excused himself, said he would be back shortly.

"Got to phone some boys back in Niagara."

When he returned, Allen had some ice waiting in a plastic bucket, a quart of J&B on the table beside it. They filled up motel glasses with Scotch and water for two. Melinda took hers neat, and she and Bob White talked quietly over their drinks, while Allen took a look at the lay of the land in his *Golf Digest* encyclopedia. After they had had their drinks, and Allen and Bob White had gotten them some sandwiches, they sat on bed and chair eating. Allen suggested they might want to stay there for the next day and rest up, and maybe Melinda and Bob White would like to look around a bit. Bob White agreed, and Melinda smiled and nodded.

"You found a good possibility, huh?"

"Yeah," he laughed, "I think I did. Pretty good-sized private club. Looks quite tight: a lot of water, Scottish-type rough and fairways. Do you mind?"

"No, no," she said, "why rush it? I'm tired too. And I could go for a little rest and maybe some sightseeing."

"Fine. You can drop me off in the morning. I'll find a way back," Allen said.

They dropped him off in the morning and went about their business. There was a farmer's market fair nearby in Medina. Melinda and Bob White drove there and took pleasure in seeing the prize vegetables and smelling them. They bought some peaches and a couple of good-looking apples, a bunch of red cherries, three nectarines, and a stalk of sweet grapes and found a nice park in the heart of the town, near the city hall, and made a picnic. When they were finished eating, they drove out of town to a winery they had learned of from a brochure in the motel room. Melinda did the driving, and Bob White sat over by the door, a little half turned toward her, watching her hands on the wheel.

The winery had an odd, heavily stained wooden building for a tasting room. It looked like some kind of cathedral, and they stood at the counter in the high-vaulted central room inside of it, tasting various wines. The wines were just okay, nowhere near as good as what Allen and Melinda had gotten in California while they were there. These were fruitier, closer to the land, and a little raw. There was a meadow and a lot of hilly land behind the cathedral, and there were a couple of picnic benches out there and a stand of thick trees. They sat in the sun, and Bob White showed her how he could make a pennywhistle out of a twig he had found at the foot of one of the trees. They handed the whistle back and forth between them, playing and testing each other with the identification of simple tunes. Melinda pointed out the way the sunlight hit among the trees, the way of the shadows there, and how she would go about doing them in charcoal. As she spoke her fingers moved in the remembered gestures. She itched a little for it, but not much. She knew she now saw better than when she had tried hard to see while drawing and doing pastels, and she felt it was the seeing that had been the point all along; she didn't need to render it anymore.

When Bob White moved closer to her on the bench and put his arm around her, first putting his large hand on the side of her face and pressing it down to his shoulder, then holding her shoulder firm in his palm, she was not startled, nor did she feel uncomfortable in the embrace. His lips were a little sticky with wine, and when he kissed the top of her head and withdrew his mouth, a few hairs came away, and he used his free hand to remove them from his mouth. He didn't feel like a father or a brother to her, but he was not embracing her as a priest might or a lover either. She couldn't give a name to the quality of the touch. She realized that she could make love with him and that he would be wise about her illness and how weak she was. It would not be exactly passionate, but it would be as if passion were a kind of guarding prevention against intimacy. What they would do together would be much deeper than passion; it would not take physical stamina but would take a kind of effort that she was incapable of because of her weakness. He seemed to know something like this too, and though neither of them did anything with their bodies in contact that was translatable into an understanding, there was a kind of knowledge between them. When, after a few long moments, he did speak to her, she realized how much she needed the very fact of speaking and the words as well. She needed very little quantity anymore when it came to the larger scheme of things, but what Allen could not quite bring himself to say had started to become an absence to her in her self-involved state.

There was a family at one of the other benches, about fifty yards away, and some birds and a dog had put their song and motion into evidence. There was the occasional sound of tires on gravel in the parking lot on the other side of the cathedral and a steady, almost subliminal hum from the distant highway. It was as if a previously hidden empty space in her had revealed itself, begun to ache, and then been salved to fullness and closure all at the same time in the quick process in which he slowly touched and moved her and began to speak.

There's a place downtown Jerome, Arizona, up above the post office on the main street there. It's open there, a kind of upper-level courtyard, with pillars and six benches, where you can sit and watch the traffic, and if you look up and across and up a little more you can see parts of the sky from those sitting places. I used to sit there when I was a boy. I lived over there for a little bit. The old, retired miners from Jerome copper mine used to sit there also. They waited for their checks there. The checks would come down below in the post office, and from up above there they could see the truck coming with the mail and their checks. When the trucks would go out of sight up close to the building under them, they would wait a while, and then they would go down to their boxes and get their checks. And so I would sit there with them, usually five or more of them at a time, though sometimes less. They would cough and spit a lot. There were spittoons up there to the sides of the benches. These old men had that lung disease, and I think that they sat up there because they found it hard to get used to being inside a structure and still being able to see pieces of the sky and the other things outside. There were no windows in the mine to speak of. Maybe they liked to sit there and thought they would get used to what happened for them when they did it if they did it long enough.

It's maybe six months that I did that, and the old men would come and go. When they didn't come on the right dates, I guess

I kind of figured that something must have come up. When they didn't come for quite a while, I guess I figured that they wouldn't be coming there again. I guess I was right about that. One time there was a period of time when an old Chinese-type fellow was coming there. He was very old, and he had a braid down the middle of his back. The braid was very thin, and he didn't have too much hair in it. He did about the same amount of coughing and spitting as all the others. His coughs, however, used to really rattle a lot in his throat, and when there were other old men up there with us, they didn't seem to like to look his way too much. That old man looked at me a lot those times, and he looked at other things a lot too. There was a cat that came up there sometimes, and he looked at that cat a lot. He looked a lot and closely at people who came up there who were not old men, and when people stood in a window across the street from the benches, on the second floor, he would look closely at them also. He didn't spend much time looking at the sky above. One day his looking got to me in some way. He was on the same bench I was on, and I spoke to him.

Now I was young and somewhat arrogant in that time, and I spoke to people who I did not fear somewhat sharply at times. That way of speaking I guess had become a habit, and though I didn't mean to do so, my speaking came out sharply when I spoke to that old Chinese man. What are you looking at, old man? I said. He had been looking past me at a young woman who had come up there to get some air and was leaning against the railing that surrounded the courtyard, her face and chest pushed out, watching in the windows across the street. He could see the side of her body and the side of her face from the way she was standing. I thought this was so, since I had looked over at her myself, and she had been standing that way for quite a while, and I thought she was still like she had been. He looked away from her when I spoke and looked at my face. From the way we were, he didn't have to move his head. He only had to shift his eyes a bit. He coughed a little and swallowed. His rattle was rather quiet that time. It was like hollow sticks hitting each other if you hung them in a tree in the breeze by fishline. That's a thing to do to keep certain birds away.

Well, I was looking at the face of that woman, young man,

way she puts her body when she stands there, he said. Now I'm looking at your face. Lookie here, he said. And he reached into his baggy trousers and took out a brown envelope with a window in it. I thought it was one of the envelopes that they delivered the old men's checks in. From inside of the envelope he took out about a couple of old pictures. Two were photographs of a kind they used to take a while ago, and one was a new kind of color one. Lookie here, he said, and he handed the pictures to me. The two older ones were not as old as I thought they were. They were pictures of him taken maybe ten years before that time. He was standing with a couple of other men, in his mine gear, in front of the dark mouth of a mine shaft. The other one was more recent. He was alone in that one. Behind him were trees with sky above them; he was wearing Sunday clothes.

He just sat there and looked at me while I looked at the pictures, and after a while I started to feel a little fidgety, and I said to him, I don't understand this business. Well, it's this way, he said. You see the way I'm standing in that one, kind of leaning forward, pushing my face out at the camera? Now look at that young woman over there. You see what I mean? Now you can't see it, but in this other one I've got a face on that's somewhat like your face is when you sit up here and look around. Now we don't look alike, you know, and I don't look like that young woman. But we've all got these ways of standing and looking around inside of us somewhere.

I thought he was going to continue on there, but he didn't. He just stopped talking and looked at my face. I began to get it then. I looked back at the pictures and at the young woman, and I could see it. And I could remember seeing my own face in a mirror, and when I looked up at him, he put his face to the side, so that I could see his cheek and the curve of his nose, and he squinted out a bit. This last move of his was a little funny, but it was not really so. I could really see what he meant. He was copying me looking around, but I got it that he couldn't have done that if he hadn't had the way of doing it inside of him when he did it.

Now look around, Melinda dear. You can find a gesture of yours, or a way of setting your head, or a hand manner while talking. Maybe in that man over there or those two kids playing around there. Maybe that dog does something familiar to you that you might have done, that can give you a laugh or two. When dogs run in packs sometimes in summer evenings, sniffing around and going into yards and gathering, inquisitive beyond their good reason, they might do what you did as a child way back and maybe you can see something in it. And though it might seem farfetched to say it, it may be there are things to find that are going to stay here a while after you are no longer staying here even in these trees around here and the way maybe some of the stones here have been made as they are over time by the same kinds of things that contacted you during this time that you've been here: sun, wind, cold weather, saltwater. That is a long thing to say, and it winds me, but maybe now you could look up here and into my face some.

She did look into his face then, lifting hers from his shoulder. She had been looking where he suggested by his words that she look as he spoke to her. She turned some in her seat, facing him, and he released her but kept his hand on her shoulder, his forearm touching her neck. When her eyes got to where his face was, he smiled slightly, and then he slowly turned his head to the side, into profile. He kept his eyes in her eyes as he moved his head, making sure that she was watching, only releasing them when his head was almost fully turned. Then he pursed his lips and raised his chin a little. It was a thing she did often, she realized, when she saw him do it, when she was looking at things she felt some mild disapproval about, and as he did it she laughed lightly in a warbling way, pressing back against his forearm with her neck. Then, without turning his head back, he lifted his other hand from his lap and placed a finger beside his nose and slowly traced an age line that ran from it down to the corner of his pursed mouth. She lifted her own hand and felt a similar line in her own cheek, shallower and less mature, but running the same way. Then he turned back to her.

This time he lifted his brows slightly, causing small furrows to appear on his forehead. He sucked his nostrils in a little and raised the left eyebrow slightly higher than the right: things that she did, she realized, in moments before she broke into laughter. His left hand came up, and she saw that he was touching the tip of his thumb against the tip of his middle finger, moving them slightly together and apart. She knew she did this thing also on some occasions, but she was startled to find that they had not always been in private. He disengaged himself from her and got up and stood very straight in front of her. Then he let his shoulders slump and become rounded, his back slightly bowed, and he put one foot in front of the other, resting his weight on the straight stiff leg.

"It is the way you stand waiting," he whispered, and then he turned to the side to give her her posture in profile. "It is some possible way to stand, and I will continue it for you," he said. "Look over now at the way that little girl is standing. It is not so different either." Then he sat down beside her, and he leaned over close to her and looked in her face. "Do you see it, now?" he said. The sides of her mouth came up in a smile, and she nodded. She did see it, and she felt a welling up, but not of tears this time. There had been no tears since the miniature golf game, and she knew that tears had ended there with the thoughts of the fortunes of the little bird.

There was a welling up from the core itself. Something had broken, had opened like a stone object containing a geode. A kind of impacted air had left the core, and she could feel it pushing a few of her alveoli open again. The air left her in a silent rush, and when she breathed inward it was with some force now, because there was a place for the incoming breath to reside, and she felt in a way strong again, though she knew at the same time that the strength, though not illusory, was temporary in her body, even if it be permanent in her mind. It was strength, simply and almost embarrassingly in its melodrama, in the real knowledge of immortality and what that was about, that he had just brought to her—that she would continue on in him in that way and in the little girl and in the dog and in the stones and in the trees. She could now be both more and less than she was. Less, in that what had left her had been ego, but only that, and it was exhilarating to discover that it was only a kind of air, defined only as place and otherwise insubstantial. Its going disoriented her a little, and she had to put her hand under the seat of the bench to stay where she was. The more she would be now was obvious and unspeakable, and she knew it was not something that would be fruitful to discuss with Allen. Her remaining course was to let it just be in her and *be* her. Looking up from Bob White's eyes to his familiar brow and on over to the close-gathered family at the other bench, she saw how the bench itself, though processed, had its cuts and lines, its places of weathering, and how it was momentary center to the family, the occasion for lunch out under the sun this midweek outing.

The father spoke to the son. The mother handled something that the daughter had brought to her from the ground. It was all very tight and exclusionary, but Melinda knew that were she to catch any one of them alone, and had enough time to watch, things of herself would occur in action or become manifest in repose. And knowing this with such certainty that brought her comfort, she quit both the fantasy and the knowledge and came back firmly to the place she was sitting. She released the bench. She touched Bob White on the knee.

"What do you say, time to get back to Allen?"

"I do suppose it's about that time," he said. And he got up again and helped her to her feet. She was very light, and her eyes were energetic and crystal clear, but her legs were weak and she felt pain in her stomach when she rose and had to slump and lean against him. And then they walked, with arms holding arms and bodies brushing and touching, across the low meadow toward the wine cathedral.

The father and mother of the family at the redwood table saw them going. They did not speak to each other about it. The mother's hand moved back and forth over the ripples in the grain of the tabletop. Both of them saw that the man was quite a bit older than the woman, that he was possibly a Mexican or something else foreign, and that she was white though dark-skinned. They thought they were lovers and ordinarily would have had bad feelings about this. But there was something in the way the man and woman walked and touched against each other that they could not find it in themselves to feel anger or disapproval. They both liked looking at the backs of their bodies as they strolled away.

It was not so much the shot itself, a difficult fade around a stand of trees, that gave him pleasure as the realization which came to him when he considered it and then got ready to hit. It was a strange pleasure, not unmixed with a little growing pain. He had been thinking of Melinda all through the round. There had been no gambling possible. He was feeling a little guilty about leaving her with Bob White, and though he tried to chalk it up to conventional husband's golf-playing guilt, he knew how pathetic his attempt was and that that was not it at all. It had more to do with privateness, the intensity of this exclusionary involvement.

It may have been the sight of the goofy wishing well in the middle of the fairway that he kept catching out of the corner of his eye as he considered his shot. Whatever it was, a sense of the silliness of playing golf came to him. Why don't I just drive this fucker off into the trees on the other side and be done with it, he thought as he sighted around the bend. Maybe I could chip it into that wishing well and forget it. But the pleasure came in knowing that he probably could get it in the well, could probably knock it just where he wanted it to go in the trees, and that he had a very good possibility of getting it to the green too. He could fail at all three, of course, and of course that was of essential importance. What enriched the pleasure was the thought that he could manage to say fuck it to his other involvements too. He could just walk away and be done with that matrix as well.

This realization of choice had not occurred to him before, and he saw as he thought of it how obsessive and locked in he must have been not to have thought of it. He learned a little something about himself, and once past the learning he felt very loose and what he might have called free. The shot itself seemed almost perfunctory, though it really wasn't. It was the result of the thoughts that passed through him before he hit it that gave him room for the kind of intensity he needed to hit it correctly. He used his three-wood, altered his stance slightly, and sent it around the trees, low and very tight and swift. It carried the trap and the flagstick, hit against the slight upslope of the back of the green, bit in, trickled up, and stopped about ten yards from the hole. The two men with him applauded and yelled loudly. He bowed to them and tipped his cap. Somewhere deep in him he realized the pathetic nature of the thing. He wanted very badly to get back to Melinda, and the want felt very good to him. When he got to the green, he sank his rather long, downhill putt for an eagle.

They got to the Cape around noon and headed down the highway that ran along its center. They could see neither the bay nor the ocean from the road, but they could smell the salt in the air and taste it, and they didn't feel landlocked. Melinda sat in the corner of the backseat and looked out of the window at the familiarity of trees and shrubs. Bob White sat at the door in front, looking at the Cape map, making provisional markings on it with a pencil. He touched the point of the pencil to his tongue often before making his marks. He was wearing glasses, and neither Allen nor Melinda remembered seeing him wear them before. When they got down the Cape to Seaview, Melinda said, "Here we are." She said it almost inaudibly, but both of the men heard her and did not speak.

"If you'll take the next road off to the left there, that would be good," she said. Allen took the road, slowed down considerably, and waited for Melinda to give further directions. She told him to just keep going, and then, when they came to it, she told him to make a sharp left. They entered a curving blacktop road that ran between fairly high pines. After about a half-mile, the road climbed up out of the small pine forest and continued along the crest of a low hill. The land now was very open and rolling, and they could see the bay about two miles away over gradually lowering moors. The road ran between houses on both sides. The houses were well apart, set on parcels of land each more than an acre in size.

"Over there," she said, and Allen pulled up across from a simple white house with green shutters and a split-rail fence running in front of it. There was no life apparent through the windows, but they could see the edge of a children's metal swing set in the backyard. The yard in front was very well kept, almost meticulous in its rows of slate walks and planted beach roses, day lilies, and heather. The clapboard on the front of the house looked freshly painted, and the roof had been recently shingled with new cedar shakes.

"Looks very well kept," Melinda whispered from her place in the back seat.

"It does that," Allen answered.

"It's a beautiful house," Bob White said, "a very good place for a young girl to grow to be a woman. Something nice to remember and think about."

"Oh, it was all right, I guess, really not bad at all," Melinda said, and then after a few moments, "I guess we can go now."

"But look at that honeysuckle blooming and that juniper over there. Been around for a while I'd guess," Bob White said.

"Yes, it was there," Melinda said after a moment. And they sat in the car across from the house for a few more minutes.

"Guess it's time to go?" Melinda said after a time.

"It's time," Bob White said, and Allen pulled slowly away, Melinda turning in the backseat, watching the house recede, then disappear as the car sloped down again and entered another small forest.

He came up and sat back in his chair when he was finished packing. The duffle was a small, tight bundle at his feet, the mouth rolled in and the cloth handle on top. They both had watched his economical movements and his sureness about the placement of things, and they had watched with an intensity that neither of them was aware of, so that the packing seemed to take a very long time, broken into such small increments, though he had accomplished it in only a few minutes. Allen felt there was something to be said now that he had finished and was ready to go, but Melinda did not have such a feeling.

"Well, time to go," Bob White said, and he stood up and took his time looking over at both of them. Melinda smiled at him and nodded, and Allen took a step toward him, lifted his hand, and spoke as he took Bob White's hand.

"Well, thanks for the company, the snake dinner, and the rest of it," he said, and he shook Bob White's hand for a long time, not wanting to let it go, but he did when Bob White released him. The Indian walked over to the motel room's sliding doors, reached behind the wisps of curtain, and pushed one of the panels aside. He turned back to them and smiled before stepping out.

"It has been my pleasure," he said. "You have my letter? I appreciate your kindness, and I say good-by now." Melinda smiled, lifting her body from the bathroom doorframe where she had been leaning.

He stepped behind the veil of the thin curtain, and they could see his shadow, his arm coming up, as he slid the glass door closed again. They heard him crunching across the gravel as he left them, and then they were alone again and together. They were silent, and they didn't speak to each other for a long time. They both knew that the nature of the closure would take a while. They had a while, and they silently agreed to let it happen in its own good time.

My Dear Melinda & Allen,

Now that I have written and look back to correct I see that I have spoken more than I had intended. There are things we have to shake ourselves free of in time. Life is one of them, fancy talk is another. Perhaps it is in the body only that we come to live. Closing in on death and other intensities is where we can best do it. The search for lost things is hindered by routine habits, and that is why it is so difficult to find them. This last sentence is not mine. I read it somewhere, but I have come to see in the words of it the kind of message that I would presume to send you as I am leaving. Let the routines and forms go. Live in the force of the habits clear through to the other side of them. You'd want of an Indian that he say profound and often mysterious things, but this is not always possible now, and it never was. Melinda, let me be the first to welcome you home with words. Allen, I bless your skill and the translation of its habits when necessary. I do not give you the history of my name now, after my going, but as a gift, I give you the two song strokes of my namesake:

Bob White

The sand grains separated as they fell, becoming a light shower and then individual and harmless bits that came to rest only a few feet from the edge in the side of the escarpment below Richard's feet. The wood stopped its vibration against the fabric of his shoulder shortly after he had kicked it. He fingered the coin medallion on his chest, feeling the individual embossments of the rods and, faintly, the wires. He saw the firelight flicker out down the beach below him.

On Monday he had been a good boy, pressing the barrel of the pistol into her forehead between her eyes as he rammed her. He had told her it was loaded, knowing she would think that part of the snuff-movie game and believe it was not loaded. He had put the hollow points into it while she was in the bathroom in the motel, and he had taken the safety off. He had known that there would be little passion in him and that he would not loose control and pull the trigger, blowing her head open when she came. She had liked it, he thought, and he had been a good boy in letting her have it, not tainting it with irony or other kinds of put-downs that she would not be able to understand but would feel were present and be brought down by. Tuesday he had struck her viciously in the small of her back, making sure that the sharp surface of the ring he was wearing bit into her flesh as he came into her from behind. He did this to make up for Monday when, after he had banged her, she had said, "That was good, Daddy! You were a good boy." On Wednesday they made it to the Cape. He got them a place in a modern motel on the highway, a little below the town of Seaview.

He turned once in a circle, very slowly, before he left the cliff. He could see the silver in the water by starlight below him, but the light was dim and the silver flashed out very hard and stationary, as if knifeblades turned to catch the light. Down the cliff to his right there were two kinds of darkness. There were the holes in the night where the cliff turned and jutted, and there was the darkness of ragged growth at the cliff's edge. Turning to the course, the jagged places became spotty. He could distinguish the rolling slopes that were the fairways. Coming around he saw the thick shaft of the lighthouse. He started then along the path toward it, his medallion swinging slightly on his neck and stuttering against his chest. When he got to the blacktop of the small parking lot, he walked to the driver's side of the car, opened the door, and slid in. She was pressed into the wedge where the seat met the doorframe on the other side.

"Hey, Gerry, what's happening?" he said as he got in. He said it quietly, pinning her with a slightly ominous edge in his voice, as if she had somehow been a disappointment to him while he was gone and there would be dues to pay because of that.

"Nothing, Daddy, just sitting here thinking."

"Thinking, huh. It's getting to be time," he said as he stuck the key in the ignition and twisted it, starting the car.

"Hey, good Daddy, I've been waiting for the right time," she said, but he thought she didn't understand what he was referring to and thought it was sex. He let it go, feeling what for him was a kind of benevolence in not taking her up on her mistake.

They drove out of the parking lot and down the blacktop road past the small clubhouse on the right. The yellow night light at the clubhouse door was burning, and it shone enough to illuminate the dark figures of pine trees and the edge of the green beyond them. He caught a glimpse of the ripple of the flag on the flagstick as they passed. When they got to the end of the road, they turned right and headed back toward the mid-Cape highway. The road that took them there was guarded from the openness of the course and the sea beyond it by high trees and brush. It could have been a road in another part of the country entirely, and as such it seemed of little consequence to Seaview Links and its fortunes.

The two of them sat on the sand of the winter berm below the lighthouse, and up the beach and away from it. It was not really cold there, but they both felt a little chill and pulled their blankets around their shoulders, gathering themselves in tight around the small fire they had built with driftwood. The stars seemed very hard in the sky, the partial moon a dark, burnished yellow and not giving off much light. Frank Bumpus talked, and Bob White listened. At times Bob White asked questions about particular people or the nature of local political affiliations. He jotted things down in a small notebook, holding it close to the fire when he wrote. Then he talked for a while, and Frank Bumpus listened, interjecting information when necessary. They tried hard to admire the beauty of the night on the beach and the sounds and look of the waves when they curled and flashed phosphorous, but they continued to feel a little cold and their admiration never really got a good start.

After a while, seeing that there was not much use in staying there, they stirred the fire in sand, rolled their blankets and, staying in close to the cliff, headed under the lighthouse and down the beach to the cut that would take them up the dunes to Frank Bumpus's house. When they got there, they drank tea and talked a little more by candlelight. Frank Bumpus got some Courvoisier and a couple of Swiss cigars out of the cupboard when their tea was gone. They drank and smoked and talked about strategy and implementation. Then they talked some about Thoreau, and Frank Bumpus spoke about the Seaview Historical Museum, where the Pamet documents were on display, suggesting they go there tomorrow and have a look at them. He said he would also show Bob White the place of the underground river that had been the people's watering place. Bob White spoke of the Indian school he knew about where the teacher, herself a Pima, had taught the students by having them assemble the skeleton of a deer from the bones brought from various places. The students were asked to do it without the aid of books or foreknowledge about human or animal anatomy. It was a good way for them to learn about skeletal structure, he said. He said that it may be that it is a good way to learn about other things as well. They talked on for a little while, finishing their brandy and cigars. When they were done, it was one o'clock in the morning, and they went to bed.

GERRY

I learned whipping and what it could be about when it was tender. And I was good at it and could teach it too. It was a way of cleaning up before lying down, properly, with a woman. And then I taught it to him, and he twisted it. I liked it that way too at first, but coming out was like going into a dream—he had so much scag and blow for me—and I didn't see he turned it to shame and guilt. You grow too old for those things after a while. It's a look back into childhood, and there comes a time to get rid of that. Forcing and saying the words, faking and pretending, don't really make it happen.

I never hit Annie very hard, just enough to sting her, to wake her up, and I talked to her all the time that I did it. The talk was about how the men, though they never really beat her, might as well have been doing the same thing, because they wore her mind down, and I told her she needed a change of attitude.

Before Annie got sick and died in the joint, the whipping stopped, and we had a good two months together before they took her off to the infirmary. We used to lie in bed facing each other, just the nipples on our breasts and the tips of our toes touching. I'd run the end of my tongue over her lips then, and we would put our hands on the curves above each other's hips. We didn't use any devices that reminded us of men, nor did we touch each other in manly ways. I kissed her eyes, and she kissed mine. I bit her ear lobes gently. I took quiet handfuls of her soft flesh. She kissed the little cups behind my knees. We rubbed our mounds together and had sweet names for them. We were never violent or aggressive, nor did we order each other to do things. I gave her a swatch of fabric from the inside of the leg of an old pair of jeans of mine. She gave me a metal comb. I took her to the window to see the birds in the high trees beyond the walls. She told me stories about dreams of flying. I read her Virginia Woolf and Kate Chopin. I gave her cigarettes. I liked the way she sighed when she saw the birds sit on the walls under the trees. She gave me a small purse that she made out of cigarette wrappers. She said she liked the way I was thin and graceful when I walked. I gave her a green marking pencil. She liked to draw pictures of natural objects on my stomach. I liked the way she hummed to herself in the morning, washing up. We painted each other's toenails with glitter.

She said she liked my eagerness, my little sounds, when I kissed her. She gave me anemones that she had saved up for. I gave her a black, domed pearl button she had admired on a frock of mine. I liked to put my knee between her thighs when we were sleeping. I liked the narrowness of the bed. She told me stories about her childhood in great detail while we were drifting off. I dabbed her tears away with Kleenex and kissed the places where the drops had rested. I liked the way her breath smelled when we awakened. She gave me her wedding ring to wear on my thumb. I gave her salted peanuts in small packages. I opened the packages with my teeth and handed them to her. I liked her smile, a little cockeyed, and her even teeth. She told me she liked my toes, and she did the little piggie game for me. I gave her some peace of mind, I think. She liked to comb my hair out by the window. We liked to walk together in the courtyard, making no show of affection but enjoying the looks of the others who knew about us. We liked it that they really didn't know anything at all. She gave me kisses in the palms of my hands.

I gave her a picture of myself to carry in her pocket. I cut the man out of it with scissors. She liked to brush against me secretly in public. I enjoyed it when she lifted me off the bed and sat me up. I rocked her in my arms when she got sick and fearful. We had secret names for each other, different ones we didn't think were silly. I gave her pieces of hard candy. She told me she was in love with me and made a small occasion out of saying it. I liked the feel of the thickness of her ankles, holding them when I rubbed her feet. We liked to stand together at the window. She gave me a hanky she had embroidered: a crewelwork crown of red vines and a small blue flower in the corner. I gave her a peach when I got it. She said she liked the way my teeth felt under my tongue. She gave me a felt bookmark with a prayer on it. I liked to look up and see her listening hard when I read to her. She mouthed the words of repeated passages. She fluffed the pillows for me.

She said she wasn't afraid of dying anymore, when she got close to it, because she had known me. We cried together when she said that. I gave her wet washcloths for her forehead when she started to get fevers. We liked to hold hands in bed like school-girls and giggle. She liked to cradle me in her arms. We chewed the same pieces of gum; I used her toothbrush, and she used mine. There were times we washed each other with our tongues, wiping each other down with a dry towel afterward. I put a wet towel, heavy with water, on her stomach sometimes to ease her pain. I liked to call her Little Baby, though she was bigger than I was. She called me Honey and Sweetheart in very natural ways and without blushing. I gave her a bar of soap, lavender and hard milled. She gave me serious God-bless-yous when I sneezed. She liked to wear my underwear tight against her body and walk around. I slept with pieces of her underwear between my thighs. I wiped her after she had relieved herself when she got weak and sick. I took nothing from her that she did not wish to give.

She gave me a pretty garter she had made from a broken bra strap and a piece of lace. I gave her warm milk laced with nutmeg when she woke in the night in pain. I liked the way she smiled up from under her half-closed lids. She said she wished things had been otherwise, and I needed to hear it. We liked to talk about imagining cooking for each other, whole meals eaten by candle-light, with fresh fruit and cheese for dessert and cool white wine. She tore a fingernail, and I sucked the blood away. She gave me a barrette with a small enameled bird on it. We sang each other to sleep. I gave her whatever I could bear to give to her, which was everything. She asked for nothing. And she opened the floodgates of my heart.

SEAVIEW

They came up from behind the clubhouse in their two motorized carts. There was a brief line up in front of them. Eddie Costa, who was their fourth and carried his sticks, had made it through, and they could see him above the crowd now as he trudged up past the putting green and toward the first tee. When the Chair reached the cart in front of him, he locked his brake and got out, leaving Campbell sitting in the passenger seat. He went to the back and got a seven-iron out.

The thick and ragged line of beachgoers numbered in the hundreds. Some carried signs and the makings for signs: *free beach, free the skin beach, freedom now,* etc. Men, women, and children, some in swimming suits, others in street clothes, young women in long colorful gowns, men in old army fatigue jackets. None seemed aggressive, but there was no break in their mass, and the carts couldn't get through. A Seaview Township police cruiser was parked along the clubhouse side of the road, and a young officer stood beside it, involved with a group of golfers. They were talking about the look of some of the women passing by. When the Chair got to the side of the front cart, he rapped his seven-iron against the tire.

"Let's get the hell on with this," he said, and he walked over to the cruiser and began talking heatedly with the young officer, pointing over at the crowd with his golf club as he talked. After a few moments, the officer nodded, pushed off the side of the cruiser where he was leaning, and walked over to the crowd. The Chair walked over with him, but halfway there the officer stopped and motioned for the Chair to move away. He returned to his cart, jammed his seven-iron into his bag, and got in. In the cart behind him, Allen could hear him speak.

"This is *some* damn business; this is some *crap!*" Allen turned to Melinda and smiled, and she smiled also.

The officer stopped the line briefly, and the four carts started up and then moved their way through to the other side. The first two turned off and headed for the fifth tee. The Chair and Allen steered theirs over to the first. Eddie Costa was waiting for them, sitting with legs crossed on the park bench to the side of the tee.

"What kept you," he said. He said it dryly, and he was not smiling.

"Some *crap*," the Chair said. "Okay, okay, let's get going boys, let's go."

The tournament was a metropolitan scramble, and the Chair had selected the teams the night before. He had needed an A, B, C, and D player for each. He'd figured himself for B, and he had put Commander Wall down for his C. But Wall had called in the morning, something had come up about hang-gliders and motorcycle gangs. Allen had come in and signed up on the previous morning, listing himself as a scratch player. The Chair had liked the way he looked and had selected him for his team. Art Campbell was a tourist who had not played at Seaview before either. He'd said he wasn't very good. The Chair had figured him for a twenty-three handicap. Eddie Costa had been his substitute for Wall. The rules for the metropolitan were simple. Each player drove from the tee, and then the team selected the best drive of the four. The other three players then picked up their balls and brought them to the place of the drive they had selected. Then all four hit second shots from that place and again selected the best ball. This way of playing continued right through the putting that finished each hole.

Melinda stayed in the cart when the others got out and began organizing their gear for play. The sun was hard and bright, but there were a few heavy dark clouds coming in, and large shadows were falling in various places down the fairway. The sun hit Melinda's face, and it was clear, both because of her posture and the chalk whiteness of her skin, that she was not well. Only Allen looked at her. The others were embarrassed by her presence, because of her ill look and the fact of the oddness of her being there at all. This was the way men had behaved toward her when she had started to work on her father's boat. But she had no urge to somehow go below and write or draw now, and she just sat in the cart. When the Chair had first seen her in the cart with Allen, he had started to object, thinking that to bring one's wife along was unprofessional, but her look had prevented him from speaking out.

From where she sat she could see across the golf course toward the lighthouse and the cliff. She felt in the way the men excluded her a kind of comfort and freedom from them, and she gave her attention to those things in the distance.

The line of beachgoers had turned at the lighthouse and were moving in the seaside rough of the sixth fairway, down over the edge of the cliff, heading for the beach below, halfway between the lighthouse and the Air Station property. Their line had thinned out, but it was long and continuous, and there didn't seem to be any end to it. The women in the line stood out sharply in their colorful clothing, and those who wore only swimming suits had bodies that were tanned, hard, and shapely, and the men in the line tended to recede and pale in the comparison. As women in the line reached the cliff's edge, some would pick up small children, holding them in their arms as they started down. The hair of some of them lifted and caught the light as they stepped over and descended. The signs and the sign makings that were carried flapped like injured birds might, and the line seemed to get slightly frenetic just before it dipped over the edge. There were men carrying outdoor cooking implements, and some carried long objects wrapped in tarps. The people wearing street clothes (she could see four of them, three men along the line, one woman now stepping over the edge) seemed as if they had been transported here from another activity. They were not wearing skuff-arounds but garments they might have used for business. Three men, it looked like, in slacks and jackets. One wore a snap-brimmed hat. The woman stepping over the edge was dressed in a tailored suit. Details from old post cards from a time when people dressed up even for the beach.

As the players organized their clubs and balls, they were all watching. Four figures appeared along the line carrying a large boxlike object, two on either side at the rear, two in the front. It looked like a casket, and the four stumbled, holding the line up behind them, and pulled back and forth against the smooth possible rhythm of carrying the object gracefully, the box bobbing and tilting. At the edge, they got some help in going over, but the object tilted up precariously anyway, and sunlight flashed momentarily off what seemed to be the object's black-lacquered underside before it slipped and disappeared, the front end halfway over and held back from crashing down by the rear men before it went out of sight. The four players around the carts had gotten fixed in their looking, their hands coming to rest on club heads and golf bags, but a slight cough from Melinda broke the concentrated effort, and they began to move again, back into their efforts.

"Better hit off now," the Chair said quietly, and Campbell moved up to the markers, stuck his tee in the ground, and put his ball on it. He hit and dubbed his shot, squirting the ball out low so that it struck the hill about forty yards from the tee, bounced high, and disappeared over the rise and into the beginning of the hard-edged shadows that stained the fairway, to where the green sat, higher than the tee, still alive and shining bright in the sun, its red flag limp along the flagstick. Not even the Chair had energy to say an appropriate thing, and as Campbell shook his head and picked up his broken tee, they avoided looking at him. Eddie Costa moved to the markers, teed up, and hit and sent his ball, straight but short, thudding it into the side hill, a good seventy-five yards from the apron. They all saw the ball hit and stick, imbed and make a wound at the sharp edge of a shadow in the sunlight. The Chair hit a fair shot also, but his was a little high, and it suffered in distance, winding up only a few yards in front of Costa's. He rapped his club on the tee, driving the head into the grass, almost imbedding it, but he did not speak, and he moved back, offering the area to Allen.

The closer Allen got to the markers to get ready to hit, the more vertigo he felt. It was something about angles. The tee was a little cockeyed and was not perfectly flat. Instead of its rectangle pointing directly at the green, it was wrenched off at a slight angle, and a ball hit straight from it would go into the heavy rough to the right. The markers pointed that way, and the one on the left was perceptibly lower than the one on the right. The hills in the fairway, and the green too, seemed slightly tilted; the flagstick did not stand straight, and under the large geometric shadows, though they seemed to try hard to right the tilting, could be seen into with concentrated effort, and under them the ground bent in wrong ways. He tried to shake it off by figuring it, judging the last hill before the flag against the green's surface, but he was not sure of his judgment, and when he hit his three-wood he could not be certain of sending the ball out correctly.

He hit it straight, but he had overcompensated, and the ball landed to the left of the green, rolled past the maw of the trap on that side, and pulled up, he thought, a little short.

"A very good hit, we'll play that one," the Chair said, but without much enthusiasm in his voice.

Allen replaced his three-wood in the bag and got into the cart next to Melinda.

"Was that a good shot?" she said.

"Not particularly," he said. The cart's foot pedal was jumpy; it lurched off, sending Melinda's head and shoulders back, and he stopped the cart and looked over at her, putting his hand on her shoulder. She said she was okay, and he helped her settle in better. He eased the pedal down, and the cart moved off more smoothly. The other cart was halfway down the path to the green. Eddie Costa had walked to his ball and dug it out of the embankment with his pocket knife. The sky was darkening. It looked like it might rain, and where the sun came through it was as if through incisions in the sky, throwing the dark shadows down even sharper.

He cut from the cart path, heading off toward the left of the green where the other cart now waited, the two men still sitting in it. Costa was looking over the line from Allen's ball to the hole. He pulled up and saw that he had, indeed, passed the trap, and that there was an open and flat chip to the hole, the ball back about ten yards on the short apron. There was a good twenty yards of green to work with, the pin cut back and right, and beyond the pin about ten more yards of flat green. On the other side of the green there was some rough, and then the cart path, and beyond that and slightly elevated from where they were, the tee for the second hole. The Chair put a marker beside Allen's ball, lifted it, and handed it to him. Campbell hit his chip too strongly, blading it slightly, and it scooted past the pin to the left and rolled over the jagged lip and into the rough backing the green. Costa, with his odd stance, struck the ball cleanly, rolling it up to within three feet of the pin on the near side. The Chair chipped close also. Allen figured that they were close enough, and he missed his shot, hitting it fat, and wound up short of the other two. They selected Costa's ball to putt. Campbell missed the putt. Costa sank it. They took a birdie three on the first hole.

Now the darkness was getting serious. Rain threatened but seemed to tease and hold back. There was very little breeze, but what there was was chilling, and Allen got his slicker out of his golf bag and put it around Melinda's shoulders. She hunched her body slightly, sliding down deeper in the seat. She seemed smaller. Allen was careful to avoid bumps on his way over to where the cart path paused beside the second tee. He got out, looked questioningly at her; she nodded to reassure him, slumped down further in the cart, and he went to the back to get his driver and walked with the three men to the surface of the tee. When he got there he saw the way the par five dropped off in the distance, noted the slight dog leg and the green off to the left and far away. He saw the Jenny Lind tower and the three domes of the Air Force Station. A little up the hill in the right rough, about halfway between it and the tower, he saw a strange, wooden-looking object. It was nothing he could place, and he squinted but could not make it out. When Campbell hit a fair shot, a little high with a slice in it, but far enough to get over the downslope of the rough and make the edge of the fairway, Costa and the Chair watched the ball, and when it landed it was on a line with the tower and the strange object below it.

"What the hell is that thing?" Costa said, pointing in the direction of the tower. "What *is* that?"

"That was never there," the Chair said. "I can't quite make it out, Eddie. Let's hit and go down and check it."

When Allen hit, he picked the line of the object and the tower above it. They were very high up, and he knew that he could get past the dog leg with what looked from here as no more than a nine-iron to the green. Such an easy hole, he thought. He clicked smoothly through the ball, jumping it out and up. It moved straight off the screws, and when it landed it rolled only a few feet up the embankment toward the rough, stopping in the fairway near the red one-fifty marker, on a line with the object and the tower above it.

"That was one hell of a shot," Costa said and smiled at him. Then they got in their carts and headed down, Costa trailing on foot behind them. Allen noticed that Costa was limping slightly when he and Melinda passed him.

As they descended, it was as if they were entering an inverted, groined dome. The trees and the hills on either side seemed to climb up around them. There was no sunlight in the fairway they headed for. It got colder as they descended, but the trees and the configuration of the land were natural protections against the breeze, and what they entered felt like a damp cavern.

They stopped their carts near Allen's ball, and then they looked up at the object. Christ, a second time—it's like that pole in Tucson, Allen thought, and felt colder when he thought it. But it was not like the pole, though it was tall, maybe twelve feet high, and roughly cylindrical in its vertical axes. It was organic and muscular looking. It was made mostly of wood, some hewn and some gathered. The spire that was its central core was a tree trunk which had been stripped of its bark and limbs until it was bare and blond, tapering and slightly twisted halfway up. On the part of its lower surface that was visible above the scrub hiding its base, it was imbedded with shells: sea and razor clams, mussels, blue points, and cherrystones. The shells were inserted carefully in the wood, in a pattern that was suggested but very complex and unclear. It could have been a kind of writing or a series of symbolic markings. The shells were set close together, though with space between them, and the blond wood showed through in contrast, outlining the figures of the shells in relief. Most of the shells were clean and smooth, but the oyster shells among them were sharp and threatening.

Halfway up the obelisk, and affixed partly to a crosspiece near its top, was the lower mandible of a large shark, pointing downward. The crosspiece was made of two-by-four pine pinioned with galvanized bolts to the tree trunk at its center. Near the ends of the crosspiece, the joints in the jaw had been attached through cleanly drilled holes with thick pieces of silver wire. Three feet below the crosspiece, where the front of the jaw had met the lip at the front of the shark's vicious snout, it was attached with heavy-gauge blond fishline. The jaw faced out at them as if they were inside the shark's mouth, looking upward. The teeth had been removed, and where they had been, and carefully selected for graduated size and shape, the upper shells of quahogs had been inserted so skillfully that the shells looked like the natural teeth of the shark, but more even and more colorful, turning the imagined shark into an instrument not for ripping but for crushing, the color in the shells turning it into some magnificent mutant.

Melinda saw it could be thought of as beautiful, and she could not look away from it. Allen couldn't look away from it either, but he could not see beyond its presence to any judgment about it. Art Campbell moved to his bag on the back of the cart, unzipped its vertical side pocket, and adjusted something in it. The Chair made a strange sound when he saw what was above the jaw and the crosspiece. Were it not that a golf glove had been sewn into the end of the limp sleeve, the wrist hung over the edge of the crosspiece and affixed there with a long nail so that the glove dangled over the wood, he might not have recognized his green slicker, the one the woman had ridden away with on the bus. The collar of the slicker was draped over the top end of the trunk above the jaw, another nail holding it there. It hung down slack behind, the tip of its zipper just visible below the crosspiece. It hung very still in the absence of breeze.

"Get it down, get it *down*," the Chair said, his voice just above a whisper, and he stepped into the cart and fell into the seat. Nobody moved at first, but then Eddie Costa started, limping a little, favoring his left leg and bent over. Allen and Melinda noticed what they had not seen before, when he was able to stand straight, that there was some slight deformity in his back. As he got on his knees and bent down to his golf bag, which he had placed on the ground of the fairway, they could see the rise like the bulge of a small dolphin running down from his collar to the middle of his back, his jacket stretching tight over it as he opened the zipper compartment of his bag. The sky was dark, and where Costa knelt, surrounded by the two carts, the darkness was even deeper. But though there was no discernible sunlight at all now, the quahog shells in the shark's jaw and the emblems of the shells below it were reflecting, and they cast light, a kind of vague aura, a rough circle of beams on the ground where Costa knelt. He noticed it and glanced up, and his eyes gleamed in it for a moment before he looked away and down.

He reached into his bag, but he seemed tentative and uncertain.

The first thing he took out was a dark and richly colored Paisley shawl, and he spread it on the ground beside the bag. Then he started to take various objects out, searching. He placed them carefully in rows on the square of the shawl as he removed them from the bag. With each thing removed, he had to reach into the zipper compartment deeper to get the next. Soon he was in up to the elbow, still searching. They all watched the objects accumulate. Near the end he was getting desperate, hesitating each time he reached in. The beams of light, now seeming to come from some source in the shell teeth themselves, grew brighter and slightly red around the shawl and the man digging in the bag as the sky continued to darken. He was in up to his shoulder. They could see his hand hitting against the vinyl, like some small animal in the pouch, as he searched, still on his knees, his cheek pressed into the zipper of the slit, his eyes closed. Then he withdrew his arm and sat back on his haunches, bent over, his arms hanging, his hands in the rough fairway grass. Where his cheek had pressed the zipper there was a line like a red scar running from his eye to the corner of his mouth. He seemed to snarl and whimper at the same time. He cocked his head, almost sheepishly, glancing up at the fixed smile on the jaw. Then he lay out flat on the ground, opened the bag's slit, grasping the zipper on either side, and put his arms and head into it and began to inch forward. Their mouths were open as they watched him go in.

"Get my ankle!" they heard his urgent, muffled voice in the pouch. The Chair slid from his seat, circled the carts, and moved in behind him. He got down on his knees and reached out and took Costa's right ankle in both hands, keeping his arms extended, his body as far away from the man in the bag as he could get it. There was a slight jerk, and the hump slipped into the slit. He was in the bag now almost up to his waist. There were rumblings like thunder coming from over the hill and the other side of the course. When he was in the bag as far as he could go, he stopped moving, and the Chair somehow knew that it was time to pull back. It took effort, the body seemed to fight against withdrawal, but it came slowly out as the Chair pulled at the leg, urging the breach. Finally, the hump popped out, and then the shoulders, turning, and then the head. The head turned back, as red as a newborn, and looked at the Chair intently.

"Keep pulling," Costa hissed. The Chair pulled, and Costa's arms came out, and then his hands, and held tight in them he had the end of a braided rope, and it uncoiled as it came like a length of placenta. When he was out, he rolled over on his back, his body bowed because of the bulk of the hump under him, his chin extended, his chest heaving as he sucked for air. He jerked his left foot, and the Chair released his ankle and fell back on his haunches. Melinda sat in the cart watching, her hands crossed over her chest. It was clear to all of them that they had to wait for Costa to come to himself again, and while they waited and listened to his gasping, they gazed at the shawl and the objects that covered it, starting at the upper corner. Somehow, it seemed proper to read it from left to right, and then down, as if it were a manuscript, wampum, or some other written message.

The first row contained a small carved wooden whale, a match-book with *Richardson's Funeral Home* printed in gold letters on a deep blue-felt background across its surface, a crumpled and faded post card with a picture on it, a moonstone medallion, a snakeskin wallet, a baby's rattle, and a small wire loop, like a garrote, that obviously had something to do with fishing. In row two: a spool of fishline, an oyster shell, a packet of Red Man chewing tobacco, a lure, a white plastic barrette, a bag of peanuts, a small Diamond matchbox, a hemostat, a plastic bag full of rotten blueberries, a bird whistle. The third row: a small stuffed bird, a curved Kelly clamp, a red-checked bandanna, a little silver spoon, a gutting knife with a scrimshaw handle in a tooled leather sheath, a book of shadow signs, a black-lacquered thumbtack, a dolphin ring. And in the last row: a small dark bottle, a syringe in a plastic tube, a silver thimble, a golf glove, a razor blade, a plastic paperweight with a blue flower in its center, a piece of wooden doweling, a coil of thin wire, four small charms on a ring (three human figures and a putter), and a glass sliver of moon.

It all meant nothing they could have agreed upon, but what it meant to each of them displayed itself in posture and movement. Campbell got closer to the back of the cart and put his hand on the open mouth of his golf bag. Allen shifted in his seat and looked over to where his ball had come to rest and its line into the green. The Chair looked back at the spire and the shark's jaw, then back at his soiled knees, and shuddered. Melinda breathed through her parted lips, sucking in air like Costa, and continued to stare at the shawl. Then, gaining sufficient breath, Costa rolled slowly over onto his stomach, put his palms on the ground, and pushed back up to a kneel. He reached back by his foot, grasped the end of the braided rope, and pulled it forward to his knee. He flicked his wrist, rolling a loop across his forearm and catching it in his other hand. He leaned back on his haunches and thrust his arms out in front of him, palms up, the three-foot braid that sagged in the middle held at arms' length and offered to the Chair. The Chair shrank back in his seat in the cart, pushing in the air in front of his body, and shook his head.

"*You* do it, Eddie."

Looking at him, and with arms still extended, Costa did a strange turn with his hands and wrists, bringing them together in slow trick. When his hands came apart again there was a small nooselike loop tied in the rope. He rolled back on his heels and pushed forward again, coming to his feet, then limped to the back of the Chair's golf cart and, using the little noose, tied the rope around the bumper. The Chair craned around in the seat to watch him, and when Costa finished with the tying, he rose up from the back and looked again at him.

"The rest is yours," Costa said. The Chair got down out of the cart then, slowly, but with some resolve.

"Give me the fucking thing, *give* it to me!" he said, and Costa handed him the end of the rope. He took it and looked up at the spire briefly, then headed toward it up the side hill of the rough. The others watched him and did not see Eddie Costa gathering the objects in the Paisley shawl, shoving them back into the slit in his golf bag.

The Chair climbed awkwardly, slipping back at times, grabbing at tufts of scrub for purchase. When he reached the base of the odd cross, he was careful not to touch it. He took the rope in his left hand, held the end of it in his right, a good length of braid between them. His first cast missed the mark, and he had to do it again. On the second throw the end dropped through the half ring of the shark's jaw, sliding between two of the bottom shell teeth. He played the rope up, the weight of it moving the end down toward him. He was close to the spire, and he had to force his head back on his shoulders to see what he was doing. From where the others were, the perspective seemed to put him almost under the shark's jaw, and it looked as if he were offering his vulnerable neck to it in some ritual of acceptance. The rope's end seemed to avoid his fingers as he reached up to it, and only after what seemed a long time did he get a hold of it. As quick as he could he tied it, and then he backed down the hill awkwardly, keeping his eyes on the jaw.

When he got to the surface of the fairway, he turned and headed back to his cart, waving Campbell away from it with an impatient gesture. Campbell lingered near his bag, and he had to jump clear when the Chair put the cart in reverse, jammed at the gas pedal, and twisted the wheel to get it to turn in a tight little circle so that it faced away from the side hill and the spire. Then he drove it forward to the other side of the fairway, slowly, until the braid lifted up off the ground and became taut. He had his left arm back over the seat of the cart, his head turned, watching the spire. A few heavy drops of rain fell, spotting his knit shirt at his biceps. The sky was very dark now, and the only strong light was in the aura around the spire, the polished shells softly gleaming. He pulled forward, and the jaw seemed to vibrate. They could all hear a kind of humming coming from the taut rope, and the Chair could feel it in his body and in the cart. Then the back wheels of the cart began to turn slowly, guttering down into the fairway earth, throwing up sand and tufts of grass. The spire held. The Chair threw the cart into reverse and moved it back a few yards. Then he raced it forward, snapping the rope up from the fairway this time. When he reached the end of his tether, his head snapped back, the wheels guttered deeper, and the front end of the cart came up like a bucking horse a good three feet off the ground. The spire shook, and two shells spun out of the shark's jaw, but it held again.

Allen and Melinda watched what was happening in the darkening day. Had they been able to step away from it, it might have been funny, at least in some way ironic in its incongruity and inappropriateness. As it was, it was purely mad. They watched the spire shaking and holding, the Jenny Lind tower above it dark and very stationary, the cut windows in its stone like vacant eyes.

The deep groin of the fairway was exaggerated in its depth by the darkness. The slopes of the rough on either side seemed to press in and down on them. They thought they could hear sounds—heavy implosive thuds, motors, kinds of cracking, unidentifiable—over the hills toward the sea, but they were not sure of them. The overriding sound was that of the whine of the cart as it moved and jerked. The Chair moved it back and forth. He raced up the fairway and down it. He headed again across it. He tried various angles of pull. The cart wheels were hot and smoking, and they could smell rubber burning and oil in the air. Twice, the cart came close to flipping on its side, but with unexpected nimbleness, and like a sailor leaning over the gunnels of a small skiff to keep it righted, the Chair thrust his body half out of the cart, using his weight to keep it down, holding the steering wheel, his feet hitting the pedal.

The braid kept falling slack and then leaping up, taut and humming, from the fairway. The spire held, but then, very suddenly, it stopped holding. The Chair was trying the cross fairway attack again, his body hunched down and ready for the violent jerk. When he reached the end of the rope, there was a sharp crack, like the splitting of a large rock, and the rope broke. The cart raced across the fairway and halfway up the hill into the rough on the far side. When it went as far as its momentum and power could take it, it turned in a tight circle and came to rest, its nose butted up against a small pine. They had all watched it go up and were looking that way, but then they heard the sound behind them and turned to where the Chair was looking from where he sat with his chest against the wheel up in the rough, and they saw the spire slowly falling toward them.

Though it was over forty feet away, they each shrank back a little as it tipped. The arms of the slicker waved disjointedly, and its body billowed out with air. The golf glove flicked its fingers on the wood of the crosspiece. The changing perspective in the fall made the shark jaw seem to broaden its smile into a grin. The wood sighed, and shell teeth began to fly out of the mouth, turning and spinning in the air. Then the spire was perpendicular to the line of their vision, and they could not see its complexity. When it hit and disappeared in the side hill scrub, there was little sound.

The Chair brought the cart down out of the rough, the trailing braid wiggling and ascending like a massive decapitated snake up toward where the cart had been; the tip disappeared into the scrub and went up to where it was looped around the pine. He stopped the cart alongside Allen and Melinda's, and Costa spoke to him.

"Do you want that fucking slicker?" The Chair could not speak for a moment, but he shook his head.

"I *got* what I wanted," he finally said. "Now let's finish this hole!"

Only Allen knew immediately what the Chair meant. Campbell and Costa seemed a little bewildered, as if they had forgotten why they were there, in golf carts, halfway down a fairway. Melinda was already, in her different nature, slightly separated from any events. Allen stepped out of the cart, and as none of the others moved, he spoke.

"Okay, I'll hit then." He walked over to where his ball was, stood back ten feet behind it, sighting along the line. Because there was no other movement, the others watched him.

The ball sat five feet down from the entrance into the rough running along the fairway toward the green. It was on the flat, and he would have a good place for a stance. He was about a hundred and sixty-five yards from the front of the second green; the pin stood twenty-five or so feet back to the right and on the high side of the slope. He figured he could go straight at the pin with a wedge, get it to bite and pull up quick. The green had begun to glisten; the rain, though the drops were still infrequent and far apart, was steady now and real. The drops were large, and he figured that the green had softened a little already. The shot gave him nothing interesting to negotiate. He turned and went back to the cart, grabbed the head of his eight-iron, and pulled the club free of the bag. When he got behind the ball again, he looked up the groin of the slowly dampening fairway and thought about the lines.

The lines were best when they arced. There were lines in the air and lines on the ground. The lines on the green were visible to anyone when it rained. You could retrace the putt after it was finished then. The ball would make a kind of trough, pushing the drops to either side in its roll and bending the wet grass down before it. When the rain had been heavy, a small rooster tail of water would rise up behind it, and as the tail shrank the ball would slow in its pace, and when it stopped the tail would stop. And then there would be a trail like a snake left behind when it had passed through sand. You could see every detail of the breaks the ball had negotiated, how it had fought against them or rolled comfortably with them when the pace was right, taking it to finish somewhere near the hole or in it. If you watched long enough, the trail would begin to disappear as the grass rose up again in the trough and the rain fell. It would leave the surface of the green in increments, starting from where the head of the putter had rested, the end of its tail becoming faint and slowly vanishing as you looked up it toward the hole or the final resting place of the ball near it. It could be almost as if the movement of your eye along the line registered and then canceled it, until, when your glance reached the presence of the ball or the absent place in the green where the hole was, there was no longer any use for the line, and it was gone.

But this was for anyone to see, and for him it was the lines in the air, the gentle and hooked arcs and graceful fadings and dips, that gave him better pleasure. He felt it as a kind of geometry he could trace back to his body, and when things were exactly right, he knew it was an actual aura emanating from him, and in that extension beyond his body he experienced a unique kind of power. At least he thought of it as unique, felt that there was enough difference in it, though he had heard that archers knew of a similar thing. The line would start out in the bundle of hiss that sat in the muscle of his heart, that tangled and self-regulating system of twisted and complex nerves which made the heart go and in turn extended its influence, making his whole body operate.

After the planning, but before the hit, it was as if the bundle of hiss tensed a little, became a different kind of system and potential. It was as if it became one continuous long nerve coiled in the flesh of his heart. It was as if it unraveled slowly, sending itself like a catheter into a pulmonary artery and from that to the brachial and down into the wrist of his left arm and into his thumb, where it pressed into the grip of the club. And a moment before the club face struck against the ball, and as the ball itself seemed to swell in that way it did, reaching out to the club face

to touch it, the visible letters on the Golden Ram sharpening in
their outlines, it was as if a small hole opened in the end of his
thumb and the tip of the nerve came through and there was a
kind of synapse, an electric arcing, between his thumb and the
ball, and the arc continued into the air when the ball shot off the
etched surface of the club face, and the lines began. It was not
an unraveling. It was as if the air were a surface on which the ball
could trace and map its path, but it looked like a filament of gold
or silver, depending on the place of the sun, and it stayed and
marked its arc until the ball had descended and found out its
resting place. He felt, at certain special times, that the line was
somehow part of his body and that his influence throbbed along
the line and was connected to the ball until the shot was finished,
when the ball came to rest.

He moved up to the ball and got slightly down in his stance
and addressed it. He had decided on a half eight, a slight punch-
ing fade, to take the ball low and left, then bring it back right
so that when it hit in the apron it would be coming in on an
angle from the left and would have some side spin in it. That
way it would roll up the hill toward the right back of the green
where the pin was. He figured it would stop close and would get
them their eagle. He shifted his feet, lifted the club head from
the ground, then replaced it, then did that again, sighting his line
in, picturing the filament he expected to come this time. Then he
brought the club head up in a half backswing, began the slight
hip-shift toward the green, brought the club down and through,
dug into sand in the crude fairway in front of the place where
the ball had been, and the force of the swing brought the club
through and up.

His head was pulled up by his arms; he looked to see how the
ball flew and caught sight of it when it was already a good fifty
feet from him. Then the line began to materialize, silver this
time under the dark cloud cover. The ball, etching the line,
reached its apex and then began to descend, turning its arc to the
right and in toward the green. But his eyes stopped at the apex,
and they widened. There was another line there, this one a dirty
white, and it cut across the top of the arc, dividing the air above
the fairway from high rough on the left to an equally high place

on the right. His concentration broke. He quit watching the ball, got up from his stance, and turned to the others, but he kept his club head in the air and pointed with it.

"There's another line," he said. They did not know what he meant at first, but then Campbell saw it too, and he pointed.

"There!" he said. And when the others saw it, it was shaking and whipping slightly, and their eyes followed along it to the right, and they saw some rustling in the scrub high up in the rough, the kind of movement a small animal would make or a large bird foraging. But the thing happened too fast for them to judge the movements. The bird leapt up from the brush so quickly it seemed to materialize in the air a few feet above it. Like a great hawk, or an osprey, or an eagle even, it danced and fluttered on stiff wings, and the absence of the glare of sunlight or the backdrop of shadows was such that they could see it very distinctly. It was not a bird at all but a small man with wings. His face was in profile, his chin up and his jaw-set, arrogant, but austere in its stillness. He wore a feathered headdress and fringed shirt and trousers, and in his small right fist he carried a tomahawk. He dipped down a little and then rose quickly as the line connected to him snapped taut. Then they heard the rustle in the paper as the high breeze above the still fairway caught him, sending him higher.

"There's the flyer!" Campbell yelled, and their heads jerked to the other side, following the line to where it entered the brush, and they saw only the curve of the back before it disappeared over the hill, the line still taut and the kite climbing higher, quickly, until it was directly above the fairway and very high. They watched as it disappeared into the clouds and the rain that was falling, weighty and a little heavier now, wetting their upturned faces.

Allen went back to the cart and got his umbrella from the attachment on his bag, opened it, and handed it to Melinda. The Chair had his out already, and he sat in the cart under it, shivering slightly, though it was not so cold, just a little wet.

"We've got to hit up and get out of here," he said. "We're taking too much time!" He looked back toward the tee, but there was no one there, no other team, waiting behind them. His voice was still a little raspy and shaky, but he had recovered a little from the events, and he got down, dropped his ball, and struck it quickly, taking no time for a practice swing. His shot was long enough, but off to the left.

"Come on, Eddie, Campbell, let's go!" Eddie went over quickly to the place from which Allen and the Chair had hit their balls, dropped his, and hit up also. Campbell seemed not to want to leave his golf bag, but he too went over and hit, then trotted back to the cart and got in. Then the carts started and headed up the fairway toward the green.

The clatter of the two carts prevented any other noise from reaching them, and it was only when they pulled up and stopped at greenside and the motors wound down that they could hear the distant sounds coming from the direction of the lighthouse and the other side of the course. Melinda thought she could hear a horn of some kind blowing in short blasts. They heard dull thuds, faint and distant, and what they took to be the sounds of voices yelling.

"This must be it," Campbell said, and he got down out of the cart and went to his bag in the carrier. The Chair turned and saw him reach into the slit and work at something. When his hand came out and up, he was holding a small semiautomatic rifle.

"Christ!" Costa said, when he saw it.

"Now, just a *minute!*" the Chair squeaked.

"*You:* shut the fuck up and stay here," Campbell said, pointing at the Chair with the short barrel. "This is government business." And he started toward the left in the direction of the third green, far up the hill. He trotted slowly in a half-crouch, the rifle hanging at the end of his arm vertical to his body.

Allen could see the flagstick out of the corner of his eye, and he turned a little that way and saw that his ball had ended where he had planned for it to end. The line was in the green, from where the ball had bounced up from the apron in a slowly turning curve to where it now rested, only about three feet from the flagstick and the hole, with an uphill lie and a putt that seemed from where he was to be straight in. He had a physical urge. His body wanted to lift up out of the seat and get down and go over and make the putt, get the ball down for their eagle. It would be easy, and he wanted to get it over with while there was still a chance for it. He needed to close it, to finish the process that he had started at the tee. It would be open-ended otherwise, like the future had been before Melinda's illness. A good part of the future was buffered because it was circumscribed and contained now. The parameters in which prediction took place were clear and understandable, and he could handle them, like he could handle golf. But the ball was there, and it seemed to throb in the waiting, because its potential was so directed and narrow. It yearned for its death in the hole, and he throbbed and yearned with it. He felt he had to get it soon or he might not get it at all, and if he did not get it it would not just change things and push him out and away from the focus, because there was room at least for some painful stretching, but it would break him: the focus was taut, and he had real fear. He thought of the danger inherent in the system of the Tensegrity Sphere that Melinda had spoken of that day in Aspen. He fought to get out of the cart, and he fought to stay in it at the same time. He heard the sharp intake of breath beside him, turned his head to Melinda, and then looked where she was looking.

Campbell was halfway to the crest of the hill when the rifle came up and across his body. His right hand grabbed the stock, and as he came to the ground he dug it in in front of him, breaking his fall with butt and elbows, then quickly had the stock to his shoulder and the rifle sighted at the torso of a boy who had appeared, trotting on and over the upper green, coming down the hill toward them. The boy was looking back. His arms hung at his sides as he ran. His canvas workbag bounced and rattled its contents against his right knee. When he turned and saw the prone man with the weapon below him, he pulled up, dropped the bag with a thud to the ground, and raised his arms, his palms elevated and open in front of him. Campbell came up off the ground quickly, his rifle still at the ready, but then Allen saw the release of tension in his shoulder and saw him raise the barrel of the weapon, using it to motion the boy toward him. The boy picked up his bag and began to come down in a half-skip. When he reached Campbell, the man turned and came down the rest of the way with him. They could hear the structure of the boy's voice, the rhythms in the talking, well before the two reached them.

"Chip," Costa said, turning to the Chair as they approached the carts, the boy already in mid-paragraph, his eyes blinking, his skinny body doing its little dance.

". . . and who would imagine such dark power to thwart us? Simple beachgoers, a brink of a sunny day (though some clouds), and the Chipper snatching a few deserved winks up under the truck (a toke or two to soothe him) . . . *Hey*, Chair! *Hey*, Eddie! . . . then comes Sammy, rapping the running board, and calls him out. With much eye-rubbing and half stagger up from slumber's appassionato, he and the other lad trot over to see the ladies from cliffside. My, my, naked and two-toned down there! a good four hundred souls to the Chip's calculations. Warm and dumbstruck I was, though felt a few wet drops to cool me. Magnifico! clean fleshy pleasures! arms alink with Sammy: two jaunty lads just watching. But some (watchamacallit) ritual of sorts going on down there: flappy *freedom now* and *skin beach* posters hooked up, and that darkling dangeroo casket for a burial of stuffed pillowed man with Air Force Station uniform on him. Felt a kind of chill, I did. Some people in dressed-up wear, heads atilt and looking up to cliffside from the beach. And then the whales!, Chair! and a few souls pointing and dancing, until the beachy masses turned seaward, the Chipper's eyes, I bet, as big as pumpkins! great bodies aroll and *some* splashing! It was *something*, Chair! *You* seen it Eddie, you an ocean bucko, now and previously, the *Chip* knows of it . . .

"And I am desirous of clear word power now that I have come here to tell you. There were twelve of them to my count, and that is accurate, because I was on the high prominence of the land's overhanging figure and could see their backs, massive and glistening, when they rose and blew their silver fountains, the sun sparkling the spectrum of colors in them. Half dark over the land it was now, the clouds threatening, but seaward it was shining. The one closest in seemed to be pilot, the pivot on which they made their turning. They came, fanlike, around the lighthouse point, their row uniform, running out from their pilot into the deeper water, some space between them but a pattern in their rise and dive. The massive back of the third one out showed itself like an island, and I could see the city of barnacles and other sea life and caught wood and rigging there, a ruined city: crushed temples, viaducts, remnants of streets and busy squares, streaming riverbeds, benches and cupolas, trellises for the hanging of seaflower shades.

"The fourth in the line seemed overshadowed by this giant's size and complexity, and as if to assert its own mastery, its head came up once, and its jaw, encased in a sheath of leather skin, showed itself, and its upper lip curled back, and I could see those yards of heavy white bone as the massive head stood for a moment straight up in the turbulence: a graceful sea-arch and a dark cave entrance. The force of the pilot turning the line seemed to suck water out, and the shore swell pulled back to sea in riptide, and sand bars came up, the small clear pools forming inshore, driving the heavy turbulence out and away from the few bathers, the water flooding away from them, until those up to their necks and bobbing were now no more than ankle deep and gazing sea-ward, their feet sunk in wet sand. And then the little naked and brown children were jumping up and dancing on the beach, and some were lifted on the shoulders of men and women, and the dolphins came.

"I picked out three to start with, one to each side of the far whale in the line, and one to his tail, a little back to avoid the hard banging of that fanned mass as it pounded the water down by the ton. Then another came and shot like a new metal barrel from a great depth and sailed in the air high over the back of the largest whale, sliding in on the other side with no splash, as if the water had parted for his entrance.

"Then there must have been fifty of them, males and females both. They came up in concert, as if a single complex of mind brought them. They formed loops and lines in the air, and they looked like elegant charms on some invisible bracelet of intention. Over and under the whales they went, and I could hear their fluted talking and their racial yells. Some stood on their tails and raced backward no more than ten feet in front of the whales' heads, then flipped over and dived. And the whales too were talk-ing and making a music, but their sounds were deep and foghorn-like and vibrant, like the largest of organ pipes. The dolphins sounded like piccolos in counterpoint, and it was as if the two languages were of the same root. The line moved along the shore slowly, and the sea was like a giant amphitheater, a massive musi-cal progress taking place on it, clouds of sea birds creating a roof over it, the sea itself the soft stage. The bodies on the beach leaned toward the sea intently, and even the children stopped their movements, and all of the world seemed, for a time, changed . . .

"And then comes the *Chiefie* and his crew! And I am as if *zonked* at the sight. In a dozen boats and drifting down coast and turning in and dressed in full Injun regalia, the Chiefie standing in a prow, with headdress, face paint, and *tomahawk!* O naked brothers, sisters, children, all jammed in from the sea and seaside cliff as if caught in ambuscade! And the pilot turned the line of whales seaward. It was as if they had prepared the coming of Chief Wingfoot and were now going, and behind them the dolphins fell into files of mimicry. I could no longer see their eyes. They came up, dived, and came up again behind the whales. They moved together, and I felt that they had given up thought then and were totally of a real magic, at one with their body motors, moving with natural and quiet grace toward their better world.

"But now the *Chiefie* was pilot, and his Quahog People boat boys were coming stately into the whales' vacancy. The sea itself had come back in to shore, and old Chiefie's boats were riding the returning swells. The Injuns began to pop over the gunnels and into the surf, waist deep, and pull the boats to beach. And the naked and dressed folk were moving again, but this time back and against the escarpment below the cliff. Indeed, old Injun visages were doing their number on them as of old. But when they hit the beach, the Chief stayed in the prow pulled up on the sand in surf and pointed to the bucks to head right and left and to turn boats over and get down behind them.

"And the dear Chipper and his cohort Sammy are watching all this with some intensity of eyeball and head connection, when— oh presage of darkness!—the Chipper hears the roar of horn and motor at his rear, and when he turns—O dear lady in cart!—the twenty or so and dreaded Devil's Advocates on motorcycles, four abreast, scorching macadam, up to the lighthouse, where the Chip sees now the townie cruisers with gumball lights ablinking and the chubby and local coppers waiting with clubs withdrawn. His eyeballs are affixed there, but he has look enough to see *more* of the Chiefie's redskins back of the hill and coming over the eighth fairway, over underground river below ground, creeping up in a line, and the Advocates peeling off before they reach the cruisers and cooking along the rough to the seaside of the sixth, *right* on toward your *humble* Chipper and Sam! And Chip's eyes want a definite closing, for some of the beach folk are over the crest now, and the Advocates coming along it, driving them back, and hitting into a few, set aroll with bruises and sand scrapes. A woman is clipped head on and carried, with flabbergasted Advocate and motorcycle all in a slow twisting, over cliff and down to scatter souls struggling up, and the woman staggering to foothold on the scarpside sand to rap Advocate soundly with straw basket on groggy noggin.

"And mucho yelling and down-coast movement from the coppers at the cruisers then. And back to the left, on clubhouse road, I see three khaki jeeps and the troop truck coming, see Injuns hunkering down and digging in for action . . . Oh, oh scheiss! grab the bag handle and skitter away, Sammy and Chipper running to the sixth tee and over the shoulder catch old townie constables hot on Advocates' heels, some stopping to aid Skin Beachers, others running in pursuit with clubs waving, and behind them, the troop truck unloading, Injuns and Air Force boys in standoff, and the press corps arriving with wheel screech and old war horse photographers jumping out and already snapping. And *then*, the Devil's Advocates' air flyers acomin'! Dark and shadow-laden bike boys hanging from huge rigid wings and drifting high out over the sea, coming around lighthouse promontory point, such monstrous birds! and dipping slowly down from the sky and approaching cliffside, heading our way. And the Chipper then has quick and acute recognition of the Advocates' diversionary ploy. Their motorcycle force turns into the sixth fairway, forms wagon-train circle, chains and clubs revealed now, waiting the coppers' coming, while the flyers drift, free and unopposed, along the escarpment, bringing the promise of yet *more* chaos!

"Sammy hits down quick into the brush, and the Chipper brings eyes up from him and sees the final and distant whale swells, a spout, hint of the magic bracelet, the distant sky of birds, the place of horizon. He reaches out for it, wanting to be there, but it is no good of course. Hears roars to his left, landward, cries, and in the air the slap and shadow of dark wings above him, and the Chipper is finally fast in cutting out! . . . And, well, here I am, and I am possessed with no more breath for message."

His arms dropped to his sides, coming down from the animated, jerky, and sometimes strangely graceful gestures. The Chair and Costa gaped; they had understood the words but were having trouble comprehending the import of the events. Campbell moved in to get down to specifics, rough casualty counts, and the possible current state of things. His hand came up in a gesture intended to keep the others quiet as he moved toward Chip.

Melinda saw it first and saw Campbell catch it in the corner of his eye and stop and turn. She pressed in and behind Allen's shoulder, as Campbell fell back, bringing the barrel of the weapon up. A wing tip came first and threw a shadow down over the carts and the five figures. There was still no sun, and a shadow did not seem possible, but it was there, hard edged and huge, cutting its shape in the fairway where it met the apron, cooling the wet ground, causing the grass blades to flatten out. The tip was directly above the thin spire of the flagstick on the upper green, and the limp red flag came up and rippled out, showing its white number three. There was then a torque movement, as if the wing tip had been driven through by the flagstick, a slight turning that brought the tip of the other wing into view, and then the whole thing rose up, showing its expanse of underbelly to them. Their heads were craned back, their necks exposed, and they felt as one might feel lying in an open casket in an open grave, a uniformly dark sky above him, no clouds, the edges of the grave hole framing the vacant and still picture. And then a thing of movement entering the picture, at his feet, known first by feel, and coming up to where it moved into his vision, and his wishing for the higher vacant view, as the dark wings and the oblong body of some death flyer moved up and hovered and became still in the air above him.

It seemed to stand up on its tail for a brief moment. It had caught an updraft as it reached the near edge of the green where the ground fell off and rolled on down to the carts, and its wings were full of air and taut and open, lifting it almost straight up. They saw the ribbed struts in the wings and the scalloped ends of the fantail and the feathered half-moon curves of the ailerons. The field of the convex surface of the undersides of the taut wings was black, and there were various figures in the field looking down at them. In the umbrella dome of the left wing, the figures were human and animal, but there was no place to focus, no clear order, and they throbbed and took precedence like dream images, lurid in their Dā-Glow colors and comic-strip rendering: a man in uniform, in chains; starved desert animals in cages; a snake swallowing a bird; a miniature woman, handcuffed, half out of a tent; a small coffin; the head of a man in a golf cap; a transfixed dolphin on a spear; a coinlike medallion in a gloved hand.

In the dome of the other wing, and partly following the ribs and struts, there was a huge geometric figure, a rough circle of red sticks and green wires that did not touch each other, extending to all corners of the field. They had had to fight to focus on the specifics in the left, but when they looked in the right wing their pupils dilated, and they could take in the whole of what they saw there. It was like looking up into the high skeletal expanse of a cathedral dome. It was airy, and there were a lot of spaces in it, and yet it seemed to press down and contain them.

And then they saw the beginning of ripples in the two domes, and for a moment the figures in them became animated and strangely alive. The tail of the hang-glider lifted as it came up and moved out from the slope into the air above them, and they saw the head of the oblong figure between the wings cock to the side slightly and look down and over at them. He was wearing a black aviator's cap, hugging his head tightly and buckled under his chin; his eyes were big and insectlike in his flight goggles. He wore a scarf of red silk around his neck, and it rippled out the way the flag had on the green. From his shoulders to his feet he looked embryonic, like a spire encased in wet leather, as if he were a gigantic mutant butterfly only half out of the cocoon. His arms were out and moving, manipulating the steering mechanism, a bar that seemed driven sideways through his neck.

His head came to a stop when his gaze reached them, and they saw him push the bar, lifting the glider so that it stalled and seemed to stop dead in the air, with wings snapping taut and full of the air. Then they saw his right hand drop to his belly and touch the weapon that was slung there and looked like a large and misshapen vestigial organ running from his groin to his upper chest. He quickly got it loose, dropping his left hand from the bar also, and swung it down from his body and out, his arms dangling low now. The weapon was coming around, the barrel dipping down toward them, and they could see the barbed, blue steel of the spearhead and the rubber tubes of the catapult. And then they saw sudden and fleeting indentations in the leather below the flyer's chest, his body lurch, and a shower of little pellets fall. They heard the quick, dull blasts as Campbell fired his rubber bullets, and the rifle was halfway lowered when they glanced at him. When they looked back up, they saw the glider stop hovering and begin to rotate. They saw the flyer's still and unconscious body in its trussing, arms limp and slightly waving, and the top of his hanging, leather-encased head.

"Another one!" the Chair yelled, and they all turned to the left and saw the second glider drift down over the hill, back, and a little over the high rough halfway down the fairway near the red one-fifty marker. Campbell trained on it, but he did not fire. Midway through his turn he saw the third one come over the ridge.

"Get *down!*" he said, and he turned and headed for the rough that ran uphill toward the Jenny Lind tower and the Air Force domes above it. He ran low and zigzagged, and the spears sent from the gliders missed him as he disappeared; they struck and vibrated in the brush beyond the green's apron in his wake. Allen jumped half over Melinda in a turn, pulling her against his chest, and rolled as gently as he could, bringing the two of them out of the cart and down to the ground behind it, where he lay over her, on one knee, his crouched body supported by his right hand on the cart's side. Sighting across the seat, he saw Eddie Costa fall and roll, clutching his golf bag along his body, until he got half of himself under the Chair's cart and the golf bag quickly adjusted against his exposed side. When Costa went down, Allen could see Chip running.

He was headed in back of the green, hitting into the pines in the direction of the sea. His run was a little like a mimicry of Campbell's run, a half-lope and stutter step with some darting and weaving in it. He turned all the way around once, looking back. There was a muffled burst from above and down the fairway, and Chip stopped his turn and seemed to dive backward into the higher pines. The trees caught and held him, and he landed standing, arms thrown back and out, tangled in the branches. Allen saw him caught, his head cocked to the side, his eyes wide open, and then he saw the beginning of the seepage across his body. It came out at his thin waist and formed a belt of blood there, and there was a place in the middle where the belt had a buckle, a filmy, convex, moonstone shape. For a moment the fluids paused in the belt of holes, and the boy looked girded with many colorful and rich jewels, like those set in the belts of champion wrestlers. His mouth opened and closed on the air, but no sound issued. He wanted to speak, it seemed, to finish or at least add to his story. He pulled his left arm free from his bed of pine and reached out in a sweeping and vague motion.

He either indicated the apron, beckoned to Allen, or gestured for his workbag that sat in the open beyond the carts. Then the jewels of fluid began to break and fall, and his arm came down; his hand moved to his buckle and his palm pressed into it. The fluid oozed between his fingers and began washing down and across his groin and thighs. And as if the buckle had been some kind of switch, as his palm pressed into it his eyes went out; they rolled back in his head, and the lids fell to cover them over. His mouth continued its effort to speak, and then it stopped doing that. Then the noise and the concentrated effort shut down, and it was very quiet.

The rain had stopped, but there was still no sun, and the sky remained uniformly dark. Allen heard the creaking and the yaw and the sound of slapping lines above, and he looked up and saw the unconscious figure hanging from the rigging between the great wings and slowly coming down. The glider turned gradually in a half circle, then caught some air, moved up a fraction as the domes in the wings filled and stretched taut like membranes, and came back around again, lowering. The man's head and arms hung loosely down, but his feet and legs were still tight together.

Allen kept his hand over Melinda's face, and when he brought his eyes down from the glider, he saw the Chair standing alone, his arms raised and his hands in fists. He was looking up at the glider, and then he looked down and back to where the second and third had come over. The third, the one with the rifle, was struggling in a gust of air, the flyer jerking at the bar for elevation. The second was climbing, and it looked like it might make the other hill and reach the domes. It was halfway across the fairway in its climb. The Chair swung toward it, shaking his fists and yelling.

"That's enough, that's god*damned* enough!" he screamed. "Stop it! Stop it! This is a *golf* course!"

Allen saw the little metallic glint and the movement in the small, trussed-up figure. Then the rush of air came, and the spear descended. The Chair opened his extended fists to fend it off. The force of the hit turned him back, and Allen saw the surprise in his face as the spear stuck quivering in his thigh. The Chair looked down at it, then shook his leg tentatively as if to free it. And then he backed up, limping, toward his cart; his hands were fists again, and he was shaking them and yelling at the flyer.

Costa came up from under the cart and threw his bag and body into the rear carrier as the Chair slid awkwardly into the driver's seat and hit the pedal. The cart turned, throwing Costa halfway out, and headed down the fairway. As it picked up speed, the spear began to wobble in the Chair's thigh, and he slowed down, meandering, to avoid bumps. Costa was bouncing in the carrier, but he held tight to the back of the passenger seat. They reached the dog leg in what seemed a long time, headed around it, and were out of sight.

Allen got up in reflex to follow the cart's going, but then he saw the glider, the one with the rifle in it, coming down in the fairway about fifty yards from them. It was only ten feet from the ground, and he saw the flyer's leather legs kick free of the rigging and the man hang down from his shoulders and waist, his legs dangling and dancing, his feet getting ready to hit. His hands held his weapon, but it was caught in the trussing and the straps on his sleeves, and he was jerking and moving it to get it free. Allen reached to his golf bag on the back of the cart and grabbed a club head and pulled up and out, sliding the club free. He looked around, saw Melinda's figure crouched, and behind her the flagstick and his white Golden Ram sitting on the green near it. He looked back and saw the man's feet hit and stumble, and the tip of the right wing came down and scraped the ground. He was struggling to stand, jerking at the rifle, and he looked to be trying at the same time to get at the safety buckle that would release him from his wings.

Allen turned and ran toward the flag. He could feel that the pitch of the club head in his hand made it a four-iron. He threw the club head out and away from him as he moved, spinning the club and catching it by its grip. Approaching the ball, he had a brief, sudden urge to hood the face of the club all the way down, to make the club a putter, knock the eagle in, and finish the hole. When he got to the ball, he stopped and turned quickly into a hitting stance. He sighted down the fairway at the landed glider. The man now had his footing, and his weapon was loose in his right hand. Allen saw him reach for the safety harness, his left hand and arm across his belly. Then he threw his left arm out and away from him, and the straps of the harness fell loose. The left arm and hand came back to the rifle as the man squatted slightly, bringing the weapon to his shoulder. Allen could see the bulge of the silencer at the barrel tip as it came around. Behind the grounded flyer, the wings stood up, full of air. They began to lift slowly, rising up and tipping forward over him like some large protective umbrella.

Allen saw the drops of rain. They were gathering on the sides of his hands, along his right thumb, and a few glistened on the shaft. His hands were in his grip and well in front of the ball, the face of the four-iron hooded slightly. He looked up once and saw the red flash at the end of the barrel. Then he looked down at the ball and focused on the *Go* letters and the space between them and the face of the club. He saw the spatter of red drops at the base of the shaft and felt the bite in his left forearm.

Then the club shaft was rising back and up, his left fist tightening. He forced himself to stay down on the ball, to keep his left arm rigid, to cock only at the wrist. At the top of his backswing, he put all of his concentration in his left shoulder, imagining it to be a joint in a piece of heavy machinery. When the club came down to the ball, he tried hard to literally snap and break his tendons and ligaments loose from their insertion in bone, to break his wrist with the force.

Before the club hit, he had a stab of guilt at what he was about to do to the green; he wondered if it would scream in outrage. The power in the swing carried him sideways, almost off his feet, and when the shaft came over, righting him again, it arched in its whip around his neck and hit him sharply in the right shoulder. His head came up. He saw the clean, odd slice of divot he had cut move out and up, and then he saw the man jackknife under the wings, the rifle fly up and out as the Ram hit him in the stomach. There was a sharp echoing crack down the fairway. The man was driven back five feet or more. His hands met his toes as he sat up in the air. And then he fell and the wings came down over him, and Allen could see his body lurch and squirm, hitting against his canvas covering. Then Allen felt something brush against his cheek and turned and faced the open palm. He looked up and recoiled. The man hung directly above him. He was under the wings and close to the red sticks and green wires that did not touch each other. He could hear the flyer's deep breathing, the creaking in the rigging, and he could smell the leather. He dropped down and dived and rolled. The scalloped edge of the wing caught his arm, and he jerked it loose and rolled again and came up and ran to Melinda.

He could see above her and the cart six dark gliders coming over the hill's crest. He lifted her up quickly and put her in the seat, then ran around and jumped into the driver's side, hitting the gas pedal as he entered. The cart lurched forward, bounced as it crossed the wing tip, dug grooves in the apron of the occupied green, got beyond it, and started into the rough and up the hill toward the stone tower. The hill steepened quickly, and halfway up the cart slowed and coughed and quit. Allen jerked the wheel to the left, bringing the cart sideways, and it began to tilt. He rolled toward Melinda, trying to use their combined weights to keep it from falling, but it continued slowly up. He grabbed her around the waist, squeezing her in the crook of his left arm. As he rolled with her, he reached back with his hand and got a hold on the mouth of his golf bag. They left the cart and fell into the rough. The bag ripped loose and the cart turned over on its left side and bounced and slid downhill. Allen threw himself over Melinda, pressing her in the brush. He had his golf bag in his left fist, and they were hidden in thick growth.

He stayed down over her for a long time. He kept his face pressed in the side of her neck; his cheek was pricked by pine needles, and the shallow tear in his forearm hurt him a little.

Once he looked up, wondering about the six gliders, and saw them give it up. He caught them when they were very high, near the level with what he guessed was the hill's crest. There was a strong breeze there, forcing the gliders back. They turned, dipped, and angled for position, but none was able to negotiate the crest. One by one, they peeled off, bending away from the Air Station and toward the sea.

As his eyes came down from the sky, they rested on the stone tower. It was a good seventy-five yards up the hill from where they were. Still, it seemed the thing to do, and he brought his face back down to Melinda's and told her what he thought. She nodded sharply in agreement. He pulled his golf bag up beside him and slowly rose to a crouch. He checked the sky again and found it empty. He checked the hills across the fairway, looking down it and up to the hill over which the first glider had come. Then he looked to the green where the downed glider lay. It was still. He could not see the place where the flyer with the weapon had been struck by the Ram, but he could hear nothing from that direction. He looked back behind the green into the brush in the direction of the sea. The boy was there, hung in the pines, almost graceful, silent and still. And then he saw the body slowly falling in, the pines closing over it, and Chip was gone from sight.

From the direction of the lighthouse and the distant side of the golf course, where they could not see, they could hear only the muffled sounds of motors, some voices raised in command, and the creak of machinery. Allen reached in his bag and fingered through the club heads until he felt his three-iron and pulled it free. He got up, slinging the bag over his shoulder as he rose. He had the iron in his left hand, and he reached down with his right, took Melinda's arm, and helped her to her feet. She staggered a little, but he held her while she steadied.

"You get in front," he said. He got her there, and put his hand in the middle of her back, his arm out stiff. He used his three-iron as an awkward staff, and he pushed what strength he could into her, leaning forward, so that she could make it uphill. They went in tight little zigs and zags in order to cut down the steepness of the incline. They kept their heads down in their effort.

Allen glanced up occasionally in order to steer them. With less effort and time spent than he had anticipated, they came to the wet, stone base of the small tower.

Richard's intention was to kill him on the eighth green. He had seen that the eighth was set no more than a hundred feet from the public road that ran parallel to the high, jagged cliff, the golf course between it and the sea. The eighth was also set down in a shallow valley protected from wind, and the rough that ran from behind the green and continued all the way to the road was almost a forest. The pines in it were high and straight and very dense, and they started very close to the green's back, just beyond the sand trap behind it.

He had seen him and his wife and the other three at the first tee through his binoculars, from where he stood against the car at the lighthouse parking lot, and he figured he had close to two hours, safely an hour and a half. He would get Gerry and something to eat, then he would come back and wait for them. The road to the lighthouse was crowded with walkers heading for the beach, and it had taken him a while to get past the clubhouse and away from the course.

When he got back to their motel room, Gerry had their things packed and ready in the way he had told her to. He told her to get in the car, and he took her to a drive-in on the highway where they got some food. On the way he told her that she was to keep quiet and stay in the car and that, if she was good, he would find a good way later of giving her something she would like. When he got to the road that headed to the golf course, an hour and a quarter had passed, and as he came to the turn toward the lighthouse, he could see something was going on and that his plans might have to change.

He passed a policeman standing beside a motorcycle near the place where he had intended to enter the pines on foot. Up ahead, he saw a cruiser blocking the mouth of the lighthouse road. Some people were standing around on the road, but the land sloped up from there, and little could be seen in the direction of the course and the sea. He slowed but did not stop, passing the lighthouse cutoff.

"What's happening, Richard?" she said in the seat by the door. "Just shut up and sit there," he said.

He continued along, west of the course, until he passed the entrance of a campground and came to the road that moved off left, at an angle, to the Air Force Station, and then he stopped the car. He could see that the Air Force road ran along the down-coast edge of the golf course. Above the ascending road, up and to the right of it, he could see the three white domes. To the left, and also well up and toward the sea, he saw the parapet of the stone tower. There was a sign, marked *government property, authorized vehicles only*, at the mouth of the road, and a short way up it, at a turn, he could see the nose of a green military truck sticking out. Two men in uniform, with rifles in their hands, stood in front of the truck. He turned the car around and went back to the campground. When he got there, he parked in front of a small building near the road. The building was white cinder block, and it had a sign above the door, marked *office*. He went in. Gerry stayed in the car. In a few minutes he came out with a paper in his hand and a canvas packet under his arm. He got into the car and checked the simple numbered map on the paper. Then he drove around the building and entered the open meadow behind it. There were a number of campers and tents, and as he entered the central dirt carpath that ran down the middle between them, he saw short sticks with numbers on them and the spokes of driving paths moving off to both sides. He turned at the second spoke, driving very slowly; when he came to number forty-three he stopped the car and got out.

The meadow was about three hundred yards deep, from the road to the hill that started up toward the golf course. He could see there were a good number of men in military dress lining the perimeter between the meadow and the course. Some of them had weapons slung over their shoulders, and some had side arms. A number of the campers were milling around along the line, talking and looking up the hill behind it. There was smoke rising in the air in places from beyond the hill. The rain and the uniform and heavy cloud cover had begun to move off. It was still cloudy, but there was some hazy sun in places brightening the day a bit. He turned and looked over to the right and behind him. There was a low white building, the back of which came up close to the pines that covered the hill running between the campground and the Air Force Station road. The sign on the front of the building read: *showers/men*.

He told Gerry to get out of the car and help him. The tent was small, a one-man pup, and they got it up quickly. They took what they could find out of the trunk of the car, making the camp appear serious. Then he told her to get back in the car and wait. He told her she could get in the tent when she wanted to, but that the car and the tent were her only two places. He smiled at her, tight-lipped, giving her the rules. The tent was very small and uninviting. He got his blue robe out of his suitcase and his shaving kit. Then he got in the tent, took off his shoes and socks and rolled them in the towel he had with him. He rolled his pants to the knee. When he was ready, he got out of the tent and headed over to the white building in his robe. When he got in, he checked the stalls to see no one inside of them. The place was empty, and he figured they were all outside, checking the military action. He went to the screened window at the back of the building, raised it, and with the heels of both hands knocked the screen out. He put his shoes and socks on and made a bundle of his robe and towel and shaving kit. Then he got through the window, dropped to the ground, and stepped into the pines.

He headed up through the trees in the direction of the sea, passing to the right of the line of Air Force men. It took him a good ten minutes to reach the crest of the ridge. When he got there he looked down and saw the second fairway. He could see the green and the dark object on it, though he could not identify it. He saw the golf cart turned on its side to the right of the green in the low rough. Above him, up the ridge in the pines to his right, he could see the top of the stone tower. He took his binoculars out of his shaving kit and trained them on it. He saw Allen, his head and shoulders visible, at the parapet, standing still and looking out. Allen seemed to be alone, his wife nowhere in evidence. He dropped his kit and towel and robe in the brush. He checked his pistol and shoved it down in his belt. Then he headed up and along the ridge. He was starting to buzz a little, and he would have liked to hurry. But the pines were thick, forcing a slow pace. He figured it would take him a good twenty minutes to get there.

They struggled together up the enclosed spiral. He stayed to the outside of her and pressed his hand on the cold stone for support, his bag scraping against the curve as they ascended. She wasn't limp, but she was staggering, and it was little more than his body on one side and the inner wall on the other that she felt was keeping her up. She knew it certainly wasn't her breath, because she couldn't get much of it, and she was trying to mask her wheezing, keep it from bothering him, and that too took its effort. It took them a long time, but the tower was under forty feet high, and when they finished climbing, she had something left.

They came out into the cool of the late afternoon air, and she found that if she leaned back against the tower's upper core she could stand. He let her do it, slipping the bag from his shoulder, leaning it against the notched parapet. It was still heavily overcast, but it had stopped raining, and even as he watched the cloud cover again, the sky began to clear, and some sun came through, and there were soft shadows on the stone. He looked at her, and they both managed parts of smiles. He stood at the parapet that came to the level of his lower chest and looked away from her and out. He had expected the sight line to be better than it was. He could see the whole of the upper green on top of the hill over which the gliders had come, but he could not see much farther. Off to the right, and higher still, he could see the sixth tee and the tall brush at the sea's edge that came up to it. There were two hand carts in front of the tee and what looked like a couple of golf bags lying on it. Smoke was rising in places across the course, from sources beyond his vision. There were no longer any sounds of the kind they had heard earlier. He could just see the edge of the green below him and the far edge of the fairway running back from it. He could not see the cart or the gliders from where he was.

He turned back from the notched outer wall and walked to where she was leaning against the inner core and pressed against it beside her. Their shoulders touched, and he felt a little stab where he'd been hit when his forearm brushed her, but he did not move it away, and he put his hand down and took her hand.

"It's kind of like we're little people on top of a rook from a chess set," he said, and she laughed halfheartedly in agreement. His other hand came up and touched her cheek and then came down again. They stood, leaning and looking over at the wall in front of them. The sun brightened the notches in some places. It was as if they were waiting for something. She had been waiting for her breath to come back, and it did. He had no idea what he might be waiting for. They continued to stand there, each gathering strength and as long as they had that task, their postures didn't seem awkward to them, but after a while his mind began to fidget, and he felt he had expectations. They were here now. They had done things. They could even smell the sea. They were so close to it, they could walk over to it were the circumstances other than they were. What had happened down below had not thrown either of them. They had been so much in it that they had not had space to think about it, but now they had that space and time.

She felt her illness coming back to her, unsullied again, and she sensed she had the final closure back, contained in her body, and she had no need for talk, explanations, or plans. He had none of what she had, and he felt odd and restless and uncomfortable. He would have talked, and he did feel that talking would be very useful to him, and he tried hard to think of something to say, but he could not think of a single thing. Half-ideas formed in his head, but when he tried to move them into words they seemed to dissolve and go away. She knew that when he had touched her cheek fleetingly a moment before, that had been it, about all she would get, not near enough, but all.

She did not exactly wonder why the young boy messenger had to die so violently down there. She needed nothing in the way of philosophical explanation of such things and never had. But he was so sweet and harmless, she thought, the place of his death so isolate from human concern, and she did think that it would have been good to note the circumstances through tender talk. Who else was left to give some proper weight to his passing but the two of them here? She said a silent prayer of sorts for the boy, something outside her own concerns and Allen's as well, something she realized was in all ways beyond him as a possible thing to do.

When she was finished, she thought to help him out, and she said:

"Help me to sit down by the wall there, please."

He took her arm and helped her over to the wall and squatted down as she lowered herself. Then he got up and got his golf bag and brought it over to her. When he moved it, he felt something about its weight, and then he remebered the gun and the binoculars he had put in the zipper pouch. He handed the bag down to her so she could use it as an awkward pillow, and she took hold of it, propping it up beside her against the outer wall, and leaned against it. The smell of its leather was familiar and almost human. He reached in and pulled his four-iron by the head out of the bag's mouth, and then he squatted beside it and got a handful of Rams out of the small zipper compartment and stood up.

"The gun and the binoculars are in the pouch," he said. "I guess I better do something, better go over there and see what's up, get us some help out of here, okay? Will you be okay?"

"Okay, right," she said. "I'll be here. Be careful."

"Okay," he said, and he seemed ready to speak again, to say something more extended, but the air came out of his mouth without any words in it except, "Bye-bye." He raised his hand and waved his fingers at her, and she raised her own hand and waved in the same way back at him. He turned then and went to the opening in the core, and then he started down the spiral.

She appreciated the soft breeze that came in through the half-open window on the other side. She was where he had told her to stay, pressed in the wedge between seat and door, her right leg up and stretched out on the seat. Her arm lay in her lap, and the breeze cooled the sunburn she had gotten from having it on the window sill as they were driving cross country. She could see much of the staggered line of uniformed men at the edge of the campground. She watched them, but they did nothing of interest. After the group of Indians came down the hill from the golf course and one of them had spoken with one of the uniformed men, she watched as some of the guards left and the Indians took their places. The Indians wore various kinds of headdresses and buckskin shirts, but from the waist down they were dressed in jeans and work pants and tennis shoes. They looked, even in their rough wear, more interesting than the uniformed men, more various in their gracefulness in standing. She watched to see if they did anything she could spend time with, but they, like the military men, did very little.

She knew she was not biding her time any longer. It was just that she felt inert right then, and the thing she would soon do would get done when she felt like doing it. It was not an important thing at all for her. It was just to make a formal ending. She was already done in the way she had to be, and after she went and got in the tent, she would just do what she wanted to do.

It was no specific event. He had done nothing out of the ordinary, and she could not really even think of it as a slow accumulation of things. It was not her birthday, though she had been thinking recently of its passing a month ago, and she had been thinking of Annie, too, but not in any serious way. All she knew was that when she had awakened in the bed in the motel that morning, she had heard some birds singing outside; she had listened to their clear songs, and then she knew that she would be going.

She sat for a little while longer, and then she swung her leg down off the seat and turned in it and opened the door and got out of the car. She walked around the car and went to the tent, where he had told her, with that smile of his, she could also sit if she felt like it. It was not that she felt like it, but that she wanted to feel this last limitation to see if it would be like she thought it would be. She got in the tent and sat down in the cramped space. The canvas was catching the sun that had come through the clouds, diffusing it, and there was a golden glow inside the tent. She couldn't sit straight up without hitting her head on the top, and she sat hunched over. She could feel just how foolish it was to sit there, and she thought he would think she would try it in the way she was doing now, but that he would think she would feel some pleasure when she did it. It did feel nice, in its way; the light was fine, but what she felt had nothing to do with rules. She sighed, then opened up the flap of the tent, pushing the slit open. She pushed up from her haunches and crawled out through the slit, head first, turning her shoulders slightly, and got to her feet and stretched her body.

She went back to the trunk of the car, opened it, and got her suitcase out of it. It was a small canvas case and very light, and she lifted it easily. She didn't close the trunk. Then she went back to the passenger side of the car, put her suitcase on the ground, and got in. She reached up to the rear-view mirror and took hold of the medallion that hung down on its thick chain and slipped the chain from around the mirror, taking the medallion down. It was the one he usually wore, but it belonged to her. She held it in the palm of her hand and jiggled it. It was heavy and solid, and she could feel the embossed complex of rods and wires with her fingers. Then she took the chain in both hands and slipped her head through the opening, putting the medallion on.

She got out of the car and picked up her suitcase from the ground. As she bent to lift it, the medallion swung slowly at the end of its chain. When she rose up, she heard the two sharp notes of a bobwhite. They came from the hillside to her right and were very loud; she could tell the bird was close. They seemed to cut through what overcast was left and be part of the quality of the coming sunlight. She turned away then, from the direction of the sea, and leaving the tent and the campground, she began her walk to the highway.

Richard was no more than a hundred yards from the tower when he saw Allen materialize in the dark, vacant space of the cut-stone opening that was the doorway. He was a little away from cover and at a level with the base of the tower, and when Allen stopped in the frame, a golf club in one hand across his chest, a fat bulge in the bottom of his left pocket, Richard thought he was looking directly at him and had an urge to jerk the gun from his belt, raise it, and fire. But then Allen was gone, having turned out of the opening, moving quickly to his right and trotting into the pines behind the tower. In a moment, Richard could no longer see him. He stood in his tracks, felt he wanted to enter the dark doorway, made his decision quickly, and started to run toward the tower. When he got to it, he cut around it as Allen had done and started after him. The growth was thick, and there was some sunlight in it, but he knew nothing about tracking and could not read signs, so he guessed at the direction Allen had taken, and moving in a slight crouch, though it was not necessary—the pine growth was higher than a man—he stayed on his level on the ridge and headed in the direction of the sea.

It took Richard no more than ten minutes to get there, but that was enough time for the sweat to have risen out of him. What he had thought was a trail had petered out, and he had to struggle through heavy growth that cut at his arms and tore his clothing in places. His gun kept slipping down into his pants at his belt, and he had to stop often to adjust it. Once he tried to put it in his pocket, but his pockets were small slits and he couldn't get it in. He tried carrying it in his hand, but that was no good either; he needed both hands free to push the brush away before him. Finally, he came to the edge of the cliff.

He was half way over it before he knew he was there. The pines ran right up to it, he was a little dizzy from the pace and work of his movement, and he stepped over the edge. It was only reflex that made him grab at the pines. He went over, but he had a hold on a thick branch, and he jerked himself back from the edge and stood still on the lip, breathing heavily and trying to listen. There were birds singing, and there was the heavy sound of the breakers coming in, and there was no possibility of hearing anything else, so he stood still and waited until his breath could return to normal. The beach was empty. He was standing above a small inlet, and he could not see very far to his left or right. He picked pine needles from his shirt fabric and from his hair and pants. The beach and the sea below him were beautiful in their emptiness and solitude and unconcern, but he was not moved by them. When he had his clothes adjusted, the gun set firm in his belt, he began to work his way to the left along the edge of the cliff.

He had gone no more than thirty yards when the growth around him began to thin out. The cliff sloped down slightly, then up again in the distance, and at the place where it crested the growth got high and heavy. He saw that to his right the escarpment running down to the beach was more gradual in pitch than where he had almost fallen over, and he moved to the edge and stepped over it, getting himself below the lip so that he would have some cover as he moved on to the next crest. He worked his way along below the edge, and when he got to the higher pines, where the cliff steepened sharply again, he came back over the lip. He entered the pines and stopped and listened again. He could hear something quite close to him at the cliff's edge. He could not identify the sound, but he knew it was Allen. He edged as quietly as he could through the thick stand of pine, and before he got to the edge of the cliff, he saw him.

There was an open place, a kind of sea perch, at the cliff's edge. It was surrounded by heavy growth, and there was a path at the back of it that headed into the golf course. The area was a rough rectangle, about twenty-five-feet long. Allen was standing at the far end of the rectangle, away from Richard and facing him. The Golden Rams were on the ground in front of him, and he was standing over them with the golf club in his hands. He chipped one ball and then another, hitting them cleanly and with sharp little clicks, sending them in the air, about a foot off the ground, ten feet down the rectangle. Then he went and got the balls, brought them back, and chipped them again.

Richard watched him and began to fear him. The thing he was doing was very odd. It was outside of Richard's previous experience of what odd might be, and he felt that he wanted to understand what was going on. Was he waiting for him, biding his time in this way with his golf? It didn't look like it; there was something more serious about the way he hit the balls, something very concentrated, contained, and in no way casual, and there was such obvious skill in it that Richard felt fear in knowing that he had no skill that could be compared to it. Then he began to like the feel of the fear he had, and when Allen walked back after chipping the balls for a third time, Richard stepped out from the pine cover and entered the open space. He did it as quietly, but as quickly, as he could, and Allen heard him and turned around and faced him, dropping the Rams on the ground.

They stood at opposite ends of the enclosed rectangle. They were alone together in a peaceful place, and yet it did not seem so peaceful: the clouds were moving and changing; there was light action in the sky, and the shadows kept altering their shapes between them. They could hear the surf rushing, and they caught glints from the sun hitting into the swells in the corners of their eyes. They both felt a need to speak or do something at least that would join them to the action of sky, ground, and sea, some kind of activity, some committed entrance to the changing world. Had they spoken out, casually, they would have brought up talk that was directed into the fixtures of the past, their time together in that solid place; they would have spoken, sentimentally, about life directions, or shared musical taste, or women, or the touchstones of common events. They knew enough of where they were to know that the talk could not be of the future and felt the hollows in their stomachs in knowing, finally, that it was indeterminate; useless to speak of it, a foolish enterprise. And what of this present, Allen thought, how escape from that?

It was Richard, finally, who found the way to handle it, but it was incidental that it should be him; it could as well have been Allen; there was not much difference. They both shifted a little at their ends of the enclosed space. They did tentative things with their knees, hips, and shoulders. The high brush seemed to push in on the three closed sides.

"This is it, man," Richard said. "Are you ready?"

"I'm ready," Allen said, and he adjusted his grip on the shaft of the four-iron.

They both felt the romance of it, and they both liked the feeling. Their brief words seemed to echo in the air, and they felt a strange kind of gratitude that each had spoken the words correctly and with sufficient drama. Each waited for the other to make his move. They felt they stood there for a very long time, looking at each other.

It was Richard who moved first. His hand came across his stomach and groped for the gun grip in his belt. He got it and jerked at the weapon. But the hammer had gotten hooked in his belt loop, and it would not come free. The crotch of his pants pulled up against his groin as he twisted and jerked again. Then Allen was moving. He fell into his stance and started the club head back quickly. When it came to the level of his shoulder, he squeezed the grip in his left hand and began to whip the club down at the swelling Ram. But it came down too quickly, and he knew that the head was gone. It had left the shaft in the force of his backswing, had probably loosened when he had hit the hang-glider pilot, and it was flying behind him, spinning in the air into the brush. He saw Richard jerk again at the gun, the bottoms of his pants almost to his knees, the whiteness of his shins ridiculous above his black tennis shoes. He came automatically through the

242

swing, and as his head came up, the tip of the headless shaft passed over the top of the ball, then continuing over his left shoulder. As he brought it down again, he pointed it at Richard as if it were a rapier, ineffectual at this distance, and then he saw the gun come loose as the belt tore free, the pants fly ripping away, and Richard's hand thrown up from the force over his head with the gun in it. He had an urge to leap for him, but before he could do it the gun came back down, and Richard, with right arm extended, fell into a crouch and brought his left hand to his right wrist, aiming at Allen's chest. They both stood very still. Then Richard grinned at Allen, and then he pulled the trigger.

There was a sharp pop, like the sound of a child's cap pistol, and then, for a moment, there was nothing, and then the bullet came. It appeared in the mouth of the barrel, seemed to pause there for a moment, and then it slid out into the air, rose slightly, and when it reached its arc it began to fall. When it hit in the rough grass in the space between them, it disappeared, making no sound. Richard fired again; another bullet came out, arced also, and fell between them. When he pulled the trigger for the third time, nothing happened at all.

They went at each other then as if they were in the same dream. They both felt heavy-footed, and they tried to drop their instruments, but could not release them. Richard stumbled toward the cliff as he threw his arm out, trying to get rid of his gun. His pants were falling, and he reached down with his left hand to get them, but missed, and they came down around his knees. Allen whipped at him with the headless club shaft, but he did so as Richard reached for his belt, and the shaft sailed over his head, the force of the intended blow spinning Allen around. When he came through his turn again, they had come to the lip and were falling. Allen reached out for Richard, groping for something to hold to at his neck, but there was nothing there. He caught only the edge of his collar, briefly, jerking Richard's face close to his own. There was a place in which they were embraced and turning, where they could not see land or sky. The sea was empty and without limits, and there were no horizons.

She sat in the shade on her tower, leaning against the central core. She had thrust the golf bag away from her but had taken the binoculars out of it first. If she went to the notched edge of the parapet, she could let her hair down and he could climb up it and come to her. But her hair was dark and short, and she knew that if she had golden tresses she would cut them also, for only in that way could she be who she knew she was and not some romantic shadow. But it could be the witch who would climb up, who was really some dark wish in the story. She had never been one who was much inclined to wishing, and she could accept her choices and their results. Anyway, the story had been his story, she realized, and she was no more than the end of it, the tail at the end of the tale.

Would it have been better, really, some other way? She felt it might have, but she was not inclined to regrets. Still, she thought, when one is in such a position, one might be allowed the indulgence of sweet dreams of another life. She learned the back of her head against the central core and closed her eyes in order to conjure up the possibilities of some past. She was not moved by memory, however, and she soon came back to herself. She spent a few moments in gathering strength and resolve, and then she pushed against the cold stone behind her and struggled up to her feet and crossed slowly and carefully to the notched edge facing the golf course.

She lifted the compact binoculars to her eyes and began scanning the distances around her. They were very fine glasses, powerful but very steady, and they brought the distance to her sharply and in bright delineation, as if things far away were circled in her control and influence. She had always thought of them as an extravagance, but Allen had not.

She pointed the binoculars in the direction of the sea, but she could find nothing to focus on there. It was just pine tips and the sky above them. The sea itself was not within view. She didn't look down at the fairway below the tower, nor did she train on what she might have seen of the rest of the course from where she stood. She turned slightly to the left, leaning in the notch, and she found that she could see to the highway running down the middle of the Cape. There were some cars moving there, and finding a landmark she remembered she lifted the glasses to where she thought the house was, but there were trees and hills in the way, and she could not see it. Then she brought the glasses back to the highway. She saw the cars again, and then she saw a slight figure, a woman, standing with her thumb out, a suitcase on the ground beside her, hitchhiking in the direction of the mainland.

The woman was at the bottom of a long and gradual descending of the road, and beyond her the highway moved gradually up again, until it disappeared over a western rise in the distance. She was low where she stood; it was getting late in the day, but she was in sunlight, and when Melinda sharpened the focus, she could see the textures of her clothing, the strands of her loose thin hair, and the heavy chain and emblem hanging from her neck. The suitcase on the ground beside her was boxy and cheap; her clothing, while not so cheap, seemed to be a box for her body to hide in: it guarded against definition, and it was only when a breeze pushed at her blouse that Melinda could see that her breasts were small. She was bent over slightly, her posture was poor, but it was familiar, and she had placed one foot slightly in front of the other. Her elevated arm was thin; her thumb, out in the air, was delicate, and she wore a ring on it. The cars were passing her by. The fine glasses were not heavy, and Melinda had adjusted them carefully so that their cups fit comfortably over her eyes.

The car came over the rise in the slow lane. It was moving slowly, and it only had to brake slightly and pull off the highway in order to roll up and stop beside her. It was an old convertible, almost an antique, a 1955 Buick Century, dark blue with shining whitewalls and a white, rolled-down top. It was very well kept but not fanatically so; it looked serviceable, weighty, rounded, and strong. It had a number of chrome porthole circles in the side of its front fender.

There were three women in the car, two in the front seat, one in the back. Their arms were resting in visible places, on shining window sills and over the white roll of the folded-down top. They were smiling, and their arms and faces were brown. They were leaving the Cape after a sweet week in the sun. They had their hair gathered, hooked up with barrettes, combs, and colorful ribbons, in different and careful styles, loosely but held back enough to handle what breeze would come into the open car. They wore bright blouses of natural fabric, just a little flamboyant, but tasteful. The one who was driving the car was about forty; the other two were somewhat younger. The driver lifted her hand up, and the woman beside her reached out and opened the door.

There was a moment in which the slight figure paused in the open doorway. The inside of the door was patterned with blue and white rolled-leather ribbing, chrome handles with clear plastic buttons with little blue flowers in them, and deep pouches. Someone had hung a plastic bag of fresh fruit over one of the handles: dark plums, small oranges, and bright yellow bananas; there were a few walnuts in the bag also. With the door open, the brown legs of the three women were visible. In the front seat, the legs formed a pattern, those of the driver (a little thicker in ankle) a compliment, seen over, between, and behind the fine thinness of those of the passenger. The woman in the back seat had her legs crossed, a brown sandaled foot hanging down in the air. They all wore loose skirts with Paisley and silk-screened designs.

She lifted her head up to their faces, and as her head came up her whole body lifted, pushing its form out against her blouse and skirt. She lifted her arms up and stretched and smiled, and the three women laughed lightly, and they raised their arms also, beckoning for her to enter. She stepped into the back seat, putting her suitcase in the corner, herself beside the woman there.

The woman in the passenger seat in the front pulled the door closed, and as the car moved slowly back on the highway, she turned in her seat and began talking. She moved her hands as she spoke, and she had a way of touching the tip of her thumb against the tip of her middle finger, moving them slightly together and apart from each other while she was making a point or listening to one of the others. The car moved up the gradual westward slope of the highway. The four women were talking and laughing. The breeze began to lift strands of their hair as the car picked up speed. As the car came to the crest, the woman in the backseat handed something to her new companion. The woman took it and looked at it. She nodded her thanks, and then she brought her hands up, arching her body in the seat. She reached back and began to gather and order and hook up her hair. Then the car dipped over the western crest and left the field of the glasses.

EARTH LIGHT

And now have I come to walk this somber plain at the final edge of evening. There is earth light under it, of course, but no shine yet. Our small fires mark the perimeter, lit in the faces of governments and the press, and our young boys are loose now behind them, but they keep it quiet. Militant before, they are now awe-struck and a little unbelieving. The occupation is all political and a matter of visibility and negotiation. They cannot spill, methodically, our blood yet; they have to sit down and talk some.

It is some cheer to Frank Bumpus (who meets already with them, in the name of Chief Wingfoot) that the talks will include the Chairman, a good buffer for us, though he be injured and limping, to keep things knotted and confused for a good long time. He grieves some for his wound, but more for the purely innocent, the young boy: workmanly pro. The mad products, in their borrowed and tortured uniforms, have laid him low. He was a victim of what his own people (Thoreau and Bradford, no heeded correctives) have, predictably, brought forth.

A worn brown fedora, with a tern feather in its band; a leather vest; a brace of golf bags; an old flying cap; a new Golden Ram; various weapons, clubs, spears, and chains: these are the products of my reconnoitering. I carry Frank's old wooden golf club as a staff. There is some scarring, but only the traps are deeper wounds, and these have been salved a bit by their filling of sand. The greens, like gentle haircuts, and the careful cutting of the aprons and rough lines do not give us much pain. Theirs was a kind of ritual also, having to do with land, and mostly in respect of it, though in the service of a game. But not for Allen. Soon I will take a cart over and check the stone tower.

It has all been matters of priority, but tempered by being in one place at one time, sane, because one cannot be elsewhere. Thus, they are mostly insane; they find it hard to be where the body is. For Melinda, in her circumstance, it was possible. Being elsewhere was only, properly, a story. And so I tell one for myself and for the two of them.

When I was a boy I had a fine and secret name. I liked it, but I had no use for it. I could not speak it outside my family, and my father, who was very conservative as those things went at that time, seemed nervous even when he whispered it to me when he instructed me. This rubbed off, and I avoided its use entirely. I could say it now if I wished. It would be okay to do so, but I have not said it in a long time, and it would come rusty to my mouth, and so I will keep silent on that account.

Now I was a child of great virtue, I thought, and I dreamed about the future and how I would have various successes when I got big enough to have them. I felt I had evidence to predict this. I rode well, was sufficiently easy with people, if a little sharp and arrogant, and women seemed already able to see a man in me, and they did not touch me much when I was with them. In this time I am talking about, we lived just outside Jerome, Arizona, that copper mining town, in a time when the mine was thriving and there seemed to be as many executives around as there were miners. Maybe too many chiefs, as some might say in some circumstances. There were inspectors and a lot of well-dressed people in offices. I used to see them come and go, in white shirts, from where I sat above the post office there. Well, in one summer I did get tired of all that sitting around, and I headed out to the edge of town to the golf course there, to see if I could find something to do.

There may be some passing historical import in what I will say now, maybe not. In Jerome they had a bowling alley, and they hired mostly Mexicans as pinsetters there. Sometimes town boys would get jobs there, but they didn't last. The story had it that Mexicans could stand the heat of the pin pit better in the summertime, and it was also said that they had bigger hands. There was one they told about, name of Manny, who could get five pins in each hand at a time. That was the whole rack of pins, and after a strike was thrown, he could have those pins racked up and down on the alley in one stoop, before even the ball got back down that trough they have for its returning to the thrower in such places. Some of the stories about the Mexican hands went on a little, and they got upward even to their ancestors, and into myth, and that the size of the hands came from miraculous acts early on down south in Mexico. There were of course the other stories, those about big hands for swimming across the river to get into America without passing through customs at the gate, but these were not told often, and when they were it was mostly by those who had no sense and could not set pins either, and they were of little matter. If it hadn't been for the cheap four cents a line that the Mexican pinsetters were paid there at that bowling alley, they would have had the corner on a very good market indeed.

I say passing historical moment here because machines have now taken over, and nobody anywhere sets pins anymore. I tell about these Mexican pinsetters as a kind of analogue, because I got to be the first Indian caddie down that way, at the golf course over there. The thing had to do with vision instead of hands in my case, but really it had to do with familiarity of a kind of looking and concentration. The thing was that I could follow the flight of the ball, on and off the fairway, and see where it landed or went into woods or lower rough. I knew how to mark it when it went out of sight, and I knew how to select my marks so that when I moved from beside the man who hit it I wouldn't loose them or be fooled by seeing them from another place as I got closer to where the ball was. I had done it with birds and small animals, and I had played games in which doing it was important. It was no big thing, and it was not an Indian thing. Any old farm boy can do this thing.

When I got down to the course there and asked for a caddie job, the man who ran the place said he would see about it, and he took me out to a tee, and he hit a good number of balls all over the place and told me to go get them. I had them all marked, and I brought them all back right away, and he hired me right then. The money was not good money, but it was better than four cents a line, and I was young and had some curiosity, a thing that can lead a young boy to learning and a man to possible ruin. I caddied a little on that first day, but the thing and the place were so new to me that I didn't see much.

On the second day, I went out early with four of those mine executives. There was a town boy there with me who was a little surly seeing me there, but he was okay. He watched after two of the bags, and I carried the other two. It was a very nice morning; it was sunny but cool for that time of year, and it was good to be outside at work, I thought. I spent some boy's time thinking about how I was out there doing "a job of work," a phrase I had heard men say.

A pleasant first thing I found out about golf that time was that there were a lot of silences in it, and I could hear the birds singing, some sharp-noted and some like flutes in trees in the rough. But I don't want to talk on about the qualities of weather or the shape of the course or give some atmosphere to this business more than is necessary here. What I want to get to is what could be called the home truth that came to me there, a kind of cracker-barrel truth I guess, though not in a saying like most but in a story, and as such to be gotten out of it.

The four men were very good golfers, and this meant that I had very little work to do. Their shots were straight, and their movements over the ball were economical and spare. When they walked to where their balls landed after they hit them, they did not waste time or space but went in straight lines, and they knew what to do to save steps around the green and on it. Their play was a matter, I could say at my age now, of exquisite, exclusionary form. Its aim was a kind of complete noninterference. It was mechanistic; it was not animal nor human. And it struck me that it was an awkward thing for bodies to do as well. And I tried to imagine some translation of the skill, but there didn't seem to be any. And on top of all this, here we were outside, and to play it right it seemed you had to stay, as far as possible, unaffected by birds, wind, the wave of grasses, the light, the faces of your fellows, their thoughts, the nature of your lie, the new blueberries, trees and small animals, the sheen on the morning-glories, but not by the future.

And that was the home truth. You had to do something here that locked most everything else out of here so that you could get to something over there, and when you got over there you had to do the same thing over again. I got it then that I, with my secret name, was just a boy, but that I had come to that time when my mind was most always reaching and imagining what it was like to be a man, and that I better "get off the dime," as I had heard men say. And I saw that these men, executives and important people, had, in their concentration and the obviously serious pleasure they took in it, a place in which they lived and remained boys, and that it would not stretch it much to think that they were also victims of an improper human thing. Though graceful in play, they were not where the age of their bodies placed them. Their secret names might just as well have been Blue Dot, Top Flight, Ram, Hogan, X L, or Spalding.

And so, about halfway through the round, I found myself standing off to the side as my two men hit their approach shots to the green. They were both powerfully concentrated, close to each other, but not in awareness of one another. And if there was any association between them to be figured, I surely could not figure it. And I, their caddie, from my position, task, and distance from them, well beyond the lines and hook-ups in their matrix of play, might just as well have not been there at all.

I stood straight and stiff and still off to the side, and I did not look in the direction of the play but up the fairway to where the green looked down at us, and I waited. It struck me then that this was no thing for a man to be doing with his time. And when they hit their shots, and I was trailing behind them, I just let the burden of their bags slip from my shoulders and down to the fairway grass. They walked their straight lines, and I turned and started along mine.

It was not so straight, that line, but when it turned it only yielded to necessity. I reached the cut grass of the low rough, and after I had passed over it, I entered into the natural rough, the growth that went on and away from the golf course. That rough was not manicured like the other; it was more complex, and it was not to be defined in terms of anything other than itself. It was not so soft to walk on, but I think I remember it felt right under my feet. It was when my feet entered that complex that I heard the voice of that quail in the brush beyond where I was headed. He was singing the two notes I took from him and am now known by. That is the story of my brief career as a caddie for lost men and how I got my real and public name.